Shattered Energy

SHATTERED ENERGY

A Memory in time

Athena Plencner

Current Words Publishing | Los Angeles

Shattered Energy

Book 1: A Memory in Time

Editor and Publisher: Dianne Pearce
Cover art: Gary "Guf" Frayer
Design: David Yurkovich

ISBN: 978-1-957224-68-8 (paperback)
ISBN: 978-1-957224-69-5 (ePub)

Published by Current Words Publishing, LLC
Los Angeles, California
currentwords.com

To my family.

Thank you for your unwavering support.

Shattered Energy

Chapter 1

Every morning began the same, with fire, blood, and death.

This morning was worse.

Ariyana jolted upright in bed.

"Glacin."

His name escaped from her lips in a harsh whisper as her lungs constricted and every muscle in her body seized. Frozen in pain, she toppled out of bed onto the soft throw rug. She hit hard on her right side, her arms refusing to move to brace her fall, and air exploded from her lungs. She coughed and wheezed as her lungs fought to get enough air.

She had lit a fire before going to bed, hoping the warmth it provided would offer her some comfort when she awoke, but she had not anticipated the differences that this morning would bring. Unlike other mornings, today she woke up before her dream consumed her sleep, and now her body lay painfully immobilized on the floor, her eyes staring deeply into the yellow and orange flames. Her face and shoulders grew warm while a contrasting icy throb began to pulse within her chest. Her muscles strained, and her bones ached from the contracted grip they had on her body.

But none of that mattered. He was dead, or more accurately, was about to die again.

She knew what was coming. She could feel it overwhelming her like a rising tide. She narrowed her eyes, trying to will the golden flame in front of her into a turquoise glow. She hoped that she could catch a glimpse of him, unscathed, before she accepted the reality that he was gone, still gone, and worse yet, only existed in her dreams…her only dream.

Most people woke from their dreams with glimpses of events that they could barely piece together or maybe just a feeling that the thoughts that came to them during their slumber were pleasant or traumatic. This was not the case for Ariyana. Her dream came to her every night, unyielding, and tore through her sleeping mind like a cancer bent on destroying her from the inside out. She didn't get the luxury of fragmented pieces that didn't make sense. It was a clear event, with a start and a finish, and it held more detail than a scripted film.

The dream had first come to her in the early morning hours of her sixth birthday, and even now, twenty-four years to the day later, each night that passed only brought more pain. It never got easier.

The effects of the dream stayed with her for a while after waking. Her skin burned where she had been injured, her muscles ached from overuse, and her mind was plagued with anguish. She couldn't control it.

The icy throb inside her chest intensified, spreading throughout her body with each pulse of her heart. It expanded until she could no longer feel the heat from the fire in front of her against her skin. She had never woken up from her dream before, and she wondered if this was always what happened before her dream consumed her. Her wheezing became worse. She was taking in less air with each strangled breath. The warm air of the room burned inside the cold walls of her lungs.

Instinct urged her to try to pull herself closer to the fire, but her body refused to respond. She choked on one last breath before the features of the room around her morphed from wooden walls and a wooden floor to stone. She saw her own breath dance in a small puff of cold air before the full weight of her dream bore down on her.

Chapter 2

The chamber was darker than normal. It was only illuminated by the low silver flame that danced along the silver feathers that covered parts of her body. That flame was also lower than usual. Ariyana assured herself that she was keeping a low profile inside the chamber so that her light didn't alert anyone or anything to her presence by shining through the tunnels and caverns around her. In truth, though, she was afraid, and the strength of her flame was reacting to that fear.

She hadn't been separated from Glacin since the moment that they joined and became companions. Nor had she ever been left alone inside the rock tunnels and caverns without the flames of other Draxins burning and casting their light all around their intricate colony.

Ariyana felt panic building inside of her. With her right foot, she dug her talons into the stone floor, leaving three deep scars in the grayish granite. She contracted the muscles along her strong, prehensile tail, causing the long, silver feathers that were bundled at the end to sharpen into a blade-like tip. She whipped it against the stone, sending a shower of sparks across the chamber and into a shadowed corner. They quickly vanished, creating the illusion that it was the darkness that had swallowed them up.

She stepped back, squeezing her eyes shut. Her hearts pounded in her chest, and she wanted to pull herself into a ball. She wanted to wrap her arms around herself to convince herself that she still had shape, but the darkness didn't care that she had shape. Its cold expanse would swallow her up and let her drift alone as it had once before.

Something hard hit her back. She gasped and whirled around. The wall. She shook her head to try to clear it. She hadn't realized that she had continued to move backward during her panic attack, but was grateful for the hard impact, as it seemed to knock her from her thoughts.

Now, she was right next to the opening of the chamber. She heard the harsh, uncertain sounds of a nearby battle. They echoed down the tunnel. Glacin was in that battle, and it worried her to think that one of those howls could be his.

She should be out there with him, fighting by his side, not hiding away in their chamber, hoping that he would return. But she was not permitted to help fight their battle. She was not Draxin. She was foreign to his people and not fully trusted. She belonged to Glacin, their companionship accepted by the queen, but not the people as a whole. She was sure the main reason the queen didn't want her out there was that she believed it was Ariyana's fault these new creatures appearing in the sky were launching this unprovoked attack.

The thought angered her, and she lashed at the floor, sending a shower of sparks out into the tunnel this time. They didn't extinguish like before, though. They caught in a current of some kind, flared slightly, and drifted down the tunnel like they were trapped in the wind. But it wasn't the wind.

Ariyana reached out and ran her fingers through it. It was an energy current. It flowed from the outside through the tunnels, and it was connected to danger, to a threat that wasn't targeting those who were fighting outside. It was targeting something deep within the colony, something…her breath caught in her throat as realization hit. *No!*

She bolted out of the chamber and into the darkness of the tunnel, relying on memory and the scant light that her flame provided to guide her way.

Ariyana and Glacin had a strong connection and communicated with each other through their thoughts. When he left to fight, he had put up a strong mental block to keep her out of his mind and his thoughts out of hers. She could break through it if she pushed hard enough, but she wouldn't. No matter what she found in here, she knew that one small distraction could be fatal to him or to those he was trying to protect. She readied herself as the tunnel walls flew past in her peripheral. He was serving his people by fighting outside, and she would prove herself by protecting what was in here.

Ariyana tore into the queen's egg chamber, her chest heaving from exertion. Her muscles coiled, ready for attack. The feathers through her hair, along her forearms, down her spinal ridge, and along her tail sharpened and ignited into a brighter, silver flame. She held her arms up in a fighting stance as her claws and talons lengthened, and her tail whipped up and arched over her shoulders.

The queen's clutch of eggs burned golden-red in the center of the chamber. Its flame not only illuminated the massive chamber but the horrific face and sharpened limbs of an enemy as it dug its way out of a fracturing hole in the rock floor about fifteen yards behind the clutch.

The floor vibrated, and then there were dozens of them, chewing and digging their way in. She didn't think. She charged into the chamber, leapt over the large clutch, the fire licking at her feet and tail, and landed with a hard slap at the opening of the hole. She drove the tip of her sharp tail over her shoulders and into the middle of the creature's face. Its shrieking cries filled the cavern and her mind. The contact with the creature created an instant energy connection that tingled uncomfortably along her skin and painfully through her thoughts. She recoiled from the creature, yanking her tail from its head, desperate to sever the connection, and watched it disappear into the darkness of the hole.

It was unclear whether she had injured it or killed it. Her mind was a mess of noise. She grabbed her head, overwhelmed by the barrage of shrieks, and stumbled backward.

Multiple sharpened limbs burst through the rock floor around her, one catching her across the calf and slicing it open. She fell back toward the eggs and cracked her head on a protruding rock. Her hold on her mental block loosened, and an image of her companion flashed through her mind. She gasped and pushed back on the image, shutting him back out. She hoped that none of her emotions or images of what was going on had made it through to him.

The hole exploded open; rock shrapnel filled the chamber, pulling her focus back to the threat in the chamber. She pulled her head into her chest, covering the side of her face and neck. She felt the nick and burn of small injuries across her skin, but nothing large had hit her. She peered between her two arms. The air was thick with rock dust, but it wasn't thick enough to conceal the dozens of creatures that scurried from the hole to surround her and the eggs.

She cautiously pulled herself into a squatting position and peered behind her. Relief filled her when she saw that the eggs sat unscathed in their rock nest. Her eyes roved around the chamber. She slowly rolled herself onto the balls of her feet and balanced half her weight onto her extended hands. Three creatures moved forward out of the thickest part of the dust cloud and stood about ten yards in front of her.

The creatures were three times her size and stood on six legs. They chittered in sync with one another and were answered with chittering noises from the creatures behind them. None of the creatures were quiet. Some were screeching, some were chirping, and others were chittering. She focused past the noise of it and heard what she was looking for—there was a rhythm to it. They were communicating.

The three creatures took another step forward, allowing her to see them more clearly. Their back legs were stacked with thick muscles and supported by large two-taloned feet. Their torsos were long, lean, and flexible. They had four arms that came off their chests, and each arm ended in a deadly point that was as sharp as a spear. Their coloration was a mixture of browns and greens with irregular white outlines. Their bodies appeared rough and jagged in some places, but their strength and agility were evident. The features on their faces were pulled back toward bony protrusions coming off the backs of their heads like skin pulled grotesquely over a skull. They had slits on their faces where eyes should be, and their mouths were hidden by two large black mandibles.

The air around her was thick with dust and tension. Ariyana peered down at the fractured floor. A loose, long flake of rock lay two inches to the right of her right hand. She glanced back at the three creatures in front of her. The truth was a siren of noise inside her mind, telling her that peaceful creatures didn't burrow through miles of rock to meet a new species. They weren't here to become allies.

She lengthened her claws and slammed them through the wider end of the flake. In one swift movement, she stood, broke the flake free from the rock floor and brandished it to the side like a weapon. The feathers through her hair, along her spinal ridge, and down her tail rose, sharpened and blazed.

Two large, bat-like ears pricked and rotated forward off the protrusions on the heads of the three creatures in front of her. The slits on their faces widened, revealing yellow, oval eyes. They reared up on their hind legs, emitted a high-pitched squeal, and charged her.

Ariyana didn't hesitate. She leapt at the middle creature, grabbed its mandible, dug her talons into its thick exoskeleton, and shoved the rock flake through the juncture where the head met the thorax-like body. It shrieked, gurgled, and stumbled backward, swiping at its face with its front limbs. She secured both of her hands on its mandible and wrapped the talons of her right foot around the rock flake. She pulled her body up and stabbed her left claws through the creature's right eye. It shrilled, reared up and right, and knocked into the creature next to it. She pulled its head to the side, yellow, viscous fluid oozing down her arm, extended her body, and pushed the flake forward with her talons. The flake tore through its neck with a wet crunch, and its head slapped against the side of its thorax, still attached by tendrils of flesh. It convulsed and crashed against the rock floor.

She landed, rolled, and popped up to face the two creatures rushing toward her. They showed no regard for their own kind as they stepped on the fallen corpse, piercing it with their sharp limbs.

They slammed their front limbs into the rock floor, and red, serrated ridges extended from the forearm joints all the way along their outer edges to the sharp points. They hissed at her as six red and orange wings unfolded from large plates on their backs. They vibrated against each other, creating a high-pitched chirping sound. The other creatures in the chamber answered with their own high-pitched chirping.

Visibility in the chamber was worsening as the thick cloud of rock dust accumulated in the still air. She couldn't see all the creatures in the chamber, and the echoes made it sound like she was surrounded. Her mind filled with images of being corralled by dozens of creatures displaying identical poses to the two in front of her. Her rock weapon was gone, lying somewhere under or around the dead creature, but she didn't let that deter her. She rushed forward and leapt at the closest creature.

It anticipated her move, though, and adjusted to the side. She landed awkwardly on its thorax, missing its mandible and slamming against its upper wing instead.

It bucked wildly, trying to dislodge her, and the other creature reared up next to it and took a few failed slashes at her back. She dug her left claws deep into the forearm of its wing and latched her right claws onto the thick exoskeleton on its thorax. She whipped her tail up at its face and drove the sharp tip down, impaling it between the fleshy meat below its eye and its right mandible. It jerked back, shrieking, and whipped its head from side to side. Her right hand tore free, and her body weight fell onto her left arm. The force of her fall caused her tail to rip through its face, tearing off its right mandible. The creature screamed, jerked to the left, and reared.

Yellow, viscous fluid splattered across her body, causing her to lose her grip, and she fell hard against the floor. She felt a rush of energy to her side and rolled onto her back. The other creature's front legs impaled the ground on either side of her shoulders, narrowly missing her.

Unfortunately, it didn't fare as well as she had. It had moved in for the kill too quickly, and just as its legs narrowly missed her shoulders, the front legs of the rearing injured creature speared through its head and upper thorax, killing it instantly.

She rolled out from under the two creatures before the second set of legs speared the floor. She jumped up and crouched in front of the eggs.

The injured creature pulled itself free and swiped at its mangled face. Thick fluid oozed from the wound and splattered on the rock floor in yellow splotches. It stepped toward her and hissed through a mouthful of now-visible sharp teeth.

She stayed low to the ground, her weight on her toes, and her tail arched over her shoulders. A crunching sound to the right pulled her attention away from the creature in front of her. She had been so focused on the three creatures that were attacking her that she wasn't thinking about the rest of those in the room. They had all moved to the other side of the clutch and were busy chiseling away at the stone nest around the burning eggs. "No!" she screamed, standing up and pivoting toward them.

Movement flashed at her side. Ariyana whipped her head back toward the creature and dodged left as it drove its left leg down toward her head. She wasn't fast enough, though, and it sliced her outer right thigh.

The creature drove forward, swinging its right leg in a wide arch toward her neck. She leaned back to avoid the blow, but the injured leg gave out, and she stumbled. The creature's leg caught her diagonally across the chest and knocked her on her back at the edge of the clutch.

Her head slammed against the floor, and an explosion of light blurred her vision. A rush of movement over her body was her only warning before burning pain exploded through her shoulder.

Chapter 3

Ariyana's vision cleared instantly. The creature's front limb was impaled through her right shoulder. She tried to cry out, but her seizing lungs denied the release. Pain lanced through her body like magnifying bursts of lightning as the creature slowly lifted her off the ground. The red serrated teeth of the limb dug deeply into her flesh, securing the creature's hold on her.

Numbness spread from the wound with each beat of her hearts, smothering the pain with its dark tendrils. The numbness didn't bring relief. It brought a sense of panic and approaching death as it spread. She dug her left claws into the limb for purchase and struck at the creature's face with her tail, but she missed.

Her tail and left arm fell weakly against her body, and fear crept its way into her thoughts. She could barely move, and her breathing labored. The physical pain was gone, but it was being replaced with shame and guilt. *She'd been left behind for a reason. She wasn't strong enough. She had failed her companion and his people by not protecting their unborn young.*

The creature lifted her up toward its face. Yellow fluid oozed from its missing mandible over its sharpened teeth as it ground them against each other.

"No," Ariyana moaned.

Piercing cries filled the chamber, and the creature raised its head and hissed.

Massive jaws closed around the creature's thorax, tearing through it in one bite, severing its neck and limbs from its body.

Ariyana fell, hit the floor, and crumbled onto her right side, her weak legs unable to hold her body weight. The creature's head hit the ground with a wet slap next to her face. She moaned and rolled weakly onto her back, trying to grasp the segment of limb in her shoulder.

Relief, concern, and anger blasted across her senses. She looked up as her companion lowered his head into view. "Glacin," she whispered.

He rumbled in his throat and threw the creature's body across the chamber, hitting two other creatures and slamming them into the wall. He towered above her. Glacin unfurled his wings, and the sharp turquoise feathers along the forearms bristled, vibrated, and blazed with turquoise flame. He snaked his long neck toward her, the creature's yellow fluid dripping from his fangs and sizzling in the small burning feathers along his jawline.

Turquoise flame danced in his crested feathers and around his eyes. He turned his head to the side, and his silver pupil constricted to a sharp four-pointed star in his black eye.

Trouble. Glacin said, his voice filling her mind like a warm liquid.

She choked on a cough and rolled her eyes. The word came out as a statement, not a question. "Is now really the time to –," she started, but movement above Glacin's head pulled her attention to the chamber's ceiling. A handful of creatures had climbed the walls and were making their way across the ceiling to a point just above Glacin's body. "Pull this out. Now," she said, glancing at the severed limb in her shoulder. "And we can stop these things from trying to get to the eggs."

Can't. The red teeth excrete a toxin. Pulling them out seems to make it worse. Two have already died from this, and their body size was greater than yours.

She glanced around the chamber. The creatures had formed a tight circle around them. They chittered at each other, the sound turning into an eerie echo around them. "It's hard to breathe," she wheezed. Sadness washed over her, but it wasn't coming from her. "Glacin?"

He peered down at her. *This is going to hurt.*

He rounded on the creatures, giving her no time to react, and used his wing and tail to shove her into the middle of the burning clutch behind her.

The impaled limb and her wounds ignited. Ariyana screamed. The numbness vanished instantly as every nerve ending in her body caught fire, and her blood boiled. She hoped that she would lose consciousness soon so the pain would stop.

Wait, no! What was she thinking? Glacin was out there alone against an unknown threat. He'd pushed her into the flames of the clutch for a reason. A contraction coursed through her muscles, and a vision of each unborn hatchling contracting in its egg flashed through her mind.

She rolled to her side and yelled out for Glacin. *She couldn't feel him. Could he feel her?*

Another contraction seized her, and this time a vision filled her mind of the queen and her mate, Evix, fighting the creatures in the night sky. The pain began to ease, and the next contraction didn't bring pain. It brought a renewed strength that coursed through her veins.

The flames around Ariyana began to pulse, and her hearts began to beat in time with them. Each pulse brought more strength and connection. She could feel each unborn hatchling and saw flashes of the queen tearing and biting through dozens of creatures that were only illuminated by her brilliant golden-red flame.

Ariyana threw her arm out, dug her claws into the rock, and pulled herself up and onto her knees. She forced her eyes open and could see the faint glow of turquoise jumping and dancing through the raging golden-red flames around her.

He was moving more slowly than normal.

She reached up to pull the limb from her shoulder, but it was gone. She peered down and was shocked to find that her skin was healed and unsinged.

A burst of energy raced through her body as the flames around her pulsed intensely in sync with the throb of her hearts. Ariyana felt her body become a vessel for raw, untamable fire and bolted to her feet. She zeroed in on Glacin's flame, and, without thought, she leapt toward it, roaring his name.

The pain hit her mid-air like a kick to the chest, and she landed hard, short of her intended mark, lost her balance, and collapsed to the right, clutching her chest. The clutch's flame had cut her off from her connection to him completely, but now she could feel the full weight of the truth. He was wounded badly, so bad in fact, that a portion of their bond had shattered.

She looked around, trying to find Glacin, desperate to see him with her own eyes, but it was impossible. The creatures stood between her and her companion, and she could only see the faint glow of his flame on the other side of the chamber.

A few creatures had turned to look at her when she landed, but the majority of them were focused on Glacin and were slowly advancing on him. Even though she couldn't see him, she knew that the creatures were encircling him, cutting him off from her and from the tunnels behind him. Ariyana righted herself, howled, and charged the mass of creatures. She took three long strides and leapt onto the closest creature's thorax, digging her talons deep into its exoskeleton. It shrieked and threw its head back. She grabbed onto its face, stabbing her long claws into its eyes. The creature reared up, squealing, and flailed its four front arms. She pushed her body weight forward into its upper thorax and pulled its head down toward the floor, forcing it forward into the center of the mass.

It slammed into four other creatures. She dug her claws in deeper and pulled its head down further, driving it forward in an agonizing panic. It used their bodies like stepping stones, impaling them with its flailing limbs, and made its way through the mass of creatures.

In unison, the mass of creatures turned their attention from Glacin to her and the creature that she had taken hostage. They swung and stabbed at her, but she had secured herself up high on the creature's thorax, so they missed. The creature that she had forced forward didn't fare as well, though, and multiple limbs pierced through its body. After a few more steps, it stopped flailing, gurgled, toppled to the right, and crashed to the floor.

She leapt from its head, over the last few creatures, and landed a few feet away from her companion's side.

Glacin was no longer standing. He was on his belly, panting, and soaked in his own blood. There were a handful of creatures on the other side that were tearing and ripping into his black scales. Everything was covered in his turquoise blood, including each of the creature's hideous faces. The only feathers on his body that were burning were the ones on his upper neck and face.

Rage consumed Ariyana. She charged the creature closest to her. It had ahold of Glacin's left wing forearm and was tearing off chunks of scale-covered flesh to get to the bone. She jumped onto its back, climbed up its thorax, and grabbed both of its mandibles before it could sink its teeth into her companion again. She dug her claws deep into the flesh above the mandibles. It pulled back and shook its head wildly from side to side, trying to dislodge her, but she held tight, digging her claws in deeper. Finally, it lifted its head up high and exposed the unprotected crease where the head met the thorax. She swung her legs up, grabbed its thorax with her talons, and stabbed her tail through its throat over and over again until the creature began to sway. She jumped as the creature tumbled backward. She landed, rolled to her side, and knelt in front of her companion.

Their gazes met, and a lance of pain more intense than before tore through her hearts, doubling her over.

Chapter 4

Ari…Arissss.

Her name floated through her mind on wisps of agony and broken promises. Her body felt cold; her companion's warmth was leaving her. She was losing him.

Ariyana crawled forward, reaching for him. The cold sense of loneliness that she was always fighting was debilitating. She was drifting again, lost and alone in the empty vastness of space. She couldn't lose the only thing that had ever meant anything to her—she wouldn't.

She cried out against the panic, forcing herself to pull back from her own fear. But it was too late. Her distraction had left her wide open. Glacin's eyes filled with panic, and the energy behind her shifted. Two limbs impaled through her upper back and slammed her to the ground. The side of her head hit the rock floor, and her vision filled with white flashes of light that seemed to dance around Glacin's face.

She choked on a cough, and silver blood splattered across the rock floor. She couldn't breathe. She clawed at the ground, trying to drag herself to him.

The chamber filled with an echoing screech. It vibrated off the walls and around her mind, which called out for Glacin, hoping that she had enough energy to make a connection, to get through the noise.

A roar filled the chamber, and heat blasted across her body.

The creature was torn from her, and the pain was replaced by the warmth of a muzzle. It caressed her from shoulder to face, warm breath playing through her hair. *Remember the connection that we share…you don't have to be alone anymore.*

"Glac—" she began, but he grabbed her in his jaws, cutting off her thoughts. She felt a rush of air, and then pain exploded on her right side and back. The chamber around her disappeared in a blaze of golden-red. Glacin had tossed her into the middle of the clutch's fire again.

Her wounds ignited, and the contraction of the burning clutch began to pulse inside her. This time was different, though. The energy filled her immediately, and Ariyana could still sense her connection to Glacin. She felt everything, from the panic-inducing shattering of their bond to his sorrow and regret. There was no time to waste.

Ariyana pushed everything aside and concentrated on pulling energy into her body. She deepened her heart rate, forcing each pulse to push blood through her body faster. To her surprise, the clutch responded to her needs. Each unborn hatchling contracted in its egg to match her pulse rate, sending jolts of energy through her. She jumped to her feet, shaking. Her body felt electrified. Her silver flame was laced with ribbons of golden-red fire.

Agony exploded through her hearts, causing her to stumble backward. She looked up just in time to see the creatures rip both of Glacin's wings off. He howled, and his head collapsed with a wet slap on the rock floor.

Ariyana's body began to tremble, and the chamber filled with a sound that she had never heard before.

It was rage-filled, and yet empty.

It was darkness, and yet filled with blinding light.

It was billions of voices, though it emanated from one.

It was the soul of the universe that shattered inside her.

The chamber walls groaned and vibrated around her as if they were an extension of her body. She clasped her hands into fists at her sides. Her claws tore deeply into her palms, and blood poured from the wounds, silver blood that burned with black fire. Her pupils dilated, black consuming her eyes. Then, the feathers around her eyes ignited into black flame. It streamed from her eyes like liquid fire, moving through her hair, along her spinal ridge, and down her tail until every silver feather was consumed by black flames.

She roared, and rocks exploded from the chamber walls, raining down on the creatures around her. Ariyana stepped through the clutch, and as she walked, her black fire bled into the golden-red flame of the clutch, consuming it until everything around her burned ominously with dark flames.

She leapt from the edge of the clutch and grabbed the nearest creature. She clasped onto its face and dug her claws into the flesh behind both of its eyes. She was about to tear through its head when she felt it. It flowed into her fingers like liquid heat, rushing toward the throbbing chill in her chest. It radiated from every cell in its body. It was heat; it was energy; it was sustenance.

She drew in close to the creature's face and stared at it. Its eyes swirled with ribbons of bioluminescence that called to her…that made her…ravenous. How was it possible that she wasn't aware of this emptiness inside of her?

Everything fell away except for that hunger. She needed the creature's energy, craved it. Without thought, she pulled it into herself, filling every hungry cell of her body. The creature whined and squealed loudly— sounds that she registered, but didn't tie meaning to. Instinct drove her to both pull harder on the energy and push farther on the connection that she felt. The creature in her hands was bound in some way to every other creature on the planet. As she pushed the connection out, she felt a wildness take hold of her. Had she ever felt so free before? Her mind soared through the swarm of creatures, through the expanse of space, filling her need by absorbing their energy.

Ariyana barely registered that her connection brought her mind to another planet. All she felt were hundreds of thousands of creatures. The thought of filling herself with all of their energy thrilled her, but the moment that she pulled on the first of it, a horrific image flashed through her mind like a rock wall and knocked her backward, cutting her off from the swarm.

Her claws burst free of the creature's head, and she fell back as if she had been struck in the forehead. She landed on her feet, and the creature hit the floor next to her, bursting into burning ash. This set off a chain reaction, and all the creatures in the cavern disintegrated into the same burning ash.

Ariyana dropped to her knees on the rock floor, her ash-covered hands lying palms up in her lap. She felt disoriented and hungry for more.

Her feathers still burned with black flame. She searched the cavern for more creatures, but it was empty, swirling only with ash.

Please.

A familiar whisper drifted through her thoughts.

Please.

It was louder this time. It was warm, it was home. She shook her head to clear the hunger that consumed her mind.

Glacin! The realization shattered the obsession to absorb more energy, and her silver flame blazed through the black, like the sun breaking through a dark storm.

Glacin's body came into focus in front of her, and she choked back a sob. She rushed to his side and pulled herself into his head, tucking herself between his neck and lower jaw. His black scales and turquoise feathers were wet and dull with his blood. The feathers on his eye ridges were the only ones that were still burning. She stroked the scales around his eye.

"I need you to get up," Ariyana begged. "I have to get you outside. I need to get you out to the water."

"Help!" she screamed, her eyes wildly searching the cavern for someone to help.

The scales along his throat vibrated softly, and he opened his eye to look at her. The four-pointed, silver star in his black eye, which marked their unique bond, had faded thin.

It is already…too late. The energy of my ancestors is falling from the stars…to take me…to my resting place.

Ariyana looked up and realized that the burning ash around them looked like falling stars in the night sky. Glacin's mind was too weak to realize that they weren't outside. She squeezed her eyes shut, and tears streamed down her cheeks. His people believed that when they died, their bodies must be outside under the open sky so that their energy could be released and protected by their ancestors, but Glacin was in a chamber, and there was no open sky to witness his passing.

She jumped up and pushed on his massive head. "Get up!" she yelled. "Glacin, get up! Help me get you outside. Please! Help!" she screamed again, hoping that someone was close.

He rolled his head to the side and knocked her over. She scrambled back to his side.

"Please," she cried. "Please get up. Don't leave me. I need you. I can't do this without you. I can't go back to the emptiness."

No tears. No emptiness. One day...you will feel the truth.... You have never been alone.... You have always been more than you can ever imagine.... His voice trailed off in her mind. The feathers along his eye ridge burned out, and the silver star in his eye disappeared. The last thread of their bond shattered, and the energy inside her hearts broke. His body disintegrated into ash and fell through her fingers, plunging her mind into darkness.

A piercing noise filled the chamber, and she pressed her palms into her ears. She fell forward into his ash and curled her body into a fetal position. She cradled her head in her arms to protect her ears from the noise, and she lay there and cried and begged for death to take her.

Chapter 5

The piercing cries morphed into a strange, yet familiar sound, but the pain remained, sharp and steady in its determination to consume her.

Instead of pushing it away, she let it build.

Let this pain kill me! Her thoughts demanded. *Let it shatter inside me until it shreds not only my insides, but the bonds that hold my essence together. Let me bleed out. Let me die....*

Instead of death, though, an unrelenting pressure built on Ariyana's chest. Her shoulder blades dug into an unforgiving surface, and she was finding it more and more difficult to breathe. The pressure quickly overshadowed the pain of mourning for her companion. Frustration grew inside of her, a dangerous spark in the darkness that still blanketed her. She pushed back against the pressure to free herself.

Her body was jerked roughly, and pain exploded in the back of her head. She tried to move her arms but was met with more resistance. She wondered if she might have missed one of the creatures, but quickly dismissed the idea. She had craved the energy of those creatures more intensely than she had craved anything else, including her bond to Glacin, and she had felt each creature's energy flow into her body. She didn't miss any of them. This was something else, something that didn't make clicking piercing noises.

Her frustration grew, and it intertwined with the anguish of losing Glacin. She feared that whatever it was, it was here to take away more than his life; it wanted her memory of him too. She bucked her hips, and something fell hard against her upper body, painfully slamming into her mouth. A sound filled her ears, a faraway sound that stirred a memory that was beyond her reach.

The pressure on her mouth eased, and she bit down in defense. Her teeth cut through something fleshy, and a slight salty taste coated her tongue. Her head was jostled back and forth, and the familiar sound in her ears became loud and full of urgency.

Something grabbed her chin in an iron grip, and the scent of citrus filled her nose.

Her eyes popped open, chasing away the darkness, and an angry face came into view. "Ariyana!" it yelled.

There was that sound again. She knew that word. That word had pain associated with it, pain that she didn't want to remember. She couldn't deal with any more pain, and she pushed back on the memory.

"Ariyana! Damn it, let go!" it yelled again, and the pain increased on her chin.

She peered down. She had its forearm in her mouth.

No, not "its." His. She had his forearm in her mouth. She knew this man, and she knew that the memory of this man was associated with the pain of the word that he kept saying.

She let go and pushed him back, roughly. She wiped at her mouth and clumsily pulled herself into a squatting position. Her body ached and felt foreign to her. She looked down at her hands, and they were just that, hands; no claws, no silver skin, no feathers, no ash, no blood: just human hands.

"What the hell is wrong with you, Ari?" he barked. His face morphed momentarily into the face of one of the creatures from her dream, then instantly flashed back to normal.

She felt emotionally feral and yelled back a primal roar.

Confusion and concern flashed in his eyes, momentarily overshadowing the rage.

She scanned her surroundings. The cavern was gone, Glacin's remains were gone, and it was all replaced by a furnished room, lit by a soft yellow light in the corner and a small fire in the fireplace. She was crouched on a mahogany floor and surrounded by matching wooden furniture.

She couldn't hold back the memories any longer, which were rushing into her mind. She knew this place. She knew this man. Her eyes drifted back to his, which had now resumed their angry glare.

"Devyn?" she asked. She had intended to just say his name, but it came out as more of a question, and she regretted it the moment she said it. His nostrils flared, and his face reddened.

"Who the hell else would it be?" he snapped, standing abruptly and grasping his injured arm to his chest. "Damn it, Ariyana! You lied to me!"

She threw her arm up onto the bed and lifted herself up to sit on the edge. She arched her back and stretched her arms behind her to ease the ache in her muscles. She concentrated on stabilizing her breathing back into a steady rhythm. Each inhale was still painful, but it was easing slightly.

Her thoughts were another story. Her therapist called this her *Transition Phase*. Simply put, her mind and body were transitioning from dream to reality. On a regular night, she could settle her thoughts quickly and mourn Glacin's death in her mind without Devyn being the wiser, but on a day like today, it was impossible. She had two things working against her: the first was that it was her birthday; the second was that today marked the fifth six-year cycle of her dream.

She didn't understand how it was possible, but her dream grew more and more detailed and intense every night, building to a peak on the morning of her birthday every six years. The dream continued to build from there every night thereafter, but was always the most extreme on that six-year mark.

As the pain eased in her body, she noticed that a new sensation was replacing it. The sensation that she felt before the dream consumed her: the deep chill in her chest, like an icicle pierced between her breasts. She rubbed her knuckles against the spot on her chest and was surprised that her skin was ice cold.

She was exhausted and didn't have the strength to have the argument that she knew they were about to have. Glacin had just died, and her soul felt crushed. She could still feel his blood and ash on her skin and smell the cold rock of the egg chamber around her. She longed to be held and told that everything would be okay. Devyn started pacing in front of her, and she sighed. That clearly wasn't something that was going to happen.

Devyn was right: she had lied to him. She had been lying to him for the last year and a half, but he had given her no choice.

Chapter 6

Ariyana's first dream came to her in the early morning hours of her sixth birthday. Her parents had been very protective of her and had made sure that she wasn't exposed to any violence through what she read and watched on TV. She didn't have any experience with death, and certainly had never seen someone killed so brutally. She awoke screaming and crying. Her parents and brothers tried to soothe her. They told her that it was only a nightmare built out of her imagination. They assured her that she was safe and that nightmares were dreams that rarely occurred.

They were wrong.

The dream came back night after night after night to torture her. After a few nights, her parents were concerned and took her to a doctor. Her childhood became very difficult and lonely over the course of a few short weeks.

She saw more specialists than she cared to remember and was immediately treated like she was broken. It didn't matter who she saw or what their specialty was, they couldn't cure her. The dream still came, and the isolation and treatments continued.

Her family grew more protective of her, and her twin brothers, only a year and a few months older than her, never let her out of their sight. Friendships, outside of her best friend, Lexa, were difficult, and relationships were impossible.

For Ariyana, the memory of her life before her dream became but a dream itself, something untouchable and hard to reach. Her life became a whirlwind of medical professionals trying to fix her broken mind, cure her illness, medicate her sickness.

She hated those words just as much as she hated the doctors who spoke them. She never felt broken, ill, or sick. She just felt heartbroken and alone.

She grew up quickly, learning how to tell her family and doctors exactly what they wanted to hear, and her best friend, Lexa, was the only person that Ariyana confided in.

Lexa was as protective of her as her family was, but in a different way. Whereas her family sought to protect her from herself, Lexa sought to protect Ariyana from the world. She never treated Ariyana like she was sick or broken. Lexa treated Ariyana like she was important and special to the world; a world that could hurt her if Lexa wasn't diligent in watching over her. Lexa and Ariyana were inseparable.

Things changed when Ariyana and Lexa were in their last semester of college. They had pushed through four years of college quickly and were set to graduate at age twenty-two. They had their lives mapped out and were going to leave the day after graduation to travel the world. Lexa spent nights keeping Ariyana's mind occupied before they went to bed, talking about the adventures that they were going to have.

Then, Devyn walked into their lives.

Ariyana had never dated anyone before. When she was young, her parents wouldn't allow it, and when she was in college, she was worried about trying to explain her dream. She felt pretty confident that waking up screaming in the middle of the night would lead to her date running for the door.

Devyn didn't make her feel worried about that, though. She felt drawn to him, and he to her. She told him everything on their first date, and instead of pushing her away, he seemed to pull her closer, wanting to keep her as safe as Lexa did.

Devyn incorporated himself into their friendship quickly, even joining them for a couple of months to travel around after graduation.

Ariyana and Devyn's relationship progressed as quickly as their friendship. They married soon after she turned twenty-three, and she got pregnant right away with twin boys. They were excited to start a family, and the prospect of becoming parents pulled them closer together. They would spend hours each day talking about everything and planning for the arrival of their children. Ariyana felt lucky to be in love, and though she still had the same dream every night, the sadness that she felt upon waking was nothing compared to the joy that she felt about the babies growing inside her.

Ariyana felt free to be herself, and the pain of being controlled and forced to take multiple kinds of medication as a child to stop her dreams felt like a distant memory. She and Devyn promised each other to stay honest and true to one another.

Everything changed the morning of her twenty-fourth birthday, though. Ariyana's dream consumed her completely that morning. Devyn was startled awake by her whole body convulsing next to his. Then, she started to scream, a scream so intense that it sounded like her soul was being ripped from her body.

Devyn panicked and rushed her to the hospital, concerned about her life and the lives of their unborn sons.

When Ariyana came to, her water broke, and she went into labor. After three hours, her sons were born and safe in her arms. She felt an instant connection to them. Their eyes were open and full of awe. They studied her face with their eyes, and reached for her with outstretched hands.

Her dream had hit a new level of intensity, and though the details of Glacin's death had been more graphic, sadness did not dare enter her heart in that moment. Ariyana was consumed with love for the two little boys in her arms. She looked up to share that moment with the man that she loved, but instead was met with the eyes of a distant stranger. The Devyn who was looking back at her held no love or companionship in his eyes.

Devyn argued with her, raising his voice in a way that he never had before, making their sons cry. He demanded that she go back to her doctors and resume her medication. She begged him to change his mind. His face remained hard and uncompromising as he let her know that if she refused, he would make sure that she never saw their children again. He told her that he finally saw the truth. She had put their children in danger by ignoring her condition, and he said that he didn't feel that she could be a fit mother without medication.

Ariyana felt cornered and heartbroken. *How could she chance losing her beautiful sons?* Devyn had years of medical records from her parents to show any judge that there was something in her life that she could not control. So she took the only path that she could see in that moment, returned to the doctors and started taking the medication again. The medication made her sick and her mind slow, but it seemed easier for her to be sick so that everyone else could pretend she was normal.

Their marital relationship suffered because Ariyana felt less and less like herself. She still tried to be honest with Devyn, talking about her feelings around the dream, telling him that the medicine was making her sick and wasn't working, and trying to build a family with him, but he continued to push back. He refused to listen to her whenever she mentioned it, telling her that she was just looking for attention.

Finally, a year and a half ago, she couldn't stand feeling sick and started lying. She stopped taking her medication. She trained herself to wake up in the early morning and move to another room in the house before her dream came on. She also took the medicine with her on her morning run and threw it away.

She hated lying to him, but hated feeling out of control more.

Everything had been fine up until this morning—the morning of her thirtieth birthday and her sons' sixth birthday. The dream had grown in intensity again, and she couldn't control her screaming or her body's reaction to the dream. Now, here she was again, staring into the hard, uncompromising face of the man who was supposed to love her unconditionally.

Chapter 7

"Are you listening to me?" Devyn asked sharply.

"What?" she snapped.

"Are you kidding?" he shot back. His neck muscles were tense, and his hands were shaking. "You have no room here to give me attitude." He shoved his injured arm in her face. "What the hell, Ariyana?"

The skin around the bite mark was red and starting to bruise. She had broken the skin with her two upper central incisors, and he was bleeding slightly. The wound wasn't very deep, and, at most, he would just have a nasty bruise for a couple of weeks, but, still, she had never hurt anyone during a dream, and the sight of the injury made her flinch. "I'm sorry for biting you. I think you must have scared me. I thought that you were—"

"Stop it!" he yelled, pointing a finger at her. "I don't want to hear it. You lied to me. I will not give your nightmare power by talking about it."

She stood up. "Would you please just listen for once? I couldn't take that poison any longer. It made me feel sick and like I was walking through life in a fog, never truly myself. I'd been telling you that for four-and-a-half years. I told you that I was miserable and that that poison wasn't helping. All it did was trap me in my own mind in the morning. The dream still happened. I just couldn't wake up from it."

"What part of 'I don't want to hear it,' don't you get? I don't want to listen to your excuses," he said. He turned around and stormed out of the room. She heard him rummage through something in the bathroom. Then, he stomped back into the room and threw something at her.

She flinched and caught it against her chest. She looked down and saw her medicine bottle. She looked up at him in confusion. "I just told you that this stuff makes me sick, that it's not working, and that it's trapping me inside the dream, unable to wake up. Don't you care about that?" she asked.

"I care about the fact that you lied to me. I care about the fact that you bit me. But no, I don't care about the excuses that you have right now. The way I see it is that when you take the medicine, neither our children nor I wake up to you screaming and thrashing about. Seems like it is working just fine to me."

Hot anger raced through her body, and she threw the bottle at his face. He jerked his head out of the way, and it hit the door behind him. "I'm not sick, Devyn!"

Devyn crossed the room in a long stride and grabbed her by the wrist. She yanked it free. His eyebrows pulled together, and he shoved his injured forearm in front of her face. "You're not well either," he snapped. "Normal, healthy people don't do this to their spouses, nor are they plagued night after night by the same nightmare. It's not about what makes you feel comfortable. You have to think about those around you and how you might be influencing them."

His words hit her like a backhand to the face. He used the words "normal" and "healthy" against her. She hated those words and what they meant.

She broke eye contact and looked over at the window. It was still dark outside. The clock on the nightstand said it was 4:45 a.m. The window was cracked open, and the wooden blinds were moving from a light breeze that was blowing in. Today was the first day of fall, and Ariyana could already feel a chill in the air. She took a deep breath, and her nostrils filled with the sweet scent of pine. This was the best time of year to visit her parents' cabin. She loved being high in the mountains, but even the things that she loved about celebrating her and her sons' birthdays up here weren't enough to change the fact that she was done being treated like a broken doll.

Every doctor that her parents had dragged her to had used words like *normal* and *healthy* to let her know what she lacked in this world, and now Devyn was doing the same. It felt like a betrayal. Yes, they struggled in their relationship, and he demanded that she take medicine for her dream, but he had always left those hateful words alone. He knew that she suffered from the trauma of being a lab rat as a child and was careful about the words that he used when they fought.

That wasn't the case today.

The chill in her chest throbbed, and she reached up to massage it.

Devyn turned toward the door, picked up the medicine bottle, and placed it on a small table by the door. "I'm going to go clean up my arm," he said, without looking back at her.

She looked down at her own hands, expecting them to be covered in blood and ash, but they were clean. She continued to stare at them. There was something else about what he had said that was nagging at her. It dawned on her, and she looked up.

"Who am I influencing?" she asked.

Devyn stopped abruptly with his hand on the doorknob. His shoulders were tense through his thin t-shirt. "What?" he asked with a small hitch in his voice.

"You said that I have to think about how I might be influencing someone. Who are you talking about?"

He turned his head and peered into her eyes. His anger, demand, and stubbornness were gone and replaced with nervous energy.

"It's strange," she continued, "the boys always run in when we have an argument."

He continued to stare and didn't say a word.

"Where are the children, Devyn?" she demanded.

His eyes softened, and he walked over to her. He ran his hand down her upper arm and cradled her elbow in his hand. "I think it's time for you to start thinking about the boys and how your behavior is affecting them." He flashed her a condescending look when he said the word "behavior."

Her breath caught in her throat. She tried to step away from him, but he tightened his grip on her elbow.

"Don't give me that look. I didn't say that you were a bad mom. I would never say that. I just think that your obsession with this nightmare is negatively influencing them. They adore you and want to protect you. We've both heard them talking about their dreams and how they see the same thing night after night. The doctor says that they are experiencing a type of "sympathy pain" after six years of watching your reaction to your nightmare. It's not real, Ariyana. They just don't want you to feel alone."

"Screw you," she hissed and pulled her arm free. "You are just as small-minded as all of those doctors are…, and my family. I told you everything when we first went out. I was honest with you the whole time that we dated, and you promised me you would never let anyone take away my right to choose how I dealt with this." Tears burned in her eyes. "I think that the real truth here is that *you lied to me*. You have no right to threaten to take the boys away from me unless I take these meds." She stomped over, grabbed the medicine bottle off the table and pushed it toward him. "I'm sorry I would rather not feel sick all the time," she began, and then the medicine bottle caught her attention. She pulled it closer to her face to read the label. She looked up at Devyn in shock. "This is dated two weeks ago, from Dr. Jensen. Why do you have a new prescription for me from my doctor? How did you get this?"

He raised his head and rolled his right shoulder. He always did that when he didn't want to talk about something. "I had to ask him a few questions and, let's be clear here, he is our family doctor, not just your doctor. I have as much right to talk to him as you do. Also, it's not a new prescription; it is a refill. I called it in for you … to help," he responded in a casual tone.

She narrowed her eyes at him. *He was lying.* If something was going on with him, he would just tell her, not give her a vague response about having a few questions. The questions must have been about her. Unless—

"Why aren't the kids in here?" she blurted out, realizing that he hadn't answered her question about the kids. She stepped to the side to walk to the door, but he stepped in front of her, blocking her path. Anger and panic flared in her chest, intensifying the icy throb. The little hairs on the back of her neck rose, and goose bumps prickled down her spine. "What have you done?" she demanded.

"I haven't done anything wrong. I agree with Dr. Jensen on this. He feels that if we can get in front of this now with the boys, we can break it before it becomes a habit."

She lunged forward and shoved her forearm into his chest. "What did you do?" she yelled.

He was a foot taller than her and was twice her size in muscle mass, but she caught him off guard, and he slammed back against the door. His eyes widened in surprise for a moment, then narrowed into irritation.

"What the hell has gotten into you?" he barked. "You are acting irrationally. Can't you see how unhealthy this behavior is and how unhealthy it would be for the boys to see it?" He pushed her arm off his chest, causing her to step back. "You act like I am some kind of villain, set out to poison you and our children. Stop being so dramatic. All I did was give the boys something to help them sleep. It's no different from taking a Benadryl." He rolled his eyes and shook his head.

"You're wrong," she said, taking one more step away from him.

Ariyana felt like a fist was closing around her heart, and she was struggling to keep it from constricting inside her. She was still reeling from her dream. For her, Glacin had just died, and dream or not, the loss felt real. She also hadn't had a chance to work through the new details that revealed themselves in the dream this time. She had seen herself do things in her dream that alarmed her.

Now she was standing in front of a cold and distant man she did not know. This was not the man whom she had fallen in love with. How could he not understand the consequences of his actions? It was true that she had lied about taking her medicine, but that was nothing compared to Devyn seeing her doctor behind her back and deciding to give the children medication without talking to her first.

The chill in her chest began to throb again, and she noticed that her proximity to Devyn was becoming uncomfortable. She was sure that she was imagining it, but swore that she could feel his body heat even though he was a few feet away from her.

She squared her shoulders and crossed her arms. "You need to get the hell out of my way," she said sharply.

"You're blowing this out of proportion," he said in a condescending tone. "You're the one in the wrong here, not me. You've been lying to me for a year and a half."

Her body was shaking. "And you've been ignoring me for six! Move!" she yelled. She pushed past him and threw the door open, making sure to hit him with it. She crossed the hallway to the boys' room, opened the door, and stepped inside.

Chapter 8

Her senses were always heightened after waking up but never to the extent that they were this morning. Stepping into her children's room was like stepping into a thorn bush. Every inch of exposed skin prickled.

The air was thick with distress.

The weak glow from the small night light in the left corner of the room cast eerie shadows over the strained features of their faces. Their minds were restless, though their bodies were tense and completely still.

Their beds were positioned in the right corner of the room at a right angle to each other. When she had put them to bed that night, their feet were facing each other at the corner, but at some point they had shifted, and now their heads were touching at the corner, and they were holding hands.

Devyn hadn't left the room across the hall. She could feel his eyes on her, watching her slow advance into the room. She knew that he wanted to see her face when she realized that he was right, but he would have no such luck. Anyone willing to open their eyes would see that these children were in a state of distress. *That was the problem, though, wasn't it? Devyn had chosen to turn a blind eye to each of them, her included.*

Ariyana approached the boys slowly, each step a challenge due to the tension in the room. Her eyes adjusted to the limited light, and her heart sank. Their foreheads were covered in tiny beads of sweat that glistened as their heads twitched on the beds. Their eyes moved wildly under their eyelids.

They were dreaming.

She cast a look down and behind her, catching a glimpse of Devyn's shadow in her periphery. *The coward hadn't moved. How could he not see what was so clearly in front of him?* His sons might not be on what he considered a *real medication*, but they were just as trapped as she was. Their little minds were locked in sleep—locked in the darkness of the dream that filled their thoughts.

She closed the distance between them and collapsed to her knees at their bedside. She never wished that her dream would become theirs. This was the first morning, outside of the day that they were born, that she had woken up screaming, so she'd never had to explain her outbursts to them. They were so young. She didn't want to burden them with her pain, and yet, even though she didn't talk to them about it, they always seemed to know.

They would wake up soon after she did, running in with concerned looks and warm snuggles, gently stroking her cheeks and forehead. As they got older, they'd started asking questions about the creatures that she kept to herself, and two weeks ago, they asked about Glacin. She had been so careful for so long, but they knew about it anyway. In her heart, she believed that they could see what she saw. She knew that it didn't make sense, but, for her, it didn't have to. They were her sons, and they shared a deep connection to her soul.

Now, here they were, hands clasped so tightly that their knuckles were white from strain, and she was responsible. She reached out to soothe them and wrapped her hands around their tiny, joined fist of tangled fingers.

The moment her skin made contact with theirs, images blasted through her mind as clear as if they were in the room: a black, burning scar of smoke through the morning sky, three black crescent moons set against a pale background, and blood, pools of its bright crimson color surrounding and splashed across grey granite rocks.

A deep growl filled her mind, the sound replacing the images, and increased in intensity until it felt like her body was humming with it. The sound took over her thoughts like a siren's call in the ocean. She concentrated on it, reached out toward it with her mind, but instead of being met by a destination, a single word tore through her thoughts, instantly breaking the connection.

Aris!

She toppled backward onto her butt, breathless and confused. The cool, comforting smell of fall wafted around her. The smell was faint, but oddly noticeable considering the windows in her children's room were closed.

The icy ache in her chest had increased, and she protectively placed her hand over the spot. It felt like a dark hand had pierced through her chest, wrapped around the icy spike, and squeezed, chilling her deeply.

There was a rustling behind her and a murmur of words that she didn't care to listen to. She pulled herself back up onto her knees in front of the boys.

Surprisingly, the strain was gone. Their hands were still clasped, but not in distress…in comfort. Their skin was dry, and their faces were peaceful. She reached out and placed both of her hands on their clasped hands. She was grateful when nothing happened, no images, no sounds, just their perfect sleeping faces.

As identical twins, their facial features and body types were exactly the same except for two interesting differences: Alec had dark brown hair and sky blue eyes; Kai had white-blonde hair and emerald green eyes. The doctors had told her that it was rare to see these kinds of differences, but not unheard of. For Ariyana, it wasn't any stranger to her than the fact that they were born on the same day that she had been.

She reached out, first smoothing Alec's hair off his forehead and then Kai's, and then she bent down and kissed them both on the forehead.

They didn't move, and her frustration surfaced again. It didn't matter that their dreams had settled. Devyn had had no right to make this decision on his own.

She shook her head. That wasn't it, though. That wasn't what was fueling the growing frustration and anxiety inside her. Yes, she was furious with him, but what she saw and heard when she touched their hands felt more urgent, more ominous.

The ache in her chest made her feel like something had a hold of her, and the images and the word that tore across her thoughts, though she didn't know what they meant, felt like a warning.

She stood abruptly.

She had to get out of the cabin; she had to get away from Devyn.

She turned on her heel, quickly left the children's room, and pushed past Devyn and his mumbles of weak concern. She pulled her sleep shirt off and tossed it at him. She rummaged through the top drawer of the dresser and pulled out her running clothes. She was grateful that she'd had the forethought to store some clothes in this extra room the night before.

"What are you doing? It's 5 a.m. You can't go running right now," he said. "We need to talk about this before your family shows up later. You can clearly see that the kids are fine. You can see that you were wrong."

"Oh, can I clearly see that? You're an idiot, Devyn." She stomped over to him and glared up into his eyes. "You're blind here," she hissed, pointing at his eyes. "And here." She poked her index finger into the middle of his forehead, hard enough for his head to flinch back. "And I will do whatever the hell I want."

Ariyana threw her stuff onto the bed. Then, she put on a sports bra and a running tank top and quickly pulled on a pair of shorts and some socks.

"This isn't going to work if you're going to act like that. You're the one in the wrong, and you're projecting onto me. All I've ever done is try to protect this family and keep us healthy and together."

She grabbed her shoes and slowly turned her head to look at him. "You're delusional," she snapped. "This," she gestured wildly in a circle, "is not protection. This is control. This is your way, or no way at all. And I am tired of it. I am not sick, and instead of listening to me and trying to help me, you've pushed medication onto me and threatened me. So, you're damn right! We do need to talk about this, but not until I've had a chance to think about what I need from now on. Not until I've had a chance to think about what's right for me *and for them*." She stabbed her finger toward the children's room.

She looked down, slipped her shoes on, and stood to look at him again. "What kind of person drugs their own children?" she asked, her tone full of disgust.

His eyes widened. He opened his mouth to talk.

"No, shut up," she barked, and pushed past him out into the hall. "I don't want to hear your excuses," she called back, throwing his own words in his face.

Chapter 9

Ariyana stood on the edge of the wooden porch, staring at the white stone path that led into the woods at the back of the property. The pine trees stood like shadowed sentinels against the clear, dark sky. The full moon was behind her, low in the sky but still above the tree line. It made the stone path in front of her glow and the woods beyond appear full of shadows and mysteries.

Her heart was pounding, and she couldn't catch her breath. She was overwhelmed with conflicting desires: wanting to hit Devyn; wanting to collapse onto her knees and cry; wanting to run as fast and far as she could. Her heart hurt, her soul ached. *Devyn was being unreasonable. Why was it hard for him to see that she needed him to support her for who she was, not who he wanted her to be? Why couldn't he see that he was wrong? She would never have made a decision like giving the children medicine for something that wasn't medically necessary without talking to him first.* She hated the medicine, and she hated that he just assumed that the children were *tainted* with her issues.

She jumped off the porch and stomped over to the pine tree in the yard next to the stone path. The air was crisp against her flushed skin, but it didn't bring her any relief. She felt like she was suffocating. She wanted to be herself, free from hiding who she was, and free from being forced to be the person that she wasn't. She clenched her fists, yelled, and kicked the tree.

Ariyana started as the grass rustled behind the tree, and a figure stepped out into the moonlight.

"Don't kick," Lexa teased, holding her hands out playfully, as if Ariyana were wielding a dangerous weapon. She chuckled at her little joke and jumped from stone to stone on the path like she was playing hopscotch. Her straight, jet-black hair was pulled up and away from her heart-shaped face into a high ponytail. It danced around her shoulders while she jumped. When she reached Ariyana's side, she did a dramatic final pounce, landing on two feet to face her. Her honey-colored, almond-shaped eyes sparkled with mischief.

Lexa was striking and fierce. She was the type of person that stood out in a crowd. She was five foot ten, with a lean and long muscular body. She had always been a natural runner. Her skin was flawless and sun-kissed. Even now, in the moonlight, she had the perfect outfit on to accentuate her tanned skin: olive green, short running shorts, sports bra, and tank top. She studied Ariyana for a few moments, her eyes darting back and forth between Ariyana's eyes. "Running again?" she asked, raising an eyebrow.

Lexa's double meaning was not lost on Ariyana, and she narrowed her eyes at her. "I'm in no mood for your tongue-in-cheek today," she said and turned back toward the porch.

"Well, when my best friend isn't in such a bitchy mood, she usually likes my tongue-in-cheek," Lexa said, her lips in a feigned pout.

Ariyana turned back and glared at her. "Are you trying to be disgusting or funny?" Ariyana asked.

Lexa flashed her a *who-me* grin and said, "Both."

"Fun," Ariyana said, not hiding her annoyance as she sat down on the end of the porch. "Why are you here so early? You're supposed to be here later when my family shows up."

"Don't play hard to get," Lexa responded, walking over to her. "You know why I'm here." She gestured to her outfit and tapped on her temple with her index finger. "I was staying in a hotel in town, and something woke me up at two. I couldn't fall back asleep. I felt like I needed to be here…so here I am, ready to run."

Ariyana's chest throbbed, sending icy pulses through her heart and lungs. The sensation was intensifying. She reached up and massaged the spot. She looked down at her hands and saw a flash of them covered in blood and ash. She flinched and started vigorously rubbing her hands together.

Lexa sat down next to her and placed her hands over Ariyana's. "What doesn't exist can't be wiped clean," she said soothingly, all humor was gone and replaced with concern. "It was worse, wasn't it?"

Ariyana felt tears start to burn in her eyes, and she looked away. "Do you remember what I've told you about what I look like in the dream?"

"Of course. Tall, pale-skinned creature with swirls of silver all over your body, silver feathers that burn with silver flame, long tail, claws, and talons. Or, in one word, incredible."

Ariyana straightened and gave her a sideways glance. "Not this time," she said.

"What do you mean?" Lexa asked. "More detail seems to come into focus for you with each dream, but the dream itself doesn't change. It starts the same and ends the same, and you've always been the same creature. So, what are you saying? 'Not this time?' What? What was different?"

"The part about how I stopped the creatures was really clear this time. Glacin was dying, and he had just saved my life for the second time. I could feel our bond shattering, and something inside me changed, like a switch. When I stood up in the clutch's fire, I could sense the insect-like creature's energy," she said, turning to look into Lexa's eyes. "I can still feel it inside of me. It was an energy that their bodies radiated, but I couldn't see it until that moment. And I didn't just see it, I could taste it … I could feel it. It woke something up inside of me that I didn't want to control—a hunger, and it changed me. Black fire consumed my silver fire and the clutch's fire. It wrapped around my body and filled my mind. I leapt at the closest creature and buried my claws deep into its brain. I connected with its energy, and I pulled it into my body. Once I started, I realized that I could connect with all the creatures on the planet and syphon their energy through the creature I was holding. I couldn't stop. I wanted more. I wasn't thinking about saving Glacin or the clutch behind me, or about the creatures that I was killing. The only thing that I wanted was to satiate my hunger. I tried to push the connection further to other creatures on other planets, but something stopped me. It was like slamming into a wall. It hurt and left me crazed for more, but if it hadn't happened, and if Glacin hadn't been able to pull me back from my hunger, I don't know what I would have done. I killed all of those creatures, Lexa. What does that say about me?"

"It says that I shouldn't mess with your internal demons," she responded matter-of-factly.

"I'm being serious."

"So am I. What do you want me to do? Psychoanalyze you? I don't know how to do that shit, and, honestly, I know that you don't believe in that shit anyway. I know you believe there is more behind this dream, and I don't have the answer to that. I do know pain, though, and yours is very real. I don't believe that these new details mean that you have evil inside of you. I think it shows that you were willing to do anything to save Glacin's life."

Ariyana gave her a weak smile and sighed.

In reality, Ariyana wanted to snap back and say, *If I was so willing to do anything to save Glacin, then why was I only focused on my hunger, not him?* She also wanted to admit to Lexa that it wasn't just the new details that were bothering her. This dream felt more real than any other had before. If she focused, she could remember how her body felt when she moved, how the flames felt along her skin, and how her senses came alive when that energy flowed through her body. But she held her tongue. How could she admit that her body, as it was now, felt more foreign to her than the body that she inhabited in her nightly dream?

Ariyana clenched her jaw, not wanting the words to spill out of her. *Maybe she should consider that Lexa was right; maybe there was a better way to look at this.* Ariyana tended to focus on her failure in the dream, that she failed to save her companion, and now she was also focusing on the ruthlessness that she saw in herself as she pulled the energy out of each of those creatures. Instead of trying to figure out the inner meanings of the dream, maybe she should focus on what Lexa pointed out: she didn't fail because she had given up. She did everything that she could to try to save Glacin and the clutch. That was important to remember, even if that "everything" involved an ability that terrified her.

Lexa was also right about knowing pain. It was what had connected them when they first met.

Lexa and her father had moved into the neighborhood about two months after Ariyana turned six, and she was the new student in Ariyana's kindergarten class. By that point, Ariyana had lost Glacin every night for two months, and the emotional trauma of the dream was taking its toll on her. Watching her companion die every night added what felt like years to her young life. She was quiet and did not interact with the other kids in her class. She was already seeing multiple doctors throughout the week, and even kids as young as six could be cruel in their stares and whispered talking.

Ariyana remembered Lexa coming into the class and being introduced, but she'd had no intention of getting to know her.

Lexa had had other plans.

Lexa was drawn to Ariyana the moment that she met her. She saw the pain that she felt in Ariyana's eyes. Ariyana knew death, just as Lexa did.

Lexa's parents were in the military. Her mom was deployed overseas when Lexa was four and a half for what was supposed to be only a six-month deployment. Lexa had been very close to her mother, who had sworn to her that she would return on her fifth birthday. Three days before that, her mom video-called her and informed her that her deployment had been extended another four weeks. Her mom was going to miss her birthday. Lexa was devastated that her mom was breaking her promise to her. She told her that she hated her and slammed the laptop shut, refusing to open it when it rang again.

On the morning of her birthday, two military officers came to their home. She watched from the kitchen as they talked with her father. She couldn't hear what they were talking about, but her father kept adamantly shaking his head. Then, the man who had never shed a tear in front of her, collapsed forward into the two officers, crying. They helped her father into the living room, and as they were about to step out of the hallway, her father made eye contact with her. She knew the truth immediately—her mother was dead.

In that moment, she took the full weight of her mother's death onto her shoulders. It was her fault; it was her words that had left her mother broken and susceptible to mistake.

Lexa, being only five years old, took her guilt and wrapped it up in rage. Though she remembered seeing her father collapse all those years ago, she had no memory of leaving the kitchen. All she remembered was that one moment she realized her mother was dead, and the next, she was screaming and hitting one of the officers as her father tried to pull her off of him

Lexa cried for twelve days straight. Death changed her—her pain, her heart, her soul. She was a different child after that. She and her father moved around a lot after that, trying to find a place to settle down and heal, and that's when Lexa found Ariyana.

It was clear to Lexa the day that she first saw Ariyana that she was suffering from loss. It was different from Lexa's loss, but it was still loss, and Lexa had felt that Ariyana needed her. She had an intense need to protect Ariyana, and though Ariyana was hesitant to connect, Lexa never let her be alone. It had taken them a couple of years to truly become inseparable, but once it happened, it was impossible to find one without the other. As they grew older, their bond grew stronger. They were attuned to each other.

Even to this day, it surprised Ariyana just how much Lexa could feel what she was feeling, and vice versa. Lexa accepted her for who she was and what she believed, no matter how crazy.

Lexa bumped her shoulder into Ariyana's, and she turned to look at her. "So, tell me, what else happened. Your dreams are the most intense every six years. I'm assuming that all of this isn't just because the dream was bad?" Lexa said, shrugging her shoulders. "Does Devyn know that you haven't been taking your medicine?"

"Yes," Ariyana answered and looked down again.

"What happened?" Lexa asked, and Ariyana heard the excitement in her tone.

"I guess that I was screaming, and he tried to wake me." She bit her lower lip. "I bit him," she said softly.

"I'm sorry, *what did you just say?*"

Ariyana turned and looked at her. "I bit him on his forearm."

Lexa's eyebrows raised in alarm, she pressed her lips together, and her chin started to quiver.

"Don't," Ariyana scolded.

Lexa burst into laughter, tipping back onto the porch and rolling from side to side.

"It's not funny."

"Yes, actually it is! He's a big guy, and you're like what? One hundred and fifteen pounds? He can bench twice that on a bad day. He's just pissed cause your feisty butt got the better of him."

"It's more complicated than that. He's mad because I lied about taking the medicine. He thinks that I'm negatively influencing the boys and is throwing the same threats in my face."

"It's your body, your life, your choice. You stopped for a reason. Maybe he will listen after he stops being butt-hurt about you biting him. I mean, how did the kids take it? Did they freak out? They have such a strong connection to you. I'm sure that they just want to protect you."

"They didn't come in," Ariyana said. She stood up and looked at the sky. It was changing from inky black to dark purple. The sun was rising. "Devyn gave the boys something to help them sleep without talking to me. They didn't hear anything."

"What?" Lexa was by her side in a moment.

Ariyana turned and met her gaze. Her honey-colored eyes burned with anger. "I told you it was more complicated," Ariyana said.

"Yeah, you could say that. What are you going to do? This isn't okay."

"I don't know. It was awful. I went in to see them, and they didn't wake up." Ariyana felt her emotions starting to rise again as Lexa grabbed her arm.

"Hey, it's going to be alright. You know that, right? We can fix this. You don't have to take that crap anymore. He can't force you. And he can't just give the kids medicine without talking to you about it first. We'll find a way. I promise. Now, come on, it's your birthday. Let's run some of this stress off, come back and clean up, and after that, we'll figure out the rest. Okay? We can't solve everything right now, but we can run until our lungs burst. I mean, yours will probably burst before mine since you're so old now. It might be hard for you to keep up." She sucked in a breath between her clenched teeth and shrugged her shoulders playfully.

"I'm two months older than you," Ariyana stated, shaking her head at her.

"I know. I'm still twenty-nine, so young and so beautiful," she said, flipping her pony-tail behind her. "Try to keep up."

Lexa took off toward the tree line.

Ariyana smiled and took off after her. She wanted to take a moment to be lighthearted. Unfortunately, as she attempted to catch up, she couldn't shake the nagging feeling that she should have told her friend about the images that she had seen when she touched her children's clasped hands.

Chapter 10

The air felt icy as she ran, and it easily cut through the thin material of her running clothes. She welcomed the feel of it, though. It balanced her body temperature with the chill in her chest.

Her body settled into its natural rhythm quickly. The ground rushed by in a blur, and the steady thump of her feet echoed around her. She fell in about twelve feet behind Lexa and maintained that distance between them. She was grateful for her friend's presence but needed some time in her own thoughts.

They followed the white stone path to the tree line, and, without breaking pace, Lexa led them into the thick pine forest. The cold air was fragrant with the scent of pine trees and granite.

They had run this trail many times before. In daylight, it would have been easy to see the well-worn path beneath their feet, but now, in the dark, they relied on memory to carry them forward.

The moon was still high enough to pierce through the trees behind them, and that provided Ariyana with enough light to see flashes of Lexa as she moved in and out of the shadows. Her long black hair swung back and forth, her leg muscles flexed with each step, and her warm breath surrounded her in puffs. Lexa made running look easy and beautiful at the same time.

Ariyana loved to run as much as Lexa did, but she didn't look as graceful. It had taken her years of training to find her pace, whereas it had come naturally to Lexa. Ariyana always felt like her body wasn't quite balanced correctly for running, like something was off, but she always pushed forward and eventually found a pace to keep up with her friend. Unfortunately, though, that didn't mean that they were on common ground. Ariyana may have found a way to keep up with her, but that didn't mean that Lexa was running at full speed. It didn't happen often, but on occasion,

Lexa could go from graceful gazelle to fierce predator in a matter of seconds and take off without warning. It was a sight to see.

Lexa was similar to Ariyana when it came to needing time in her own thoughts, and she used her running as a way to work through the horrors in her own mind. There were no secrets between the two of them, and just as Ariyana's dream was more intense on some nights than others, the memory of losing her mom affected Lexa more deeply on some mornings. These were the mornings when Lexa ran more like a fierce predator, as if she could hunt the memory down and destroy it. Luckily for Ariyana, on this morning, Lexa was maintaining the pace that she needed to keep them both together.

They pushed deeper into the forest.

Ariyana began to notice that the chill in her chest was pulsing in time with her heartbeat and was growing into a cold burn through the upper part of her core. She sucked in two deep breaths and exhaled forcefully to stretch her chest and lungs, but it didn't help. She rolled her shoulders and took two more deep breaths. This time, she noticed what she had missed before. There was no warmth to her breath. The air inside her lungs was cold and ghosted invisibly past her lips with each exhale.

She slowed down a little, wondering if that had ever happened before. She was about to call out to her friend, who was charging forward, when she noticed another strange sensation—a hum in her mind.

It was faint, and it felt like a light pressure on the top of her skull.

She stopped and scanned the trees around her. It had grown lighter, and the black of the shadows was being chased away. She could see enough detail of the trees around her to know that nothing seemed out of place. She looked up to the tops of the trees where patches of grey-purple sky peeked through.

The sun would rise over the mountains soon.

The chill in her chest changed from a throb to a hum and matched the hum in her mind. Her body felt electrified.

"Do you feel that?" she called out to Lexa. *No response.*

Her head snapped toward the direction that they had been running in. She had assumed that Lexa had heard her stop and stopped running herself, but she was completely out of sight.

She jogged forward a few paces and stopped suddenly. The hum intensified with each step, and it now felt like her entire skull was vibrating. She called out again, and still there was no response.

She grabbed her temples. She felt like her eyeballs were shaking in her head. "Lexa! Something's wrong. Where are you?"

She could hear the desperate plea in her tone. This wasn't like her friend. Lexa was always aware of her surroundings and never let Ariyana out of sight for too long. Even when she sprinted forward in a burst of energy, she would loop back after a few moments, let Ariyana catch up, then run alongside her briefly before pulling slightly ahead again.

Ariyana took a few more steps, and the vibration traveled down her spine, sending flares of pain out along her nerve endings. She stopped and squeezed her eyes shut. Light flashed behind her eyelids, and the same images filled her mind again: a black, burning scar of smoke through the morning sky, three black crescent moons set against a pale background, and blood, pools of its bright crimson color surrounding and spattering grey granite rocks.

The images left as quickly as they came, and her eyes popped open. She felt breathless and frigid. Something was very wrong. She pushed forward, ignoring the increasing vibration and sense of foreboding. She had to get to Lexa.

She burst through the tree line into a huge meadow and stopped abruptly. The sight in front of her might not have seemed out of place to anyone else, but to Ariyana it was wrong. Lexa stood twenty feet in front of Ariyana, off the trail. Her back was to Ariyana, and she was perfectly still. Her body was rigid; her face was angled up at the light purple and pink sky; her arms were at her sides, and her fingers were fully splayed. Her muscles looked contracted, as though her body were under enormous strain.

Ariyana opened her mouth to call out to Lexa, but her words were cut off by a sharp lance of pain through both temples. She clenched her teeth and pressed the palms of her hands against her temples, willing herself to push through the pain. Her eyes darted around the meadow. She had no evidence to suggest that they were surrounded by danger, but her body felt what her eyes could not show her. She charged forward, following her instincts. She had to reach Lexa.

Ariyana was an arm's length away from Lexa when many things happened at once. She reached out to touch Lexa, and a burst of light flashed across the meadow. This coincided with the sun's first light peaking over the tops of the mountains to the east, but they were independent of each other. The flash of light reached them, and Lexa fell backward like a plank.

Ariyana, taken off guard, caught Lexa's head before it hit.

Ariyana gasped when she saw that Lexa's eyes were wide and unseeing, and she had trickles of blood coming out of her right nostril and both ears. Her body held no warmth, was pale, and clammy to the touch.

Ariyana was reaching toward Lexa's cheek when a three-taloned foot stamped down next to her. Something rough grabbed her around the throat, and the next thing she knew, she was flying through the air.

Chapter 11

Ariyana awoke suddenly, pain seizing the breath in her lungs and her voice in her throat.

She was lying on her left side with her right arm over her head. Her right hand was tangled in her hair and pinned between her head and something solid and cold.

There was a slight ringing in her ears.

She forced a breath out and sucked a quick breath in. The smell of dirt and blood filled her nostrils. *What happened?*

Her head was heavy, and her eyelids didn't want to open. She felt confused and fuzzy. She knew that lying on her side on the ground wasn't normal but the "why" escaped her.

Her body ached all over, and the chill in her chest felt like it had intensified, making her feel abnormally cold. She wanted to curl her legs into her body to keep her core warm, but her legs wouldn't cooperate. Her body didn't want to move.

She concentrated and realized that there was something else there. It swam at the edges of her awareness. It was distant at first, unfocused and overshadowed by her pain, but as she concentrated on it, it became obvious.

Danger.

It surrounded her like a thick fog. Every nerve ending on her exposed skin was warning her that she was in trouble.

Her memory rushed back: Lexa bleeding; the three-taloned foot; feeling a rush of air. *Something must have thrown her. But what?*

She heard a rustling sound in the grass. It wasn't right next to her, but it was close. It had an aggressive rhythm to it, almost like stomping. It didn't sound like an animal, though; at least not an animal that she was familiar with.

She stopped trying to force her body to move, kept her eyes closed, and mentally took stock of her injuries. Her body ached, her left side felt raw, and her head was pounding; *maybe a concussion, that would explain the heavy, fuzzy feeling.* Her left arm hurt, and her right hand felt swollen; her legs seemed okay, but the fact that she could freely wiggle her left toes told her that her shoe must have come off.

She pulled her head forward gently and moved her hand across her scalp. *Her fingers still worked.* She wasn't sure if anything was broken, but she could tell that she had less strength in the hand. As she moved to raise her arm from her head, she noticed that her hair was wet and warm. *She must have instinctively protected her head from injury.* She had still hit her head, but it felt like her hand might have taken the brunt of the damage.

She lay her hand down in front of her face and slowly leveled her head so that she could open both eyes.

It was bright, and everything was blurry. She wondered if it felt brighter because of the head injury. She squinted and blinked rapidly to try to clear her eyes. All that did was make the colors more distinct.

She almost groaned in frustration, but froze when a pale figure moved into her field of vision and began pacing back and forth. She watched it move, desperately straining her eyes to make out what it was. It was tall and awkward in its movements. It was blurry, but gave off an air of agitation and strain. As it moved, she noticed that the chill in her chest pulled toward it. No matter what direction it moved in, she noticed a distinctive shift in the throb in her chest in that same direction, like the pull between two magnets.

The pale figure stopped and stomped loudly. The hum at the top of her skull started again, and she squeezed her eyes shut against the pain it added to her existing headache. She heard a series of clicks, grunts, and growls, and her eyes popped open.

Her vision cleared instantly, like being pushed out of a dense fog. The only problem, though, was that the scene in front of her didn't make sense. She'd either hit her head harder than she'd thought, or she had officially lost her mind.

Chapter 12

Two creatures stood about forty feet in front of her with their backs to her. *Well, more accurately, one was kneeling down, and the other one was standing over it. Even then, saying that it stood was an understatement. It towered over the other one. It looked like it was ten to twelve feet tall!*

The one standing had pale, lavender skin with dark purple marks that swirled across its exposed body. It stood on the balls of its three-taloned feet, causing exaggerated bends in both its ankles and knees. Its hair was as white as freshly fallen snow, and it had three long, black horns on its head. The horns came off the back of the head, not the top, and they ran parallel to the body in an elegant curve. They were uniquely shaped. They curved up in a sharp point at the crown of the head before curving down and away from the shoulder blade area of the back. The two outer horns were symmetrical. The third was a little smaller, starting a little lower and in the middle of the outer two. This third horn pointed toward what would be a spine if the creature were structured like humans were.

The one standing had chopped its white hair around its horns in an irregular style, whereas the one kneeling had long, elaborate braids around its horns. This one had only two horns, and they were much smaller than those that the standing creature had.

The standing creature grunted and clicked at the kneeling one while constantly shifting from one foot to the other. Its body language conveyed discomfort and maybe urgency. Ariyana wondered why. *Were they possibly hoping to avoid a conflict with other humans, though they showed up prepared and dressed for battle?*

They wore plates made from a strange material connected together in various locations across their bodies like armor. The plates didn't look like they were made of metal: there was no shine to them, and they didn't appear to be a natural part of their body. The plates were mostly brown with little bits of green here and there, and they were outlined in white.

The creature that was standing had plates that covered its broad shoulders and upper arms, and continued along its back in a way that mocked a flexible spinal column. The creature also wore a thick brown cloth that covered its mid-section, hips, and upper thighs. From what she could see with its back to her, it had plates that ran from mid-thigh, across the knee, to mid-calf. The only shiny thing on its body was something silver that was tied to its waist.

The only human characteristics that they shared were that they were bipedal, had two arms, and a head. Aside from that, there was nothing like them on Earth. That small fact alone should have been freaking Ariyana out, but it wasn't. There was an unmistakably dangerous energy in the air that she couldn't ignore, and yet there was also something familiar.

The creature that was standing shifted its weight by stomping its right foot against the ground. This abrupt movement pulled Ariyana's attention to its three-taloned feet. She stifled a gasp. How had she not noticed it before? She knew those feet!

In her dream, she never caught a glimpse of her face—there were no reflective surfaces—but she knew what the rest of her body looked like for the most part. More importantly, she knew what her legs and feet looked like, and right now, she was looking at a larger version of them.

A nervous excitement filled her. She had spent years trying to make sense of her dream. *Could it be possible that some of the answers were standing right in front of her?*

There were some obvious key differences, of course: they were missing a tail, their skin coloration was different from hers in the dream, and they didn't have any feathers.

She put some of her weight onto her left arm to lift herself when the standing creature moved to the side. Ariyana sucked in a breath.

Lexa.

She was lying on her back, motionless, between the creatures. The one who was kneeling was beside her, moving her head back and forth and lifting her right arm. She caught a glimpse of Lexa's face and had to stop herself from yelling out. Lexa still had blood trickling from her nostrils and ears, but now she had what looked like fresh tears of blood streaming from her eyes.

All thoughts of sharing similarities with the creatures and every trace of nervous excitement disappeared and were replaced with a protective rage: *injured or not, she had to get to her friend.*

Decision made, she quietly slipped her remaining shoe off and used her toes to remove both of her socks. She pulled her legs into and under her body, carefully shifting herself into a slow crouch. Every little crunch of gravel and every snap of small twigs beneath her made her freeze and hold her breath, but the creatures never looked back at her.

She kept her eyes locked on their movements, shifting her weight from one foot to the other foot, positioning her body into a low sprinter's stance. Her body ached and complained, and her head pounded, but it still complied. She leaned forward onto the balls of her feet and outstretched her hands into the gravel. The fingers on her right hand brushed a rock, and she glanced down at it. It was the perfect size.

She heard a crunch, and her attention jerked back to the creatures. The standing one was shifting again. This time to the right. Now it stood right in front of a small granite boulder. Ariyana's eyes glittered with anticipation. *Just what she needed.*

She sprang forward, scooping up the hand-sized rock into her injured hand, which ached but held tight. She covered the distance between them in six long strides. She ran up the boulder between them and leapt onto the creature's back. She dug her toes into the crease between its back plates, grabbed its left horn and bashed the rock into the right side of its head. The creature whipped its head around, dislodging the grip her toes had on its back and flinging her body over its shoulder. It grabbed her by the neck, its sharp claws wrapping completely around her, and pulled her off its shoulder. She grabbed its wrist with her left hand and slammed the rock down against its forearm. It dropped her, and she landed hard on her butt. It reached out for her, and she spun around to avoid its grasp. Its claws missed her arm but raked across the exposed skin of her back. She bit back a cry and tried to maneuver away from its grasping hand. She wasn't fast enough, and it grabbed her ankle.

It yanked her toward it and up into the air. She waited until she saw its chest and kicked out with her free leg. She struck it square in the center of its chest, and it dropped her again.

She landed on all fours and saw Lexa. The kneeling creature had moved, and Lexa was alone. She ran over to her and spun to face the creature, positioning herself between it and her friend.

For the first time, she saw its face. It had an oval-shaped face with pronounced eye ridges and a strong jaw, making it seem more angular than rounded. It had large, almond-shaped eyes and high, sharp cheekbones. Its eyes were incredible. It had three half-moon pupils in each eye.

Her children's vision flashed through her mind. *The three half-moons set against a pale background.* She exhaled loudly.

It took a step toward her. Its movement pulled her out of her distracting thoughts. She shook her head to clear the vision and hardened her stance.

It had the same dark purple marks on its face as it did on the other parts of its body, as far as she could see, and they were pulsing from dark purple to almost black. It narrowed its eyes at her and anger darkened its features. Then, with a movement that she barely registered, it was in front of her. It grabbed her by the neck and lifted her up to its face.

It didn't have a nose like she did. Its face was flat in the middle with two closed slits where its nostrils should be. It also had two other slits, one on each cheekbone. These were closed as well with a sharp bone or tooth-like protuberance that lay across them.

It pulled her close to its face and drew its full lips back from its sharp teeth in a low growl. She narrowed her eyes and slammed the rock into the center of its temple. The skin exploded open. Milky lavender fluid splattered across her face and injured hand. It roared. She saw a flash of silver out of the corner of her eye.

She was whipped around and slammed into something hard, after which something drove through her right shoulder, impaling her to the object behind her. The pain in her shoulder exploded through her body, and for the first time, she cried out for something other than losing Glacin.

Chapter 13

Ariyana's vision darkened around the edges, and her head lolled forward. Her weight increased on the weapon, and blood streamed down her arm and off the tips of her fingers. She was vaguely aware of a dripping noise and light vibrations on the top of her right foot. *Why did it feel like her foot was wet? Was she standing next to water?* Her eyelids grew heavy. She felt so tired and wanted to sleep. The pain was slipping away like a mere annoyance at the edge of her consciousness, and she waited for the sweet bliss of passing out.

But it didn't come.

Instead, the back of her injured hand began to tingle and burn, and a bright pinpoint of light grew in the center of her vision, chasing the darkness away.

This angered her. She wanted the darkness to overcome her. She didn't want to feel the pain anymore; she didn't want to worry about being different anymore; she didn't want to dream. She wanted to sleep.

The tingle raced up her arm like a bolt of electricity and tore through the chill in her chest. It felt like millions of tiny ice crystals were shattering and spreading through her entire body. Every muscle tensed from the explosion inside her, and the bright light completely filled her vision, blinding her.

***

She heard voices, loud and angry. *They were fighting about her.*

Something bad had happened. She had no memory of what it was, but guilt and sadness curled their fingers through her emotions with a tightening grip. She concentrated on the emotions, trying to follow them back to their source, but no images seemed to be tied to them. She concentrated harder, trying to pull herself back to her most recent memory, but instead of a memory, she found a well of rage that ran deep and opened up into an expanse of loneliness. That expanse terrified her. She knew that anger and loneliness all too well. She thought that she had escaped it. *What was pulling her back?*

A loud crack echoed around her. She jerked her head up and jumped to her feet. She hadn't realized that she had her head buried in her knees.

She was alone in the rock chamber. She had her back pressed against the far rock wall that faced the opening to the chamber. It was lit with six fires: three to her left and three to her right, which were nestled in roughly carved pockets along the walls. The fire was bright red and filled the chamber with an ominous light.

A loud growl rumbled from the opening, and a body skidded across the floor in the adjacent chamber, making her jump.

Idrin stomped over, grabbed Kylor by his chest covering, and slammed him against the wall. Another loud crack echoed through her chamber. "You are a traitor to your clan, and, worst of all, you betrayed me, your royal!" Idrin yelled.

Ariyana walked over to the opening, and a massive purple tail with dark blue fire struck it, sending an explosion of tiny rocks and dust toward her. She was trapped. Arc, Idrin's companion, swung his head toward her and hissed.

The gesture was clear—she wasn't allowed to intervene. She found it odd, though, that her mind was quiet. She should have been able to hear Arc in her thoughts, to feel him, but there wasn't any sense of him. *Was he blocking her?* The thought that she was being shut out, mentally and physically, dragged her back to the expanse of loneliness that was threatening to swallow her whole. She curled her talons and tore deep gouges into the stone floor. The feeling of the solid rock against the balls of her feet helped to solidify her existence in the physical realm. *She wasn't falling*, she assured herself. *She wouldn't allow herself to fall. Not again.*

Kylor grunted under the pressure of having his head shoved into the rock, but he didn't fight back.

"I did not betray you," Kylor snapped. "There is strength in risk and honor in defeating an enemy before they can attack you first. You have grown weak, and you would not have taken the chance if I had come to you first. You would have refused to leave the safety of this planet. I took the chance that was laid before me. I took the risk to eliminate our enemy." His voice was full of anger, and though his muscles were tight from emotion, he didn't try to free himself.

"But you failed! And failure is weakness, and weakness deserves death."

"It was not weakness. We were ambushed. They knew we were coming," Kylor argued.

"You think that proves your strength? Not being ready for an ambush? You are a warrior. The strongest of our clans! My first in command! And yet, you crawled back to this planet with the blood of those that followed you on your hands and excuses in your throat. I scream for your blood, I long to mix it with the ashes of your companion and offer it to Vayle as a tribute. Your presence disgusts me!" Idrin hurled the words at Kylor like weapons. The chamber filled with waves of Idrin's anger, and it lashed against Ariyana's sensitive skin, filling her with his emotion.

Kylor's gaze hardened on her. The three half-moon pupils in each of his eyes were thin slivers. There was so much hatred in his eyes. She couldn't hold his gaze. Even though Idrin's anger was consuming her, she felt shame, but not toward Kylor. It was her own shame that made her avert her gaze.

Kylor snarled. "You have no right to talk to me about loss of life with that Tehkara in our halls," Kylor said, his words dripping with hatred. He finally pushed against Idrin and stood at his full height. "What she did was a greater disrespect to our people. I demand the right of my kinline. I demand the right to take her life."

Idrin shook his head and snorted in amusement. "Only an Aryllyn has the right to what you selfishly demand."

Kylor looked at Idrin. Confusion and denial flashed through his eyes, but only briefly because a moment later, Idrin had a hold of him. He grabbed him by the back of his neck with his right hand and at the base of his middle horn on the back of his head with his left. He pushed him to his knees and slammed his face against the wall. In one quick motion, his right hand came up and snapped the tip of the middle horn off. He released

Kylor as quickly as he had grabbed him, took a step back, and threw the four-inch piece of horn at his feet.

"You are no longer Aryllyn," Idrin said fiercely. "You are Tehkaric. I banish you and those that follow you from this planet, from our people, from the protection of our alliance. I leave you marked as the traitor you are. You and your followers will never again bond with a Draxin. You will die in disgrace—alone."

Kylor picked up the horn, stood and squared his shoulders, desperately trying to look dignified. "You are blinded, Idrin," he hissed. "She lives among us and the Draxins, yet she follows none of our laws. She will never be the prize at your side that you hope her to be. She will betray you as she betrayed my kinline. The blood still glistens upon her hands just as it will again when you least expect it."

Ariyana looked down at her hands and started. They were covered in lavender blood. She stepped back and squeezed her hands shut, trying to hide them from view. Kylor snickered, and she met his gaze. He was watching her.

Two other Aryllyns had entered and were pulling Kylor from the chamber. "Who is the real traitor, Aris?" he yelled at her. "Your guilt will destroy you, and I will be there to watch you crumble."

"Enough!" Idrin yelled. He stormed across the chamber and punched Kylor in the face. "Even now, banished, you are still blind. You have lost everything, and you still cannot see what you have done. We cannot protect both worlds, Kylor. One has to fall to save the other. You did not just crawl back with the blood and ashes of those that followed you on your hands, with your shame. You brought death to our world! You pointed our enemy in our direction. You made us weak by allowing so many to die. They will come, and Aryll will fall. That will forever stain your hands. Our people…," Idrin trailed off, his chest heaving. Then he hardened his gaze and continued, "My people will never forgive your treachery. I deny you a swift death. I deny you honor. I deny you companionship." Idrin shoved him in the chest, "Get off this planet."

Idrin released his anger into the chamber like an emotional energy storm. Neither Ariyana nor Arc was prepared as it hit them. It consumed and overtook her. The word "Tehkaric" filled her every thought.

She heard Kylor yell back a response, but the anger-filled energy that dominated her mind made his words incomprehensible. She couldn't control how she felt; she couldn't calm herself down. She continued to step backward, trying to distance herself from the anger, hatred, and betrayal. She clenched her fists and squeezed her eyes shut, but the feeling continued to build. She needed to release the building storm inside of her.

A bright light filled her vision behind her eyelids. The new assault on her senses was too much. She tilted her head back and roared.

***

The light dissipated, and Ariyana slowly opened her eyes. She could no longer see in the same manner as before. There were no physical shapes around her, nothing solid that she could touch. The only things that she could see were swirling mists of color. *No, not just color, there was something else. Every color seemed to shimmer or vibrate. Some mixed together, keeping their color while traveling through another separate color, while others remained completely separate, only touching at their boundaries.*

It should have been beautiful and, admittedly, alarming, but she was too consumed with anger over what she had just witnessed. She wanted revenge.

The feeling was as clear to her as her understanding of who she was in that moment. She knew that her name was Ariyana, she had a husband and two kids, and a best friend named Lexa. It was clear to her now, but it hadn't been when she was stuck in the vision of Kylor. She didn't know any of that then. She had felt like a different person; she had felt like she did in her dream of losing Glacin. Only this time, she wasn't watching him die; she was watching Kylor being banished for betraying his people.

She repeated his name in her mind. *Kylor.*

She knew who he was. That information was limited to a name and the knowledge that he was a traitor, but he still had a name, and a name had power. For her, in that moment, that power was rage. Not hers specifically, it didn't originate from her, but it felt good inside her chest. It calmed the chill coursing through her and gave her something to focus on.

Then, as if she had manifested it herself, a purple mist moved into her field of vision and swirled and pulsed in front of her. She didn't need to see the world as she had before to know who stood before her. *It was him, Kylor;* his energy to be exact, but him nonetheless, and he was an arm's reach away from her.

She roared and lurched forward, but her upper body slammed against something, and she stopped abruptly. She looked down but she couldn't see anything, not even her physical form. All she saw was a faint glow of shimmering, silver light, but nothing tangible. *Where the hell was her body?* This enraged her further, and she tried again, getting the same result. Something was connected to the area where her right shoulder should be, impeding her ability to attack.

She roared, amazed that the sound danced around her, though there wasn't anything physical for the sound to come from. She slammed her shoulder over and over again into the obstacle she couldn't see. A loud crack echoed behind her, but the sound didn't come alone. It came with a memory, a memory of sensations, and all at once, they came rushing back.

Chapter 14

The bright sun, the meadow, the sound of birds chirping, the smell of pine trees, Kylor standing wide-eyed in front of her, and pain— agonizing, burning pain. Her roar turned into a desperate scream. She could see everything, hear everything, smell everything, feel everything. She looked down at her right shoulder, and there was a thin, iridescent spike impaled through the flesh of her upper body. It was pierced below the clavicle, straight through her shoulder, exiting her back above the scapula, and driving into a large boulder. The flesh around the spike was torn, bruised, and bleeding profusely.

Her breathing was fast and shallow, and her heart was hammering in her chest. Her shoulder was beginning to go numb, and she could feel beads of sweat forming along her hairline. *She was going into shock.* She knew that she needed to remove the spike and stop the bleeding soon, or she was going to lose consciousness.

Her thoughts zeroed in on the spike itself. *It didn't just appear on its own. No, she remembered now. Before she fell into the vision, Kylor had impaled her to the rock with it.* This added fuel to the rage inside her.

She slowly raised her eyes to meet his and snarled. She saw a shadow of uncertainty before he narrowed his eyes and growled.

She grabbed the spike with her left hand and yanked.

Instantly, Kylor was inches away from her; one hand around her wrist, pulling it away; the other vice-gripped onto her chin.

She held his stare. "Kylor," she began, but he shoved her jaw upward, forcing her mouth closed.

"There you are," he said in a low voice. "White eyes, back to strange blue. Bits of silver in there." A growl rumbled in his throat, "I see you." He released his hold on her face and pinned her left wrist against the rock behind her. "You looked at us like strangers when you first attacked, but now I see familiarity in your new eyes. I could not have fathomed that this could be you." He pulled his head back, studying her from head to foot, but kept his body firmly planted in front of her. "Did not know that you could exist between the realms, but if anyone could, it would be you. Where did you go in your mind just now? What did you see that brought you back?"

Shock trapped her words in her throat and snuffed out the rage in her veins. *She understood him.*

The words that he spoke were not English, but their meanings were as clear to her as if they had been. She stared at him, her mouth agape. *What was happening?* She wasn't sure if it was the blood loss or the adrenaline in her system wearing off, but the reality of all the events that led up to this moment finally hit her like a punch to the gut. The creature in front of her was not from Earth. The creature that had beaten her, impaled her to a rock, and forced images into her mind was not human.

She squeezed her eyes shut. *This had to be a new dream, an extension of what she usually saw.* She tried to suck in a deep breath, but the attempt to fill her lungs moved her shoulder, and pain lanced through her arm and chest. Her eyes popped open. She'd been in pain before in her dream, but this pain was different. In her dream, the pain that she felt was only accompanied by her fear of losing Glacin. The pain that she felt now was accompanied by the full realization of who she was. Her dream identity was tied to Glacin. Her identity now tied her to everything that made her Ariyana.

She looked back at Kylor and realized that his mouth was moving. He'd been talking while she was lost in thought. Her eyebrows pinched together in confusion. "Is this another dream?" she asked. She hadn't meant to ask the question. It just rushed out.

Kylor tilted his head to the side, his face twisted in disgust. "Dream?" he hissed. The word sounded forced, like he was imitating her instead of speaking in his own tongue.

"I saw a vision of you," she continued. *His eyes widened when she said "vision," and he growled. That word clearly meant something in his language.*

"Questioning reality?" he asked. He released her wrist, turned on his heel, and bent down. His body moved swiftly in an arc; his arm curving down to grab something, his body twisting, and he shoved something into her face. Her eyes widened in shock. *No, not something, someone—Lexa!*

Her friend hung limp in Kylor's grasp. He had her by the back of the neck. Lexa stared forward, her pupils fully dilated, alive, but unaware. She seemed to peer right through Ariyana. She looked small, frail, and broken. Worse than that, though, was the blood. *There was so much of it.* It trickled from her ears, the corners of her eyes, and her nose.

"Real enough?" he asked, pushing her closer.

All thoughts of the absurdity of the situation, that these creatures weren't human, and that she should be terrified about what was going on, disappeared in an instant. The desire to protect rekindled the angry heat inside her.

She glared at him. "I'm going to kill you," she snarled. She reached for the spike again.

Swiftly, Kylor tossed Lexa behind him into the other creature's arms and grabbed Ariyana by the wrist before her fingers could circle around the metal. He pressed his body against her. It was noticeably cooler than hers. The rough material of his armor scraped against her exposed skin. He leaned into her ear, the side of his face lightly brushing against hers. "Living among these weak creatures for so long has left you confused about who is dominant here. Your threats do not concern me. To repeat, what did you see that brought you back?"

She thought about the vision that she'd seen: that he was a traitor. She thought about the rage Idrin had unleashed due to his betrayal, and a wicked smile curved at the corner of her lips. "You want to know what I saw," she challenged, shoving his head away with her own. "I saw the truth! You are a —"

He grabbed her by the face again and squeezed. She could feel his cool breath on her face. His lips were pulled back completely, revealing a mouth full of razor-sharp teeth, and his three half-moon pupils were constricted into thin slivers. His eyes looked wild as they searched her face, and his markings pulsed.

"Truth! A word that oozes falsehood, no matter the language, when it falls from your lips. You came to us with nothing but lies in your throat, and you did nothing but spill blood at our feet." He squeezed her tighter and dug the claw of his thumb into her cheek until she felt blood drip off her chin. "Tell me what *truth* you think you saw. Was it as clearly seen as the blood that will eternally stain your hands?" He shoved her hand, palm first, into her face.

It was covered in a mixture of his blood and hers. The image of her hands covered in dried lavender blood flashed in her mind. Her heart sank, and an intense feeling of guilt overcame her. She pulled her wrist away and flinched as the rough movement sent another lance of pain through her shoulder.

Time seemed to slow down around her, and it was difficult to breathe. Another emotion was overtaking her—panic. She didn't know where it was coming from, but it was tied to the image of her bloody hands. All traces of anger were gone, and she felt vulnerable and small.

These whirlwinds of emotion were exhausting to her; she sucked in short breaths of air, trying to calm both her racing mind and her erratic heart rate.

She needed to concentrate on the one thing that made her feel grounded. Lexa. She looked down and most of her view of Lexa was blocked by Kylor, but from what she could see of her, she still hadn't moved. She was perfectly still on the ground, as the other creature moved around her. *Lexa needed her, and she wasn't going to be much help unless she pulled it together.*

She exhaled with as much force as her injured shoulder would allow and narrowed her eyes at Kylor. She had so many questions rushing through her thoughts. *Why did the vision of Kylor and Idrin seem so familiar? Why did she feel like she knew Kylor and Idrin even though she hadn't heard their names until right now? Why was Kylor here? Why did her children see a flash of Kylor's eyes in their dreams?*

That question made her heart skip a beat. *Her children. Her children saw Kylor. Was it just a dream, a flash of a vision, or did they know more? Was the vision one way, or did Kylor know about them, too? What would Kylor do if her children came out here looking for her?* She hardened her thoughts against the possibility and intensified her glare.

"Enough with the doublespeak," she said. "I don't know what you want me to say, and I don't know what you want me to do. I'm feeling emotions that I can't control and seeing things that are not part of any past that I remember. I don't know why you're here, but we could chalk this up to a misunderstanding and just go our separate ways." Her eyebrows lifted in a "what do you say?" kind of way, but Kylor just stood there staring at her, hard and unyielding. All she could hear was her blood dripping at her feet and a rustling sound every time the creature near Lexa moved.

Desperation made her thoughts swim. *Did she need to try to appeal to his sympathy?*

"Look," she began, her tone softer this time. "I'm not going to attack you again. You were hurting my friend. I didn't think, I just reacted. Take this thing out of my shoulder. I can slow the bleeding and get her to a doctor." Something that she couldn't read flashed in his gaze. She hoped that it was working, so she continued, "Please. I'm begging you to understand that I don't know why you're here, and I don't want to get in your way. So, let us go, take your friend, go away, and settle your conflict with that Idrin guy."

Kylor's markings darkened. A noise that she had never heard before rumbled in his throat. Pain exploded across her right cheek, and her left temple hit the side of the rock. Pin-pricks of light flashed through her vision, and she tasted blood in her mouth.

"Would you stop hitting me in the head?" she snapped. "I already have a concussion! And whatever it is that you are trying to get out of me, you won't get it if you turn my brain to mush." She spit the blood out of her mouth at his feet.

His eyes narrowed. "We don't have a word in our language for 'Please'," he snarled, mockingly saying the word in her tone. "But I can hear the meaning in your pathetic begging. You are still just as weak and small as you were the first day I saw you. You are a disease moving about the universe, destroying everything that you touch."

Anger welled inside of her. "You know what?" she hissed. "Maybe the person that I saw in that vision had bloody hands because she had slapped the stupid off your face for what you did." She narrowed her eyes, and, through clenched teeth, she hissed, "Did that translate?"

He grabbed her left wrist in one hand and ground it into the rock wall. Then, he grabbed her face with the other and pushed her injured skull into the rock, clamping her mouth shut. "What I've done?" he roared, snapping his teeth. "Speak it!" he yelled. "Say the word that screams inside your mind. Let it tear from your throat and take shape like the weapon you want it to be."

God, she wanted to. She wanted to spit the word in his face, but he wouldn't let her.

"I could crush your skull in my hands," he continued. "I can feel its delicate hold ready to shatter. And yet you stand here, judging me for the curse that you brought to our planets. You think I am a fool, is that it? You want me to believe that you don't know who you are. You are the only fool here. I know full well who you are. A Tehkara!" he roared. "You came to my planet with promises of alliance against a common enemy. We took your hand in peace. And yet, when it became too hard for you, you ran to hide here," he motioned around with his head, "on this small planet that could offer you a new beginning. Did you clear your memory as you integrated yourself into their species? Did that make it easier for you to forget about all the blood that you have on your hands?"

He squeezed her jaw tighter and pressed her hand harder into the rock. She fought the urge to cry out.

"Your mind is tortured by it, isn't it?" he asked through gritted teeth.

She met his gaze and the storm that raged there. "I made a promise to you," he whispered.

He released her hand and held out his own hand to the other creature. He kept his gaze on her, though. Without hesitation, the other creature placed a dagger in his open hand, never once removing his gaze from Lexa.

The dagger was silver and smaller than the spike through her shoulder. It looked like a feather: a sharp feather that was fashioned with a handle where the quill should be.

Kylor grabbed Ariyana's chin in a vice grip, his sharp claws scratching down the sensitive skin of her cheeks. He was so close that it seemed like the only thing that existed between them was his rage. His three half-moon pupils were thin crescents in each of his eyes. His chest heaved, and his nose slits were wide open. Each exhalation moved the fine hairs around her forehead. His lips pulled back over his sharp teeth in a dark smile. "I changed my mind," he snarled. "I don't want to hear you speak. I want to hear you scream."

Chapter 15

His movements were so fast that her mind didn't register them until the pain hit. Her upper chest burned, and her collar bones throbbed. He pushed his hand upward against her chin, roughly shoving her mouth shut before her scream could escape her lips.

He moved his mouth close to her ear. She sucked in a deep breath through her nose. The scent of snow and sweet peppermint filled her nostrils.

"No. Not yet," he whispered.

She squeezed her eyes shut against the pain and exhaled deeply from her nose. She fought the urge to whimper against his hand as she pulled air back through her nose. Her next few breaths hitched in her throat. She concentrated on her breathing and pushed the pain to the side. *He wanted her to lose control. She had to try to maintain control as long as she could.*

Her chest began to numb, and she opened her eyes to glare at him.

He squeezed her chin harder, and it felt like her jawbone was going to snap. She grabbed his wrist with her left hand and squeezed. Or at least she tried to. Her fingers were numb, and they didn't fully wrap around his wrist.

He flicked his wrist, and her hand fell away. He held the dagger up to her face and let it glisten in the sunlight. The dark red of her blood glittered like jewels in the sun, contrasting beautifully with the shine of the silver metal. The dagger was intricately engraved to look like a real feather, and the areas that resembled the barbs seemed to dance and vibrate where they were covered in her blood.

"Familiar?" Kylor asked. "Does it call to you? It should. It was a part of you. Not much was left of you when you disappeared and allowed our planet to die. We saved everything that we found. Some hoped to connect to you, some hoped to find you, and others—those of us who believed you were a false ally—hoped it would help us defeat you if you were still alive. You will now endure the pain of all those that you abandoned and let die in your name."

He held her glare and returned it. He placed the tip of the dagger in the middle of her hairline on her forehead and slowly sliced a thin line down to the bridge of her nose. Then, he placed the point of the dagger at the corner of her right eye. He dug it into her skin until she groaned before slicing out across her temple. She sucked in a quick breath that hitched in her throat and cut off sharply with what sounded like a squeak. He repeated the same cut at the corner of her left eye, again waiting until she responded before finishing the cut. Next, he released her chin and grabbed her by the throat. He pressed the top of his hand into her chin, forcing it upward, and sliced deep gouges across her jawline. Finally, he squeezed her throat until she made desperate gasping noises through her nostrils. He violently pushed her head back into the rock, released her, and leaned back to study her.

She sputtered and coughed, sucking in breaths through the pain. Her head hung forward, she no longer had the strength to hold it up. Blood dripped off her nose and chin and added to the gathering pool at her feet. She watched it, mesmerized by the rhythmic plop, plop, plop. *It was so red and vibrant.* In that moment, she couldn't remember seeing a color that red before. More than that, though, it was familiar: pools of blood splashed against light grey granite rock.

Her children's dream.

They'd seen Kylor's eyes. They'd seen the pools of blood. If they could see what was to come, there was one thing left: a black, burning scar of smoke through the morning sky.

"The dream," she whispered.

Kylor roared at her, and she felt the energy of his hatred slam against her exposed skin. He grabbed her right hand and sliced a deep gash across her wrist, then did the same to her left. Panic slammed into her as she saw her blood pulse out of her. That panic doubled when she realized that her body was too numb to feel the pain. She was cold, and she was tired. The icy throb in her chest increased with her heart rate, and she was sucking in quick breaths of air. She was close to the final stage of shock, and the only thing that was tethering her to consciousness was a single thought: her boys. *What would happen to her boys? They were special and unique. Who was going to protect her children if she couldn't survive this?*

"Give it to me!" Kylor yelled.

Ariyana opened her eyes and squinted. Her vision was blurry, but she could see that the other creature was standing next to Kylor. He had something large and silver in his hand.

"Her current form may now be too weak to survive," the other creature said. The volume of his voice was low, his eyes were cast to the ground, and his tone was respectful. It was hard to see the details, but Ariyana noticed that the second creature's markings were lighter in color than Kylor's.

Kylor snatched the silver object out of the creature's hand and towered over him. "You are here because I allow it. You breathe because I allow it," Kylor lashed out. "The only reason that you exist is because we are the last of our clan. Do not make me rethink your existence. Keep quiet and maintain the hold on the Nexi. That is all I need from you."

Kylor grabbed Ariyana by the chin again and shook her head violently. "Awaken, Tehkara!" he barked. He held the silver object between them. "Do you feel that? It's reacting to your presence; it senses the energy inside of you. You did well suppressing it when we first saw you, but you cannot hide it from yourself."

She groaned between quick breaths. It was the only response that she had the energy to give. She didn't know what he was talking about. The only thing that she could feel was her racing heartbeat and the building chill in her chest. Her body was struggling to keep itself alive.

Kylor tossed her head back against the boulder. He balanced the object in his left hand and held the bloody dagger above it. A single drop of blood broke free from the tip of the dagger and splattered against the top of the object.

It exploded into life—dozens of thin tendrils whipped out, reaching and searching. It didn't matter how weak her body felt, that weakness did nothing to stop the fear as it burst through her the moment the object lashed out. But that fear was nothing compared to the terror that consumed her when Kylor shoved the whipping tendrils against her chest.

The open wounds along her collar bones burned instantly. The tendrils snaked up her neck and face, across her shoulders and down her arms, racing toward the cuts that Kylor had left in her skin. She couldn't see what was happening, she could only feel it. A freezing burn started in each wound, followed by a pulling sensation; not pulling on her, though, pulling inside her. Her heart was already racing, but the fear of not knowing what was pulling itself inside her body made her heart pound faster, drawing the burning ice through her veins toward her heart. The chill in her chest started throbbing in sync with her heartbeat as if it was responding to the familiar icy sensation that was pulling toward it.

The instant it reached her heart, it felt like a frozen electrical current exploded inside of her, sending shards of ice through her arteries. The pain brought a fresh burst of energy with it. She reached up, ripped the spike from her shoulder, and collapsed to her knees. More tendrils snaked into the open wound in her shoulder, causing the muscles in her right arm to contract violently. The spike fell out of her left hand and clanged against the granite rocks beside her. The muscles in her left arm contracted too, pulling her forearm up to her chest to meet her right arm.

The icy, silver metal moved along her skin like liquid and covered the deep wounds in her wrists. The blue veins in her arms turned silver, and tiny red beads of sweat broke out across her skin, small at first, but then large and dripping with each heartbeat. She was secreting what looked like blood and body fluids, leaving behind growing pale, porcelain-white splotches on her skin. This created a terrible contrast of sensations: burning chill in her body; scolding fire on her skin. The fluid leaving her was taking her body heat with it.

Each heartbeat deepened, taking over the spread of the sensation through her body. Her stomach cramped, her head rolled forward, and she vomited. She became overly aware of all of her organs and muscles as the chill spread through her body. She cried out in short bursts of sound as her seizing lungs would only allow her to take quick, desperate breaths.

Pain stabbed through the corners of her eyes and lanced through each, blinding her. She fell to her side, no longer able to keep herself upright, and smashed her temple into a rock. A burst of light filled her vision. Images flooded her mind: Glacin flying around a green waterfall that forked off a white, snaggle-toothed cliff that jutted out from a large black wall of rock; Glacin, wings spread to their fullest, basking in the glow of a red sun; Glacin diving through the air, with her tucked into his neck feathers, his warm turquoise flame wrapped around her, keeping her safe; Idrin, his hand wrapped around her throat, trying to shove a blade through her chest.

This image filled her mind and held her in its grip, just like Idrin held her throat. She couldn't shake free of it. She struggled to both free herself and keep the blade from piercing deeper into her chest, but his determination was proving to be stronger than her desperation. His eyes grew wild, he roared, and pushed with all of his strength. She felt the blade push between bones and pierce the core of her two hearts. Silver light filled her vision, and she screamed. She screamed until everything went black, and all sound disappeared completely.

***

Lexa's mind filled with Ariyana's screams. Her friend's pain was unimaginable. Lexa could hear everything, see everything, feel everything, but she couldn't move or react. She felt frozen in time as time moved around her. She felt out of control because she couldn't take control of herself; she felt desperate to help Ariyana as she watched her being tortured and beaten; she felt enraged at the two creatures as they asserted their dominance over both of them. But now, she simply watched in horror as her best friend's body convulsed and changed before her very eyes.

She watched as the main creature, Kylor, the name that she had heard Ariyana call him, walked up to Ariyana with a handful of whipping, silver tendrils and thrust them on her broken, bloody body. The tendrils wrapped around her upper chest and throat, desperately seeking out her bleeding wounds. Next, she watched as they pulled into her wrists first, her veins turning silver as they moved up her arms. They moved quickly under her skin, causing Ariyana to scream and finally rip the spike from her shoulder. When she collapsed to the ground, her body began to sweat out blood and other strangely colored body fluids, leaving behind skin that was growing pale, porcelain-white. Then, the tendrils raced up her neck toward the cuts along her jawline, the corners of her eyes, and hairline. Ariyana's body seized, and she fell over, smashing her temple on the rock as the tendrils dug into her face and eyes. Her blank eyes stared at Lexa as fluid drained from her eyes and pores.

Lexa's mind raced as the impossible played out in front of her. The blue in Ariyana's irises drained out like tears, followed by the white of her sclera, leaving behind a pool of silver that swirled around her pupils. Her eyes closed once, twice, and when she opened them again, her pupils had changed to four-pointed stars.

Ariyana's scream filled Lexa's mind again, only this time it didn't let up or fade away. It grew in intensity, building like a pressure cooker in her mind. It was unbearable. Then, like a bubble popping, everything was gone, everything. Her body was free. She sat up suddenly and sucked in a deep breath. The creature next to her jumped, and she punched him in the face. She scrambled toward Ariyana.

"Stop!" both creatures yelled in unison, but it was the one next to her that continued talking. "She will die if you touch her."

Lexa stopped abruptly. Her head whipped around. "Die?" she asked, her tone dripping with venom. She glared at both of them. "Stop this now. You're killing her."

Kylor shoved her back toward the other creature and snarled at her. "We are not killing her. We are making her whole."

"What the f—" Lexa began.

Kylor turned around abruptly and growled, cutting her off. "Quiet your shrill voice, or I'll find another way to bind you."

"I dare you to try," she challenged, shooting a look at him and the creature beside her, though she made no attempt to move toward Ariyana again.

Worry lined her forehead as she turned her attention back to Ariyana. Her skin was almost completely pale now. Her hair was turning silver as the silver liquid wrapped around each strand, moving from her scalp to the tip, the brown color draining away. Lexa's eyes widened as she watched her friend change before her very eyes.

Silver, metallic feathers sprouted from the middle of her forehead at the hairline, and ran as a crest through her hair and down her spine, forming a ridge of feathers.

Tiny silver feathers grew through her eyebrows around the corners of her eyes.

Sharp teeth elongated in her mouth.

Long, sharp, silver claws grew out of the tips of her fingers.

Her ankles lengthened.

The balls of her feet widened.

Three large talons morphed from her toes.

A large reptilian tail grew from her tailbone, covered in long, sharp, silver feathers, the sharpest at the end of her tail.

Silver swirls marked her skin in decorative designs.

Little, silver feathers covered her skin in small, strategic patches.

Then, her body secreted a liquid silver second skin that shaped itself around her private and vital areas, forming an armor around her core, upper arms, and upper legs.

And finally, a silver fire ignited across her body, burning brightly in her feathers.

After the fire ignited, her body settled down and grew still. The liquid metal had burned away the clothes that she was wearing, so now she lay in front of Lexa in her new form. All traces of humanity were now gone. She looked more like the two creatures standing beside her.

Lexa leaned forward on her hands. The creature beside her put a cautionary hand on her shoulder, and she whipped her head toward him, growling. He released her immediately, his eye ridges raising in surprise.

"Ariyana," Lexa said gently, reaching her hand toward her pale calf, but before she could make contact, Ariyana's eyes popped open, and she leapt to her feet. Startled, Lexa jerked her hand away and fell back on her butt.

Ariyana's eyes moved wildly between the three of them. She looked confused and agitated. That changed instantly, though, when her eyes settled on Kylor. Her body shook as her lips pulled back from her sharp teeth. She roared, grabbed Kylor by the throat, and slammed him against the same rock that she had been pinned against. She held something shiny in front of his face.

It took Lexa a moment to realize that it was the spike. Ariyana had moved so quickly that she never saw her grab the spike from the ground.

A wicked grin spread across Ariyana's face as she moved the spike toward his eye. "I changed my mind," she hissed. "I want to hear *you* scream."

Chapter 16

Ariyana felt Lexa reaching out to her, but she was more aware of the mental connection than the physical one that Lexa had tried to initiate. It was overwhelming, and she hardened herself against it, pushing back as hard as Lexa pushed to connect.

Her body was surprisingly responsive to her needs. She moved faster than she thought she was capable of, and she could feel the thin layer of liquid silver moving to areas where she felt vulnerable. She felt connected to the energy that swarmed around her. It flexed and bent to her will without thought.

Her body felt strange but familiar. The weakness that she had felt when Kylor beat her was gone, and now she held him easily against the rock wall. The uncomfortable heat was also gone. Her body temperature had lowered significantly to equalize itself with the chill in her chest. Kylor groaned, and she squeezed his throat tighter.

"Aris," he wheezed.

She loosened her grip slightly and narrowed her eyes, "That is not my name. It's Ariyana." The feathers along her back ridge rose and vibrated with irritation. Her tail whipped from side to side along the ground.

"No…Aris," he countered, his eyes full of arrogance. "It means 'song of the mind.' A name given to you by your Glacin."

She gripped him tighter, until no sound could escape his lips, and pressed the point of the blade into the corner of his eye. "How do you know that name?" she demanded. "How dare you speak it as if you knew him?" She pressed the full weight of her body into his, driving the strength of her position into her hold on his throat until his voice forced its way into her mind.

Enough!

She was unprepared for the forceful intrusion, and she released him, jerking away. She felt off balance and shook her head to re-orient herself. She expected him to move away from her, make an escape, but he stood there, glaring at her, rubbing his throat.

"Why did you really seek this species out, Aris? To hide from us, or from yourself?" He spit the words at her, adding more emphasis to her name.

She took a step toward him, raising the blade again, but he countered quickly and grabbed her wrist. The contact sent an electrical jolt up her arm, her body stiffened, and light filled her vision.

***

Ariyana was in a large chamber that was filled with warm light. The far side of the chamber was occupied by a spring of bright green water that bubbled slightly. It was enticing and called to her like a siren, promising comfort amid its warm embrace. But she ignored it, gave in to her anxiety, and paced the chamber.

She was confused and agitated. It felt the same as it had when she'd lost Glacin. *She was alone, but why was she alone? It wasn't because she had lost Glacin. That had already happened. So what could it be? Why did she feel so confused? Why was she agitated?* She couldn't remember how she got into the chamber. She felt sure that something had gone wrong, but couldn't grasp what that something was.

Then, she realized that it wasn't Glacin that she was looking for in her mind, it was Vayle. *Yes, it was Vayle that wouldn't respond; it was Vayle that had shut her out.*

She stopped pacing. It was too quiet in her mind. She looked at her hands and sucked in a breath. They were caked in milky lavender…Blood. *What did I do?* she thought to herself. She had no idea what horrible thing had happened, but she knew that she was responsible.

She rushed over to the spring and thrust her hands into the warm water. She vigorously scratched and rubbed at the skin, so anxious to remove the sin from her flesh that the Lielycet turned red and began stinging her. She pulled her hands away from the pain only to feel rage crash over her from behind and beat against her raw emotions.

"It doesn't matter how many layers of skin you remove. The stain of your actions will never wash clean."

She whipped around to face Idrin in the doorway. Anger and pain were etched into the features of his face. She couldn't remember a time when he had turned that anger toward her. His right hand shifted at his side, and a silver blade glinted in the light.

Disbelief and betrayal filled her, overshadowing her guilt and anxiety. She hissed at him. "What have you come here to do, my companion? Shun me as Vayle has done or kill me?" She remembered in that moment that Kylor had betrayed his people, the Aryllyns, and Vayle and her people, the Draxins. That was why Vayle was quiet, she was in mourning. Ariyana couldn't recall what happened after that, but she remembered that she was angry about the pain that Kylor had caused Vayle.

"Your actions were disgraceful among my people," Idrin snarled.

She squared her shoulders. "What of his actions?" she demanded. "He disgraced Vayle and her people!"

"His punishment was decided. You had no right to interfere!" he yelled back.

"Your punishment was weak!" She spit the words at him, hoping to piss him off.

He charged her, slammed her against the wall, and pushed the blade into her chest. She caught it in her hand and held it firmly in place, silver blood dripping onto the rock floor between them. She sucked in a breath.

"Death then?" she muttered.

He ignored her words. "Kylor's actions made the alliance weak, but it was your actions that ripped us apart."

The words tore at her just as the tip of the blade tore at her skin. She longed for the connection that she'd had with him and Vayle, but his words and actions shattered the bond that she craved. She felt more alone than ever. Vayle had made an oath to her after Glacin died, and she'd broken that oath when she pushed her away. And now Idrin, someone who had sworn his hearts and ryn to her, had a blade to her chest. He could no longer control her, and so he wanted her dead.

She glared back at him. Her hand shook around the blade as he continued to try to force it into her chest. He struck her, and her head whipped back and hit the wall. She licked the blood from the corner of her mouth but held firm.

"The Draxins want vengeance against the Aryllyns, and the Aryllyns are screaming for your blood. You had no right! You have left me no choice!" he screamed and hit her again.

She still couldn't remember what she had done, but she was hurt, so she lashed out. "I had every right," she said smugly, her tone laced with disgust. "I don't answer to them, and I'll never answer to you."

"And that's why you'll never be anything other than a Tehkara," he sneered.

Outsider.

The word sliced through her. It stung more than any mortal wound. Her eyes burned. She met his gaze, and the last thing she saw was the shock in his eyes as she released the blade, and it pierced through her hearts.

Chapter 17

She jolted back into the present moment with Kylor standing in front of her, holding tight to her wrist. She kicked him square in the chest, and he slammed against the rock behind him. She rushed him, pushed the side of his face against the rock, and pressed the blade into his throat. "Is that why you came here? To finish what he failed to complete?" she demanded.

He groaned as the blade bit into his skin, but the corner of his mouth curled into a conflicting grin. She shifted her body weight to get a better grip and apply more force to his throat, but he grabbed the blade between the hilt and his throat and forcefully began to rotate her arm away from him, out to her side. Their arms shook from tension—hers, trying to keep the blade in place, and his, forcing it away from him. Blood dripped in big, milky, lavender drops from between his fingers. Her eyes widened in disbelief. He was trying to knock her off balance. She whipped her tail out to counter and pulled the blade from his grasp, slicing through the flesh of his fingers. He pushed away from the boulder, threw his arms out to the sides and held them up in a defensive stance, ready to counter her next move. More blood dripped from his hand onto the ground between them as they moved back and forth in a semi-circle, facing each other.

"You disgust me," he said. He raised his chin, showing her that he looked down on her. "Only the weak run. And to find you on this dying planet, reeking of fear and despair, shows me that you're not worth the life that Glacin gave to save you. *Tehkara.*"

Tehkara. Outsider.

There was that word again: that added slap in the face; that final straw that broke her patience. Her parents and brothers had made her feel like she did not fit in. Devyn made her feel like she'd never belonged, and now this creature, this alien to this planet, had the nerve to call her an "outsider"? The stress of fighting for her life hadn't allowed her to question the events of what took place, but being told again that she was worthless and unwanted pulled it all into focus.

Devyn had made her feel unhealthy and unfit to be a mom.

Kylor had beaten her and almost killed her. He had transformed her body.

Her visions had shown her a world where she was equally unaccepted and was killed for it. And through all of that Kylor again shoved *that word* down her throat.

She snapped.

She whipped her tail at his leg, and he jumped to the side. She anticipated the move and punched him in the face. His head whipped to the side. She kneed him in the stomach, hard, and he pitched forward. As he curved over, she was ready, and kneed him in the face. His upper body whipped backward. When he came forward, reaching for her, she punched him in the throat, and he pitched back against the rock. She pressed the blade into his chest, over his hearts.

"How dare you! You came here and hurt my friend; you beat and tortured me; you forced this silver material into my body, changing me into...*this*; you forced images into my mind! And after all of that, you have the nerve to tell me that I am a worthless outsider? I don't know why you're here, but I sure as hell didn't ask you to come. So, why don't you take your damn opinions and leave, *Tehkaric*," she said, spitting at him the name that Idrin had called him in her vision.

His three half-moon pupils fully dilated, and his lips pulled back in a hiss. He leaned into the blade. "Do you know what I see? I see nothing but that frail, broken creature that landed on our planet all those cycles ago, fractured and mourning the loss of her companion, Glacin, because she was too weak to save him."

The feather crest in Ariyana's hair flared out and burned fiercely. She leaned in and opened her mouth to talk, but Lexa appeared next to her. "Stop!" Lexa commanded.

Ariyana's words caught in her throat, but not because her friend demanded it. The Lexa that she knew was not the Lexa that stood next to her now. Her exquisite features were still there, but now she was surrounded by a glowing honey-amber light, the same color as her eyes, and with that light came a sense of peace, calm, and comfort. Lexa's eyes had always been a perfect contrast to her jet black hair, but they stood out even more now that that same color glowed around her.

"Neither of you will benefit from the other's death." She turned and glared at Kylor. "Well, I'm still iffy about you...*prick*."

Kylor hissed and opened his mouth to argue, but she cut him off. "Are you serious?! Does your species not know when to shut up? I thought that Glacin was just a creature in her dreams, but even with that limited amount of information, I would never spit on his memory like you just did. Do you have a death wish?" She shook her head at him and rolled her eyes at his ignorance. Then she turned her attention back to Ariyana, "I'm not condoning what he did. I just want to take a moment to point out that he knows the name of the only creature that you've ever dreamed about. I also want you to look at how you've changed. You look like you've always described yourself to me after you've woken up in the morning. I should be scared, looking at you like this, but I'm not. I feel like I'm seeing you, the real you, for the first time." Lexa reached over and laid her hand on Ariyana's wrist, "You're magnificent."

Unfortunately, Ariyana wasn't ready for the skin-to-skin contact. It created a direct link to Lexa's thoughts. The words echoed through her mind over and over again, each time getting louder and louder until it sounded like someone was screaming in her mind. She ripped her wrist out of her grasp and ground her teeth together against the discomfort.

It didn't sever the connection, though, but amplified it, and her mind filled with millions of voices—talking, screaming, and arguing all at once. The blade slipped from her fingers and clanged against the granite rock. She stumbled back, covering her ears.

Lexa moved to grab her, but the other creature clutched Lexa's shoulder and pulled her away. "Does your species not have the ability to reason when danger is present?" he chastised. "She is not who you think she is any longer. She could hurt you without even realizing what she is doing."

Lexa jerked her shoulder out of his grasp. "Don't. Touch. Me," she warned through gritted teeth. "If you ever touch me again without my permission, I'll show you that I don't need stupid superpowers to stop you from moving."

His eyes widened, and he cocked his head to the side, considering her.

"It's too loud!" Ariyana screamed, dropping to her knees. "My skin burns!"

"Are you causing this?" Lexa demanded, pushing her forearms against the rough armor plates of the abdomen of the large creature that Ariyana had called Kylor. He was still against the rock, so she only succeeded in forcing a deep exhale from him, but his eyes widened in surprise for a moment before he regained his composure. He pushed her back toward the other creature as one might shoo a fly buzzing around their face. She bumped into the other creature's abdomen and rounded on him, expecting him to grab her. Instead, he held both hands up, palms facing out, and stepped back.

"Is your species slow as well?" Kylor asked. He stood up straight and adjusted his body like he was stretching out his sore muscles.

"What?" Lexa asked, offended.

"I have already told you that we have made her whole again. She clearly can't control it," he said, matter-of-factly. He moved away from the rock and approached the other creature. This put Lexa in between them and Ariyana.

Lexa rolled her eyes. "Jerk," she mumbled.

She turned her back on both of them and dropped down beside Ariyana, whose feathers were vibrating, creating a low hum in the air around them. The silver flame along her feathers sparked and sizzled. Her face was twisted in agony, and her sharp teeth were clenched. Her tail twitched behind her, and the silver swirls under her skin moved and pulsated rhythmically. It was clear that something was attacking her, but Lexa couldn't tell what it was.

"Ari—" she began, but Ariyana's eyes popped open. She grabbed Lexa's head in her large, clawed hands, palms pressing firmly against Lexa's cheeks, and stared into her eyes. Her black pupils were fully dilated, filling her eyes with nothing but inky blackness. "It burns! Make it stop!" Ariyana screamed.

Searing pain blasted across Lexa's body, like every inch of her was burning, and she cried out in unison with her friend. They remained locked in pain, tumbling deeper into their connection, into an abyss of fire.

Ariyana couldn't distinguish herself from Lexa or the pain. It all just existed in the same place in the dark. As she was losing herself, though, something small began to build—something that seemed attached to her like a lifeline. It was faint at first, but grew exponentially until two small voices broke through the chaos.

"Mom!"

Ariyana's attention snapped back to the present moment. She released Lexa, whose body went limp and collapsed to the ground. She whipped her head around and saw her two sons break through the tree line on the opposite side of the meadow.

"Mom! She's coming!" they screamed. They were so far away, but she could hear them as if they were right next to her. They both stopped and pointed up toward the sky.

She looked in the direction they were pointing. There was nothing there. She was about to question what they were looking at when the sky began to shimmer and undulate. It looked like the surface of a bubble: pink and purple colors mixed and moved around a large portion of the sky. Cracks appeared, like ice fracturing in warm liquid, and then something shattered through—a large ball of red flame covered in thick, black smoke. It was streaking across the morning sky toward her two sons, who were now running straight for her.

Time slowed down for her as she peered down at her unconscious friend and then back at her two sons. She lifted Lexa up and leaned her against the back of the large boulder. She felt sure that Lexa would be safer here when the ball of smoke and fire hit the ground. Then she stood, glared at Kylor, who was backing away with what looked like uncertainty in his eyes, and turned on her heels, charging toward her sons.

Ariyana's body was stronger and faster than it had been before. It only took her a few long strides to reach them. She dove, pulled them into her arms, and slid into a crouch as the fireball sailed over their heads. It was as big as their cabin and felt as hot as the sun. She twisted her body away from the impact and held her sons to her chest. The fireball struck on the far side of the meadow. Fire exploded up and out from the impact site, carrying debris with it.

Must protect them. She repeated the words over and over in her head: *Must protect them.*

Ariyana peered down. Alec had his face against her, bracing himself, but not Kai. His emerald-green eyes stared up at her, hopeful and curious, no sign of concern or fear.

"Don't be afraid," he mouthed and put his warm cheek against her cool skin. There was no time to question his calm demeanor. The roar of destruction bore down on them, and she braced herself, contracting all of her muscles. The thin, silver metal shifted across her skin, lining itself across her back along her feathered spinal ridge toward her shoulder blades. As the metal shifted around her shoulder blades, she felt an energy start to build. Just as the fire hit her, that energy released itself, and two large silver wings tore from her back, covered in large, burning, silver feathers. The wings seemed to move of their own accord and wrapped around the front of her body, covering her children while the blast raged around her.

Ariyana and her children were surrounded by red flames.

The flames no longer carried the heat of fire the way the fireball that had sailed over their heads did. Instead, the flames were laced with emotions—pain, anger, betrayal, and, more importantly, loss, a familiar loss; a loss that she was already connected to. One so familiar, in fact, that, as she allowed herself to feel the loss, her children left her thoughts, and what was going on around her faded as her surroundings changed.

Chapter 18

The flight chamber was dark as Vayle approached it. *It was never dark.* It heightened the sense of loss that she felt and warned her not to approach. She landed roughly in the chamber. She was battle-worn and broken. She had never experienced the loss of a mate, not directly. Vayle had felt the pain of losing one of her people, but losing a mate was different. She had only ever felt that type of pain through her shared connection with her people when they experienced a loss. It started with the Draxin's ryn, their soul. When a mate died, the energy connection between their bonded ryns shattered. Once the connection between them was gone, an overwhelming emptiness filled the survivor. It would be too much to bear, and the living companion would phase, traveling from the physical realm to the energy realm, without destination, resulting in suicide. She understood that feeling because she felt it now. She wanted to die.

Vayle flared her golden wings in the chamber, and it filled with a faint red glow from her burning feathers. She was the queen of her species, the one responsible for passing the royal energy on to the next queen when she felt she had led for long enough. But in all of her species' history, a queen had never lost a mate. Suffice it to say, the prosperity of her people was not a priority right now.

She curled her long neck behind her and peered out of the flight chamber into the quiet, black sky. *All it would take is one phase, and the pain would be gone*, she thought to herself. She started to turn when a slight *thump* beat in her chest, separate from her own heartbeat. She peered back into the darkness of the caverns, looking toward her egg chamber.

Thump…thump.

There it was again. Something was pulling her into the dark, trying to anchor her to this life.

She slowly crept in, uncertain. She came across Evix's ashes first, and she moaned. Her mate's ashes were surrounded by the ashes of the creatures that had attacked him. She pushed her muzzle through the ashes of Evix's head mournfully. It was terrible to see his bright magnificence reduced to colorless ash. She longed to curl up on his ashes and lie there forever, but soft sobs filled the cavern and pulled her forward.

She was shocked at the devastation that was laid out in front of her when she stepped into the egg chamber. To her absolute surprise, her clutch burned golden-red in the middle of the massacre, untouched and unharmed. The clutch's golden-red fire was tipped in brilliant silver flame that danced across its surface. The rest of the chamber appeared to be covered in black ash, some of which still floated in the air like burning rain. On the far side of the chamber was a large mound of ash. Vayle could feel that it was Glacin's remains. Shorn of the color of his vibrant life, his ashes somehow still held a faint silver glow. Vayle approached slowly and peered down. A tiny, silver body was curled motionless on its side in the center of what was once Glacin.

It was Aris. She was frail, broken, and bloody, covered in turquoise and silver blood, some of which still poured from open wounds. She was still alive, but barely, and she was moaning Glacin's name.

In that moment, Vayle felt grounded again. She felt a renewed sense of connection to her planet and her people. Without any doubt, she knew who she was. She was Vayle, the queen of her people. And now she was Vayle, companion to Aris.

Glacin had lived for the same thing he had died for: to protect Aris. Looking down at Aris's fragile body, Vayle knew that she would do the same. They needed each other. Vayle felt the anguish inside of Aris. Her ryn had shattered just like Vayle's had, but there was an energy much deeper than Aris's ryn that had shattered too. It was a raw, open wound that Aris was protecting. Vayle hoped that with time and earned trust they would find a way to heal each other. They had something in common, something that would help them battle the pain ahead…they both longed for release.

***

"Mom?"

Ariyana blinked and shook her head. Her boys came back into focus.

"Where were you?" Alec asked.

"Did I…did I go somewhere?" she asked, confused.

"No, not by walking," Kai replied. "But you were not in your head. And your eyes—they turned completely silver…like your hair." He playfully reached up, curled his fingers through a few strands of hair, and ran his hand along one of the feathers in her crest. "The fire isn't warm."

His statement snapped her back to the moment. Her body had changed; she was covered in fire. She jumped to her feet. Both boys slipped from her lap and landed on their bottoms in front of her. "Don't touch! I don't want to hurt you."

Alec stood and pulled his brother up alongside him. Their eyes sparkled with excitement. "Don't be afraid," Kai said. He reached out and traced one of the silver swirls on her forearm with his fingertip. When he reached the tip of the swirl, he looked up into her eyes and smiled. "Your body is different, but we can still see you, Mom. We trust you."

"You won't hurt us," Alec added.

The ground began to tremble, and a low growl sounded behind her. They both peeked around her.

She spun awkwardly. Her wings were heavy and hard to manage, but they were large, and they allowed her to conceal her children from view behind her.

"No matter what you hear, you have to stay behind me," she told them.

"But there's nothing to—" Alec started.

"Please," she urged. They both fell silent but shared a look.

The growling mixed with a rustling noise and the sounds of shifting rocks and gravel.

Ariyana steadied herself and squared her shoulders, trying to prepare herself for what was coming. No matter what she did, though, she couldn't calm the assault on her body. She felt waves of dizziness wash over her, followed by a heightened sensitivity to the noise and discomfort of, oddly enough, her surroundings. Her body felt too heavy and difficult to move. She felt a mixture of anger, betrayal, and loneliness, but again, they were emotions that weren't originating from her. They were bombarding her from an outside source.

She took a step forward. Through all the different emotions and feelings washing over her, she didn't feel fear. The last vision that she'd seen was still fresh in her mind. It was a different perspective of the moments after Glacin's death, someone else's perspective—Vayle's perspective. In that vision, she felt how Vayle felt about losing Glacin, and she felt how Vayle felt about her: determined to protect her. Seeing all of that, feeling all of that, had meant something. It meant that Glacin had existed, that Vayle was real, and, more importantly, that Vayle was here, on Earth.

Chapter 19

Ariyana's view of what lay ahead of her was obstructed by piles of dirt and rocks. She would have to climb about six or seven feet before she would be able to peek over the side, and she was hesitant to do that. One, she wasn't comfortable with leaving her children alone in plain view, and two, whatever had crashed into the meadow, whether it was Vayle or not, was conscious and pulling itself out of the hole it had created.

The growling grew louder, so much so that the air around her seemed to vibrate. She leaned back onto the balls of her feet and forced her twitching tail to wrap around where her children stood. Her wings felt heavy and awkward on her back, and she tried her best to adjust them to hide the boys from view, knocking into them more than once.

The air above the piles of dirt and rocks started to undulate, like heat coming off a stretch of pavement under the assault of a summer sun. A moment later, the undulating air turned into golden-red flames that danced above her as if a doorway to Hell had just opened up. It was both mesmerizing and terrifying to watch.

However, Ariyana snapped out of it when, without warning, a large, burning, red and gold wing shot straight up and landed with a loud *whomp* against the ground. The wing hugged the ground at first, then it pulled into an angle, giving the wing claw at the joint purchase against the ground. Three massive claws slammed down against the pile of dirt and rock in front of them, sending debris raining down around them and forcing Ariyana and her boys to move back a few steps. Her arm shot back instinctively to protect her boys as she moved, but the back of her arm hit the membrane of her wing instead. It startled her. She wasn't expecting a wing to be there, and her body flinched. Her wings shuddered and threw her off balance, causing her to stumble ungracefully.

Dammit, she thought, hoping that she'd get used to the new append-
ages. A crunching noise pulled her attention back to the claws.

They were as black and shiny as polished obsidian and were as long
as she was tall when she was human. The paw that they were attached to
was armored with thick, golden scales that glistened in the sunlight. The
claws flexed and tore deep gouges into the ground.

The mother in her screamed that she needed to swoop the boys
into her arms and run as fast as she could in the opposite direction, but her
new instincts told her it would be a grave mistake to run. Though her body
buzzed with expectation and fear, she squared her shoulders and stood
firm.

A massive head rose next, lilting one way and the other. Its golden
scales glittered in the sun, and its crest of red, burning feathers rose and
fell as it shifted to help the body beneath it balance. The eyes were squeezed
tight, and the fangs were barred.

It looks like it is in pain. She thought to herself. It was a passing, idle
thought, but the creature's head snapped forward as if she had projected it
into the creature's mind.

It?

The word filled her mind with a shrillness that she wasn't prepared
for. The word was filled with disgust and disbelief, and it echoed through
her thoughts. Then, the creature threw its head back and roared.

Loud!

This word filled Ariyana's mind with a high-pitched panic, causing
her knees to buckle slightly before she caught herself.

She mentally pushed back on the intrusion, grabbed her ears, and
screamed, "Enough!"

The roaring stopped, and the voice in her mind went silent. She
looked up and saw that the creature was still and staring at her, her head
angled to the side, one beautiful, golden-red, multifaceted eye studying her.
The flames that danced through the creature's feathers made its eye glitter
like a jewel.

Images of Glacin filled Ariyana's mind. She couldn't stop them
from coming. The creature in front of her studied her now the way that
Glacin had done in her dream before he'd saved her life. Her soul filled

with longing. Ariyana leaned forward onto her talons and stretched out her right hand. "You look so much like him."

The creature jerked its head back, snarling, and roared at her, *Deceiver! Coward!* The creature's anger lashed out at her, filling her.

"You just crash-landed on my planet!" she lashed back. "What makes you think you can just call me a liar and a coward? Last I checked, I'm standing right here in front of you. Did you see me run? No! So don't you dare call me a coward," she spit back.

The flames in the creature's feathers rose higher, and it slammed its other clawed hand down into the dirt and rocks in front of it. It lifted itself higher and stared down at Ariyana, who leaned back into her kids and angled her wings farther back to shield them.

Do not think that you can mislead me with your false emotions, Aris. You abandoned us when we needed you most. You left us to fight a war that we were not prepared to fight without you. And an entire planet died because of your selfish cowardice.

It wasn't easy for Ariyana to hear someone else's voice in her mind, especially while also being bombarded with feelings that were not her own. It made her eye twitch, and felt like a mix between eating something sour and getting a brain freeze. Once the sensation stopped, though, she was able to focus on what the creature had said. The creature had called her the same name Kylor had called her, that same name she heard Glacin say in her dream. "That's not *my* name," she stated, annoyed, "It wasn't me that abandoned you. You clearly have the wrong person."

The absolute dismissal angered the creature further, and its wing claw shot out to grab Ariyana. She pivoted quickly, linked her arm around her boys, and rolled out of the way. She popped back up, spun, and pushed them toward the tree line, screaming: "Run!" The boys looked between her and the creature in disbelief. "Now!"

They both flinched. Alec grabbed Kai's hand, and they took off toward the trees.

The creature roared louder when her children took off, and Ariyana looked up in time to see its claws coming down toward her. She rolled, the claws missing her face, but one snagged on her wing, causing her to trip and sprawl out to the side. The creature slammed its wing claw down onto Ariyana, the two claws impaling on either side of her head, pinning her down.

The contact instantly pulled her into another vision.

*****

Ariyana was surrounded by darkness and ash.

He was gone.

She was lying on her side, in a fetal position, in the middle of what was once his magnificent form. She scooped a pile of ash and pressed it against her forehead. She couldn't sense him any longer. His smell was gone; his warmth was gone; his calm, soothing presence in her mind was gone. *It was all gone!* She was left with nothing but emptiness again.

Hot tears burned down her cheeks, leaving pale scars of silver on her ash-covered skin. *How could he do this to her? How could he tear her from her loneliness and show her the warmth of companionship only to abandon her? She needed him to come back. She couldn't live like this again. How could she go back to the emptiness now that she knew what it was like to be needed, to be wanted, to be…joined?* Her ryn felt shattered and empty, and she moaned, "Glacin."

She heard something move in the corridor around the bend and opened her eyes to see what was approaching. She didn't care if it was more of those creatures coming to finish what they started. Part of her even longed for that to be the case. *At least then the emptiness would be gone, and maybe she could join Glacin with his ancestors in the stars.*

She heard another crunch but looked away from the sound. Her eyes skimmed across the side of her thigh, and the tiny feathers burning there. Her silver flame did not burn as brightly as it usually did, but that was not what caught her attention. What made her pause was the turquoise blood that covered those feathers. Her silver flame made it glisten where it wasn't concealed by a thick covering of ash.

She grabbed a blood-covered feather and ripped it from her thigh. Instinctively, she tensed, expecting to feel pain, but none came.

She cupped her hands protectively around the tiny feather and held it to her chest. His blood was the last thing she had left of his vibrant life. She lay there, holding the tiny feather against her chest, moaning his name over and over again. Something crunched right next to her, and she braced.

"Aris?"

Chapter 20

Ariyana came out of the vision abruptly, screaming his name. She couldn't stop the tears from coming. All the loneliness and emptiness that she felt every morning when she jolted awake from her dream consumed her now. Ariyana shoved at the creature's wing claw, both pushing it away from her upper body and rolling away from the creature's grasp. She leapt up and roared at it.

No, not it … her. She knew this creature just as this creature knew her. It was Vayle—whole and real, standing right in front of her. She fell to her knees. Her wings collapsed awkwardly and painfully around her, but she didn't care.

"Tell me he was real. Tell me he lived!" Ariyana yelled. But Vayle didn't respond. Vayle's wings slumped to the ground, and her chest heaved. She leaned back away from Ariyana.

Anger mixed with her sorrow, and Ariyana punched the ground. "Say it!" she demanded. Vayle's surprise filled Ariyana, and her heart sank. "Tell me that he lived…please," she pleaded, burying her face in her hands.

Alec and Kai ran to Ariyana's side. They gently folded her wings against her back and snuggled in against her sides. They didn't say anything; they just leaned against her while she cried.

A wave of anguish washed over Ariyana. It was intense and too much to bear. She couldn't control the onslaught of Vayle's emotions, and it made her own emotions worse. Glacin's death was a stab wound through her soul that had left a scar. Every night when she dreamed about him dying, the wound would break open and fill her with raw loneliness. Experiencing Vayle's loss as well as her own didn't just break open the wound, it tore it open like sharp claws violently ripping her soul apart. She tried to push back on Vayle's emotions.

He lived. Vayle's voice filled Ariyana's mind, overshadowing the emotional storm inside her. Her voice was silvery and strong and had an air of command to it. She spoke like a true leader, though her words were laced with the anguish that Ariyana felt. *All energy weaves uniquely back to the energy realm, but Glacin's wove deeper and shone brighter than any energy that came before him. He was the first of us to bond with an outsider; the first to deny the Flight; the first to ignore his queen's command.* She angled her head so that she could study Ariyana with one golden-red, multifaceted eye. *He lived and…he died protecting his companion, protecting you.*

The words felt like glass inside her soul. Ariyana had doubted herself and her sanity for so many years. She had spent countless nights desperate for someone to say those words to her, and yet they stung. They tore at her, cut at her, destroyed her. Knowing that he had lived meant that she wasn't crazy, but being certain that he had died meant just that—Glacin was gone, and she had failed him.

How are you on this planet? How are you alive? Vayle's voice cut through her shame spiral and brought her back to the moment.

"What?" Ariyana asked.

Why have I found you here, on this planet, alive? Why, after countless solar rotations, did you let me…let us believe that you were dead? Vayle's voice rose in agitation. *Why? Why deceive me? Why abandon me? I had lost so many, and your response was to flee?*

The words echoed loudly in Ariyana's mind, and Vayle's anger lashed at her like a spike-tipped whip. She cringed.

Vayle leaned toward her. *Answer! Now!*

Ariyana jumped to her feet and pushed her boys behind her.

"I don't know how to answer that," she responded, raising her hand, palm out toward Vayle. "I was born here, to human parents, and everything was normal, or whatever that means, until the moment I turned six years old. Ever since that night, I have had the same dream; nightmare, memory—I don't know. Whatever you call it, I watch Glacin die every night, trying to save me. I fail him over and over again, night after night. And truthfully, until all this happened, I wondered sometimes if I was crazy. I keep having visions and seeing things that feel real, like when your flame touched me when you crashed. And just now, when you touched me,

I saw another memory of the moments after Glacin's death, and I knew who you were. It also happened when—"

Vayle curled her claws, leaving deep gouges in the dirt and rocks. *You claim that you do not know me? Your companion! Your Nexi.* She shook her head quickly back and forth and exhaled in a way that sounded like a sneeze. *You reek of fear. You hide on this planet to escape your shame and failure. You abandoned those who counted on you. You brought war to our planet and left us to die!* Vayle pulled her head up and back. *You disgust me. I thought that you were dead. I mourned for you. But you…you moved on. You chose a new home, a new Nexi, and you created life. You created life while others died in your name.* She hissed, lifted her wings, and rubbed her feathers together, creating a low, ominous hum. *Your ryn is black and tainted. I felt you. I came here desperate to find you, but I am sickened to see you now…sickened by your treachery. Tehkara!*

Ariyana's reaction to that word was visceral. Her wings unfurled, and all of the feathers along her spinal ridge rose and sharpened. She pushed her children back with her tail and closed the distance between her and Vayle.

"Where were you when that creature cut out my soul? Where were you every night when I dreamed of Glacin's death? When I screamed his name? When I longed for the connection I felt with him?" she yelled. She pointed a sharpened claw at Vayle's face. "Where were you when he died?" Tears streamed down her face. Her emotions were vibrating inside of her. She clenched her hands into tight fists. She couldn't stop the emotions from building like a storm, both her and Vayle's emotions were combining like a violent thunderhead. She wanted to hurt someone; she wanted to attack; she wanted to…scream!

She turned away from Vayle and roared. It was primal and pure and released the caged emotions that she didn't know how to express with words.

She whipped her head back to Vayle. She was out of breath, as though she had just run a couple of miles. She sucked in a few deep breaths and unapologetically said, "I don't remember." She stared at Vayle, waiting for a reaction, but nothing happened. Vayle wasn't human, so Ariyana couldn't read her expression. She stood perfectly still, head turned so that she looked at Ariyana with one eye. Her wings remained raised. Ariyana couldn't feel anything else coming through, and she wondered if Vayle had the ability to shield her feelings in the same way that she could release them on Ariyana.

Knowing that the silence had gone on too long, she continued. "I have lived on this planet for thirty years, feeling out of place and alone, only ever feeling alive, truly alive, when I dream about him, and when I see myself in their eyes." She turned and looked affectionately at her children. "I feel Glacin's energy in them," she said, turning back to Vayle, "just like I feel it now inside of you. I don't remember anything outside of my life here and my nightly dream of Glacin, but I've never felt more complete than I do now, standing next to y—"

Ariyana's vision became blurry around the edges. She stumbled to the left, but quickly caught herself. "Next to yo—" She tried to finish, but Kylor's face filled her vision for a brief moment, and then disappeared. "You!" Ariyana yelled.

"Something's wrong," Alec and Kai said in unison.

Ariyana whipped around. Both boys were facing away from her toward the tree line. She stumbled back and fell against something solid. "Something is wrong," she muttered. Kylor's face filled her vision again, only this time it was like he was standing in front of her. His mouth was moving, but she couldn't hear what he was saying. "What?" she whispered. She couldn't breathe, and she grasped at her throat. Kylor held up the sharpened claw of his thumb. It glistened in the sunlight. She realized that she couldn't breathe because he had his hand around her throat. He put his other hand around her throat and pressed his sharpened thumb claw into the pounding flesh over her carotid artery. He leaned into her ear. "If she won't come with us willingly, we'll give her no other choice but to follow," he said smugly, breaking the skin with his claw. Ariyana instantly felt sick, weak, and tired. Kylor's face blurred completely.

"No…no…no," she muttered slowly, over and over. At once, Ariyana snapped awake, yelling *"No!"* and started swinging wildly at the open space in front of her. Nothing was there, no one was there. She whipped around and saw Vayle. Her wing claw was out, level with her body. She turned around again, searching wildly. She was confused. *Where did he go? He was just here,* she thought. *Wait! Both her boys were missing.* She turned around again. "Where are they?" she demanded, but before Vayle could respond, she turned around again and screamed: "Alec, Kai!"

Panic was setting in, and she was about to scream for them again when both boys came running out of the tree line. "She's gone!" they screamed. "So is dad," they said between breaths as they got closer. "They're both gone."

"Kylor!" Ariyana yelled.

What? Vayle's voice was full of disbelief. *What name did you just say?*

Chapter 21

Ariyana looked back. "Kylor," she said in frustration. "I saw him in my mind just now. I thought he was here, choking me, poisoning me, but I think that I was seeing him through Devyn's eyes. At least, now that I think of it, it felt like it was Devyn. I don't know. Is that possible?" She shook her head. "That's not the point. He has them, both of them, Devyn and Lexa. I don't see him anymore. What does that mean? Where the hell did he take them?"

How is that possible? Vayle demanded. *He can't be here. Only a Draxin can travel like I did. Who was with him? What were the features of the creature that looked like me?*

"What?" Ariyana asked. "What are you talking about? The only one that looked like you is you. There was no other, just Kylor and a smaller version of him."

Kress! Vayle hissed. *Impossible.*

"It isn't impossible," Ariyana barked. "Look at me. I did not look like this. I looked like them." She motioned toward her boys. "Don't tell me it's impossible. He was here, he beat me and cut me, almost killed me; he put this silver tendril thing on me, and now I look like this. So, yeah, he was here, and now he's gone, and he's got Devyn and Lexa. Do you know where they are?"

Betrayal on Draca? Vayle's voice was pensive and full of disbelief. It felt distant in Ariyana's mind, like Vayle wasn't directing the question at her, but rather thinking it out loud. Then it shifted and felt urgent, and she said, *We must leave now. This planet cannot protect you any longer. If Kylor could find you here, the Tethryn are not far behind. We must get to Draca now.*

"Where? What is a Tethryn? Unless Devyn and Lexa are on Draca, we're not going there. I want you to take me to where Kylor is, nowhere else."

I don't know where Kylor is, but my people and our allies can help. We must go to Draca. My planet. There, we will identify the Draxin that has betrayed me, and that will lead us to the Tehkaric. Vayle growled as she spoke the word in Ariyana's mind.

Ariyana bristled. That word created the same response inside her as "Tehkara" did, even though it was not aimed at her. Neither word had a direct translation in the English language, but she felt their meanings. To be Tehkaric was to be banished or labeled a traitor, and to be Tehkara was to be one who does not belong, an outsider.

Ariyana narrowed her eyes. "Go to another planet? Like, leave Earth and travel through space?" she asked in a frustrated, sarcastic tone. "Yeah, sure, and I guess I'll just jump in the recreational space shuttle I keep lying around for just this purpose. Are you crazy? I keep repeating the same thing to you. We need to find Kylor. He has Devyn and Lexa. They are hiding around here somewhere, and we need to find where that is before he does to them what he did to me. It doesn't make sense to leave the area where they were when they obviously couldn't have gone far." She gave Vayle an exasperated look.

But Vayle didn't respond. She stood there, staring, her eyes moving back and forth between Ariyana and her children. "Well?" Ariyana threw her hands out to the sides in frustration. "Are you going to help or not?"

Vayle made a noise that sounded like a sigh. *Did your mental capacity drop significantly when you took the form of this species?*

"Did you just call me stupid?" Ariyana's tail twitched, and the flame along her spinal ridge crackled.

What is a "spass sutt L" and why would you need one? Vayle asked, ignoring her question. *Kylor is no longer on this planet. He left as soon as he acquired a means to get what he wanted from you, something that we are still unclear on, and that makes him dangerous. He is gone, this I know for sure, and if you hope to find him before he decides to take his impatience out on your companions, I suggest that you stop wasting time and come back with me to Draca. Is that clearer?* She stepped forward and leaned down. *This planet is unsafe. We must leave now before others come looking for you.*

Ariyana took a step away from her, and she heard her boys do the same. "Stop talking to me like I know what you mean. This is new, this is difficult, and I don't understand. According to you, Kylor took Devyn and

Lexa somewhere away from Earth. Fine," she gritted out, though she didn't completely believe it. "But we don't breathe in space." She pointed at herself and her boys. "Yes, we, because if I'm not safe here, neither are they. So, how do you expect us to get there? Make this make sense to me."

Vayle stared at her. A light air of frustration and impatience dusted over Ariyana, and then vanished. She kept quiet, though, and waited for Vayle to respond.

We will phase. Vayle said each word slowly, carefully enunciating each syllable. *We will travel from this realm, the physical realm, to the energy realm. That is called phasing. Then we will travel through the energy realm to get to Draca, just as I did to get here. This is something that we have done many times as one…joined as companions.*

"I don't remember that."

That does not mean that you are incapable of doing it. We cannot stay here and work on the missing pieces of your past. You must trust that by moving forward, your past will reveal itself.

"How will I know what is real and not real? How will I know who to trust? What if I remember, and it's too late?" Ariyana looked down at the ground. "What if I never remember?" She didn't have the heart to voice the real question that bothered her: *What if I don't want to remember?* She looked back up into Vayle's eyes and felt a twinge of sadness. The question didn't need to be spoken to exist between them.

Vayle leaned down more and rested her chest and belly on the ground. She pulled her wings toward her shoulders and folded them along her back. She swung her long neck so that her huge head was only an arm's length away from Ariyana. She chuffed out a large breath, causing Ariyana's hair and feathers to flutter around her face.

What were you about to say before you saw Kylor through your companion's eyes? What do you feel in your ryn when you are next to me? What did you feel when you saw those memories?

Ariyana closed her eyes and sighed. She tried to settle the turbulent storm of her mind and focus on the questions Vayle asked her. What did her body's energy tell her, her ryn, or as the human's call it, her soul? She could feel Vayle's anger and sadness; they stood out, but as Ariyana concentrated, she realized that they did not dominate Vayle's emotions. The feeling that dominated Vayle's emotions was hope.

Ariyana opened her eyes and glanced back at her children. They were staring at her, expectantly. They walked up and hugged her legs.

"You feel the connection too, right?" Alec asked, his bright, blue eyes sparkling.

"Wait, what? How do you know what she asked me?" Ariyana asked.

"We can hear her," Alec stated, matter-of-factly.

"And she can hear us," Kai chimed in.

"We felt her from the beginning," Alec said. "We agree that she is angry. She's angry about the past, but not enough to ignore her connection to you…and to us." He added brightly.

"Vayle's right, Mom," Kai said. "We do need to leave with her now. There's something very dark out there searching for you."

"Kylor?" she asked.

"No, much worse," Alec answered.

"How do you both know all of this?" she asked them. "And why are you talking like you both aged ten years overnight?"

"We see things more clearly now," Kai said.

The boys turned, smiled at Vayle, and started walking toward her.

A flutter of panic filled Ariyana's stomach. Everything had changed so quickly, and that change was spreading fast—she wasn't human any-more; *hell, she was being told that she never had been*; her husband and best friend had been kidnapped and taken away from Earth; she was connected to a dragon-like creature; her children had matured in a matter of minutes, and they needed to leave Earth.

She watched her children walk toward Vayle and felt sure that these weren't the only things that were going to change. She felt a sense of fore-boding, but knew it wasn't something that she could walk away from. Her children were stepping toward the future without fear in their hearts. It was time that she did the same.

She stepped toward Vayle and put a hand on her muzzle. "I feel in my soul, or ryn, that you were my companion…are my companion, and though I can't remember, I feel that I trust you."

Vayle leaned into her touch. *That is what matters. We will figure out the rest in time.*

Ariyana nodded in agreement. "So tell me, how do we do this phasing thing?"

Chapter 22

The success of what we are about to do will fully depend on your absolute trust in what I tell you to do. It must be done without question. There is no time to explain how phasing works. All three of you need to get on my back and press your upper bodies against my scales. My flame will protect you in the energy realm. I will need you to close your eyes and concentrate on the image that I show you. You must not allow yourselves to get distracted by anything. Each of us must concentrate on the same destination. If one of us focuses on a different location, it could force us to phase. We could be thrust, unprotected, into the cold of space, or worse yet, torn apart in the unprepared entry into an unknown planet's atmosphere. Understand?

Ariyana's forehead instantly etched with concern, and doubt crept in. "This sounds incredibly dangerous." She shook her head, hoping the disbelief would loosen its claws in her mind. "How do you know that the three of us can phase safely?"

Again, I have no time to convince you. Every moment that we stay here is a moment that we leave ourselves open to attack.

"Attack? I ask you—again—what am I missing here? I was just attacked by Kylor. He took my husband and best friend to an unknown location, and now you're telling me that if we stay here any longer, we could be attacked by…," Ariyana paused, racking her brain for a possible culprit, but came up empty-handed. "By who, exactly?"

Vayle didn't hold back her frustration and impatience, and Ariyana cringed under the weight of the discomfort. *You cannot control your emotions or the emotions around you. All you can do is trust. I will spend as many planetary rotations as you need explaining the details around all of your questions, but not until I have the full force of my people around us, protecting us. Do as I have asked. Get on my back. We leave now. Aris, no more questions.*

It was hard for Ariyana to distinguish between her frustration and Vayle's, but there was no mistaking the swell of annoyance that she felt over being called by another name yet again. She didn't appreciate Vayle's complete dismissal of her concerns, and she was growing tired of being called "Aris."

"I was clear before—my name is Ariyana, not Aris, so stop calling me that," she said sharply. "I am willing to go with you, but you must assure me that it is safe for my children. I will not just thrust my children into danger."

You did that the moment you conceived them. Being connected to your legacy automatically puts them in danger. What we are about to do poses less danger to them than being your young.

Ariyana and Vayle stared at each other. It was clear that Ariyana wasn't going to get the answers that she wanted right now, and, in Ariyana's mind, it felt clear that though she had her doubts, she felt safer with Vayle than without her. The best course of action in front of her was to take her children, leave with Vayle, and ask her questions later.

Ariyana sighed.

Feeling their mother's resolve, Alec and Kai walked up to Vayle, and she lowered herself down to allow them to climb up. Her wings were tucked into her sides in a relaxed position, but she lowered them, much like a human would drop its shoulders, so that they could climb up more easily.

Alec didn't hesitate. He climbed up on top of her front arm, curled his fingers around her wing joint where it met her shoulder, and awkwardly hefted himself onto her neck. He regained his composure quickly, pushed his body up and threw his right leg over the other side of her neck. Then, he looked down at his brother with a huge grin on his face. "C'mon," he said, encouraging Kai. He reached forward and ran his hands down Vayle's neck, smoothing her feathers and wiggling his fingers in their flame. "It moves like water, and it's not hot. You have to try it. It feels…," he paused, smiling, and said, "safe."

Not needing any other encouragement, Kai scampered up, giggling, and sat in front of his brother. He mimicked what he'd seen his brother do and turned around to show Alec his excitement.

Their excitement was infectious, and it was impossible not to smile. Ariyana approached Vayle and reached out to pull herself up behind her boys. She stopped, though, when something caught her eye. It was the sun glinting off her golden scales. It made them look like liquid gold. She ran her hand along Vayle's shoulder, and the golden color seemed to swirl around her touch. It was the most remarkable thing she had ever seen.

As she watched it, though, she thought of Glacin.

She saw him in her mind, sunning himself in the middle of the day, and she saw her pale hand, perfectly contrasted, moving over his black scales. His scales had been as dark as the night sky, and each scale's black color swirled with its own light as if her touch gave each scale its own star.

Her breath hitched in her throat. *Was that a memory of him?* She wondered. She felt Vayle's eyes on her and turned to see that Vayle had snaked her neck back to look at her.

Everyone who knew him misses him. His radiance was unique in this universe, much like yours is.

Ariyana could feel her pain mirrored in Vayle's voice, though Vayle meant her words to be comforting.

"Mom," Alec said, pulling her attention to him. His blue eyes sparkled with understanding. He reached his hand out toward her. "It's okay. I'll help you."

There was no mistaking what he meant, and she offered him a weak smile. She stepped up on Vayle's hand and paused. The fact that they were leaving Earth became real in that moment, and she realized that she might not see this meadow again. She turned and looked out at the destruction that had taken place in such a short period of time: the deep gouge in the soil that spanned from one side to the other; the broken boulders; the splintered trees; the pools of red blood. It looked like a great battle had raged over this land. It was hard for her to see it looking the way that it did.

Her eyes traced the tree line on the opposite side until she found the small space in the thick pines where the trail from the cabin came out. As she watched the small opening in the trees, she imagined that she could see Lexa running, in all of her stunning glory, across the front of the tree line and out into the meadow toward the spot where Ariyana now stood. Lexa was happy and laughing and racing with a very human-looking Ariyana, who teased and goaded her friend on. It was a moment in time that had taken place many times, until today.

The vision of Lexa drew closer to Ariyana in her mind's eye, so close that she swore she could almost grab her, but then she vanished like a shimmer of smoke, dissipating in the air.

Everything had changed in such a brief period of time, and now she was leaving her home, the only home that she remembered having, for the unknown. She felt desperate to capture the image of the meadow in her mind: the way the pine trees looked encircling them; the way the deep green points of their tops sliced into the pale blue of the sky; the way the sun danced across the sky like its only goal was to warm the meadow below. It had been the only truly happy place that she had known on this planet, and she was sad to let it go.

She felt a warm tingle in her mind. It was Alec. Her connection to her children was growing stronger.

"We wear our past like a suit of armor. We think that if we hold those events close to our hearts then we won't let them hurt us again. But it doesn't work that way. The tighter you hold onto the past, the more it will cloud your judgment of tomorrow. We have to trust in tomorrow, Mom. We have to trust that it will bring us to where we need to be instead of being afraid that it will take us closer to the pain that we've already endured."

She whirled around. "What?" she asked in disbelief. The words were spoken in the voice of her six-year-old son, but they were not the words of a six-year-old, nor were the eyes that now stared back at her. His face still held the innocence that she remembered, but his eyes were burdened with knowledge, a knowledge that he was too young to possess.

Kai pushed up from Vayle's neck and leveled his mother with his own soulful eyes. "The planet is eager for us to leave. She knows that danger is coming."

"What the hell is going on?" she demanded of Vayle. "Why are they talking like they have aged thirty years in thirty seconds?"

Because you have changed! Vayle snapped, losing her patience. *They are connected to an unimaginable energy, a connection that will intensify and would be best handled while in the protection of my people. Listen to your young, listen to your planet, and let us leave.*

She looked at Vayle; she looked at her boys; she looked at the ground. "Listen?" she said and stepped back down onto the ground. She crouched down and ran her right hand across the course soil. The skin across her palm started to tingle. She buried her claws under the top layer of soil, and a presence instantly filled her mind.

Go! A very hauntingly feminine voice urged her. Then, she saw dozens of images from different perspectives of cop cars heading straight for the cabin. *Please!*

She jerked her hand back, shaking her head. *What the hell was she doing?* The people of this planet barely accepted her, and she had looked human while trying to fit in. She knew the truth, *hell, even the planet knew the truth: the people here would kill her and Vayle in a heartbeat now.* She was wasting precious time by lingering in a place that never really accepted her for who she was.

She turned, grabbed the top of Vayle's wing joint and settled in behind Alec. Her wings hung awkwardly on either side of Vayle's neck.

"What do I do with these?" she asked, flexing muscles she wasn't used to, trying to get her wings to lie down along her back.

You did not—Vayle started, but then cut herself off. *I have not had a creature on my back that had its own set of wings. Try to use them to secure yourself and your young to my neck. I will try my best to maneuver appropriately if the atmosphere on Draca tries to pull you off.*

Ariyana nodded. Both boys lay forward, and she pressed against them, drawing her wings around them and around Vayle's neck as best she could. When she felt as comfortable as she was going to get, she told the boys to close their eyes and said, "Show us."

Chapter 23

There was nothing at first except for the soft sounds of her children breathing. The sound was calm and soothing and reminded her of when they were little, settling into the first stages of sleep. She missed those quiet moments, lying with her children at nap time or just before bed. The world felt like it stood still in those moments, like she could hold onto them forever if she tried.

She wanted to hold onto this moment too. It felt peaceful and safe and surprisingly familiar. Vayle's body temperature felt the same as the air around her, which was oddly comforting. She had spent most of her life on Earth feeling like everyone who touched her, except for her children and Lexa, had scalding body temperatures. Being close to Vayle and—she hated to admit it—Kylor was the most comfortable, from a temperature perspective, that she had ever been. It was hard to be next to someone who generated a lot of heat when you felt like a spear of ice was lanced through the center of your chest.

She stretched her back muscles, relaxed her neck, and settled her head against Alec's back. She could feel the pull of Vayle's flame around her. Every tingle against her skin, every caress against her own flame held a promise of the past. All she had to do was pull the feeling toward her, like pulling on a loose string, and the story would unravel in front of her.

She felt a nudge in her mind, not aggressive, but strong enough to veer her away from her current path. She had become distracted. Her task was to focus on Draca so that they could phase there. She mentally gave her thoughts a shake to clear her mind and opened her mind to Vayle. An image immediately consumed her thoughts and all of her focus, not like a memory of something that she had seen once before, but a full sensory experience of the place in her mind. She could see Draca as if she were floating above it in space.

It was nothing like Earth. There was a mass of bright, vibrant green that covered the whole planet, and in the middle of that green were large masses that were covered in a mix of red, yellow, blue, and black. The planet was rotating around a yellow star, and it had a red moon.

She concentrated on the green parts of the planet and felt like she had just stepped into warm water. She felt humidity against her skin and smelled sulphur and salt in the air. It was nothing like the oceans of Earth, but an ocean nonetheless. Surrounded by water were large land masses that were covered in different concentrations of red, yellow, blue, and black. As the planet rotated, or perhaps as she moved herself around the image of the planet, she wasn't sure which, the largest land mass came into view. It was covered in huge, black mountain ranges that reached toward the sky, yellow trees, blue grasslands, green lakes and rivers, and patches of red that she couldn't discern.

She concentrated harder, willing herself closer to the planet, so that she could see more detail. As she got closer, she noticed large herds of animals in both the trees and in the grasslands. She focused on the ground, desperate to touch her feet to the soil so that she could get closer to the beasts to make out the details of their strange bodies.

As she stretched out her talons to the ground, though, something pulled her back. This was nothing like the nudge she had felt before. It felt like a football player had just rammed into her side.

"*Stop!*" a voice screamed in her mind, and her whole body was propelled up into the sky, into space, and instantly slammed back into her own mind, sitting atop Vayle's back still on Earth.

Her body was moving roughly back and forth, but not by her own doing, and as her mind cleared more and more, she could hear someone yelling at her.

"What?" she mumbled.

"Stop! You're hurting her," Alec demanded.

His words and his urgency brought her fully back into the moment. Alec was rotated around, his hands on her shoulders, and Kai was stroking Vayle's neck, whispering to her.

"I'm awake," she said, gently grabbing one of Alec's arms to stop him from shaking her.

She directed her thoughts to Vayle. *I'm sorry. I felt pulled instead of led. It was too difficult to break free.*

Scattered…no focus…intense. Vayle's breath came in short bursts. *I guide, or we die!*

I didn't mean to hurt you. I focused on the image of Draca as you asked me to.

No, you stopped at the physical image of Draca. We must phase to the energy image, to the energy realm, but you are too stubborn and unfocused. I would not do this except that we are too vulnerable here. You must allow your mind to be fluid, and yet strong against outside temptation. Are you clear?

"Yes," Ariyana answered out loud. She was irritated about being chastised, and her tone didn't hide it, but she also understood Vayle's frustration, and she felt a little embarrassed. Vayle was clearly agitated over being on Earth without her people. She was trying to get Ariyana and her children to safety, and Ariyana's lack of experience was not helping. So she left it at a one-word response, not wanting to argue with Vayle about her lack of patience.

The pressure around Ariyana's mind lessened, indicating that Vayle's mood had calmed slightly. Alec lay his chest back down on his brother's back, and Ariyana did the same, settling her wings back in place around her children and Vayle's neck.

Follow the flow, Vayle stated calmly, showing them the same image of Draca from space. This time, though, the image changed quickly, and a bright, glowing green orb took its place, as if the planet had been replaced by its own star. It was comforting, and the longer that Ariyana held it in her mind, the more she could feel its hold on her. It wasn't the same feeling as before. Draca called out to her like a siren on a black and starless night in an ever-expanding ocean. It beckoned her to its warm, green embrace, instead of uncomfortably pulling her against her will. She sighed, and her body relaxed against her children and Vayle.

Yes. Vayle cooed in her mind. *Hold this image as you hold your young, and it will bring us toward its safety.*

She did as Vayle asked.

She felt the pressure around her body change, causing her ears to pop. She heard a faint rustling noise, like a mouse running across dried leaves in the fall. Then, her whole body was enveloped in cool air. It pulled her in and contracted against her, cutting off all sound. It felt…soothing.

Ariyana desperately wanted to open her eyes, to take a peek at the energy realm around her, but she knew that she would lose her focus and that losing her focus would put Vayle in danger. Instead, she held the glowing green orb in her mind and let the energy around her pull her toward it.

As she concentrated, she felt hundreds of pin-pricks across her skin, and each prickle held the possibility of something, a connection. She didn't dare reach out to any of the sensations but let them play across her skin instead, before eventually slipping free of her and bouncing back to their destinations.

Ariyana felt comfortable. She didn't feel like she was battling the heat of the humans around her and the chill of the ice in her chest, which, if she was not ready for it, would feel like a zap of electricity through her body. She had been known to jump in alarm if someone touched her unexpectedly, so everyone had assumed she just startled easily. It was different around her children and Lexa. Their body heat always seemed to drop when they were around Ariyana, automatically responding to her needs, and keeping her comfortable. Right now, it felt wonderful to feel that comfort all over her body.

She sighed and leaned into it. This felt right, like she was finally heading toward the one place that she had been searching for—*home*.

Suddenly, a bright, red orb of light flashed into her mind, overshadowing the green orb. Vayle groaned, and Ariyana could feel Vayle's neck muscles strain under her. Draca's green orb flashed a couple of times and then solidified back into her mind. She concentrated on it, but after a few moments the image started to flicker, red bursts of light coming through like a fire trying to consume it.

The red orb flashed, whole again, and a gravelly voice shouted *"Aris!"* in her mind.

Ariyana grabbed her temples and groaned, unable to focus on anything but the new image in her mind and the pain that accompanied it.

Vayle's pained roar echoed through her mind.

The last thing Ariyana heard was Vayle's urgent plea of *"Stop!"* in her mind as the cool air contracted tightly on the right side of her body and pulled them instantly sideways.

Chapter 24

They exploded into the tight grip of sensory overload. It was too bright, too loud, and too cold compared to the energy realm, and the lurch in Ariyana's stomach told her they were caught in the gravity of something, free-falling toward the unknown.

They were falling sideways due to their awkward entry, and they were quickly picking up speed.

Vayle unfurled her wings to their fullest length in an effort to orient them. This caused a momentary, jerking halt, forcing Ariyana's body to press down hard onto Alec's back, but a large updraft caught Vayle's right wing, bent it over her body, and snapped her wing's forearm. Vayle's scream in Ariyana's mind was deafening. The loss of function in her right wing and fully extended left wing made her flip over and fall into a spiraling nose-dive. The wind caught Ariyana's wings as they spun and ripped her off of Vayle's back.

Ariyana tumbled out into a free fall of her own. She had never used her wings before in flight and was uncertain of what muscles she needed to flex or extend. She tumbled and spun and rolled as she attempted to straighten them, this occurring one at a time due to her lack of experience.

After another roll, Ariyana accidentally tumbled into an updraft. The wind caught perfectly under her wings and billowed them out, forcing her to unfurl them to their fullest expanse to match the wind filling them. The reprieve allowed her the moment she needed to situate herself.

Vayle was still in a spiraling free fall, and her children were tucked into the joint of her broken wing, holding on for dear life. They were spinning faster and faster, and it was only a matter of time before her children, or Vayle, or all of them lost consciousness. Ariyana had to slow them down and help them land safely.

Ariyana reacted. Before her mind had a chance to question what to do next, she'd tucked her wings in and was diving like a missile toward Vayle. She must have had some muscle memory that she wasn't aware of, though she couldn't remember having wings in her dream. She would have to file that away with the rest of the questions that she had. *Now wasn't the time to worry about the "how."*

Ariyana aimed for the injured wing that flapped uselessly in the wind. She needed to fold it in against Vayle's back and secure the boys. Then, she could help Vayle.

When Ariyana reached her, Vayle was spinning quickly, and her tail was lashing around wildly. Ariyana watched, tried to time it, and then dove in to push the injured wing closed, but she was off, and Vayle's tail whipped out, slicing across Ariyana's cheek and forehead. The force of the blow knocked Ariyana backward and away from Vayle.

Ariyana grabbed her cheek and blinked her eye rapidly. There was silver blood in it, but the eye itself was uninjured. She shook her head, trying to shake off the pain of the impact.

The ground was approaching fast.

Ariyana dove again, this time swooping down slightly before arching up to reach the injured wing. *It worked!* She used her forward momentum to push the injured wing in against Vayle's back, covering her children.

Pull your healthy wing in! she screamed in Vayle's mind. Vayle groaned but complied and slowly pulled the wing in against her back. Ariyana tucked the injured wing's claw under the healthy one and paused. Their spinning was slowing and becoming more of a wandering dive toward the planet. Unfortunately, this also meant that they were picking up speed. Vayle was not going to be able to slow them down. Ariyana knew it was up to her. She needed only a moment of distance between them. Gravity seemed to be working the same on this planet, or whatever it was, as it did on Earth, so they were falling at the same rate. Ariyana needed something that would push her out ahead of Vayle for just a moment.

The solution dawned on her instantly. The thought didn't come to her like a vision. It materialized in her mind as if she had known it all along.

Draxins burned and were capable of releasing a burst of energy as a defense mechanism. She remembered it from her dream, though she did not know what it was until now. In her dream, Ariyana was impaled to the rock floor in front of Glacin, and she felt a blast of heat across her body. The creature that had impaled her was torn from her body. It was called a ryn burst. *Draxins burned, and she burned. That had to mean that she was capable of the doing the same thing.* Just thinking about it made her spinal ridge, from the base of her skull to the tip of her tail, pulse. *This has to work.*

She climbed under Vayle and pressed her back against Vayle's chest. The tension inside her body was instantly unbearable. Her breathing became labored, and her energy centered itself between her shoulder blades.

Vayle yelled *No!* into her mind just as Ariyana released the energy in her body. A silver burst of light exploded around her, separating her from Vayle and pushing Ariyana about five feet in front of her. Ariyana channeled the rest of her energy into her wings and unfurled them. Vayle slammed into her back, nearly knocking Ariyana unconscious. She shook the fuzziness from her mind and willed all of her strength into trying to keep her wings fully open.

The ground was so close. The rocks below looked as small as they had when she'd stood on the summit of Mount Whitney on Earth. Ariyana wasn't a big enough creature to fly Vayle safely to the ground, but she was hopeful that she could at least slow their descent. She strained under Vayle and against the barrage of wind that pummeled her from the front. They were slowing, but they were still going to hit the ground hard. *She had to hold on for as long as she could; she had to save them.*

Ariyana roared out against the pain and pushed her wings out as far as they would go, expanding the tips of her wings out past Vayle's body and extending her feathers out along her wing bones to create more surface area. This helped. Vayle's large body pressed harder against Ariyana's back and her claws ripped through the membrane of her wings. Ariyana felt the tips of both of her wing bones snap upward, and she cried out.

They were going to hit. Ariyana couldn't move. She was both terrified to move for fear that if she didn't help them up to the last moment, they could hit too hard, and too exhausted to move anyway.

She braced for impact.

As they drew close to the ground, Vayle jerked her body to her uninjured side and kicked Ariyana out from under her just before they hit the ground.

Vayle crashed first, sliding along the ground on her side. Ariyana hit next, managing to get her right wing under her and sliding to a stop about twenty feet away from Vayle.

Ariyana groaned and rolled onto her hands and knees, her wings hung limply around her. She felt pain in places that she had never felt before.

"Are you guys okay?" she called out, not looking up yet. Her voice sounded funny, raspy, and weak, and the air tasted and smelled like it was stale. The temperature was cool, but the grey, coarse sand under her hands was warm.

No response.

She looked up in alarm. Vayle was lying motionless on her side across from her. Ariyana leapt to her feet and ran awkwardly over to her. Her knees buckled multiple times, and she felt like her legs were running faster than the rest of her could keep up with. She stumbled onto her hands and knees and crawled the last few feet to Vayle. She caressed the scales under her eye and along her jaw.

"Vayle," she whispered.

Vayle's eye slowly cracked open, and she groaned.

"Are you okay? Are the boys okay?" she asked, not hiding her fear.

Vayle shifted her broken wing as much as she could, revealing Ariyana's uninjured children safely cocooned there.

"Mom!" they both squealed in unison and jumped into her arms.

She felt her eyes sting with unshed tears as she kissed them and held them tight. She peered over at Vayle and smiled.

"Thank you. I am so sorry. I don't know what—" Ariyana began.

There is no time for that, Vayle cut her off. *Unless you alone can get us out of here or can connect with Idrin on Draca to have him send us aid, you're going to wish we had died in that fall.*

"What? Why?" Ariyana asked.

Can you not feel them? All of them? You have managed to pull us onto a planet overrun with Tethryn, and unless you connect with your other companion, we will all die like Glacin did.

Chapter 25

Ariyana felt guilty for pulling them onto this planet, and that feeling, coupled with the memory of Glacin's death, infuriated her. She had not meant to end up on this planet, and she had never meant to hurt Vayle, *but was it really necessary to throw his death into the mix?* She didn't think so.

Ariyana opened her mouth to argue but stopped. Her senses burst to life as if they had been dormant all this time and were finally waking up. The vibration in the air was unmistakable. How had she not noticed it earlier? What stood out more to her, though, was the cold tingle that moved across her skin as if the air were filled with tiny shards of ice. What was worse was that she knew that sensation. She had spent every morning of her life since her sixth birthday waking up to her body feeling like she had just walked out of an ice storm.

Ariyana glared at Vayle. "I can feel them on my skin," she spat out. "I've felt this before, in my dream, when I killed the first creature in the egg chamber. Are you telling me that the Tethryn, the creatures on this planet, are the creatures that killed Glacin?"

Vayle slid her arms and legs under her body and groaned as she transferred her body weight from her side to her limbs. She was in agony. Her right wing was badly broken and hung limply from her side. Ariyana could see a sharp bone fragment sticking out through her scales. The feathers on Vayle's wing were slick with red blood, and they no longer burned. The feathers along the rest of her body still burned, but her flame was dangerously low.

Vayle didn't hide her irritation. *It was not an imagination of the mind that brought Glacin to you every night. It was a memory; a memory and a warning of the Tethryn's destructive capabilities.* Vayle shook her head, like an animal would shake its body free of excess water. She groaned again. *They know you, Aris.*

Ariyana narrowed her eyes at Vayle.

Ariyana. Vayle corrected impatiently. *They do not care who you think you are. They do not care what you remember. They will attack without hesitation. They will tear into your body just like they tore into Glacin's. The time is now to make a choice: wait for your supposed imaginings to kill you, me, and your young, or reach out to Idrin.*

Ariyana's body trembled. She turned away abruptly, feeling her emotions bubble closer and closer to the surface. She didn't want her children to see the anger and upset in her eyes, though from the low moan that escaped Vayle, Ariyana was clearly projecting her emotions outward.

Ariyana took a few steps forward to put some distance between them and stared at the empty horizon. There was nothing but sandy desolation for miles in every direction. Anger welled in the pit of her stomach. These creatures, these Tethryn, were probably responsible for the destruction of this planet. They were responsible for the death of her companion, for the years of mental torture that she put herself through because of the life that they took from her. She dug her claws into the palms of her hands until she felt the skin tear. She wanted them to hurt as she did.

Anxiousness—Vayle's, not hers—flitted through her chest.

Vayle was convinced that the only way out, the only way to save all of them, was to reach out to Idrin, the Aryllyn that Ariyana remembered shoving a blade through her chest. She didn't have any context for the memory that she saw, but the image was very clear—it was Idrin with a blade, a look of pure rage in his eyes, and that same blade plunged through her chest. How could she possibly trust him?

Movement along her right arm caught her eye. The thin, silver armor along the outside of her forearm had liquefied and was sliding down to coat and protect the palm of her hand. It was reacting and moving on its own to protect her from injuries. She crouched down. *There had to be another way.*

Ariyana scanned the horizon again. There was nothing as far as her eyes could see, just more of the same coarse, grey sand, like an endless, flat desert. It was dry here. She couldn't sense any sign of water anywhere near them, and it was warm. It wasn't an overpowering heat, but the dryness of the air made it uncomfortable. The planet itself felt uncomfortable. There was gravity, but it was off from what she was used to on Earth. *Maybe it was less?* She couldn't be certain, but she didn't feel as secured to the ground, *if that was the right way to say it.*

The air also seemed stale in her lungs. At first, Ariyana could have sworn that she was more out of breath than she should have been, but that seemed to be adjusting itself the longer she stood still. She felt like her body was quickly adapting to its surroundings. She wondered if that was possible.

Ariyana searched the sky and saw that the planet had rings. They were faint in the daylight but sparkled when the sun caught their reflective surfaces. They were perpendicular to the horizon in front of her and arched over her head to touch the horizon on the other side. They were beautiful. A wistful thought crossed her mind, making her long to see those rings in the night sky under a full moon. The ground beneath her feet started to vibrate.

It is too late. Vayle whispered in her mind.

Ariyana turned around and saw Vayle pull her children into her body with her left wing. Alec and Kai looked at Ariyana with both apprehension and curiosity. Ariyana turned and looked out into the distance. The edge of the horizon had started to ripple with movement. They were coming, and from what Ariyana could tell, there were hundreds of them.

Ariyana reached out and ran her hand along the coarse sand. The Tethryn had killed her companion, and she had no idea how many others had died after that. She couldn't let them keep killing the innocent. She needed to avenge those who had been lost.

She curled her claws into the sand. Instantly, the sand around Ariyana's hand grew in size and turned sapphire blue. It vibrated and danced across her hand, and tiny ice-blue bolts of electricity sparked between her skin and the medium-sized crystals that now surrounded her hand.

Countless voices spoke in her mind as one. *Dying,* they said in a weak, sing-song voice. Images of vast mountains and huge columns of sapphire blue crystals filled her mind. They were a crystalline species that existed and lived as one, covering the whole planet. The species had one sole purpose, and that was the care, protection, and maintenance of the planet, their home. They protected its surface, cleaned its air, purified its water, cultivated areas for special plants, and cared for the wildlife that existed there. They lived in perfect harmony with no selfish desire except to exist.

The images that flashed through her mind showed her a species that worked together when the planet was struck by a meteor. The planet had been injured, the sky darkened with dust, the plants suffered from lack of sunlight, and the wildlife was going to die. The species combined their energy to heal the planet's crust, to clean and filter the dust from the air, to create habitats to keep the wildlife safe, and to re-route solar energy and water to the crystalline roots of the plants. She saw tiny, sparkly, insect-like creatures that moved seeds around, large meadows that were kept healthy and pristine, and the crystal species protecting crystal root structures that fed directly to the planet's core. She saw a species that existed in the daylight and the night, sharing the warmth of the sun and the beauty of the stars. She saw a planet that had a direct link to the energy realm that kept its species connected to everything that existed in the universe.

She felt happy and content.

All at once, those images disappeared, and Ariyana felt nothing but pain. She saw the Tethryn land and start burrowing. She felt sharp, spear-like legs stab and tear into the once-protected crust. She saw meadows of perfectly formed jeweled flowers torn from the ground, their roots ripped up and left to die. She saw creatures scramble for shelter to have it crumble on top of them. She saw the Tethryn pull energy from the ground and into their bodies without remorse as the crystal structures around them lost their color, their hold, and crumbled into flat, coarse grey sand.

The past collided with the present in a memory of death and pain as the harmony that had existed around her turned into the grey wasteland that it was now.

Save, the voices begged her.

"How?" Ariyana pleaded back, tears burning in her eyes. "How do I save you? How do I bring you back?"

No, they said. *Save all. Take last spark…and remember.*

Ariyana didn't understand. *What was the spark? And if they didn't want her to save them, who was the "all" that she was supposed to be saving?*

In response, the ground around her pulsed in time with her own hearts beating in her chest. *Her hearts,* she realized. She had not had the chance to think about her body's essential functions until this moment. She would have questioned them sooner if, for example, her breathing or heartbeat had been missing, but instead, she accepted the strength that she felt, and assumed that it was a result of her transformed body. Now, the pulse around her made her very aware of the strength of the two hearts in her chest. Her hearts beat in sync with the ground's pulses, creating her very own battle drum, and she released the rage that she held inside of her.

They are upon us, Vayle whispered in her mind. Vayle was afraid, but Ariyana did not share her fear. She would make them pay for what they had done to this world, to all of the other worlds before it, and for the life they had taken from her—for her Glacin.

She stretched her arms out in front of her, moved her silver armor across her skin to form casts around the bones that she had broken, stretched her tail to its fullest length, and unfurled her wings. Ariyana felt like a predator ready to attack. "It won't matter," she called back. "This planet is going to help us—to help me—to protect you."

What? Vayle asked, clearly distressed by Ariyana's words.

"The planet wants to give me its last spark to save us all. The Tethryn need to pay for what they've done, for the lives that they have taken." Ariyana paused and roared out, "I'm going to make them pay!"

No! Vayle screamed. *Aris, you were not capable of taking on the energy of a planet when you were fully yourself. How can you possibly believe that you could do it now in your weakened state?*

Ariyana dug her claws back into the ground. Ice-blue lightning sparked through her silver flame. She turned her head furiously toward Vayle, the tiny feathers around her eyes burning both silver and blue. "Stop calling me that," she growled. "And don't tell me what it is that I can and cannot do."

The planet responded below her, and a burst of energy raced up her arm. Her hand shot out across the ground, and blue columns of crystal rose from the sand around Vayle and her children in a protective dome. Ariyana had not consciously thought to do that, but the planet reacted to the needs of her body as if it were an extension of herself. She roared, and the ground around her cracked, spiraling out around her feet. The ground tore apart and away from her so violently that blue lightning shot out of the cracks and struck the ground a few feet in front of her, leaving big craters in its wake.

Ariyana felt the energy where her skin touched the planet's surface. She felt her control over it. The chill in her chest beat in time with her hearts, and her hearts pulsed in time with the ground, urging her to let go.

Ariyana narrowed her eyes at the protective dome and marveled at the tingling sensations of energy that swirled beneath her fingertips. *What could it hurt to let go? She had been trapped in a fog of medicine for so long, pushing herself down, making herself seem small…and normal. She didn't want to be normal. She didn't want to call out to Idrin, someone that she didn't trust. She didn't want to be contained. She wanted to let go.*

And so she did.

The energy rushed into Ariyana, filling every cell in her body, as if her body had been dehydrated and this planet's energy was the water that she lacked. Instantly, she could sense every part of the planet, from its core to its rings. She could see all of it—the grey sand that covered its surface, the dried-up areas where water had once existed, the skeletal remains of roots that poked up from the surface like tiny, fragile hairs, the dozen yellow rings that circled the planet.

And she saw them, the Tethryn, hundreds of them, charging toward her from a tunnel burrowed into the crust of the planet like a mortal wound. She could feel them too. Their sharp front legs speared deeply into the ground, and the long talons of their back legs tore long gashes into the already scarred landscape.

Ariyana's body shook and trembled as if the damage was being done to her own skin. There was no limit to the destructive power of these creatures. Even now, after taking everything away from this planet, they still found a way to mar its surface. Ariyana narrowed her eyes on the fast-approaching horde. She refocused the pain that she felt from the planet and directed it toward the rage that she felt toward the creatures approaching her. This redirection changed her absorption of the planet's energy. At first, she felt it pull itself inside of her, but now she felt herself pulling it instead.

She opened her mouth in a silent scream, teeth lengthening and sharpening. Ariyana extended her claws and talons, digging them deeper into the sand; she arched her back, straightening every feather along her spinal ridge into a sharp point; she stretched her wings out until they were fully expanded; and she pulled the planet's energy into every part of her body.

Her silver flame crackled with ice-blue lightning as it sparked across her entire body. She couldn't hold it anymore. A wisp of a voice floated through Ariyana's mind. *Crush them with the last of what we are.*

The last of the energy pulled inside of her, her eyes filled with black, and she tightened her body. She heard Vayle yell, and her children cry out just before her connection to them fell silent, and her full connection to the planet took over.

Chapter 26

Ariyana's nerve endings seemed electrified. Her body felt like it wanted to split apart from the energy coursing through it. She concentrated on the planet, allowed everything else to fall away, and let her instincts take over.

The Tethryn posed a threat, a threat that needed to be eliminated. If she had relied on her eyes alone, Ariyana would have seen that the Tethryn were a few miles away from her, but her new connection to the planet meant that she was closer to them than they realized.

She felt their strong legs as they charged forward in rhythm with each other, perfectly synced. *Too perfect*, she thought. Ariyana knew it was time to throw them off balance, give them a taste of what was to come.

She concentrated on her location. She felt the sapphire crystals shift as her talons curled through them. Ariyana felt the planet's energy spread out from her talons through the spaces in the crystals, through the spaces in the grey sand, and through the fractured rocks surrounding her. The planet's energy circled her over and over again until she was the center of a storm of energy. It was too much to contain. She cocked her head to the side and sucked in a deep breath of air, filling her lungs until her chest ached. Ariyana lifted her foot and slammed it down in the center of the swirling mass. The planet's magnetic poles shifted instantly, Ariyana becoming the new magnetic north.

Vayle shrilled behind her.

Ariyana's mind perked slightly, and she brushed the outer boundaries of Vayle's thoughts. *There was no permanent damage. Vayle was just uncomfortable.* The Tethryn, though, were a different species, and their reaction to the instant change was exponentially more drastic. They squealed, and the ones that were in front of the horde tripped over their own legs and smashed into the ground. The creatures behind them impaled them as they tripped over them. Other creatures in the middle of the horde buckled and fell into other creatures at their sides. The shift was simple, and yet devastating enough that a few clusters of dead bodies littered the ground.

It didn't affect enough of them, though. The horde adjusted quickly and scrambled over the small obstacles of the dead to continue to race toward Vayle, Ariyana, *and her boys.*

They were a couple of miles away now.

Ariyana flexed the muscles in her back. Her wings flexed and shifted in response. The planet's crust heaved up slightly, fractured, and settled again. She might have missed the movement if she hadn't felt it, but she felt all of it, both in her mind and along her skin. She sent her senses out, testing the boundaries of her reach, and stopped when she realized, with mild amusement, that she not only sensed the rings of the planet, but she could control them as well. She peered up. She drew her arms up in a wide arch from her hips, stretched them out, and then drew them back into her chest. She simultaneously clenched her fists and exhaled sharply.

The rings of the planet that streaked through the sky above her head collapsed in on themselves, starting with the outermost ring. It pinched in like an arrow had been shot through it, pulling it toward the planet and dragging the other rings along with it.

Moving the rings of the planet felt as simple, as natural, as a part of her own body, as pulling air into her lungs.

Ariyana threw her arms out in a half circle and expanded her chest. The ice and rocks of the rings began to swirl, slowly at first, then faster, creating a massive polar vortex. Ariyana swirled her right hand in the air in a counterclockwise motion, and the ice and rocks spun faster and faster, colliding with each other, and, with each collision, the ice and rocks built up their mass until they looked like spear-shaped icicles.

Ariyana's gaze fell from the sky to the approaching horde. She threw her arms down to her sides, her fingers splayed wide, and the icicles shot toward the Tethryn like hundreds of arrows.

The icicles scattered through the horde, striking the planet's surface, killing some creatures instantly and injuring others as the impact sent debris flying like shrapnel. The ground groaned and shook violently. A blast of dust and grey sand exploded up into the air and blasted toward Ariyana. Alec and Kai cried out in alarm, and she felt a twinge of fear run up her spine.

Was it their fear? Was it hers?

Ariyana pushed her hands out toward the impending cloud and pushed it back toward the Tethryn.

When the air cleared, there were about a hundred creatures still alive. They clambered over the broken ground and over the torn dead bodies of the fallen, all heading in the same direction—toward her. Ariyana felt a tug of familiarity: images of her dream flashed through her mind. She saw the Tethryn explode through the rock floor of the egg chamber; she saw the Tethryn in a circle surrounding Glacin as he struggled to reach her; she saw them tear through the flesh of his wings and rip them off. She felt her knees start to weaken, and her breath froze in her lungs. Her body wanted to crumple to the ground. She closed her eyes and moaned, "Glacin." His death was so violent, just like the death of this planet—torn to shreds, left in ashes. *What else would these creatures take? What else would they consume and cast aside?*

"Mom!"

Her children!

Her eyes popped open, and Ariyana growled out a deep breath of air as she stood up straight and strong. It was the spark that she needed to reroute the anguish that threatened to overtake her. *She couldn't bring him back, but she could save them.*

She snarled, narrowed her eyes, and stomped her foot onto the ground, which fractured under her, sending fissures shooting out in a jagged zig-zag toward the Tethryn. The ground split violently, tearing apart, and ice-blue lightning tore through the open path that each fissure created, exploding where the fissures ended abruptly in the heart of large packs of Tethryn. High-pitched squeals and bodies filled the air.

But they still charged forward.

Ariyana roared. She felt the tension of the planet's surface tingling along the palms of her hands. She positioned her hands in front of her chest like she was holding an orb of air between them. She tensed her fingers as if she was squeezing the orb, and then she twisted both of her hands in opposite directions from each other. The planet groaned around her, and the untouched ground in front of the approaching horde of Tethryn tore apart with so much force that the sides exploded away from each other. Rock, dust, sand, and ice-blue lightning exploded around them.

Ariyana stood still, her chest heaving, and listened. The rumbling of the destruction that had just taken place was fading, and she could hear the heavy sound of large rocks hitting the ground and the softer sounds of smaller pebbles. There was something else, though. She leaned her head forward to listen beyond the sound of falling rocks. There was a rhythmic sound that was unmistakable against the background noise of the explosion, and it was still heading toward her. It no longer sounded like a horde of creatures. This sounded like something that ran alone.

Alone or not, though, *this creature had power.* Ariyana felt it along what was left of the planet's surface. She felt it in the icy throb of her chest. She even felt it across her own body. Her silver second skin, which felt more like armor now, moved along her body, solidifying in areas where it instinctively seemed to know she needed more protection.

Ariyana reached out to feel and knew that whatever was coming toward her had one focus—her.

You must connect to Idrin. Vayle's voice broke through her focused thoughts. Ariyana whipped around toward the protective dome that she had created for Vayle and her children.

"I will not," she shot back.

You have no knowledge of the creature that you are about to face, and you did not defeat the Tethryn as you believe you did. They are using your distraction as a chance to surround us. We need my people. We need Idrin. Forget your stubbornness and connect.

It wasn't stubbornness, Ariyana thought to herself. *It was trust.* Her visions of him did not show her a creature that she could count on. They showed her nothing but pain and betrayal. She shook her head and chuffed. *She was strong without him. She had made it this far, and she would finish it.*

Ariyana pivoted into a crouch and slammed both of her hands on the ground. She curled her claws into the sand and channeled the energy around her back into it. Thin, blue veins of crystals shot out from around her buried fingers. A quarter mile away, all around her, a thin, blue wall of crystal shot up into the air, arched overhead, and joined together in a dome above her.

She heard loud sounds of creatures snapping like twigs as Tethryn after Tethryn slammed into the wall. She felt the force of their impact and the scratch of their spear-like legs as they viciously tried to chip their way in. She elongated her claws, pushing them deeper into the ground, and channeled more energy into protecting the dome.

"*Connect to him!* Vayle yelled in her mind.

"No!"

She felt Vayle gearing up for another demand, but the sound of shattering glass stopped her.

Ariyana's head jerked up, but it was already too late. The creature landed next to her, grabbed her by the left wing, lifted her off the ground, over its body, and slammed her onto a pile of broken rock. She cried out as she landed on her already broken wings, which she had tried to cast with her silver armor.

Chapter 27

"It has been eons of searching for you. And yet, after all that searching without success, you land in my ever-waiting hands. Patience, it seems, does in fact provide the most fruitful of prizes."

Ariyana rolled onto the ground and into a crouch. Her left wing joint throbbed along her back. She concentrated on the bones along her wingtips and strengthened the silver armor there. She slowly peered up.

The creature that stood before her was nothing like any Tethryn that she had seen. It stood erect on two strong legs, on the balls of its feet just as she did, and had two long toes that ended in sharp, black, curved talons. Its body was covered in a rough-looking exoskeleton, but it wasn't split into plates like the other Tethryn. It was continuous like human skin, but looked thick and hard to penetrate. The exoskeleton itself was various shades of brown. What made it look terrifying, though, was that it was covered in external boney protrusions. Both thighs had curved bones that protruded from the back of the thigh, curved across the thick skin of the outer thigh, and ended in a sharp points at the middle of the thigh. This made the thighs look like they were protected by grotesque rib cages. It also had the same boney protrusions out of its back that came around its sides, and ended in sharp points along the middle of its chest and torso. The bones were light green, and the sharp tips were red. This, too, looked like a lethal rib cage.

It had six red-and-orange dragonfly-like wings, three on each side, that were vibrating rhythmically, creating a high-pitched noise. It had four arms, two long on top, and two shorter ones tucked into its armpits. The two long arms hung down at its sides to its mid-calf, and each had a hand with three clawed fingers. The two outer claws were long, and the middle one was short.

Its head looked similar to the Tethryn's, as it was oval, and the skin looked like it had been pulled back too tightly across the bone. It had the same two large horns, boney protrusions that came off the back of the head, and a bunch of smaller ones scattered below those across the scalp. Its eyes were different, though. It had two large oval eyes that were forward-facing. Next to both of these larger eyes were two smaller eyes on each side, one next to the other in a line toward the temples. All six eyes had snake-like pupils, black slits in the yellow orbs. It didn't have a nose, and it didn't have any mandibles.

It stood still, glaring down at her. It was clear from its stance and the emotions that it was emitting that it thought of her as inferior.

Ariyana stood slowly, never breaking eye contact. "I have no idea who you are," she said casually.

It vibrated its wings more forcefully, and the high-pitched noise grew louder. This sound was answered by an uptick in slams and clangs along the dome wall behind her.

"Your aim is to upset me, but it will not work," it said. "Patience has long been my trusted companion, and you will not break that with a few words."

Ariyana took two small steps to the left to center herself between the creature and the dome where Vayle and her children were. The only movement the thing made was a slight dilation of its larger eyes.

"Why did you say that you have been looking for me?" Ariyana asked.

It snarled, revealing a mouth full of sharp teeth. "You will be judged for what you have done." It spit the words out like a foul taste. Its voice was rough and gravely when it spoke normally, but it became guttural and harsh when mixed with emotion.

"I will be judged?" Ariyana shot back. "They killed my companion! They killed Vayle's companion! Without provocation! They killed this entire planet and its species without thought, without remorse. And countless others. Judgment has already happened against *them*."

It narrowed its eyes at her and turned its head from left to right, seeming to peer at the Tethryn that were building up around the dome.

"Are you talking about those creatures?" it asked, its tone incredulous. Its head twitched violently to the right a few times. "I believed that it was intelligence that kept you out of my grasp. *That was clearly not it.*" Scorn was evident in its voice as it said those words and stepped forward. Two red flaps extended from the forearms of its longer arms, and its smaller right arm pulled a long silver blade from behind its back.

Ariyana spiked her feathers along her back ridge and crouched. Behind her Vayle hissed, and the creature's eyes widened as it peered around her.

"It is not possible," it said in disbelief. "Not only did you land on this planet, but you brought the queen of an entire species that has caused me nothing but annoyance. You will go back for judgment, but the queen," it turned its gaze back to Ariyana and its pupils fully dilated, "will die."

Ariyana flared the feathers on her wings and rushed forward. It hissed at her and rushed to meet her. It slashed at her, but she jumped over its body and kicked it in the back. It flailed forward for a moment, caught itself and rushed toward Vayle's dome. "No," Ariyana shouted and chased after it.

It turned quickly, expecting Ariyana's reaction, and hit her across the head. Her head whipped left, and she stumbled. It kicked her in the right side and sent her sprawling out across the ground. It leapt toward her; she rolled, and its talons dug into the ground where her face had been. She jumped to her feet, and it swung the blade it held down at an angle toward her torso.

Ariyana hopped back, kicked rock debris into its face, and as it reached up, she kicked it in the stomach. It lurched back and made a grunting noise. She jumped up to kick it in the chest, but it whipped its head up as it grabbed her by the throat. It rushed forward and slammed her up against one of the columns of the dome where Vayle and her children were. It held her tight in its left hand. It brought its right arm up high and swung it down, the red flap heading toward her face, but her wings shot up, crossed, and blocked the forearm at the wrist before it could hit her. She pulled her wings apart and pushed its arm away from her.

Ariyana's two boys whispered "Mom" behind her. Her eyes widened in terror. The creature peered around her, narrowed its eyes at her, and curled its thin, rough lips into something that she could only describe as a cruel grin.

It leaned in close to her face. "Weak," it whispered, and shoved the blade into her left side, the sound of metal against rock indicating that it had gone straight through.

Ariyana sputtered, and silver blood sprayed from her lips. Her instincts had betrayed her. They had prioritized her children for just a moment, and her second skin, her silver armor, had slid around her back to reach them, leaving her vulnerable, and the foul creature took advantage of that.

It twisted the blade in a circle so that she had to cry out. Her children begged it to stop, but begging only seemed to encourage it.

Its right hand shot out for Ariyana's face. She grabbed it before it could make contact. It twisted its claws in her grasp, reaching eagerly for her eyes. She strained. Her left hand grasped at the hand around her throat; her right hand shook as she held the other hand away from her face, and her body trembled from the burning pain that radiated from the blade that it twisted in her side.

It leaned in close, its left cheek close to her right forearm, which was keeping its hand away from her face. "Just let go so we can finish this," it said, voice low, gravelly, and thrumming with hate. "You will go back for judgment. The queen will die, and I will tear your young apart to determine what has allowed them to survive. It must be done. Creatures like you must be eradicated. Admittedly, though, they are the first of their kind, and I will take great interest in what causes them the most pain as I rip them apart, one ribbon of energy at a time."

Ariyana felt the last of the planet's energy in her body vibrate with her fury. She squeezed the hand that reached toward her face as hard as she could and concentrated her energy on her right forearm.

It felt the emotions that were building inside her and angled its head to look at her with only the eyes on its left side.

Ariyana roared at it, releasing all of her rage, and the feathers along her right forearm sharpened and extended across its face, slashing straight through its left smaller eyes.

It shrieked, jerked back, released her throat, and tore the blade from her side.

Ariyana collapsed to her knees and doubled over onto her injured side.

It took a few staggering steps away from her, clutching at its ruined eyes. Its anger quickly overshadowed its pain, and it brandished its weapon at her again for another attack

Loud explosions boomed overhead, and she gazed up. Explosions of every color burst through the thin dome above. The creature's face distorted in anger and frustration. Its patience had clearly been tested. It wanted to finish what it had started but seemed threatened by what was coming. She staggered to her feet and spit a mouthful of silver blood between them. It looked at her with pure hatred, snarled at her, turned on its heel, and flew back through the hole it had created.

Ariyana staggered, her back slamming against one of the columns. *Why are you not healing?* Vayle demanded.

Ariyana moaned in response. Her energy was fading; she could feel it leaving her. The thin dome around her lost its blue color and started to crumble back into the grey sand that it was before. Then, like a bubble popping, it exploded, sand showering around her.

Ariyana's head lulled back on the column. The boundaries of her vision darkened. She saw bursts of light in what appeared to be a darkening sky. She waited for oblivion to consume her. Then she saw a vague shadow against the bursts of lights. A large, blurry creature was descending on her; she didn't know if it was another threat. She flared her wings, and, with the last of her strength, she pushed off the column. She felt a zap of cold pain on the wound in her back and stumbled forward, overcome with exhaustion. Her feet twisted under her as she lost all sense of her balance. Her head rolled as the world seemed to spin around her, and she toppled backward. She fell, waiting for the pain of impact, no longer strong enough to brace herself… no longer strong enough to care.

Ariyana heard the flap of wings and the sliding of something through the sand, then felt strong arms wrap around her. Her head rolled toward an indistinct face. Just before the darkness fully consumed her, she heard a faraway voice, "Aris?"

Chapter 28

Ariyana drifted between awareness and sleep. Her mind was groggy, and her eyelids were heavy. She heard whispers of broken words and fractured sentences, and felt pricks of emotion across her skin. Everything was far away, like the promise of a dream unfulfilled, but nothing like the agonizing pull of the only dream that she had ever known. She felt like she was drift-ing in a vast ocean, under a starry sky, on a warm night. She wanted to stay in this in-between moment for as long as time would allow.

As soon as her mind made her desires known, though, time decided that it had other plans for her. The ocean that she was drifting in started to churn, and the faint sound of voices rolled toward her in the dark. At first, they were nothing more than whispers, potentially just a trick of the mind, but soon they built up until one word became very clear—Aris. It wasn't just the name, though, it was the voice that carried it. It was deep and mod-ulated, and in the moment of speaking that name, it was full of emotion—hope and uncertainty. She knew that voice from visions that she had had earlier.

Idrin.

Just like before, saying his name in her thoughts disturbed the peace that she had felt and pushed her closer to her conscious mind.

"Vayle told us we could stay," said a young voice.

"All I am suggesting is that you can get some rest and I can watch over her for a while," Idrin said.

"Not going to happen," the young voice snapped.

It was a reproach that she was very familiar with. *It was Alec. It was her son.*

A rush of energy filled Ariyana's body. She had no idea how long she had been out, how long her children had been without her.

Ariyana forced her eyes to open. Her eyelids were heavy, and she could barely keep them open for longer than a moment or two. The room was lit with warm light, as from a fire, and the walls looked like they were made of rock, though her vision was too blurry to know for sure.

"My request was kind," Idrin said. "You will quickly learn the ways of Aryllyn and will understand that I am not one you can question or disobey. Vayle claims that this creature is Aris, but the alliance must know for sure, and we cannot do that with you in the way. Stand aside or be removed."

The threat to her children was all that Ariyana needed to pull herself out of her haze. She groaned, pulled herself up, and maneuvered herself between her children and Idrin. She was unstable, her wings throwing her off balance, and her vision was fuzzy, but she would not allow him to take her children anywhere. She widened her stance, flared her wings slightly, and growled at him.

"You!" she snarled accusingly. Ariyana staggered left, caught herself, and shook her head to clear her mind. "You stabbed me!" She squeezed her hands into fists and released the anger that was building inside her chest.

Idrin winced, and surprise flashed through his eyes. Ariyana felt that he knew what she was talking about, but her children's confusion brushed through her thoughts as well. They didn't know what she had seen. They both circled around her to stand between her and Idrin. They held their palms out to stop her. "No, Mom, not him. That's Idrin, the leader of the Aryllyns. He came to save us," Alec pleaded.

"It was a different creature that stabbed you," Kai said. "Vayle says that his name is Raesor. She said that it was the first time anyone had seen him. He leads the Tethryn, the creatures that you fought."

Ariyana took a step back but kept her eyes locked on Idrin. His status among his people was clear and seen in something as simple as the way that he stood in front of her. His stance was dominant and regal. His three horns were larger than Kylor's and Kress's by more than double the size. His long white hair was braided intricately around his horns, and his riding skins and armor were both elaborate and battle-ready. His bone structure was strong and fierce, and his tall body was tight with ropes of muscle.

Idrin's bright eyes held hers without wavering, and as his three crescent-moon pupils constricted and dilated, she could see that they were laced with hints of green and silver. His face held no expression, but his markings pulsed with intensity, quickly changing from deep blue to dark purple in a rhythm that resembled a heartbeat. It was mesmerizing to watch, and just as Kylor's markings were different from Kress's, their markings were different from Idrin's. The markings of each curled and swirled in different patterns, like an intricate tribal tattoo.

Idrin had two main markings that she could see that swirled up his throat. They met under his chin in two points that came close to each other but didn't touch. Then, they swept under both sides of his jawline, pinched into sharp points where his jawbone met his skull, swept up over his cheeks, and pinched into points toward both of his eyes. Next, they swirled back across his cheeks, under his eyes, around his eye ridges, and finally, circled around his inner eyes into two points that met, but did not touch, the other points of the markings under his eyes. He was a predator.

"Mom," Alec said softly. He tentatively took one hand, and Kai took the other. "You have to try to control your anger. It is starting to burn all of us."

The statement shook her out of her fog. Ariyana realized she was hurting her children, and that was not her intent, *never her intent*. She shook her head, took a deep breath, and squeezed their hands. "I'm sorry," she said to them. "I didn't mean to hurt you."

The boys both sighed, and their shoulders relaxed. With the tension gone, they both smiled and wrapped their arms around her and each other in a three-person hug. She squeezed them tightly, but held her gaze on Idrin. She saw a flash of some emotion ghost through his eyes, but it was gone before she could identify it.

After a few moments of silent squeezes from both of her boys, Kai was the first to pull back. "You weren't healing. Vayle didn't know what was happening, and we rushed here to save you. Does it hurt?" Kai asked, pointing to her left side.

She looked down. There was a silver scar below her rib cage that looked like a small sun. Ariyana ran her fingers over it and softly palpated the area of the scar. It was tender to the touch but not excruciating. She looked back at their concerned faces and smiled. "It feels okay. A little tender, but it feels like it is healing just fine," she assured them.

They both let out another deep sigh, like they had been holding their collective breath, and their bodies relaxed a bit more. Big grins spread across their faces, and their eyes shone with excitement. "It is so amazing," Alec began. "We couldn't talk about it on Earth cause we had to go, but have you seen your body? You have wings and fire and feathers and silver metal that moves across your body. You look, you look…"

Both boys looked at each other, grinned, and looked back at her. "Beautiful," they said together.

She smiled and kissed them both on the forehead. Ariyana hadn't realized how much she'd needed to hear them say that. They hadn't looked at her with fear in their eyes on Earth, but, as they said, they also hadn't had a moment to really say what they were thinking. She felt her body relax slightly, knowing that they accepted her without question for what she looked like in this moment. Neither of them asked her to change back. They looked at her with love and held her. They always made her feel like she belonged with them.

"This place is amazing," Kai continued. "Look at our clothes." They turned around in a circle. "These are called riding skins. We were only wearing our pajamas, and they got ripped up when we crashed, and they gave these to us after our bath in the green water."

"Did you know that we look really different from the Aryllyns?" Alec asked. "They have lots more muscles, and they don't have nipples and…," he lowered his voice to a whisper. "They don't have private parts like we do. Rays says that we are built differently."

"How would you know that?" Ariyana asked, alarmed about what happened while she was unconscious.

"Aryllyns are not shy, Mom, geez," Kai said, matter-of-factly. "Our clothes were all messed up when we got here, and we had to get dressed after we cleaned up with you and Vayle. Rays told us that we looked different." Then, his eyes widened with even more excitement. "Did you know that the water here is smart and can talk to you?"

"What?" she asked.

"It's true," Alec said. "It calls itself Lielycet, and it talked to us in our minds while it fixed our bodies and yours and Vayle's. Look! My cuts are gone!" He held up his forearms excitedly, neither of which showed any sign of injury. "Did you know that it can heal you?"

They continued to rattle off more things that they had learned while she was asleep, and she felt her head start to spin. Ariyana had so many questions of her own now. *Who was this Rays that they kept talking about? Who were they naked in front of? How did the water talk to them in their minds?*

They were excited and full of wonder, just like any other six-year-olds might be if they were surrounded by their dream come true. Ariyana smiled despite her growing questions and wrapped them in her arms again.

"This planet and everyone and everything that lives here is so cool!" they said together.

Ariyana looked back at Idrin, who stood there patiently while they spoke. Now that they were quiet for a moment, he took the opportunity to speak. "Vayle is expecting you. I need to escort you to the egg chamber," he said.

"Egg chamber!" They both squealed.

"Mom, you have to see the eggs," Kai said. "They're way bigger than any eggs on Earth."

They pulled her forward, but she tugged back slightly. "What's wrong?" Kai asked, his eyebrows pinching in concern. "It's safe, we promise. Or do you not feel good?"

Ariyana didn't understand where her hesitancy was coming from. Her eyes jumped from Alec's to Kai's, searching their concerned looks for answers, but there was nothing there to help her. *Her children had already been exposed to so much while she was unconscious, so much that she was unaware of, and then, she woke up and hurt them with just a simple feeling. What would they be exposed to if she followed them into the egg chamber? Who would they meet or meet again, and how would she react to that?* She was worried about what they had shared already, and she felt anxious about what was going to happen. She didn't want to accidentally hurt them with her emotions.

"It's okay to be nervous," Alec told her. She looked at him, surprised. "Your skin is zapping with it," he responded. "You'll get used to who you are, but not in here." He gave her an empathetic smile. "You have to do it in there."

Ariyana squeezed his hand. Her children were changing so quickly in front of her eyes: wise beyond their years. It sparked a nagging fear that she quickly pushed down—*what if they were changing just like she had?* She didn't have the energy to dive into that question right now. She would worry about it when her children couldn't easily read the emotions on her face or her skin.

Ariyana stepped forward, the boys pulling her, and Idrin leading the way.

Chapter 29

The rock chamber that they were in was warm and cozy. The walls were full of alcoves that burned with small red fires. There was a small spring in the back corner that was full of green water. Ariyana wondered if it was the "smart" water that her children were talking about. She promised herself that she would investigate it further afterward.

In the other corner, where she had woken up, there was a pile of what looked like animal fur. It didn't look like any animal that she had ever seen, though. The furs were full of colors that she was used to seeing on birds: hues of red, blue, and yellow. It was striking. Her first thought was that she couldn't wait to see what types of creatures could be covered in such vibrant colors, but that was quickly overshadowed by the fear of realizing that she was on a foreign planet surrounded by unknown wildlife.

They exited the chamber and a long tunnel, lit in the same way as the chamber behind her, stretched out in front of them. There was another tunnel to her left and one on the right, but they weren't as long and appeared to curve in other directions. There were also other chambers in both directions: *large chambers, if their openings were any indication of their size,* and the one to her immediate right was lit with a different light.

Kai saw what she was looking at and said, "That's the flight chamber. It leads outside, and it is almost dark. They have a sun like we do, only one, but they have a red moon. Vayle says it's important." Ariyana's forehead furrowed in confusion, but they tugged her forward before she could ask any questions or attempt to veer off to take a look.

"I hope that you get to meet Rays," Alec said, his voice still full of excitement. "She helped with our clothes. Her mate is Rix; it's like her husband, and he is the head of one of the leader clans. Her companion's name is Vec. That's her Draxin. She told us that the females chose their mates; it's the Aryllyn way, but that the Draxins and Aryllyns chose each other.

Vec told us that he renamed her, like a nickname. He calls her Rays because he says that she shines like the stars. Rays told us that the eggs were seeded by Vayle and Arc. Arc is Idrin's companion. She said that Vayle chooses her mate in a great battle in the sky, and the one that wins combines their energy with Vayle's, and they seed the eggs with their combined energy. Isn't that right, Idrin?"

Ariyana couldn't believe what she was hearing. She was used to the information download of her kids. They loved to absorb as much new information as they could, and verbally download it as soon as they saw her, but it was the content of the information that was catching her off guard. "I was out for how long exactly, and you taught them the whole Aryllyn mating customs and where Draxin babies come from?" she snapped at Idrin.

Idrin turned around, his expression confused, and said, "Your new words do not translate. Both of these younglings have not stopped asking questions since it was evident that they were safe. Admittedly, we are all taken by their innocence, energy, and understanding. They are curious about customs and rules, which seem to mean the same as laws, but most of all, they have a firm grasp of boundaries. They do not overstep their place except when it comes to you. They are fiercely protective. As for their curiosity, information is shared freely among Aryllyns and their questions are welcome, especially if it helps them figure out where they belong in all of this."

"All information?" she asked curtly. He didn't respond. "They are too young," she continued.

"If they understand the questions that they have, they are old enough to understand the answers," he said casually.

"You don't get to make that decision," she snapped, stepping between her children and him. Ariyana flexed her wings and flared them slightly. She was pleased when they moved in the way that she intended. Her back and shoulders were sore, but she felt like she had a little more control over her muscles.

"Who gets to make that decision?" Idrin asked.

"I do," Ariyana said firmly, pointing at her chest. "They're my children. They came from me. I get to make the decisions on when they are ready or not ready." His markings dulled to a deep blue, his eyes narrowed, and his pupils dilated slightly. "Oh, does the word 'children' not translate? Let me—"

Alec and Kai stepped between them and gently moved her back, creating space between them. "Stop," Kai cut her off.

"Idrin gets it," Alec continued. "More than you do."

Ariyana had gone too far. She didn't need to see their faces to feel it inside of her chest. She was angry because of a memory that she didn't understand, but this wasn't the time or the place to take jabs at him.

Indeed. Vayle's silvery voice spoke in her mind.

Alec, Kai, and Idrin turned away from her and looked down the tunnel. Vayle must have projected her voice into all of their minds, not just hers, because all three of them started walking forward again.

Ariyana wondered if Vayle's comment was in regard to her thought that she had gone too far, or if it was in response to Alec stating that she didn't get what Idrin understood. Either way, it made her feel like she was on the outside, and she never liked feeling that way.

You are not on the outside. We have much to discuss.

Much to discuss with everyone? She asked Vayle in her mind, feeling frustrated.

I am only speaking to you, my companion. Vayle said, answering her unspoken question about their conversation being public. *It will take time to feel comfortable here. You must be patient with yourself. Your memories will return in time, and I will be here to support you. I am grateful to hear your thoughts in my mind and to feel your energy in my ryn again.*

Ariyana felt a rush of warmth flow through her chest. Vayle was speaking the truth as her gratitude filled Ariyana with a sense of positivity.

Let us begin.

Kai ran back, grabbed her hand, and pulled her the rest of the way down the tunnel.

Chapter 30

Ariyana stood in awe of the chamber that expanded out around her. To say that it was big was an understatement, and an insult to the expertise that clearly went into creating a chamber as grand as this one. And, yes, it was definitely a chamber that was created. There were various stalagmite structures throughout, but no stalactites. The walls appeared to be marred with talon marks in strategic locations along the walls and parts of the ceiling that she could see.

To the left of the opening where Ariyana stood was a large green spring of water where Vayle lay fully submerged except for her long neck, which snaked along the rock floor. To the right of the opening sat a large clutch of burning eggs.

The boys were not kidding, Ariyana thought to herself. *Nothing on Earth laid eggs that big.* Both of her boys were almost four feet tall, and the eggs looked like they stood just a few inches taller than them.

Another Draxin stretched behind the clutch with its long tail curled around the right of it. The Draxin was large, but not as big as Vayle. It had purple scales, dark blue feathers, and the feathers burned with dark blue flame. She imagined that the Draxin probably looked incredible in the sunlight.

Idrin walked toward the blue-feathered Draxin, and it lifted its muzzle to greet him. Alec and Kai ran to Vayle, wrapping their arms and heads around her eye ridge in greeting.

"Can we lie with them?" they asked in unison, releasing her and jumping up and down in excitement. "Please?"

Vayle chuffed and nudged them in the direction of the clutch. Alec and Kai took off, running and giggling, toward the burning eggs.

Ariyana's hearts skipped a beat when she realized that they weren't stopping. They were running straight into an open flame. She threw her arm out and yelled, "Wait!" They didn't stop, though. She ran toward them, but she was too far away. Neither of them hesitated as they ran through the fire. No screams, no bursting into flames, just pure joy as they ran up to two eggs nestled next to each other and sat down, running their hands over the burning shells. She slowed to a stop and just watched them. "Wha…?" she asked.

Safe. Vayle said. *The clutch flame is the same as my flame.* She stood up slowly in the green spring, and the rippling water sparkled with bursts of green light. It reminded Ariyana of the bioluminescent waves back on Earth. As Vayle continued to step out of the spring, the ripples increased, and the sparks of green light bolted around the chamber: under her feet, up the walls, across the ceiling. It was incredible. Ariyana kneeled down and looked closer. The entire chamber was full of veins of the green liquid. She reached down to touch it. It was smooth like crystal, and she could feel the energy moving under her fingertips. She watched it spark around the chamber and flash along the shadows of the ceiling. She couldn't help but smile. If she lay down and looked up, she could almost believe she was lying below a starry night sky.

Her children's giggles brought Ariyana's attention back to them. They were lying down on their sides, Alec on one side of the eggs and Kai on the other, facing each other. They each had one hand on a different egg, and their other hands were clasped together between their heads. Her eyes stung with tears at the sight. *It had been a rough day. They had been through things that she hadn't even known were possible, and yet here they were, at ease with their surroundings and full of wonder.*

Ariyana took a few steps toward the eggs to get a closer look. The boy's clasped hands glowed with a brilliant blue light, and the hands they ran along the shells of the eggs left behind an iridescent trail. "Ale—" she started, but something landed hard in front of her, the sound of cracking rock echoing around her.

No farther. A sharp voice cut through her thoughts.

She staggered back, caught herself, and stood face to face with another unfamiliar creature. She hadn't noticed it in the chamber when she walked in. She wasn't sure if it had jumped in front of her or fallen from the ceiling.

At first, it was so close to her face that she could only see its jackal-like snout and jet black eyes surrounded in gold. It reared up, and Ariyana took several steps back, nearly tripping on a wing, as it quickly towered over her. It had six legs, but was now reared up on four. Its main body was muscled and structured similarly to that of a horse. Its hind legs had cloven hooves, but its middle and front legs had two flexible claws that were long and black. Each foot had a curved, bone-white claw that looked like an opposable thumb. Its body was covered in scales that looked black as it towered over her. It turned its head from side to side, and two sharp, cropped Doberman-like ears perked up. She could see now that it wasn't just its eyes that were surrounded in gold: it had gold scales that formed a V-shaped mask that came down to a point on its snout and fanned out in two wings across its eyes.

Rillac! Vayle chastised, raising her crest of feathers on the top of her head and hissing in warning.

The creature, Rillac, snapped its head back toward Vayle and started pacing in front of Ariyana. Its movement was insect-like and reminded her of watching a centipede move across a branch. As it paced, she noticed that the scales along its body, which she had thought were black, were not only rippling, but actually iridescent.

Idrin and Arc moved closer, and Ariyana's children sat up, their hands still clasped.

Your name? Rillac demanded.

Its voice was hard to bear in her mind. It was aggressive and sharp. It also seemed to register in Ariyana's thoughts in different levels of intonation, like multiple voices talking at once, saying the same thing. It felt intrusive in her mind, whereas Vayle's voice was pleasant and comfortable.

Rillac's voice wasn't masculine or feminine. It seemed to be both and more, almost as if hundreds of tones of voices existed in Rillac's body. Ariyana stared into the darkness of Rillac's eyes and wondered how to address the creature in front of her.

I asked for a response. Rillac snapped.

Ariyana winced. The echo of voices in her mind was overwhelming, but when Rillac spoke the word "I" in her mind this time, it sounded singular and deep and masculine. Rillac seemed to have the ability to shift between what she would say sounded like an individual, masculine persona and, alternatively, a collective "they." She had thousands of questions, but based on Rillac's body language, she could tell that now was not the time.

Rillac swiped a clawed foot against the rock floor and swung a glaring look in Vayle's direction. *Is this creature impaired? Does it not have the ability to communicate?* He used his singular, masculine tone when he addressed Vayle.

"I can hear you just fine," Ariyana responded out loud, watching *him* carefully. She could feel multiple emotions bombarding her, and it made it difficult to concentrate. It was challenging to distinguish her emotions from those of the other creatures in the chamber. It made her realize something, though, something that she might not have noticed otherwise. She could feel where the emotions were coming from. Vayle's emotions came at her from Vayle's direction; Idrin's emotions came at her from where he was standing, and so on. She could feel her connection to them through those emotions. Rillac, who stood in front of her now, wasn't emitting anything except for his thoughts. She couldn't feel anything from Rillac.

She leaned away from him, placing her body weight on the back of the balls of her feet.

Rillac's ears rotated toward her. *There is no issue with forcing you to respond or finding others to question instead,* said Rillac, glancing over at Alec and Kai.

She narrowed her eyes. "My name is Ariyana, and my children and I are from Earth."

What is Earth?

"Another planet, clearly not anywhere around here," Ariyana said curtly.

Why arrive on Draca, Ariyana of Earth?

"A creature named Kylor came to Earth. He beat me, almost killed me, put this stuff in my blood," she held out her arms to show the silver swirling below her skin, "and when Vayle showed up, he took off somehow with my husband and my best friend. I need Vayle and her people to help me get them back."

Rillac's eyes roved over her body. *Why would Kylor attack?*

"He thinks that I am Aris, someone that you have lost."

Lost! Rillac's emotions flared for only a moment, but it was unmistakable: he was angry. Rillac quickly pulled the emotions back. *Kylor is not alone in his belief in who you are. Both Vayle and Idrin believe that you have returned. I, on the other hand, do not share in their hope. I believe that they have blindly brought both you and your young here in a misguided belief that you are someone that you are not. If we do not remove the curse of what you are from this world, another war will rain down from the skies and consume yet another essential planet of our collective people. We have already seen the destructive capabilities that you possess—you almost killed Vayle, the last of her line, and Raesor was seen for the first time on the same planet that you and Vayle crashed on. I believe that you forced Vayle down on that planet to give her to Raesor. Is that what happened?* Rillac snapped, stepping forward.

Enough! Vayle demanded, slamming her tail on the rock floor next to the spring. *I know who she is. I can feel it inside of my ryn. Idrin and Arc can feel it too. I do not believe that Raesor finally showing himself was a coincidence. He knows that it is her, and she is the one that he is looking for.*

Why are we keeping her here? Rillac lashed back. *You are risking so much just by being seen with her. There is no secret now as to where she is. He will be coming here. Here, Vayle! Are you ready for that? Are you ready to lose your planet like we lost Aryll when she abandoned us last time?* Rillac focused back on Ariyana. *Because that is what it sounds like you want to do again. Is that right? Take what you want and abandon us to suffer the consequences?* This time, she felt the full force of Rillac's anger on her. She cringed as the emotion burned across her skin. Rillac's head turned from side to side, his inky, black eyes scrutinizing her from head to toe. *Actually, you must be correct, Vayle. This must be Aris since she is exhibiting the same behavior as she did before. She was a coward then, and she is nothing more than a coward now.*

Rillac leaned in close and released a new emotion. It was released with so much force that Ariyana's entire body was consumed in a cloud of disgust. It was crippling, and her knees started to buckle. Rillac inhaled deeply and reached out to grab her arm.

She jerked her arm away and stumbled backward, trying to escape the emotional storm. "Don't touch me!" Ariyana shrieked. She didn't mean for her voice to sound so panicked and desperate, but she wasn't ready for more skin to skin contact.

She stood up straight and calmed her breathing. Rillac stepped forward again, and Ariyana braced for another emotional onslaught. She didn't feel anything this time. Rillac was holding them back again. She noticed one thing that she had missed before, though. The scent of salt and clay clung to Rillac like wisps of smoke. It tugged at something familiar on the boundaries of her mind, but each time she reached out to pull on the hint of a memory, it faded.

Rillac shifted, snapping Ariyana out of her thoughts. *We are very familiar with each other's touch. I had no intention of breaking you. Why deny me now? What are you hiding?*

They were wasting time. Every moment that they stood there, arguing over who she was or could be, was a moment that Devyn and Lexa were on an unknown planet, with unknown people, potentially closer to losing their lives.

It was possible that letting Rillac touch her could allow them to instantly connect to each other, giving Rillac what was needed to trust her, but she couldn't endure another connection today. She couldn't cope with being thrust into another vision and experiencing something that she couldn't control. Not now. Not when she had too many questions and no answers, and when the only thing that mattered was getting Devyn and Lexa to safety.

Ariyana glanced at Vayle and back at Rillac. *If skin-to-skin contact wasn't an option, she would have to rely on words.* Rillac wanted to make sure that she wasn't hiding anything, that she was telling the truth.

Ariyana took a deep breath and chose her words very carefully.

"The only life that I truly remember is the one that I lived on Earth. Ever since I was six years old, I've had the same dream night after night. I see the Tethryn kill Glacin over and over and over again. It never changes; it's always the same. I can never save him. My parents on Earth thought that I was crazy—how could a little girl dream of such horrific, detailed things night after night without something being wrong with her? I was poked and prodded and tested and researched until I learned that I didn't fit their idea of a 'normal' child. I learned that the quickest way not to be treated like I was sick or insane was to pretend that there was no dream, to pretend to fit in." She looked at the ground. "But that didn't stop the pain, didn't stop the suffering. I lost him every night. I never felt normal, never felt like I belonged there. When Kylor showed up and touched me, I saw things that didn't seem like visions. They felt like memories. I can't tell you that I am Aris. I don't remember being her. I only ever remember being myself. But now I'm seeing things, more things, flashes of things that feel real. I don't remember abandoning any of you. I don't remember a war. I just know that things are changing inside of me; they are changing for my children, and I don't know what that means. I also know that there are two people out there who need my help, and sitting here arguing with you about who I could or should be won't help them. I didn't come here to put you in harm's way. I came here to ask you to help me."

Do you believe that by divulging the tale of your suffering to us we will take pity on you and give you whatever you need? Your presence alone is harmful, whether you remember who you are or not. You made us believe that you had died; you left us to fight your war; you abandoned us to die—for our planets to be destroyed. Now, you come back and claim that you have no memory of us; you ask for our help; you state that you will simply leave after we put our lives on the line to save your new companions, and you have no intention of rectifying the wrongs that you committed? Did I sum that up for you? You are a coward, Aris, and I will not put my people in danger again in your name. Rillac turned to look at Vayle. *My word is banishment. Take her back to the Earth that you found her on and leave her there, weak, alone, unprotected, and let Raesor find her there instead of here. We've done too much already.* Rillac looked at Idrin. *Do you agree?*

Before anyone could answer, Ariyana stepped forward. "Rillac, I didn't even know that you existed before today. Help; don't help; I honestly don't care what you or your people choose. You've wasted enough of my time already. Tuck your tail, run home, and hide. Your fear clearly has more control over your actions than you believe it does."

Rillac's black claws straightened into sharp points and the white claws twitched. *Fear? I have no fear of you. I did not fear you when you were actually something. I certainly have no fear of you in this weakened form. You don't even know who you are, let alone what you are capable of.* Rillac's scales rippled, seeming to hiss as they shifted. *The fear that you sense lies only in you.*

"Be careful," Ariyana stated, her voice even.

Or what? You will leave? We already know that you are capable of that. Why do you not show us what else you are capable of, or can you not remember that either?

Her body started to shake. Ariyana couldn't hold the anger back any longer. "We have people like you on Earth, you know? They talk a lot, but they don't say anything important. They show their strength by step-ping on others instead of building them up. Overall, they are sad, worthless people that eventually end up where they belong; on the bottom. I didn't come here because I wanted to be here. I came here because Vayle said that this was the only way to get my husband and friend back. I certainly didn't ask to come here to get crap from you. I —"

A wave of despair washed over her, and a deep moan echoed through the chamber. Ariyana looked up and the look in Vayle's eyes made the words she had just spoken echo back through her mind. She was so clueless sometimes. She looked over at her children, and their faces were etched in sadness. She had lashed out at Rillac but managed to hurt everyone else instead.

She turned back to Vayle. "Vayle, I'm sorry. That was uncalled for. I was angry, and I am concerned about Devyn and Lexa. I didn't mean what I said."

Or maybe you meant what you said; you just did not mean for her to hear the truth, Rillac chimed in.

"Shut up," Ariyana snapped. "Is it your job to twist words and create conflict where it doesn't need to be?"

It is my job to say what needs to be said, whether you want to hear it or not.

Both of you stop, Vayle said quietly. *Rillac stay. Everyone else leave.*

Ariyana felt a wave of protest flow through her, but it wasn't her own. She looked over at her children. They were staring intently at Vayle, who responded with a nod. They nodded back and continued to run their hands over the eggs that lay between them.

"Alec, Kai," Ariyana called to them, expecting them to come with her.

No, they stay, Vayle replied. *They are safer in the flames of the clutch than anywhere else on Draca. Only those that are bonded to the energy of the clutch may touch the flame, and at this time, only I, you, your young, Idrin, and Arc are bonded to that energy.*

Ariyana turned to her children, and they looked at her expectantly. She nodded at them, and they relaxed again. "I understand," she said. "Please know that I am truly sorry for my rudeness." She turned and left the egg chamber.

Chapter 31

The tunnel was thick with emotion. Ariyana was upset about her argument with Rillac, but that wasn't the source of the raw feelings that swirled around her and scraped against her exposed skin. She wondered if, in time, she would be able to block everyone else's emotions from her mind and shield them from her body. It was debilitating to feel the emotions of others as intensely as she did, and she knew that something that debilitating could be dangerous if it occurred at the wrong moment.

Arc's blue flame glowed brightly throughout the tunnel. The rock walls, already lit with red flame from the fires that burned in the evenly spaced alcoves, appeared to move as the two colored flames interacted uniquely with each other. In some areas, they fought for dominance, in others, they swirled around each other, and, stranger still, in large patches, they blended together. Each light acted as though it had a mind of its own.

As she drew closer to Arc, it was clear that he was agitated. His head snaked back and forth like he was battling unknown urges in his mind. She wondered if the behavior of the light around the tunnels was a reflection of his inner turmoil.

Idrin stood silently by Arc's side, his right hand pressed against his left folded wing. There were no words spoken between them, but there was clearly a conversation taking place.

Ariyana's chest filled with despair, and she groaned, unable to control the building storm within her.

Idrin peered over at her, studied her, and patted his companion's wing. Arc let out a high-pitched squeal followed by a throat rumble and strode away. The effects of Arc's emotions on her decreased with each step he took. She let out a shaky sigh. She looked back at Idrin. He was staring at her. She peered over his right shoulder, down the tunnel toward her chamber, and then, finally, back at him. He made no attempt to move aside so that she could pass and gave no indication that he was going to leave. She would have to pass him. Resigned, she walked forward.

"Arc has not been permitted into the egg chamber since Vayle and the clutch went into hibernation. Finally seeing their clutch and being asked to leave yet again has filled him with a sense of hopelessness," Idrin offered voluntarily.

Ariyana stopped, crossed her arms, and glared at him incredulously. "What?" she snapped, her tone sharp and cold.

"The emotions that you feel from Arc. I wanted you to understand," he replied.

"You believe that explaining Arc's emotions is all that I need to understand what is going on? It doesn't come close. Hell, it's not even where I would want you to begin. What was all that crap in there?" she demanded, gesturing toward the egg chamber.

"Crap?" he said, pronouncing the word roughly. "I do not understand the word, but your feelings are clear. You are frustrated by what took place. But you are forgetting your place among us. You are expected to obey the laws of this world and its leaders. In that chamber, you did nothing but disrespect our ways. You insulted us and, in the next breath, demanded our help to rescue your new companions. Why should any of us tolerate your insolence and offer you aid?"

"I do not owe you any respect! There isn't one person in that chamber that seemed to know what you did to me or why I disappeared. That means that you didn't tell them what you'd done." She jabbed a finger in his face, and her silver flame burned more brightly. Her wings shifted restlessly. "You are not my leader, not my royal. You are a liar! I don't have to obey anything that you say." His pupils fully dilated, his markings darkened, and the slits on his cheekbones widened as he sucked in a deep breath. His anger lashed out at her, but she held her stance.

"You saw a moment," he barked. "A moment does not know truth. Time knows truth; energy knows truth. You are too afraid of your own shattered energy to see the truth that exists around you. If you cannot see through your own broken shadows to see yourself, then how do you expect to face your enemies?"

"You sound pretty entitled for someone who shoved a blade through my chest."

His markings paled, and his breath hitched. There was something about her bluntness and her words in that moment that threw him off. His eye ridges pinched together like he was caught in a faraway thought. "We rarely agreed on anything, and it was well known that we fought," Idrin said softly. His gaze locked onto hers. "You were not ready for any connection in your life outside of your companionship with Vayle. Our bond was one of necessity only, a show of true alliance between our people. It seemed your goal was to challenge me and my people's laws every planetary rotation." His lips curled slightly at the edges. "In truth, I did not mind it. It became the foundation of who we were together. You became the middle ground of who we all were—two species trying to find our way together, not one dominating the other, a coexistence unlike any other. But you did the unforgivable."

The vision that she saw of her bloody hands, Kylor's banishment, and his demand for her life filled her mind. She looked down at her hands. "I killed someone," she said, her words barely a whisper.

"Kylor's three elder kin. You spared Kress, the youngest and weakest of his line, leaving him alone to carry his name and defend his clan. Though banishment is our harshest punishment, you destroyed the last of what he had by slaughtering his three kinno."

It was her turn to feel her breath hitch in her throat. Her mind fought to protect her from the shame and disgust that she felt raging inside her. Her mind whispered, *He's lying, It's not possible*, and *You're not capable of that*. But deep down, Ariyana knew that it was true. She could feel small fragments of memory filling in the gaps of the vision she saw. She saw herself staring at the blood on her hands and knowing that it belonged to Kylor's brothers, or kinno, as Idrin called them. "But—" she began, only to stop. She wasn't sure what to say.

He looked at her knowingly and continued, "After Kylor's fate had been decided, it was time to deal with you. I went to your chamber, full of rage, blade in hand." He peered down at his right hand as if it still possessed the phantom weapon. "I rushed in, ready to take your life as our laws demand, but then I saw you. You were curled and small against the rock wall, your hands raised in front of your face. They were covered in dried blood. You were shaking, and your eyes were full of confusion and shame. I could feel your pain in the chamber itself. My rage vanished, and my hearts ached over what you were going through. I dropped my arm to my side." He dropped his arm to his side as he re-lived the moment. "The movement caught your notice, and you glanced up. I softened my hearts and reached out to you with my other hand. I longed to see your need for my help in your eyes." He closed his eyes for a long moment and sucked in a deep breath. "But all you saw was the blade in my hand. Your expression transformed before my eyes, confusion and shame dissolving into distrust and anger. I opened my mouth to explain, but you attacked with a quickness and viciousness that I had never seen before. Your eyes darkened, and your silver flame turned black as night. You tore at my flesh, bit at my neck, and fought to tear the blade from my grasp." His markings pulsed as he recounted what had happened. The details of their fight had not only burned into the memory of his mind but also the memory of his body. "It did not take long for you to lash out verbally, and that is when our fight changed. Up until that point, I had only defended myself. I had not struck back at you. My only desire was to keep you occupied until you calmed down, but the darkness inside of you only grew. I allowed you to anger me. I struck back at you with matched fury, and before I knew what had happened, my blade was pierced through your chest. I will never forget the words that I spoke that day, but what I see the most when the sky is dark, and the caves are quiet, are your eyes when you, the true you, came back, and the realization hit you—shock and despair. I held you, desperate to save you, but you dissolved into silver tendrils. You were gone."

Anguish swirled around them. Idrin's chest heaved.

She knew that feeling all too well, though it was not hers in this moment. She empathized with the bone-crushing grief and powerlessness that came with loss. He was struggling to breathe with just the memory of what had happened.

Ariyana also felt a pang of doubt slip through the emotions around her. The memory that Idrin shared felt true. She couldn't remember experiencing it herself, though, and she doubted his emotions now. She couldn't control how other individuals' emotions affected her, and she couldn't help but wonder if he was trying to manipulate her. It didn't make sense that he wouldn't have told anyone what had happened.

"Why did you lie? Why did you keep this from all of them?" she questioned. "If what you say is true, why would you allow all of them to believe that I had abandoned them?"

"It is far more complicated than that," he replied flatly.

"It doesn't seem all that complicated to me. In one version, you're the terrible person; in the other, I am."

"As I said, it is far more complicated than that."

"Yeah, so uncomplicate it," she pushed.

He narrowed his eyes. "You talk of abandonment as if your leaving could be the only version of it. You abandoned everyone on this planet and mine the moment that you acted on your vengeance and took the lives of three innocent Aryllyns. You did not think of what it would do to all of our collective people and the fragile alliance I was trying to maintain after Kylor had acted of his own volition. You turned your back on what we were trying to accomplish. Tell me, what would it have mattered whether they thought you had died or thought you had run?"

"Are you really asking me that question?" she snapped. "You are just as blind as that Rillac in there." She stepped closer and flared her wings, her feathers humming with energy. "It matters, Idrin, because in one scenario, you're the one holding the blade in my chest."

She ground her teeth together and waited, expecting him to respond. He only continued to stare at her. He even kept his emotions tightly reined in. "You're holding some part of the truth back, Idrin," she continued. "And I just can't trust everything that you've told me."

She pushed past him, but he grabbed her arm. His claws bit at her flesh. The contact made her skin burn. It wasn't his body temperature per se; it was his rage that felt too hot against her skin. He pulled her close to his face. His warm cedar scent filled her nose. "You talk of trust as if we, alone, must earn yours," he hissed, his sharp teeth bared. "You fail to understand that it is *our* help that you need, and unless you earn our trust, your companions are as good as dead." He snarled and released her roughly. She stumbled back a few steps. Without another word, he turned on his heel and followed the path that Arc had taken, leaving her there in the quiet of the tunnel.

Chapter 32

Ariyana stared down the tunnel, even after she couldn't see Idrin any longer. His words had hit her hard. She felt angry and fought the urge to stomp after him to give him a piece of her mind. *How would that help?* She thought to herself. *Better yet, why was she angry, really? Was she angry with him for being blunt, or was she angry with herself because he was right? Everything that she had said, everything that she had demanded, hell, everything that she had thought had been selfish. Devyn, Lexa, and her children were depending on her to keep them safe. She wasn't acting in their best interests, and she certainly wasn't acting in the best interests of anyone gathered in the egg chamber.*

She'd expected everyone on this planet to help her because she blamed them for her current predicament. Ariyana had listened to the memories that were shared with her—she'd heard the words that were said and felt the emotions that were emitted—but hadn't accepted any part of it as being her true past. She had felt the truth of what they were saying, and some of it fit the visions of what she had seen, but was she ready to accept that at some point she had been Aris? She started taking small steps down the tunnel toward the chamber she had woken up in.

She thought back to her six-year-old self. After the first few months of reliving Glacin's death in her dreams night after night, she had convinced herself, even as a little girl, that Glacin had been real, that somehow he had existed. Now she stood face-to-face with the truth of that. Glacin was one of Vayle's hatchlings. He had been the most unique.

If something that she had already accepted as being real was now proven to be true, why was it so hard to accept that it was true because she had lived here long ago? That it was true because she wasn't who she thought she was?

She stopped at the entrance to the chamber and peered inside. It was lit with the same flame as the tunnel, glowing with warm, inviting light.

Inviting, yes, but its offer of comfort didn't hold the answers that she was looking for. She was caught in an internal struggle. Granted, she wasn't sure how much time had passed, but it felt like she and Devyn had argued just that morning, the morning of her thirtieth birthday and her twin sons' sixth. It was supposed to be a happy day full of celebrations, but it had started off rough and got worse from there.

She had fought a creature from a different planet, and it had beaten her, almost killed her, and transformed her. Devyn and Lexa had been taken who-knew-where. She had fought the creatures that had killed Glacin in her dream, adding more proof that her life couldn't have started on Earth.

How could she have known about those creatures? How could she have dreamed about them night after night if she hadn't faced them before?

Then, broken and beaten, Vayle had brought her here to face more creatures that claimed to know her, and what did she do? She managed to piss off three different leaders from three different species from three different planets.

So much had changed in what felt like so little time. Kylor had two people that she cared about, and she had no idea what he was doing to them. Flashes of what he had done to her on Earth ran through her mind, and her body reacted as she tried to push the rising panic down. Her hearts pounded; her silver swirls pulsed under her skin, and her flame crackled.

She hadn't had a chance to see what she looked like in a mirror, but from what she could see, it was clear that all traces of her humanity were gone. Her new body felt different, reacted differently, seemed impossible to control, and was easily overcome with both her own internal emotions and those of others.

Ariyana peered down and studied her arms and torso. As if the sharp, silver feathers that burned with silver flame along the outer edge of her forearms weren't surreal enough, the liquid, silver metal that moved across her skin like a protective barrier was impossible to wrap her mind around. Currently, it covered her breasts, mid-section, and lower half like a sleeveless one-piece bathing suit. As she watched it, it spread out in patches, some covering her left shoulder and her forearms, and some covering the tops of her thighs. It was light and moved with her body. In truth, she barely knew it was there, but she noticed that it was strong enough to protect her as long as it was in the right location. It had acted like armor when she was trying to destroy the Tethryn on the dying planet, moving and reacting on its own and covering her vulnerable areas. She had relied on her instincts in that fight, and her second skin had followed suit. Her fight with Raesor, on the other hand, had not been successful. She had become more emotional, and her second skin, her armor, had been too slow to protect her.

She slumped her shoulders and her heavy wings sagged uncomfortably. She knew that if she could identify the correct muscle movements, she would be able to control her wings, and she wondered if she would be able to do the same with her armor.

She stretched her left arm out and watched the silver liquid move over her forearm. It slid around the base of her feathers like water filling in the gaps between trees, cuffed around her wrists, and appeared to solidify into a metal forearm guard.

Once the liquid metal stopped moving, she noticed that her left arm was humming with energy. Actually, as she paid attention to the sensation, she noticed that the entire left side of her body was humming with the same energy. She glanced left. There was a large opening down the tunnel that glowed with a natural light that reminded her of the sunlight on Earth. She turned and walked toward it.

Ariyana cautiously peered into the chamber. It was larger than hers, at least three Draxins could fit inside it at one time, and it opened to the outside. The sun was low in the sky and shone in through the large opening on the other side of the chamber. From her position, she could see some green wispy clouds in the sky around the sun, and mountain peaks at either end of the opening.

The chamber itself was empty. There were a couple of alcoves on either side of the large opening, but they were empty as well, devoid of any flame. The only thing that filled the majority of the chamber was sunlight, and its energy seemed to vibrate as the sun slowly set.

Ariyana thought about Earth's sun. She didn't remember its energy vibrating around her after her body had changed, but she was fighting for her life, so that one little detail might have slipped her notice.

She stepped into the chamber. The sunlight was warm against her skin, and it felt like tiny bursts of lightning zinged up her arms where it touched her. She lifted her palms toward the light and watched the silver swirls under her porcelain skin dance around each other. Ariyana flexed the muscles in her back and managed to lift her wings up. After quite a few uncoordinated tries, and realizing that her chest muscles did most of the work, she moved her wings forward and finally unfurled them. The sunlight was warm against them, and the vibration from the energy felt soothing against the tired muscles and healing bones.

Her wings now lifted, Ariyana realized she had forgotten about her other new appendage. She had a strong, long, prehensile tail. This seemed much easier to control. The muscles along her spinal ridge and those in her tail were very strong. By simply flexing certain muscles, her tail flicked from side to side, curled around her, or whipped aggressively back and forth. It felt nice to be in control of something.

Unbidden, Idrin's harsh words echoed through her mind, *You fail to understand that it is our help that you need and unless you earn our trust, your companions are as good as dead.*

She sighed. Did she have the time that she needed to get used to her body and earn their trust so that she could save her husband and best friend? Earning their trust could mean accepting that this was her new life, her new body…a new life for her children. If she decided to believe that this wasn't temporary, she would have to accept all of the terrible things they told her she was responsible for. She would have to remember. Was she ready for that burden? It was hard enough living with the burden of Glacin's death, something that she struggled with every day. The rest could be unbearable.

According to Idrin, she was a murderer. She had killed Kylor's three brothers, his kinno. Now that same man, the one that she had taken everything from, could take everything from her. Tears burned in her eyes. Everything felt either out of reach or impossible.

Ariyana walked the rest of the distance through the chamber to what turned out to be a ledge. Her breath caught in her throat. She was thousands of feet off the ground. She had assumed, when she woke up, that the extensive cave system was underground. She was wrong. They were in a tunnel system that wound through a huge mountain range. She poked her head out and looked up. There were still a few hundred feet of climbing left before reaching the jagged peaks above.

Ariyana examined her surroundings. There was familiarity in the rocky peaks that surrounded her, but only in the features themselves. The mountain range spread out in a large circle, reminding her of a caldera. The sun was a small gleam of light on the other side of the range. The last of its light illuminated the foreignness of the planet around her—green lakes and rivers, long red grassy fields, clumps of yellow trees, and creatures that tested the wildest parts of her imagination.

Ariyana clutched the side of the rock wall to her left. Panic rose in her chest, her heart rate increased, and she felt a lump in her throat. She closed her eyes to hold back her tears and whispered to herself, "I'm so far from home."

You are far from quite a bit it would appear.

Startled, she whirled around, slamming her wing and tail into the side of the rock entrance to her left. "Rillac," Ariyana said, wincing from both the pain of hitting the wall and the discomfort of Rillac's echoing voices in her mind. She wondered if she would ever get used to it. Rillac strode into the chamber with the grace of a predator on the hunt. She felt exposed with the thousands of feet of open air behind her and took a few steps to the right to put the rock wall behind her instead.

Rillac's head casually turned back to look at the empty tunnel. *Arguing with your companion again? So many things to say. So many things to feel. What could you possibly be at odds about now? Does he tire of your weakness again? It must be so disappointing to know that you were someone capable of such power and strength but have been reduced to nothing more than a sniveling, weak liability. Is this simply what you have become, or do all humans share this characteristic?*

She glared at Rillac. Clearly the discussion with Vayle about her, Devyn, and Lexa's futures had not gone in their favor. "Did you come here to get your hits in before Vayle told me to get off her planet?" she snapped.

There was no response. Rillac stood perfectly still, staring at her, scales rippling.

Something felt off. She couldn't feel Rillac in her mind. Hell, she couldn't feel anything from the creature standing across from her—no thoughts, no emotions, nothing. Hoping to coax Rillac to talk about the discussion with Vayle, Ariyana began, "Will Vayle—"

Not here for Vayle! Rillac's sharp, individual voice cut through her thoughts. It was loud and unexpected. She winced and reached for her temples.

Rillac was in front of her before she even knew what had happened. He grabbed her by the throat and shoved her against the rock wall behind her. Her head snapped back. She heard a crack, felt pain explode in the back of her head, and flashes of light danced in her vision. Her mouth opened to scream, but Rillac squeezed harder, cutting off any sound.

Rillac's head turned and lowered down so that one inky-black eye stared at her. She saw her own foreign face staring back at her in the depths of his eye. Two silver eyes, their four-pointed star pupils dilating in horror and panic, before they vanished inside a flash of bright light as her mind became the center of a storm of rage and agony.

Chapter 33

She sat on Vayle's back waiting for her companion to settle.

They had just landed on a large island in the middle of a vast turquoise ocean. It was the only land mass on the entire planet, and it was inhabited by an advanced species that was capable of complex reasoning. They had built intricate shelters and a complex bridge system that allowed them to farm some types of marine plant.

She and Vayle had agreed that the island's species appeared to be an ideal candidate to approach about joining their alliance. They did not appear to be violent, so it didn't seem highly likely that they would be attacked for visiting, and the planet was rich with life and vitality, meaning that there was a high probability that they would want to protect their planet from the Tethryn.

Vayle sat on her haunches and supported herself with her tail. She kept her wings unfurled, her feathers raised, and her flame bright and strong. She was careful not to growl, roar, or hiss. It was a display of power, not aggression.

The species was neither alarmed nor bothered by their presence. They continued whatever work had occupied them when Vayle landed.

The species had six legs. Some walked on all six, others on four, and some on two. Their stance depended on the task that they were working on. Those on the bridges, harvesting marine plants, knelt on all six of their knees as they pulled vegetation from the water, while others who carried heavy baskets of the plants walked on two legs, lugging a heavy basket in the other four limbs.

They had long, muscular bodies, canine-like heads, and bodies covered in iridescent scales that changed colors as they worked. They were mesmerizing to look at, but their lack of interest in their presence was concerning.

Are you sure this is a good idea, Vayle? Maybe this species isn't advanced enough to communicate. That would make an alliance very difficult and would limit any support that they could offer.

Do not allow fear to cloud your path forward, my companion. Vayle responded gently in her mind. *We both agreed to follow Glacin's path, and that means allying with any species that can strengthen our fight against the Tethryn. We must save as many species and as many planets as we can.*

I agree. I just…, she trailed off, gazing out at the turquoise water. The sun was low in the sky, and it glistened off the tops of the waves, *reminding her of him.*

Vayle's wing joints shifted slightly under her legs, her version of a small sigh. *The ocean dances like Glacin's flame. I feel the difficulty inside of you, Aris. These alliances remind you of what you lost. Though you walk a path that feels lonely, you are not alone. My ryn is a part of you, and I would die to protect you.*

She reached her hand between the feathers of Vayle's crest and ran her fingertips along the sensitive scales. *That will never be necessary, my ryn.* Vayle's flame burned more brightly along her crest in response. *I am ready.*

Vayle tucked her wings into her sides and lowered onto her front arms, settling her belly onto the ground and wrapping her tail along her side. Vayle flexed her sharp, red tail feathers in a final display of power before lowering her left shoulder to allow her companion to dismount.

Ariyana slid down gracefully and landed on the white beach. She expected sand and was surprised when she landed on solid, smooth, flat white rock. There was still no response from the creatures. Ariyana took a couple of steps forward: "My name is Aris, and this is Vayle," she called out. "Is there one among you who is the leader? Is there one among you who can speak for all?"

The wind blew lightly through Ariyana's silver hair. It was warm against her skin and smelled of ocean and sweet vegetation. But nothing else happened. There wasn't even any talking going on between them. It was unnervingly quiet except for the rhythmic sound of plants being pulled out of the water and feet shuffling against the stone.

Ariyana took a couple more steps forward. "We have come with a proposition," she tried again, raising her voice slightly. "Is there someone among you who understands?"

A few more long moments passed, and nothing happened. Ariyana looked back at Vayle and was about to tell her they should go back to Draca when she heard a rushed shuffling and a steady click of something hitting stone.

She turned back to face the shelters. Along the main walking path through the shelters, everyone was scurrying around in what felt like a mild panic. Baskets were dropped and pushed to the side, vegetation and stones were collected from the smooth ground, and everyone rushed into two single-file rows to bow their heads to the ground.

The scurrying and cleaning settled quickly into order, and the largest of the species appeared. Its scales were also iridescent, but it had chosen a pattern that would have set it apart from its people even if its size had not. Its large black eyes were set in a band of gold, and as it walked down the main walkway toward Ariyana, its scales rippled black.

Ariyana stood tall and squared her shoulders. It stopped a few feet in front of her and looked down. It stared at her, expressionless. It was tall but had nothing on Vayle. It peered up at Vayle for a moment before looking back down at her. Ariyana put a hand on her chest and said, "Aris." She tilted her head to the side in the direction of Vayle and said, "Vayle." Finally, she reached her hand toward it, palm up, and nodded her head in a way that she hoped meant "And you are?"

The creature stared at her outstretched hand and shifted its head to the side to study her with one eye.

She sighed, not knowing what else to try. Her shoulders sagged slightly, and she began to lower her hand. Its hand struck out, grasping her by the wrist so quickly that she barely registered its movement. Vayle snarled and her feathers vibrated, but Ariyana held her other hand out toward Vayle to say that it was okay. Then, she turned her attention back to the leader in front of her.

Its hand had two long, flexible, black claws and one small, curved white claw. One black claw held her hand in place by curving under her wrist, and the white claw scraped slowly over her pale skin. Ariyana locked gazes with it, intent to show that she was not afraid. It tilted its head to the side and squeezed, its razor-sharp white claw piercing deeply through her skin.

The searing pain brought her instantly to her knees, and she cried out.

Vayle roared, unfurled her wings, and slammed her tail against the ground, shattering a deep gash into the stone. The creature held one of its arms out like Ariyana had done earlier. Vayle hissed but did not advance any further. The creature moved that same hand to Ariyana's temple.

Ariyana's scream stopped, but her mouth remained open like the sound was stuck in her throat. She threw her head up toward the sky, and her back arched. Her entire body looked like it was straining.

Just as quickly as the creature had grabbed her, it let go. Ariyana fell over. Vayle advanced on her quickly, sliding her tail between her and the creature, and nudged her with her muzzle. Ariyana was breathing heavily, but between gasps, she stroked the front of Vayle's nose and whispered, "It's okay; I'm okay."

Vayle bared her teeth at the creature and growled.

Ariyana wrapped her fingers around Vayle's fang and pulled herself to her feet. "I am unharmed. The creature was connecting. Its name is Rillac. Rillac is the leader of these people, the Torins, and they speak through their minds as the Draxins do."

Vayle was still agitated, but she settled a little. She kept Ariyana next to her even as she gained her ground and balanced herself. Ariyana affectionately ran her hand over her eye ridge and nodded her head at Rillac. "You saw why I am here, yes? You understand the need for an alliance?"

Rillac gave a short nod.

"You have my word, Rillac. We will ally to make our planets and our people stronger. You saw that we fought the Tethryn, and we were triumphant. We will stand together; we will fight together, and through our partnership we shall thrive."

Rillac gave another short nod. *Our bond is as strong as our word, Aris. You will be held to your oath, to your promise.*

***

Bright light filled Ariyana's vision again. She squeezed her eyelids closed. She tried to move her head back and forth but found that her range of motion was being restricted. She felt cold, hard stone against her back and realized that her lungs were burning.

Her mind raced. She desperately tried to piece through both the events that she had just seen and her current impairment. It was disconcerting to be overwhelmed by these visions, these memories; her own and yet not her own.

What did you see? The voice was sharp and cut through the confusion. Her eyes popped open.

Rillac.

Rillac's hand was still wrapped around her throat, and another one was locked onto her jaw. Panic rose inside her chest. She couldn't breathe. Her hearts pounded against her ribs. She wondered if Rillac could feel the strength of the two organs as they pulsed against the vice-like claws pressed against her vulnerable skin.

Ariyana grasped at the hand around her throat and shifted from side to side against the wall. Her wings had been in an awkward position when Rillac pushed her back. This meant that they were pinned tightly between her and the wall. They were useless, and the healing bones ached from the pressure of the jagged surface behind her.

She was becoming desperate. Her tail slammed against the wall. Realization filled her eyes. Ariyana leveled a glare at Rillac. She flexed her tail feathers into a sharp point and whipped it at Rillac's chest. One of Rillac's middle arms flew out, caught her tail, and gave it a nasty yank while simultaneously pulling her a couple of inches away from the wall and slamming her back against it. She heard the cracking of bones and fire ignited in her wings. Her bones had snapped where they were trying to heal. Her mouth opened in a soundless cry and tears burned in the corners of her eyes.

Rillac eased up just enough to let the faintest wisp of air through her throat. She struggled and gasped, but Rillac wouldn't ease up any further. He gave her enough air to survive but not enough to talk or scream.

Ariyana tried to call out to Vayle or Idrin but couldn't get past the anger in her mind no matter how much she fought to get through. As she concentrated on it, it wasn't just anger that she felt, it was rage, and though she felt it with every fiber of her being, it wasn't hers.

She stopped thrashing and concentrated on the small bursts of air that she could get into her lungs. She stared at Rillac. *You hate me this much?* She asked in her mind.

Rillac stared back. *Rage is an easy emotion to control.* The words were stated in Rillac's singular voice, rough and precise. *It is consuming and blinding for those that feel it. Based on your reaction in the egg chamber, you cannot control emotions or how the emotions of others affect you. It was also clear that you cannot control the memories of your past that arose when one touched you. What did you see?*

Let. Go, she responded. Annoyance flitted across her mind.

I was clear. You would be held to your oath. You said that we would stand together, fight together, and thrive through our partnership, but when the fight finally came, you ran.

I told you before, I did not run. Her own anger was starting to break through the rage that Rillac was forcing upon her.

Right. You were forced, Rillac said, sardonically. *Whatever took place all those cycles ago, one fact remains: at some point, you made the decision not to come back.*

Ariyana's eyes widened. There was nothing to say to such a blunt statement. Every argument would fall short because no matter what she said or claimed not to remember, Rillac was right: the Aris that they knew hadn't come back. The meaning behind Rillac's words conveyed everything: the truth of what happened in the past and the truth of what was staring Rillac in the face right now. That no matter who she was, she wasn't who she used to be. No longer able to hold the weight of Rillac's stare, Ariyana looked down at the floor.

No argument? No excuse? Rillac asked derisively.

She glanced back up into Rillac's eyes. *There isn't anything that I can say that you want to hear, so what's the point?*

Rillac's head turned to the right to gaze outside, and then turned to look at her again. *You are correct. There are no words that you could utter that would make any difference at all. Torins look to actions over words. What will you decide this time?* Rillac's head tilted to the side, and the golden scales rippled around those inky-black eyes. *Will you come back?*

Wha—

The question barely had a chance to register in her mind when Rillac squeezed her throat tighter, pulled her forward, and shoved her out of the cave opening.

Chapter 34

There was no air in her lungs to scream. All she could do was gasp as her arms flailed to grasp one of Rillac's limbs. Her wings whooshed forward, and her hair whipped into her face. Time seemed to slow for a moment as she fell backward into nothingness.

Ariyana's face twisted in terror but quickly morphed into fury as she watched Rillac's body leisurely turn away from her.

Time abruptly returned to normal, and she plummeted toward the foreign ground below.

Rillac's mental block had broken the moment that she was released, and many things happened at once. She heard Vayle's anguished roar—she wasn't healed enough to save her. She heard her children's screams of protest. She heard and felt Idrin's demand for Arc's help. She felt Idrin running, and she felt Arc's urgency as he raced to his companion's side. Moments later, she saw them explode out of the cave opening and dive toward her.

But it was too late.

She felt it in Arc's pained realization of her location and heard it in Idrin's urgent demand to dive.

Her survival depended *on one thing alone.*

Her mind raced back to the dying planet that she'd accidentally forced Vayle to phase to before coming to Draca. Ariyana's mind replayed it: she had wings, and she could fly. She figured it out once; *she could do it again.*

Her wings were painfully, loosely flapping around her as she fell back-first toward the ground. It felt like she was stuck in a free fall in the middle of a parachute. The tips of both of her outer bones on her wings were broken, and the wind was causing them to whip around violently. It was excruciating.

Ariyana knew that she couldn't just unfurl her wings while falling backward. It would slow her fall, but maneuvering would be too difficult while upside down. She needed to flip over.

She folded the tips of her wings down toward her body. Luckily, only the lower bones were broken, the joints were fully intact. Once her wings were safely tucked behind her, Ariyana threw one of her arms out, tightened her body, rolled to her front, and exploded her wings out to their fullest. The membranes filled with air, jerking her to what felt like a stop, though she was still falling, just more slowly now. It didn't help that the tips of her wings were bent backward preventing her from capturing as much air as she could. It also meant that she wasn't getting the proper air flow over her wings.

Ariyana took a deep breath and concentrated on the silver armor on her shoulders, willing it toward her wing bones to form casts along the broken tips. Amazingly, she felt it respond. Once this held, she flew straighter and glided rather than fell toward the ground.

She wasn't slowing quickly enough, though, and the ground was approaching fast.

Her vision sharpened, and the area around her transformed before her eyes. She saw bright colors moving around her and about the surface below. It was like the energy of the planet had taken on a life of its own and was showing her the way.

The sun was setting, and as it set, the heat was shifting all around her. It was rising quickly in large, orange updrafts. All Ariyana had to do was position herself in the middle of one of these, and it would take her back to the cave opening, where she would, appropriately, rip all of the arms off Rillac's body.

She angled herself in the direction of the nearest updraft but realized with a groan that she would hit the ground before she reached it. *I need to try something else.*

She rotated her wings forward Pand backward in a flapping motion, but she didn't have the power needed in her muscles to slow her fall. Ariyana's agitation grew.

Idrin yelled something. Arc was reaching the limit where even he wouldn't be able to pull himself out of a terrible crash if he didn't pull up.

I have moments left.

Her body began to tense, and a feeling of pressure tingled around her skin. Ariyana's eyes focused on the ground with a clarity that she had never had before. It wasn't that her eyes were picking up more detail along the ground itself; it was that she could see the details of the flow of energy. She saw it move and gather and swirl and rush toward a single point below her.

She felt the air around her do the same. It moved and gathered and swirled and rushed around her. Her flame crackled and hissed. Her feathers raised. Her wings curled in of their own accord. The pressure became so great that she couldn't hold it around herself anymore. Ariyana willed it out with a flap of her wings, and bright, silver light exploded from her body.

It emanated from her like a flash grenade, the force of the blow knocking over trees below her, dislodging rocks, propelling Ariyana upward, and knocking Arc back.

The explosion filled her wings with hot air, and Ariyana soared upward, flipping ungracefully head over feet into the closest updraft. The strong current of warm air caught under her wings, jerking her out of her uncontrolled flipping and rocketing her upward.

She whooshed past Arc. He was disoriented from her burst of energy and was trying to regain his balance. When Ariyana flew past him, he twisted and tried to make a rapid aerial shift to go after her, but caught an updraft awkwardly and tumbled into a short spin. She heard Idrin holler something in frustration and felt Arc lose a few dozen feet of height. Arc's rapid adjustment, while off balance, had cost them.

They weren't in any danger and didn't need her help. Ariyana glared at the rapidly approaching cave opening. She had her eyes set on one goal, and she wasn't going to stop until she had the opportunity to throw Rillac out of the opening. *Let's see if Rillac likes to fly,* she thought to herself. She gained more height. She didn't need to flap her wings. The upward rush of air was all she needed to gain momentum.

Once she was slightly higher than the cave opening and could clearly see Rillac, still walking away, Ariyana folded her wings and dove.

She didn't flare her wings to slow down. She shot into the cave opening and slammed into Rillac with so much force that they both sprawled across the floor. Ariyana leapt up and flapped her wings, hovering over Rillac.

"Did I come back, Rillac? Did I?" she roared, her sharp teeth elongating. She pushed her anger through her body and felt her body change in response. Her wings and talons lengthened. Ariyana grabbed Rillac by the neck with her talons and flapped hard to lift his body partially off the ground. "Want to throw me out another window, asshole?"

She flapped her wings harder, lifting Rillac higher. She whipped her tail around and sharpened her tail feathers, pointing the sharpened tip toward Rillac's face. "You had so much to say before," Ariyana snapped. "Why so quiet now? Want to tell me how weak I am? How pathetic? Huh? Do you? Cause I sure as hell can't hear you now. Should I squeeze harder, you prick? Better yet," she flapped backward, dragging Rillac toward the opening, "let's see if your dumbass can fly?"

Arc burst into the chamber behind her and slid forward. "Aris!" Idrin yelled.

Ariyana didn't bother to look back at him but yelled, "That's not my damn name!"

She was angry, and she wanted Rillac to pay for everything that had just happened. Hell, she wanted Rillac to pay for what Kylor had done to her, too. Ariyana didn't hold her anger back and let the emotion rip from her body. Rillac, Idrin, and Arc moaned.

"Oh, can you not control that?" she chided. "I should tear your throat out for what you did."

"Mom!" Alec and Kai yelled.

The word hit her like a splash of cold water to the face. Ariyana's talons released so quickly that Rillac didn't have time to react. She heard a heavy slap of limbs on the rock floor.

Ariyana landed, immediately feeling self-conscious. She kept her back toward them. She ran her hands over her mouth as her teeth shortened to their previous size, still sharp but not as long. Her wings and talons returned to their previous size as well. She rapidly blinked and took a few deep breaths, trying to bring her emotions under control.

She heard their soft footfalls coming up behind her. "Boys, wait, please," she begged.

A gentle hand touched her forearm, and she jumped. Ariyana didn't know if she was more afraid of potentially hurting them or of them being afraid of what she was becoming. She looked down to see their innocent eyes peering up into hers, imploringly. They didn't have to vocalize the question that they were asking. It hung in the air.

Idrin had dismounted and was walking up to Rillac. They were quiet, but she didn't trust that nothing was being said. Her anger quickly rose again. "What are you saying, Rillac? What lies are you spewing?" Ariyana snapped. Alec and Kai both took one of her hands and squeezed gently.

"Vayle has demanded that Rillac not speak again until we are in council with her," Alec said.

"Vayle is asking for calm, mom," Kai said. "She demands our presence."

Without another word or look, they pulled her toward the egg chamber.

Chapter 35

To say that Vayle was angry was an understatement. Her heavy, rhythmic steps echoed through the tunnel. Ariyana could feel the charge in the air, growing in intensity the closer they got.

Her children still led her forward, seemingly unaware of the energy around them. She wondered if they didn't feel it all, or if they felt it and were ignoring it. Either way, after what had just occurred with Rillac, she didn't want them to be in the middle of whatever was about to happen.

She pulled back. They both stopped and looked at her, eyebrows raised questioningly. She pulled their hands together, laying one on top of the other, and squeezed. "I want both of you to head back to the chamber where I woke up. Stay there until I come and get you, okay? There is a lot going on right now, and I'm not sure what I'm walking into. I would feel better if I knew both of you were somewhere safe."

They exchanged a look, peered back at her, and shook their heads in unison. "When she sent us to get you, Vayle said everyone has to come back," Alec said. "She said it's important."

"And that we would be safe," Kai said. They turned and led her forward again.

She was conflicted. As a mom, she felt the overwhelming urge to keep her children safe and the desire to be the one person that they relied on for direction. It might be true that having them in the same chamber as her could be the safest place for them. It might also be true that they had every right to know what was going on, since it did involve their father, but shouldn't she be the one to choose that? She still felt terrible for what she had said earlier, but she didn't feel like that gave Vayle the right to usurp her in her children's eyes.

On the other hand, though, she was no longer on Earth. She was on Draca, a planet dominated by the Draxins, who were ruled by their queen, Vayle, who was used to giving orders and having them followed immediately. The intricate details of what being a mom meant to Ariyana wouldn't be a high priority to Vayle right now.

Walking into the egg chamber felt like walking into a thunderstorm. Her children released her hands and ran over to the burning clutch. It would have seemed like it was a replay of the last time Ariyana saw them running over there, except this time Vayle was a mass of seething rage.

Rillac walked slowly past Ariyana toward Vayle. He walked on four legs with shoulders squared and head held high. There wasn't anything about Rillac that screamed remorse or shame for what had occurred between them. He appeared confident and unapologetic.

Vayle roared and hissed at Rillac, moving side to side in a manner that looked as if she was readying herself for attack. She reared up on her hind legs, unfurled her wings, flared her feathers, and beat her wings toward Rillac. Her feathers hummed and burned, and warm air circled around the chamber, which was impressive due to the chamber's massive size. Vayle dropped to her front legs and slammed her tail down on the rock floor next to the green spring. The impact of her tail sent a red flash through the green water like a ripple. She slammed her tail down again, and this time the red flash spread through the green veins in the chamber like bursts of red lightning.

Ariyana jumped back, startled, as the flash of red shot toward her along the rock floor. "What is that?" she squeaked, her voice higher than she had intended.

Silence! Vayle's voice boomed in her mind. The sound of her angry command, combined with the lashing of emotions in the chamber, threatened to buckle Ariyana's knees, but she clenched her teeth and remained standing.

You are here because I allow it! Vayle continued, sharply. Her voice was crystal clear in Ariyana's mind but her words were not directed at her. Vayle was focused on Rillac, while projecting her conversation to everyone. It was a strange sensation. It was like being next to a campfire and feeling the heat, but not being in the direct path of the smoke. *Draca is my planet and while you stand on my soil, you follow my laws.* She roared to add emphasis and Arc roared back.

Ariyana hadn't been paying attention to Arc and was now surprised to notice how worked up he was. His flame burned brightly and his fangs were bared.

It is I who dictates the rules of our alliance, not you. You are here because I sent for you. You and your people travel the universe because I allow my people to work with you. My decision was clear when you left my chamber earlier, and yet you took it upon yourself to act against what I decided. Choose your words carefully, Rillac. The energy bonding us wears thin.

I meant no offense to you, my queen. Rillac responded slowly, saying each word deliberately. *If you look past the danger, you will see the reward.* Rillac turned slightly and gestured toward Ariyana whose lip curled into a snarl. *You detailed the events that took place on the crystal planet that sparked a semblance of who she used to be.* Rillac continued, ignoring Ariyana's reaction. *I simply recreated something similar in the hopes that it would happen again. My only desire was to hasten her progress to bring her back to you. In some ways, it was successful. She has more control over her body now, and another memory came back. We are in a better place than we were just moments ago.*

"That's crap!" Ariyana protested.

Idrin grabbed her arm and gave her a stern look.

"What?" she exclaimed, throwing her free arm out to her side in exasperation. "He essentially threw me off a cliff in the hopes that I wouldn't splat into a hamburger out there on the ground. And now you look at me like I can't be pissed because he was doing it for the *greater good.*" On the last two words, she'd added a snarky tone. "I vote that we throw *you* out of the cave opening. Maybe it will help me remember something else."

Idrin squeezed her arm, and she jerked it away. "Stop trying to cow me," she demanded, glaring at him.

Enough. Vayle didn't yell the word this time, but her tone had an edge to it. *You do not understand the ways of any of our people. There is no room for weakness out here. Survival is achieved through strength.*

"Are you kidding?" Ariyana shot back. "You're telling me that it's okay that he threw me out of the cave? So, what in the hell does that mean? Every time I struggle to remember something or don't do things that you would expect, you're just going to toss me into the flames or out of a cave?

What about my children? Will you treat them the same way if they don't do what is expected?"

Vayle's wings slumped. *There are words that you use that do not translate. I do not condone Rillac's actions. Rillac is aware of the line that was crossed and is not indicating that we should do it again.* Vayle stepped toward Ariyana. *We do not mean you any harm. I do not mean you any harm. In essence, you were physically born on this planet and grew up with my people. You bonded with Glacin, and together we thrived. When he died ….* She slumped to the floor. *We found solace in each other. You and I bonded. Whether you remember it or not, you became my companion. That clutch,* she nodded her head toward the burning clutch, *has as much of your energy in that flame as it does Arc's, Idrin's, and mine. I would not be telling the truth if I said that I did not want you here as you were before, but I am grateful to feel your energy again, no matter how it appears now.*

Vayle stopped and stared at her for a few moments. Sadness washed over Ariyana. The chamber was quiet except for the crackling of the clutch's flame.

Aris, she continued, but Ariyana tensed. Vayle let out an exasperated breath. *Your aversion to that name makes no sense to me. It was a gift given to you by Glacin, not a word of insult driven into your ryn. You must choose a name, something other than Ariyana. But I ask that you truly think about your dislike of the name Aris. It is who you were to us,* to him.

Ariyana knew why the name bothered her but didn't feel comfortable discussing it with the current company. She wondered if Vayle had the same trouble with the name Ariyana that Ariyana had with the name Aris: being uncomfortable with the unknown. It was difficult for Ariyana to go by the name of a person who had lived a life she couldn't remember. It was probably difficult for Vayle to call her the name of a person who had lived a life without her in it. Vayle was correct, the name was a gift, a gift from her companion. But she lost him; she had been unable to protect him, so how could she possibly deserve the name?

"Ari," Kai called out. "My mom's best friend always calls her 'Ari'."

Vayle nodded at Kai, and he beamed. *It is decided. We will call you Ari.*

Ariyana smiled and nodded back. It was a good compromise. She would have to thank Kai later for being so brave.

Ari, I sent Rillac to bring you back to the chamber for a reason. As we are on my soil, I decide how we proceed, and I do not agree with the counsel that I have been given. You are my companion, and you have my support no matter what you decide. You have others that are close to you that need your help. I will help you, even if that means that the outcome will be you leaving us again.

Idrin huffed in protest.

Vayle's head whipped toward him. *You forget, my ally. Arc may be your companion, but he is my Draxin and my mate. He is bound to follow my rule whether you agree or not.*

At that declaration, Arc lay down on the ground in full submission. Vayle raised her head in dominance before turning back to Ariyana.

I will not let you or your people suffer. It does not matter what consequences we face for helping you. You have my, our, help with no expectations. I will never force you to stay. It is enough to know that you are alive. You do not owe me anything, and you do not need to earn my trust. I give it as willingly as I give my life. I am at ease with dying as long as I know that you are safe.

Ariyana's hearts constricted. She didn't deserve Vayle's trust or her life so freely given. Images of her first meeting with Rillac came rushing back. She remembered the devotion and protection that she had felt in that memory when it came to Vayle. She felt those same things now.

Ariyana squared her shoulders. She realized that she couldn't just take what she needed from Vayle, her people, or her allies. Whether Vayle believed it or not, Ariyana needed to prove to her that she was capable, that she was strong, and that she was worthy of calling Vayle her companion. If possible, she also wanted to avoid a war with Kylor and his people. She wanted to confront him about what happened on Earth, but she didn't want Devyn and Lexa to get caught in the crossfire. If she brought an army with her, that increased the likelihood it could happen.

She walked toward Vayle and ran her hand over her eye ridge like she remembered seeing herself do in her earlier memory. Vayle leaned in and half closed her eye.

"No," Ariyana said softly. Vayle stiffened, and confusion drifted around her body. "Hear me out. Idrin's an arrogant prick, but he had a point. I can't just demand your help and leave you to suffer the consequences. And…" she let the sentence hang in the air as she turned and glared at Rillac. "Rillac's a complete ass, but he did help me to figure some stuff out about my body. Though mark my words, Rillac, and yes, you can take this as a threat, if you ever try that shit again, no one will be able to stop me from ripping your throat out. Got it?" She didn't wait for a response. She turned back to Vayle. "Let me show you that I am strong, that I can do most of this on my own. At the very least, let me paint the target on my back. If it's just me, it might not be taken as an overly aggressive act, and Devyn and Lexa might not get executed right away due to an approaching army. Let me try to earn some of your lost trust back."

Chapter 36

It took what felt like hours of arguing, negotiating, and explaining to finally agree on a plan for Ariyana to rescue Devyn and Lexa *somewhat* alone. Her children disagreed angrily with every point that she made, but luckily had fallen asleep before she had convinced everyone that it would work. She knew that they would be furious with her, but hoped that they would understand the logic of the decision later. Right now, they were peacefully lying next to each other, hand in hand, around the two eggs that they were fascinated with earlier.

Surprisingly, Rillac was quiet through most of the discussions. Rillac had a few snippy things to say in the beginning but grew quiet once Vayle seemed like she was leaning more toward letting her go. Ariyana watched Rillac out of the corner of her eye as she, Vayle, Idrin, and Arc continued their discussion. It was unnerving after all of Rillac's insults and arguing to have silence and motionlessness. At times, she even wondered if Rillac had fallen asleep.

Once the plan was settled, though, Rillac perked right up, declaring that it was time to go back to Tor, where Rillac's chosen people would phase with Idrin and Arc to read the energy signatures in the energy realm. Ariyana found it strange that a species that relied on the Draxins for planetary travel would have a natural connection to the energy realm. *If they connected so easily, why couldn't they phase themselves?*

Ariyana also questioned why they didn't just go to the last planet that Kylor and his people were banished to. *Wouldn't there be a strong chance that they would still be there?* Rillac, of course, had a response to this too, pointing out to Vayle that somehow Kylor had traveled to Earth. If that was possible, it was also possible he had changed locations to another planet or, potentially, was keeping Devyn and Lexa on a separate planet so that he wasn't putting his people's lives in any more danger.

Ariyana felt sure that her questions were legitimate, but Rillac found a way to dismiss her concerns each time. She was trying to accept the fact that there was a lot that she didn't know, but it didn't help that she couldn't shake the feeling that something was off. She wasn't sure what it was yet, but she was determined to find out.

Idrin and Arc left promptly to take Rillac back to Tor.

Ariyana walked over to the clutch and looked down at her sleeping children. She and Vayle were alone. "Is it true what you said earlier?" she asked.

Which part?

"Is it true that part of my energy is within your clutch?"

Of course. Your energy is a part of me because we are bonded. When Arc dominated the flight, I chose him as a mate. Arc's energy combined with mine to seed the clutch. You and Idrin were a natural part of that, as you are my companion, and Idrin is Arc's.

Ariyana sighed and ran her hand lightly over the outside of the flame. The red flame sparkled with tiny bursts of silver light where her hand trailed, and she couldn't help but smile. The flame felt like Vayle, warm, comforting, and strong, and where the tiny bursts hit her skin, she could feel herself.

"What does it mean to you when you say, 'seed the clutch'?" Ariyana asked, peering back at Vayle. "Does that happen before you lay the eggs, or does it happen after? I don't know what you call it. Does it happen when the eggs are inside your body or outside your body?"

Vayle's amusement drifted through Ariyana's mind. *It is okay if you do not remember. I would rather that you asked the questions instead of keeping them inside of yourself. It feels as if you are trying to remember. That makes my heart warm. Draxins are an energy species. That is why we are able to phase from the physical realm to the energy realm. When it is time for hatchlings, I lay the eggs before the flight. Another Draxin must dominate the flight in order for me to choose them as a mate. Once that happens, I use the additional energy provided by my mate to both locate and create an original energy spark for each hatchling. Every Draxin is unique.*

"So, when we became companions, my energy was used to help you locate and create an original energy spark for each of these hatchlings?" Ariyana asked, making sure that she was following.

Yes.

"Does that mean that the hatchlings are not alive until they are seeded?"

My hatchlings are alive before the seeding, but they will not grow and thrive until they are seeded with their own energy spark.

"Are you giving them their soul or ryn?" Ariyana asked gently.

The queens that came before me believed that to be true. Are we not truly alive until our ryn ignites?

Ariyana smiled and laughed softly: "Yeah, maybe in more ways than one."

Vayle considered her quietly for a few moments. *Maybe. I am curious. If you do not know this, how did you seed your young? You are not Draxin, but you are an energy species. Where did you locate and create the energy spark for them? And why did you decide to have them share it?*

"What do you mean 'share it'? Ariyana's face pinched in confusion.

They are separate and unique in their ways, but they share a ryn. You cannot feel it? It is rare for Draxin hatchlings to share a ryn, but they can choose it. It is not decided by the siress. The hatchlings make the choice to share their energy in their eggs. Maybe your young did the same thing when you seeded them.

"Question before I get to that. What is a siress?"

I am a siress, as are you. We have the ability to create our young, and we are the ones responsible for locating and creating their original energy spark. The other side of that is a sire. Arc and Idrin would be sires.

"Got it," Ariyana said with a smile. "Alec and Kai were created physically. Humans need something called a sperm and an egg to create a child. That is how Devyn and I created them. I don't remember giving them an energy spark."

You may have looked human, but you cannot change the energy that is within you. You may not have been in control of the process. It is clear that they are a part of you and your energy.

Ariyana looked back at the burning clutch and ran her hand over the flames again. "Possibly," she said, pulling her hand away. She studied her children through the flames. "I swear they look like they've grown since we left Earth. Hell, they were different before we left. They spoke like they had gained years of knowledge in mere moments, but now it looks like their bodies are changing, too. Their skin looks like it is glowing, and the roots of their hair seem lighter." She turned and looked at Vayle imploringly.

"Earlier, when they were holding hands, I swear I saw their hands glowing with blue light. Did you see it too? Do you know what it was? Do you think that they are going to change like I have? Are they going to look like me?" The barrage of questions left her in a rush, her voice becoming more panicked with each question.

Vayle considered her for a few moments before leveling her gaze on Ariyana. *Your young are changing both mentally and physically. They share an energy that is becoming tangible, much like yours is now. They used that energy on the crystal planet when your emotions were inhibiting your ability to heal. You were bleeding out, and the battle overhead, combined with the ryn bursts from the Draxins, disoriented you. They touched you with a burst of blue energy, and you lost consciousness.* Vayle paused for a moment, studying Ariyana. *What is yet to come is shrouded in the unknown for everyone. I do not know what lies ahead for your young, nor do I know what they will look like, just as I do not know what each of my hatchlings will look like when they break free of their shells. This is what it means to live. I feel as though you should take comfort in the ease with which they have adapted.*

Ariyana nodded slightly but couldn't hold back her regret. "I'm terrified for them," she whispered. "I'm so scared that I won't be able to protect them from what's happening to them."

It is natural to care about someone so much that you fear the unknown.

The meaning behind Vayle's words didn't escape Ariyana. She related to what Ariyana was feeling. Her words revealed the truth behind her pain. Ariyana felt an overwhelming urge to apologize for her portion of that pain, but Vayle cut her off.

I will admit, seeing you with two younglings caught me off guard. You and Glacin believed that you were not meant for young of your own, and when he passed, you held true to your beliefs. You denied Idrin a kin-line conceived with your energy on many occasions. It was an argument that dominated much of your time together. What changed?

"I don't know. I don't remember feeling that way. I was human, and there was no reason to be cautious about having children, aside from being plagued by the same dream night after night." Ariyana cast her eyes to the floor and arched a brow. "What's interesting is that we weren't trying to have children at the time that I got pregnant. Humans can take a medicine to make sure that they don't get pregnant, and I was taking that. I thought that it was strange that I still got pregnant, but maybe it makes sense now. The medicine must not have been as effective for someone like me."

Why were you not interested in having young as a human?

"My dream was intensifying, becoming more detailed. Devyn was struggling to wake me up and claimed that I was becoming violent. We were so focused on my health that we didn't talk much about starting a family."

Devyn is the human companion that you wish to save?

"Yes," she said, glancing over at her children. "He's my husband."

Ariyana could not only feel Vayle's eyes on her, but she could feel Vayle's thoughts exploring hers.

Earlier, in this very chamber, you detailed a difficult life on Earth. You described a people that refused to accept you for who you were: a people who tortured you and cast you out when you proved abnormal. The pain of what you shared feels like a wound that has never had a chance to heal. Did Devyn accept you as you were, or did you have to pretend with your companion as well?

Ariyana glanced at her children again, wringing her hands together briefly before dropping them to her sides. "It's complicated," she said, tersely.

It is not, Vayle said bluntly.

Ariyana started to pace. She didn't know what to say. Humans were different from Draxins. It wasn't Devyn's fault that it was hard for him to see past her obvious differences from other people. No one else probably had to deal with a wife that woke up screaming every night due to the same *nightmare* that never changed and never went away.

You are agitated.

"It's too difficult to try to explain to you why humans are the way they are. They are just different, and some find it challenging to deal with someone as unique as me."

Vayle blew out a large breath of air. It was still hard for Ariyana to feel past her own personal agitation, so she wasn't sure what Vayle was feeling.

What about the other human that Kylor has taken?

"Lexa? I've known her for most of my life," she paused when Vayle made a strange throaty noise, "most of my life on Earth," Ariyana corrected. "I met her soon after I first started having the dream, and after I had seen a lot of doctors. She used to tell me that she felt the same pain that she saw in my eyes and was drawn to me."

Why did Lexa suffer?

"She had lost her mother not long before we met, and she blamed herself for her death. We were only a little over six years old, and yet, somehow, she said that she could see that I had lost someone too, and that I blamed myself for their loss. I felt a kinship with her, and even though our scenarios were drastically different, she accepted me just the way I was. I remember telling her that I had lost a dream companion, and that I had no right to compare that to the very real loss of a mother, but she never batted an eye at what I felt, never called me crazy, and never cast me aside. She said, 'Pain is pain, loss is crushing, and dream or not, you clearly, truly lost something in your short life.'" Ariyana smiled, "It's crazy to think that Lexa felt that way when she was barely seven years old. She's a remarkable person." Her smile fell as she thought about where Lexa was. She sighed. "I need her. She grounds me." A twinge of sadness washed over Ariyana.

She is a true companion. I am warmed that you were not alone during your time on Earth. But I question your need to save this Devyn. He is not a true companion.

"We have a history together, and he is their father," she said, gesturing at her children with her chin. "You see, I not only had Lexa in my life, I had them too. He gave me the greatest gift: he made me a mother, he made me their mother, and that is something that I will never be able to repay. The least I can do is minimize his exposure to all of this and get him back to Earth."

You think that he will go, willingly?

"I don't know."

Or do you think that he will fight you for his young?

"I don't know."

Do you think that he will accept you even as you are now?

"Vayle! I don't know," she said in frustration. "I can't just leave him there because I'm afraid of how he will look at me. He deserves to know the truth. He deserves to go home."

And what do you deserve?

Ariyana's forehead pinched. "I don't know that I've really thought about it."

Will you sit with me as you once did? Vayle's voice in her mind was both hopeful and tired. She settled her wings snug against her back and lay down on her stomach. Her body leaned to the right, exposing the long scales on her belly. She coiled her head toward her stomach and her tail toward her head. When she was settled, she eyed Ariyana expectantly.

Ariyana felt a pang of embarrassment. She couldn't remember how she used to sit with Vayle. If she had still had red blood in her system, her cheeks would have flushed with a rush of it. *I can't remember,* she whispered in her mind.

Calm surrounded her.

Vayle lifted her tail, laid it across Ariyana's back, and gently pushed her toward her stomach. Once Ariyana was inside the circle of Vayle's body, she settled her tail back down by her head.

Ariyana stared into Vayle's eyes, folded her wings in close against her back, and sat down slowly against her. She curved her tail around her right side and adjusted her wings so that they comfortably splayed out on the floor on either side of her. She leaned back against Vayle.

Chapter 37

The icy chill in Ariyana's chest settled a little. Vayle's body temperature was the same as the air around her. It didn't scald her the way Devyn's did. It was comfortable, since it eased the harshest effects of the chill.

Vayle's stomach heaved with a deep breath, and she made a rumbling noise in her throat. It was soothing, like a cat purring. *I feel concern over what lies ahead. Do you truly believe it is best for you to do this alone? What will happen if Devyn shrinks from you in disgust or rails against you in hatred? You do not appear to be in a healthy mindset to stand before him. Your time on that planet has split you internally. When you are here with me, and when you think about Lexa, you recount your memory of Glacin as a dream, but when you talk about your time on Earth or your interactions with Devyn, it is a nightmare. Glacin's death is a wound on both of us. For you, though, that wound rips open every night when you close your eyes. It appears that when Lexa was with you, you were able to heal until the memory returned, but when you were with Devyn, the wound burned and throbbed only to consume you once more when the darkness came.*

Ariyana's head hung heavily against her chest. *Vayle had seen things so clearly in such a short amount of time. She couldn't stand before Devyn and show weakness. She wouldn't. She would stand before him as she did on Earth a couple of days ago. Was it a couple of days? She wasn't sure how much time had passed.*

No matter how long it had been, she would confidently urge him to leave with her to see his children. If he refused, well, then she would drag him from that planet whether he appreciated it or not, Ariyana thought to herself.

"I will not fail," she stated, happy that her voice sounded so confident. "I realize that rescuing them alone or potentially facing Kylor alone doesn't seem wise, but I can't ask any of you to go. I can't expect any of you to take on that risk for me or for people you don't know. We also have no idea what Kylor will do if I show up with an army. Only he and Kress went to Earth to find me, I guess. I'm not completely sure what his goal was, but he didn't show up with all of his people. He also didn't immediately kill us, which, if that were his intent, I would imagine he would have done it right away. Again, I'm guessing. I just don't want him to kill them in response to an army phasing onto his planet." She sighed, "Besides, I will need all of you to keep my children safe while I am away." She lay her head to the side on Vayle's stomach. "I want to show trust to earn yours, Vayle, and deep within my soul, or ryn as you call it, I do trust that you would die for them."

Ariyana's body suddenly felt warm, like it was surrounded in a soft blanket, as contentment and joy flowed in waves off Vayle's body. After a few moments, though, the waves held an edge to them. Vayle was struggling with something.

"What's wrong?" Ariyana asked.

Did Idrin recount what happened between you and Kylor?

"Yes," she whispered. Her guilt made her want to hide from the things that Idrin told her, but if she did that she might lose Vayle's confidence. She cleared her throat. "He said that I killed Kylor's three elder brothers, his kinno, leaving only himself and his youngest kin, Kress, alive."

Correct. Kylor led a group of Aryllyns and Draxins in a secret venture against Raesor. We do not know why he did it, but I do know that every Draxin that followed him that day, every Aryllyn that supported him, was killed. His own Draxin companion, Karth, used the last of his strength to get him back to Draca and died at my feet. This failure and treachery led to him being cast out as Tehkaric. I was swallowed by my anguish, and it soon consumed you. It brought your own loss back, and you retaliated. There are rumors still that you walked the tunnels like a black fire that burned out the light of the stars. Shame filled the space between them. *It was my fault. I should have mourned with you by my side, but instead I shut you out, I turned you away, and you had to find an outlet for your own growing sense of loss. Idrin's verdict was simple when it came to Kylor's treachery, but when you took their laws into your own hands, you changed the energy flow. You not only angered your companion, Idrin, and brought shame on your bond, but you also angered the Aryllyn people. They wanted your blood. Kylor wanted your hearts. In the end, many Aryllyns followed Kylor in a shared hatred for you. And it is those Aryllyns that you will confront when you leave. You will not be able to lose your focus because if you do, they will tear you apart.* She curved her head closer to Ariyana, each exhale of her breath playing through the strands of her hair. *Hear me, Ari. Risk nothing but the path you have resigned yourself to take.*

Save only your companions and leave the rest to itself. Trust in these words. Kylor and his people want you dead. It cannot matter how your Devyn reacts because it will only take one mistake for one of Kylor's people to get their claws on you. Vayle's breathing picked up, and her heart hammered in her chest. The panic wafting off her smelled like sour smoke. *Do not underestimate your reactions, whether to Devyn, to Kylor, or to the Aryllyns you might encounter. I cannot lose you from my life again. I will not survive another loss.*

Ariyana felt the sting of tears behind her eyes. Vayle's words filled in the blanks where she still had questions after talking to Idrin.

Ariyana had no idea how she had earned the companionship that Vayle showed her now. *Wouldn't it be easier if she wasn't here any longer to torment Vayle's life? Hadn't she already brought the queen enough pain? She'd failed to save Glacin, she started an interspecies incident, she must have faked her death, though she couldn't remember why she really went to Earth, and then, all of a sudden, she'd resurfaced with new companions and children.*

The more that she was getting to know about who she might have been, the less she was liking herself, or this *Aris.*

She leaned her head against Vayle's muzzle, resting her forehead against the smooth scales. Vayle wasn't just concerned that she would get hurt, she was concerned that Ariyana would disappear again.

She ran her hand along the side of Vayle's snout. "I cannot make you promises that I cannot keep," Ariyana said, soothingly. "I have no intention of not coming back to you after I get Devyn and Lexa back. We will figure out what to do next together."

Vayle's body eased in relief, and her flame lessened to a low burn. She looked and felt like a different creature now that her muscles weren't straining under her scales. She had been so wound up before that it looked like she might pounce at any moment, but now, Ariyana could see the lines of fatigue and pain around her eyes. She needed to rest, and she needed to heal.

Yes, together.

Chapter 38

Ariyana and Vayle sat together in silence.

The soft sounds of her children sleeping and low hum of the flame surrounding the clutch echoed throughout the chamber.

Vayle hadn't fallen asleep yet, but her slow rhythmic breaths told Ariyana that she was getting close. Her emotions weren't helping her in the slightest. One moment Vayle was content, and the next she was full of anxiety. Since Ariyana wasn't used to being overwhelmed by someone else's emotions, they were wreaking havoc on her already raw nerves.

As a human, Ariyana had only had to worry about her own inner turmoil. Her body wasn't used to dealing with the physical bombardment of emotions against her exposed skin.

Right now, sitting inside the circle of Vayle's body, when Vayle felt content, it was like sitting under the warm sun on the first day of spring, but when Vayle felt anxious, it was like being abraded by an iron sponge. On top of that, it made it harder for Ariyana to control her own emotions. Being physically forced to feel something made her own body reproduce the same emotion. It made it difficult to know where her emotions began and Vayle's ended.

Ariyana settled into the crease of Vayle's front arm and stomach. It meant exposing more surface area of her body to Vayle's, which increased the sensations that she was feeling, but it also meant exposing more of Vayle's body to hers. She wondered if she could settle Vayle down enough to sleep.

Ariyana closed her eyes and took three deep breaths. When she felt Vayle's contentment, she reached out with her mind to the other emotions in the chamber. Granted her children were asleep, but the tranquility that they felt was palpable. She concentrated on the emotion, and after a few moments, it expanded out of her in rhythmic waves. Vayle audibly sighed, the last of her tension leaving her, and crossed over completely into deep sleep.

Ariyana let out another deep breath. It wasn't easy to reach out to other emotions and channel them into someone else. Her body had been tired before, but now she felt exhausted. She tilted her head on Vayle's stomach and stared up at the dark ceiling. The clutch's flame cast interesting, patchy shadows in places where rocks jutted out. Her small, silver flame, in comparison, only created small bursts of light within the red light that danced all over.

The more that she watched her silver light dance in bursts in the red light, she noticed that the green veins of water running throughout the entire chamber were also lighting up with tiny green flashes.

She watched in awe and felt a sense of belonging overtake her. Her silver light might have been small in comparison to the red light and green flashes above her, but, small or not, it was a part of that, and it shone bright and true.

Ariyana peered back down at the sleeping Draxin around her. Vayle exuded peace and tranquility, just like her children, and she had helped with that. It would take her time to figure out how to use this new body, but the content, sleeping Draxin coiled around her showed her it was possible. It made her feel hopeful.

She stared back up at the ceiling. It wouldn't matter what happened when she confronted Kylor, and Ariyana didn't care what Devyn said to her when she went to rescue him. She was determined not to lose this sense of belonging. It was what her children made her feel, what Lexa fought for with her, and what Vayle desired to get back. It was what she'd had when Glacin was alive.

Ariyana's breath caught in her throat as the chamber around her dissolved and morphed into another chamber.

No, she begged internally, as the chamber continued to morph around her. She couldn't lose him again right now. She desperately tried to force the dream from taking over, but it was already too late.

"Glacin," she choked out as barely a whisper, as her old chamber solidified around her, and the dream took complete hold of her.

***

Aguish tore through her.

Someone was screaming, but she didn't know who it was.

There was no light.

The smell of burned ash filled her nostrils, and the only sound around her was the unknown scream. Yes, that scream knew her pain: *it echoed it.* That scream came from the shattered soul and shredded heart of her loss. That scream knew her, sought her out, and destroyed her. There was no way to survive this pain.

She longed for death. She couldn't live in a universe without Glacin.

"Mom!"

The word broke through her pain like a break in a black, stormy sky, allowing one small ray of sun to shine through.

"Mom!"

Something was shaking her roughly, and she felt a hard impact on the side of her face. The impact was hard enough that it registered through the emotions and noise.

"Mom!"

Everything collided back into the present. The screaming was coming from her. The pain across her scalp was from her claws tangled in her hair. She couldn't see anything because her eyes were squeezed shut.

She stopped screaming and heard two familiar soothing voices asking her to come back to them.

It was Alec and Kai.

She was curled into a fetal position on her knees.

The chamber vibrated with emotions, and they weren't just hers.

Her body ached, and it felt like she was ripped open and bleeding. She moaned and lifted her head, forcing her heavy eyelids to pry apart. There was something large and blurry in front of her, but she couldn't get her eyes to focus. A blast of warm air puffed across her face, and a burst of hope blasted through her body. The blurry image in front of her moved, but it was hidden behind a wall of smoke, smoke so thick that not even color could shine through.

Ariyana slammed her hand down on the floor, dug her claws in, and pulled herself forward. She heard Alec and Kai call to her, but they seemed so far away. She wanted to go to them, but she needed to get to the creature in front of her first.

The outline was familiar. It had to be him.

She dug her other hand into the floor and pulled herself forward again.

This dream was finally different. *He had come back to her. He was alive.*

She pulled herself forward again. Every muscle screamed, every bone ached, but she didn't care. *She would pull herself over fire and glass to get to him.*

She was close. She could see his fire dancing in the smoke now. If she could just get through the smoke, she could see his beautiful turquoise flame again.

She could hear Alec and Kai yelling in her ears, begging her to look at them.

How could they not understand? she wondered. *He was right here. One more pull, and she would be able to see the soft scales of his nose through the smoke.*

She pulled, looking up, a muzzle pushing through the smoke in front of her.

The image in front of her morphed. She saw a flash of sharp fangs tear through a Tethryn in front of her, biting through its entire thorax, and its head hitting the ground next to her in a wet slap. The Tethryn body was thrown across the chamber, and his face came into view, his fangs dripping with yellow blood.

"Glacin," she whispered, her voice thick with emotion, but the black scales covered in yellow blood transformed into shiny gold scales, as though the smoke that she was seeing was blowing away, revealing the true image behind it.

Ariyana pushed back in horror, screaming: "No!"

She scrambled away, but her back ran into something smooth and unmovable. Tears streamed down her face as she still tried to escape the truth of what stood in front of her.

"No! He's dead, he's gone. No, I can't. Please!"

Two young boys sat on either side of her. She knew them: they were her children, but she was lost inside her grief, drowning. They clasped hands in front of her, said something that she couldn't understand, and placed their other hands gently on either side of her face. An ice blue flash of light filled her vision. She felt her body calm, and fatigue rushed her.

The last thing Ariyana saw before she passed out was their worried glances and Vayle's head snuggled close to her body, her multi-faceted, jeweled eyes full of concern.

Chapter 39

Awareness slid through Ariyana's consciousness like gentle hands trying to wake her. Multiple sensations registered at once: her body felt sore, but no longer battered; her mind felt raw, but no longer lost; her soul felt wounded, but no longer shattered.

Her memory of what had happened slowly returned. She had felt at peace, like she finally belonged, but then her dream of losing Glacin crashed over her in an unexpected wave that consumed her and pulled her in. When she came to, her disoriented thoughts were not ready to comprehend a Draxin standing in the chamber with her. She was desperate to believe that Glacin had survived, that she had changed his fate, latched onto the thought that the shadowy Draxin in front of her was him. But when Ariyana realized it wasn't him, it was too much for her to bear, and she found herself deeper in her grief than she had ever been before.

Ariyana remembered that it was her children who had found a way to ease her mind and put her to sleep, but the memory of what they did was difficult to interpret. She thought again about the flash of ice blue light she'd seen before she fell asleep. It was the same light that she had seen earlier, emanating from their clasped hands.

As she drifted through her thoughts, Ariyana became aware that there were voices around her, some floating just out of reach and others caressing lightly through her mind.

She lazily opened her eyes, but her heavy eyelids slid shut in the next instant. She was awake, but her body was overcome with exhaustion. In that brief glimpse, Ariyana saw her two sons standing in front of Rillac. Kai had his arms crossed over his chest, and Alec was pointing an angry finger up at Rillac's face. Rillac loomed over both of them on four legs, with two arms splayed aggressively.

Her body was sluggish, but what she saw made a familiar urge rise inside her—*the urge to protect*. It was pure instinct that made it rise inside her. She was their mother, and Ariyana didn't like Rillac's stance, nor did she like her children's body positions. There was something else there, too. A distant memory that held a warning that was just out of reach.

"You're dumb!" Alec's voice broke through. "Just like all those other adults on Earth. You treat our mom like you know what's best, but you don't listen to her. You don't see what she sees. You don't feel what she feels. You judge what you don't know!"

Careful youngling. Rillac's voice echoed across her thoughts like a million warnings all saying the same thing. It was sharp and demanded obedience. *Violence against the queen will not be tolerated.*

Rillac's tone raked across Ariyana's mind, and her urgency grew. Adrenaline surged inside her, and her muscles prickled with anticipation as if they were hungrily absorbing oxygen that they had previously been denied. She pushed against the smooth surface behind her. Her head felt heavy and lolled back and forth as she tried to regain control of her muscles. She opened her eyes, but her eyelids hung half closed, and her vision cleared and blurred as she tried to focus. She got her right leg under her and moved her tail to keep her balance. Her weakness was frustrating.

"There was no violence," Kai snapped. "She was lost inside her grief, stupid!"

Rillac growled, and Ariyana heard the sound of rippling scales.

As if the sound itself took shape in her thoughts, her memory rushed back. Ariyana saw the image of Rillac's hand around her throat as he violently shoved her back against the wall, quickly followed by Rillac tossing her out of the cave opening to fall to her death. A renewed strength filled her, and a feral growl tore from her throat. She pushed herself fully to her feet and flared her wings. "Get the hell away from my children," she demanded, glaring at Rillac. Her body wavered slightly to the right, but she didn't react to it. She kept her eyes locked on Rillac's face.

It awakens. Rillac hissed in her mind. *You have shown great weakness and lack of control to this point. I do not hold much confidence in your return.*

"Do you ever try to be likable?"

Do you ever feign dominance? Rillac's words were carefully chosen.

Ariyana watched Rillac's carefully schooled expression, waiting for it to crack, but it remained steady. Rillac didn't even think that she could pretend to be dominant or strong. "You're an ass," she snarled.

Rillac's scales rippled. *Insults do not mean anything if they do not mean anything to my people.*

"Think of the worst thing that you could be, double it, and that's you." Rillac's body looked like it had bristles as the scales stopped in mid-ripple. Ariyana sneered.

Vayle abruptly lifted her head, cutting off Rillac's potential retaliation. All heads turned toward her.

Another argument will not settle the distance between the two of you. Only action will. We are all hurting, but fighting within the alliance will not heal our pain. A deal was struck, was it not? Vayle's head whipped toward Rillac and the flames on her feathers around her eyes sparked all the brighter. Ariyana wondered if it was her version of a glare.

Rillac, still standing tall on four legs, nodded once in agreement.

It has been decided. Vayle continued. *Arc and Idrin will take Ari to Kylor to save her companions. She will do this alone. When she is done, Arc and Idrin will return to bring all three of them back to Draca. Simple. All that complicates it now is your fighting. We now agree that the fighting is done, correct?*

Everyone nodded, except for Alec and Kai. They stared up at her with shocked, horrified expressions. Ariyana angrily admonished herself. Her children had fallen asleep when they finally made a decision, and she hadn't had a chance to talk to them about it.

"That's not true, right?" Alec asked, his voice urgent.

"You've already fought Kylor, mom, and it didn't work out so well for you the first time," Kai said, his eyes moist with tears.

Ariyana knelt down and wrapped both of them in her arms. "It's not what you think," she soothed. "I'm not planning to confront or fight Kylor. Rillac knows where I need to go, right?" She emphasized the last word aggressively and cast a dirty look at Rillac. Without getting a response, she continued as if Rillac had agreed. "All I'll need to do is sneak around, grab your father and Lexa, and reach out to Idrin with my thoughts to come get us. He'll only be a thought away, ready to get us at a moment's notice."

"Why alone?" Alec pressed.

"Why can't Idrin and Arc stay and help you?" Kai added.

Ariyana sighed and pulled back to look at both of them, a small smile on her lips. "Vayle is too injured to come with me," Ariyana began, pushing back strands of hair from both of their foreheads. "Idrin and Arc need to come back here to protect her and both of you. Rillac will be busy coming up with some nasty comments while I'm gone." She rolled her eyes and bumped her shoulder on Alec's shoulder. They both gave her concerned smiles.

"You're trying to be funny, but we can both tell that you're not telling us the full truth," Alec said wryly.

Ariyana kept the smile on her face but knew that she wasn't hiding the strain in her eyes. How could she possibly explain to both of them that she could be putting all of them in danger just by being here and that by going alone, maybe she could keep them away from that danger?

Vayle rested her head on the floor next to the boys. *Idrin is just as connected to her as I am. He will never be far, just as I'll never be far from either of you. You will stay here, safe with me and my clutch, while I continue to heal. While Ari fights for her mate, will you stay and fight for me?*

They looked at Ariyana, knowing the tactic that was being played, but nodded in agreement nonetheless. They wrapped their arms around her again. Their fear washed over her, and she felt a pang of guilt. Ariyana had been honest about what she said to them. Vayle couldn't go and Idrin and Arc couldn't leave Vayle unprotected, but the other part of the reason was to keep all of them as safe as possible. She also knew that she needed to prove herself, to prove her strength.

Ariyana felt torn. Her children needed her, but they needed their father too. She couldn't abandon him and Lexa because she was afraid of the unknown. Her children might understand in this moment that it could be safer to leave Devyn and Lexa with Kylor until Vayle was ready, but at some point, they would grow to resent that decision if something happened to their dad.

"All three of you come back…," Alec began, his eyes moist.

"No exceptions," Kai finished, a single tear rolling down his cheek.

"No exceptions," Ariyana repeated, trying to force a confident smile. "My body is different, stronger. I understand more about it now than I did when I fought with Kylor back on Earth. I don't know everything, but I know enough, and both of you know that I can't wait any longer. I have to get them back for us." She kissed Alec on the forehead and kissed Kai's cheek where his tear had stopped.

They nodded and stepped back toward Vayle, leaning against her neck.

Ariyana stood and stared at Rillac just as Arc and Idrin entered the chamber. "I assume that the only reason you are here, gracing us with your presence, is that you know where I need to go," she said, her voice cool and surprisingly calm.

Rillac's head tilted to the side before turning to look at Idrin. Rillac and Idrin shared a look that Ariyana couldn't read. Rillac gave Idrin a small nod and abruptly turned away from her.

Chapter 40

After lots of hugs and kisses and promises of coming back to her children and menacing glares and threats to stay away from her children directed at Rillac, Ariyana nodded affectionately at Vayle and followed Arc and Idrin out of the chamber.

"We will head to the flight chamber," Idrin said over his shoulder as they walked through the tunnel. His words were followed by an image of the chamber that opened up to the outside, where Rillac had thrown her out.

The image came up so suddenly and without prompting that Ariyana questioned whether or not she had recalled it or if Idrin or Arc had shown it to her. It didn't feel forced or overpowering, but it didn't feel natural either. She remembered that phasing took intense concentration on a single place, and she had not done so well the last time. Maybe they were trying to prepare her for this next trip.

She shrugged it off as they walked into the flight chamber. Ariyana was surprised that it was still dark. She had assumed that all of their arguing and planning, combined with her getting caught up in her dream and being forced back to sleep, would have cost them the whole night and even most of the morning, but, based on the obsidian sky, it looked like morning had not yet arrived. A bunch of questions ran through her mind. She wondered what constituted a day on Draca. Was it similar to Earth's twenty-four hours, or was it longer or shorter? Could it be that she'd slept through another entire day? That question made her panic. She had not been able to get a firm grasp on the passage of time on this planet yet, but she knew that for Lexa and Devyn, any amount of time in a foreign place with strange creatures was too much time.

She peered over at Idrin and Arc. They were both staring at her. As heightened as her panic was, they were probably feeling it too. Ariyana approached Idrin. One of his eye ridges arched as he watched her. "How many hours did it take us to come up with a plan, find Kylor, and deal with my dream drama?" Ariyana asked. Idrin and Arc shared a look. Ariyana was getting annoyed about that. It seemed like it happened a lot when she spoke.

Before she could question Idrin about it, he answered. "We do not measure our planetary cycles in what you call 'hours.' We are not familiar with that." Idrin looked at Arc again.

Ariyana wondered if it was because the words that she used did not translate into words that they knew. But just before Idrin turned back to face her, she noticed a quick flash of something else between them. They were keeping something from her.

"We measure time by light versus dark, and when it is light, we go by the position of the star in the sky. The only time that has passed is one full night. Our star is getting ready to rise now." He nodded toward the now indigo sky.

Ariyana was relieved that not much time had passed but also frustrated that she didn't know how to translate that into what she was used to. If Draxins didn't measure time in hours, then how would she know how much time there was in a day, and how could she compare that to Earth? *Then again*, she wondered, *why did that matter?* It wasn't important to compare Draca to Earth. This planet was nothing like Earth. There was no job to get to on time. There were no appointments to keep track of, no businesses to keep open. It didn't make sense to keep track of minutes or hours, or even days or weeks. It was only important to watch the star slowly move across the sky. Maybe it was just her attachment to her humanity that was forcing her to look for similarities here.

"It is necessary for your mind to be clear so that we can travel to Ora without incident," Idrin said, pulling her from her thoughts.

"Ora?" she asked.

"Ora," he repeated, correcting her by rolling the 'r' sound and extending the 'ah' sound for a moment. It sounded beautiful when he spoke it. "In Aryllyn, an Oracin is a survivor. Kylor calls his planet Ora, meaning *to survive*."

His tone and explanation were oddly comfortable. Was it just his arrogance that Ariyana was picking up on? The chill in her chest started to throb in rhythm to her heart rate, and she pushed the heel of her palm against it. Something didn't feel right.

"A connection cannot be forced between you and Arc," Idrin continued. "Arc is my companion, not yours, so we will not be attempting to phase the way that Vayle did when she tried to bring you here. Arc and I will be *leading*," he said, adding emphasis to the word. "You will follow without question."

Ariyana bristled, "What is that supposed to mean?"

"We cannot risk being pulled onto another planet full of Tethryn because you lose control, or take it from Arc. Raesor would not lose again if you happened to crash on another one of his occupied moons or planets, and I will not allow you to injure Arc or me by forcing us to crash. You already did that to Vayle. You will not get the opportunity to do that to Arc."

His bluntness stung. Ariyana hadn't meant for anything to happen to Vayle, and she certainly didn't need his help to feel guilty about her lack of control.

Arc's head swung toward her. His multifaceted, purple eyes bored into hers. Ariyana shifted slightly and sharply flicked her wings out. She couldn't hear his thoughts and couldn't break his gaze. It felt like he was waiting for her to challenge Idrin, to say that he was wrong, that she'd had full control, but instead, she kept her lips pursed into a thin line. Idrin wasn't wrong, no matter how gruffly he spoke. She felt guilty because she had lost control, and she had no right to do the same thing to Arc.

Arc nodded as if she had said the words aloud and turned his head toward the opening. He took the last few steps until his neck fully extended outside and his front claws dug into the cliff's edge.

Idrin walked up to Arc's side and pulled himself up onto the base of Arc's neck. Idrin peered down at her. His regal sitting position was both imposing and breathtaking. It was only once he sat astride Arc that she noticed how much the two blended together.

Arc was a magnificent Draxin. His upper body was held high on his front arms. His purple scales shimmered under the blue flame of his dark blue feathers. He looked like the night sky covered in bursts of star-light. Idrin's riding skins were covered in patches of blue, and he was wearing more skins than armor compared to before. If he'd crouched down low along Arc's neck, he would have been camouflaged. This was also enhanced by the bold, dark blue, symmetrical curves of the markings that swirled up his neck, across his cheeks, and around his eyes. Now that Idrin was mounted on Arc, Ariyana could see his true predatory nature.

"Agreed?" Idrin asked, his voice holding a hint of annoyance.

"What?" she fumbled, his voice pulling Ariyana out of her quiet observations.

Idrin narrowed his eyes, and Arc gave her a sideways glance.

"As was discussed, Arc and I cannot stay while you look for your companions. We must phase in and out as quickly as possible. The Tehkaric could be drawn to Arc's presence, and I will not risk a full attack where he could be captured or injured." Idrin's head tilted to the side, and his brow ridge rose. "We will leave you at the base of the range. You will travel toward the rising star until you see the cave opening. We believe that your companions are somewhere inside. Once you have them, leave the caves and open your thoughts to me. We will do the rest." He rested his hand on his thigh and leaned out toward her. "This must be done quickly and without notice, or it may not matter what your hope for your younglings' future is, because you will not be around to witness it. Agreed?"

Ariyana's eyes widened, and her lip curled in a grimace. "Can you say anything without following it with the threat of death?"

"I am not the one threatening you. You threaten yourself," Idrin said smugly.

"Great pep talk. Super motivated," she mumbled sarcastically.

"I may not understand each word that you say, but your tone is clear. This is not a light undertaking. You decided to do this alone. You decided to draw attention to yourself and yourself alone. If you fail, you will fail alone. That way, many others will not fall in the wake of your defeat. You chose this path, now walk it. You claim that I have arrogance, but you hide your weakness behind those claims. Insulting others will not help you save your companions. Only strength and truth will do that. Now fold your wings and come. Our opportunity grows thin." Idrin's face settled into a determined expression, and he reached down to her.

Ariyana stared at him. *Man, she would love to smack the smug, determined expression off his face.* He annoyed her, and she couldn't help but wonder if he did it on purpose. She broke eye contact with him and stared up and back at her wings. She was finally starting to get used to which muscles needed to move in order to execute specific wing movements. She was also capable of a greater range of motion than she had seen with the birds on Earth and the Draxins around her. All she needed to do was roll her shoulders up and out in a half circle and the tops of her wings folded down along her back. She flicked the bottom of her wings out a couple of times before folding them tightly against her back. She was proud of herself and looked up at Idrin, her expression radiating excitement, but her excitement quickly faded when she was met by his tightly drawn-together eyes and scowling mouth.

He still had his hand extended toward her. Ariyana's shoulders slumped, and, bracing for an onslaught of memories, she reached out to grab his hand. He snatched her wrist, causing her to flinch, and yanked her up on top of Arc, her back pressing against his chest as much as her folded wings, spinal ridge, and tail would allow. She exhaled a shaky breath and waited for the rush of memories to overwhelm her, but nothing came. She wondered if it would be easier each time they touched. *Maybe she was learning how to block him.*

His right arm held Ariyana tight, so tight in fact that she could barely squirm under his embrace. Her tail lay over his left leg and stretched out behind him along Arc's back. She was uncomfortable. The position was very compromising, and it didn't feel right to be held this way by someone who wasn't Devyn. She felt the swirls on her cheeks move faster under her skin, reminding her of a blush, though it lacked the flare of heat that preceded the sensation.

"I need you to clear your mind and allow me to consume your thoughts," he said, his deep voice breathy across her ear.

His warm cedar scent drifted around her. The word *'consume'* floated across her thoughts like a gentle caress, and she felt her body relax into him. She felt a wave of connection surround her, and she closed her eyes. "Consume," she breathed, her head lolling back against him. His body temperature was warm but not overwhelming, and it made her skin tingle with longing.

"After you feel your thoughts entwine with mine, you must let go completely. Aryllyns and Draxins are energy species such as yourself. Energy species have energy centers. An Aryllyn's energy center is located at the base of the skull. I can sense through my contact with your skin that your energy center is in the same location as it was before, also at the base of your skull. Aryllyns call them akra points. I will fully connect with you through contact with these points. My thoughts will be yours and yours will be mine," he continued, pressing her closer. "Arc and I will lead you." He gently pressed his forehead against the back of her head. It lolled forward, her chin pressing against her chest and the back of her neck fully exposed. He ran his left hand along the top of her shoulder toward the base of her neck, his claws trailing across her sensitive skin.

Ariyana exhaled and felt the pull of Arc's energy center beneath her. She fanned her fingers out across Arc's neck, instantly finding his sensitive scales under his burning feathers.

The connection was immediate. Arc's memory drifted across her thoughts. The flight chamber dissolved away, and the egg chamber solidified in its place. Vayle had Arc by the neck, and she was flapping her wings wildly. Arc's mouth was open, bearing his sharp fangs, and he was crooning loudly. They were preparing to seed Vayle's eggs.

"Ari!" Idrin yelled, but it was as if he was far away, which didn't make sense because he was standing in front of her.

He placed his hand on the side of her neck, cradling her jaw, "Aris." Her name was a gentle invitation on his lips, so different from the urgency that she'd heard a moment ago. "The energy of our ryns wishes to unite just as theirs are," he said. His hand slid slowly toward the back of her neck, and his lips moved again, only this time they uttered no sound. He stared at her with eyes full of anticipation and hope.

Her hand moved up to cover his with hers.

"What is that?" Idrin's voice yelled out, still far away. This confused her even more. The Idrin in front of her had not spoken, and he still stared at her with hopeful eyes.

Each time Ariyana had been pulled into a memory, she was consumed completely by that memory. Each memory fully absorbed her and played out before her eyes, not allowing her to do anything but participate in the moment as it had occurred. This time was different: Ariyana felt like she was half in, half out of the memory. She was witnessing the event as it took place but knew that she didn't belong there, and, more importantly, she could still hear the Idrin outside the memory. The realization of what was occurring pulled her away from the events of what had taken place and narrowed her focus on what she felt—an overwhelming sense of need. Whether that came from Idrin or the Draxins, she wasn't sure, but, due to her time on Earth, it translated into desire.

Idrin had no way of knowing that the way he held Ariyana and the way that he touched her would spark such a reaction, but it was Arc's memory that pushed her over the edge. "Stop," Idrin moaned, his deep voice laced with strain.

Arc's front leg collapsed. Both Ariyana and Idrin lurched to the right. Rocks fractured off the ledge. Ariyana heard the rocks crumble and crash along the rock wall as they plummeted toward the ground. The sounds should have been a warning for Ariyana, but she remained locked in her building desire.

The rough movement and sounds were enough for Idrin, though, and he yelled out "Arc!" in a desperate attempt to pull his companion out of Ariyana's control.

It didn't help.

Arc's other leg collapsed under him, and the Draxin's body began to pitch forward out of the flight chamber's opening. If Arc didn't react soon, they would all follow suit and plummet toward the ground just like the rocks had done a few moments earlier.

Ariyana groaned, and Arc mimicked the sound. His right arm curled under his chest, and his side hit the edge with a sickening scraping and tearing sound as if his scales were grating along the rocks.

"Trech!" Idrin cursed.

He pulled Ariyana's hands off of Arc with his right hand and secured them against her sides. With his left hand, he grabbed one of Arc's long neck feathers and tugged it back so violently that the sharp feather sliced through Idrin's hand.

Still no response.

"Trech!" Idrin cursed again. Arc's weight was pulling them forward, and soon it would take Idrin all he had to secure both of them to Arc's limp body as they tumbled to the ground.

It wasn't what Idrin had wanted to do when he planned to take Ariyana to Ora, but now she had left him with little choice. He held onto Arc's feather with his left hand, though it sliced through more flesh, and he released Ariyana's body with his other. Once free, he slammed her forward onto Arc's neck and roughly covered the back of her neck with his open palm, careful to make sure that his fingertips instantly connected with her akra points at the base of her skull. *Enough!* he yelled directly into her mind, instantly connecting to her and severing her contact with Arc. Ariyana's body went limp, though her mind raged against Idrin's hold on her.

Sudden awareness made Arc yowl. His body lurched as he tried to regain his balance. Unfortunately, Arc's body was more out of the opening than in, and all his lurch did was hasten his fall. His back talons tore through the stone ledge; his large tail whipped and hit the side of the opening, showering Idrin in rock debris, and, finally, he roared as he flipped out into the emptiness of the air and fell toward the rocks and ground below.

Arc, still disoriented, fell back first, his claws and talons reaching and tearing at the empty air. The force of the fall held Idrin in place on Arc's back, and he used his body to keep Ariyana secured.

Arc's mind was turbulent and panicked, so Idrin dug his heels into his companion's shoulders. *Gain control!* Idrin yelled the words into Arc's mind. He didn't give Arc any room to doubt, argue, or question. He dominated and expected him to comply.

Arc's roar cut off like he had been punched in the stomach. He flared his left wing, and the burst of air that filled it forced them to flip over. Then, he flared his other wing, and they caught an updraft that sent them soaring upward, leaving the threat of the ground well below them.

Two Claw! Now! Idrin demanded, keeping his words brief and his emotions tightly bound inside himself. Without question, Arc complied and adjusted their course, heading toward the highest peak of the caldera.

As the sky brightened, the jagged pinnacle looked like a white fang piercing the sky. Its ledge jutted out into two sharp claws fifty feet from its peak, and those two claws glowed bright green from the Lielycet falls that cascaded over both sides. It was Idrin's favorite spot on the mountain range of the caldera, but, in this moment, it held no appeal. Its assault on the sky only intensified his dark mood.

Chapter 41

Arc landed hard on the ledge, staying close to the rock wall of the pinnacle. Idrin threw Ariyana roughly to the ground. She landed on her left side. Her temple smashed against the ground, and her left arm, splayed above her, splashed into the stream of green water.

Ariyana had been locked in her mind when Idrin forced a connection with her. It felt like he had trapped her inside a prison of shadows. There was no escape, and no matter how loud she screamed, her voice only echoed back as an assault against her. The connection severed the moment that he released her, but it wasn't enough time for her to brace herself against the impact. She barely had time to realize what was happening before she hit. Her ears rang and bursts of light flashed in her eyes. Her left hand started to tingle. The tingling escalated quickly to bursts of pain across and throughout the entire hand. It felt like she had shoved her hand into a beehive.

Pain cleared her mind, and she pulled herself up into a low squatting position, cradling her hand against her chest. Her pale hand was covered in red droplets. She thought she was bleeding, but her pale skin reminded her that her blood wasn't red anymore.

A burst of movement in front of her caught her attention. The flowing green stream was rippling with tiny red waves from the stream bank closest to her. The droplets on her hand pulsed and burned against her skin in time with the ripples before her. She shook her hand toward the stream to dislodge the last of the droplets.

Idrin's anger washed over her, and she felt him jump down. He landed a couple of feet away from her, cracks radiating from where his talons dug into the rock.

Ariyana snarled, twisted, and pushed herself up to meet his furious gaze. "What the hell?" she demanded.

"What was that?" Idrin growled, motioning toward Arc.

Realization of what had happened dawned on Ariyana. Her eyes widened in a moment of embarrassment and then quickly narrowed on him in a fresh wave of anger. "*That* wouldn't have happened," she argued, waving at Arc, "if you hadn't overwhelmed me with your feelings and the memory of Arc and Vayle seeding the eggs."

"Those feelings did not come from us," he spit back, gesturing between himself and Arc. "Aryllyns and Draxins do not feel *whatever that was.*"

Ariyana stepped back, breaking his intense gaze. She thought back on everything that she had felt and seen. A fresh wave of embarrassment washed over her. She remembered that Idrin had exuded a feeling of connection, and that the memory held an urgency or need, an almost instinctual urge to seed the eggs with energy, but it was she and she alone who had felt desire. Her humanity must have made her feel the precursor to what Aryllyns and Draxins engage in by instinct. Most humans would feel desire before mating, a longing to connect, *but*, she realized, *Aryllyns and Draxins must not need the same emotional connection prior to procreating.*

Ariyana couldn't stop the spiral of humiliation that overcame her. She couldn't control the way that she felt, and she couldn't stop overwhelming them with the same emotions. It felt equivalent to pushing herself onto another person against their will. *Why did everything have to feel so overpowering?*

Ariyana took another step away. *This was why they didn't trust her.* She had just added more proof to their claims that she was not only a danger to herself but to them as well. *This was how she'd almost got Vayle killed.*

Idrin grabbed her by the wrist and pulled her close to him. "Stop!" he demanded. "You cower like a weak youngling when you should be gaining skill over the experience. There is much that I do not understand about your new temperament, but if there should be truth between us, I cannot say that I really understood it before. Aryllyns follow Aryllyn law, Draxins follow Draxin law, but you…you do not follow a standard set of laws or rules. You were Aris; you are now Ari." He raised her arm up and squeezed her wrist tighter. She grimaced and tugged against him. The silver armor around her forearm liquefied and moved toward his hand. "You behave as my grasp on your wrist. You tighten your hold around something you cannot control when you should be focusing on why it is happening. You need to find the balance inside of yourself."

He let go before the armor touched him, and she grasped her wrist, rubbing on the aching skin.

He lifted a brow ridge at her.

She looked down, realizing what she was doing, released her wrist, and held her arms down at her sides. "It's not as easy to control as that," she stated, briefly meeting his gaze.

"Is it control or is it understanding that you are looking for?" He lifted both eye ridges this time.

"Asks the Aryllyn that put a blade in my hearts," she stated smugly, giving him a challenging glare.

"Enough," Idrin growled.

Both his tone and his glare held a warning that made her want to look away, but she forced herself not to back down. "Why?" she spit back. "You can't behave as if it wasn't your lack of control over me that caused you to do what you did. You can't just stand there and tell me that I have to let go of my control and focus on understanding. What part of any of this," she spread her arms out wide, "doesn't have to do with control?"

His nose slits opened and he exhaled loudly. "As I stated before, it is far more complicated than you think. You were aggressive and argumentative. It did not surprise me that you would not accept the ways of an Aryllyn siress, and, as I also stated before, I knew that our bond was a bond of necessity, not one of true companionship, but what I did not know was how tightly you held your control in place. Neither you nor Vayle let on to the inner turmoil that you battled with. It did not clear itself in my eyes until you lost all control. I was willing to guide you through the unknown terrain of your pain and anguish until you turned on me, until you showed me that without your control in place, you were too wild, too lost to trust."

"Then, why in the hell are you telling me to let go?" Ariyana looked at him in exasperation.

"Aris," he stopped and shook his head. "Ari, you hide behind a veil of anger when we talk about the past. While coated in that anger, you refuse to listen; you refuse to learn. In the next moment, you talk highly of your control and ability to handle anything and everything that comes your way.

It has not proven true, though. You hurt Vayle; Rillac was able to best you with emotions alone, and, just now, you almost sent Arc into a free fall to his death. Why will you not see?" His eyes bore into hers, and he took a step toward her. "You lost control and ran from us. You went to a planet full of a species that suffocated you more than you felt like you had been while here. Now you are back, and your control is more fractured than it ever was before. In my ryn, I believe it is time to figure out who you are without the full weight of that control. You need to find your balance."

"And what? That will be the secret to how I can save Devyn and Lexa?"

Idrin closed the distance between them. He raised her chin with a claw to meet her gaze. The three crescent moon pupils of both of his eyes dilated and constricted from half-moons back to crescent moons as his eyes roamed back and forth between each of her eyes.

"No." His tone was softer this time. "It is not something that is achievable prior to retrieving your companions. You will need to look within and determine how best to get where you need to be. For now, I warn you of this because it is when you lose control that your true weakness shines through."

Ariyana shifted her head so that his claw pulled off her chin, but she did not move away from him. He ran his claw through a lock of hair at her chin, grasping a few strains and rubbing them between two fingers.

"Weakness is a trait that is not accepted among Aryllyns," he continued. "We eradicate it at birth."

"How Spartan of you," she sneered.

He narrowed his eyes but continued, "Tehkaric or not, if you are caught by Kylor or his people and display any weakness, they will kill you no matter who you claim to be. Kylor journeyed to Earth to locate you. If his intentions were simply to kill you, he would not have joined you with your essence. He did that for a reason, a reason that we must discover. You will not figure that out if you succumb to your weaknesses."

"Your faith in me is inspiring," Ariyana groaned, rolling her eyes. "I get it, Idrin. Don't be myself right now, but hurry up and figure out who I am later so that I can stop annoying all of you. Does that sum it up?"

"Your way of speaking is exhausting," he said.

"Add it to my pile of things to fix." Ariyana shook her head and turned away from him. She walked along the green stream, careful not to step in the water. She didn't want it to turn red again and burn her. She walked to the edge of the left-pointing ledge. She had never seen anything like it. The ledge jutted out in two distinct points, creating a V-shape between them. The green water pooled around the rock wall of the pinnacle and flowed in a stream toward the fold of the V and cascaded down in a thin waterfall toward a waiting lake below. Ariyana studied the mountain range around them and was surprised that the pinnacle they were standing on now was the highest point. She turned around.

"How is this possible?" she asked Idrin. "How does the water get up here? Does it rain here often?"

His brow ridges pinched together in confusion. "What is water and rain?"

Ariyana pointed at the green stream at his feet. "That is water, and rain is water that falls from the sky."

"That is Lielycet, not water," he stated, pointing at the stream. "Lielycet is many of the same species, too small for the eyes to see, but so many that they live in great gatherings across the planet of Draca. Lielycet goes where it wants to go. It flows through cracks in stone; it dances in air when the temperature of the night air changes and cools, and it falls from great heights to play in the air currents of this world."

"Are these Lielycet here connected to the ones in the caves, the ones that my children were speaking about? But Vayle bathed in it to heal."

"Lielycet depends on Draxin, and Draxin depends on Lielycet. It is the true companionship of this planet. It is also why Aryllyns are able to survive here. We have grown to depend on it as much as the Draxins do."

She bent down and ran her finger along the edge of the streambed. The Lielycet didn't turn red this time, but a green tendril snaked up her claw. It twined itself around her claw and moved up to the middle of her finger. The silver armor that had formed around her wrist liquefied, and a single silver tendril snaked down the back of her hand toward the Lielycet. Both approached the other cautiously. They touched for a brief moment, pulled apart, and snaked back to their original locations.

Ariyana let out a deep breath. She hadn't realized that she was holding her breath. She glanced up at Idrin. He was watching her. "It's remarkable," she said softly.

Idrin held her gaze. "As you see, it is connected to you as well." His tone said it all. She was caught up in all of her emotions and was missing what was right in front of her.

"Why does it turn red and burn?" Ariyana asked.

"The Lielycet defends itself by stinging whatever has hit it hard enough to injure it. It releases a small amount of toxin to get the attacker's attention, causing the attacker to leave the Lielycet gathering immediately," Idrin replied.

Ariyana thought back to the egg chamber when Vayle had slammed her tail down on the rock floor. Vayle must have injured the Lielycet with the force of her blows. The Lielycet had responded by rippling with red waves and sending out bursts of red sparks.

Ariyana stood and faced Idrin. "What happens if someone is stung too many times? Can someone die from their toxin? My children have already bathed in the springs, or gatherings, as you call them. Are they safe? I don't want them to get hurt because they are too rough while bathing."

"Rays showed them how to be gentle and careful. She would not allow them to get hurt."

"Why didn't I get to meet Rays? Actually, come to think of it, why haven't I met any other Draxin or Aryllyn aside from all of you?" Ariyana asked. She scanned the horizon and the ground below. "Why does it seem so empty here?" She glanced back at Idrin.

"Vayle and I agreed that it would be best for us to keep your interactions isolated from the rest of our people until things have equalized out. Many of our people are still hesitant about you and your intentions," Idrin stated.

Ariyana nodded. His words stung, but she understood. She could barely handle her own emotions, let alone the emotions of others, and she kept falling into memories without warning. She didn't want to cause any further issues among Vayle and Idrin's people, especially those who were unsure of her. She couldn't help but remind herself, though, that she was about to venture onto a planet where the majority of the people there were more than hesitant about her: they probably wanted to kill her.

Ariyana peered out across the caldera in the direction of where she could feel her children's energy. Her children seemed to be more emotionally stable regarding everything that had taken place so far than she was. They were probably both more receptive to the changes taking place around them. She felt a pang of uncertainty.

"You are still worried about your young," Idrin stated matter-of-factly.

She nodded without turning around.

"Vayle will not allow any harm to come to them."

Ariyana felt the truth of what he said. Her children were safe here with Vayle, but she didn't have the courage to tell him the truth. Idrin could feel her uncertainty and assumed that the feeling was tied to her children.

Idrin believed that her control was fractured, comparing her emotional state now to the person that he'd known before. That knowledge did not fill her with the confidence that she needed to stand before the man who'd pushed her away, the one man who'd made her feel like she wasn't normal enough to be loved for who she was.

Could she stand in front of Devyn as she looked now and be strong under the scrutiny of his gaze?

Ariyana felt the warm embrace of unconditional love surround her. It coated her body in a protective layer like the thin, silver armor that had become a second skin. She knew that that love was from her children, and she smiled. Not that long ago, Ariyana had stood before Devyn on Earth and demanded that he see her for who she was. She would do the same again.

Ariyana squared her shoulders. Idrin was right. She needed to do some soul-searching and discover who she was so that she could figure out where she belonged. But, right now, she needed to help Devyn and Lexa, and hopefully unriddle what Kylor needed without getting killed or making things worse.

Ariyana met Idrin's gaze. "Okay, Idrin, you said that the only way that phasing will work is if you and Arc are in full control—that you need to lead and I need to follow. I won't fight you anymore. Take control and take me to Ora."

He nodded once and turned on his heel to walk toward Arc. Once mounted, Idrin leaned over and held out a hand to her.

Chapter 42

The next thing Ariyana knew, the sun was shining on her face. She remembered taking Idrin's hand, mounting Arc, and then everything went dark.

It didn't feel like she had been stuck in a prison this time. It felt more like an isolation tank, like Idrin had shielded her from all sensations for a brief period of time.

Ariyana slowly opened her eyes, and her breath hitched in her throat. It wasn't just her surroundings that had changed. It was cooler here than it was on Draca, and the air smelled of rock moss and river stones. She was facing the sun, and its low position in the sky brought out the vibrant colors of the scenery around her.

To Ariyana's left, there was an expansive meadow of blue and grey grass. To her right, there was a large boulder field that led up to a range of jagged mountains. The rocks were made up of a mixture of light and dark grey stone. In front of her, there was a large scree field that appeared to fan out from a thin valley in the mountain toward a patch of large trees. From this distance, the trunks appeared to be black, and the sun glinting off the leaves showed that they were dark green with blue edges.

A light breeze was blowing from the valley toward the trees, and as it played among the leaves, it made a hissing sound like hundreds of snakes were calling out a dire warning.

The unfamiliar hum of the planet's energy, combined with the eerie sound of the wind, made Ariyana shiver, though she could not feel its cool touch. She could not claim that she had been used to being on Draca, but this planet held a sense of foreboding that put her on edge.

Idrin grabbed her left hand, startling her, hooked his other hand under her right arm, and briskly dismounted her from Arc's neck. He leaned down and held her gaze. "Follow the star," he said, pointing toward the scree field and the trees. "This mountain range will travel a few paces in that direction. You will find the back caves. Explore the caves, find your companions, bring them out here, and call to me in your mind. Find your strength. Do not be discovered."

Before she could ask a question or even respond, the air around Arc rippled. An icy chill wafted toward her as if from an open freezer door on a hot day. The ripples crystallized, cracked, and melted away, leaving no trace of Arc or Idrin except for a crisp burst of air.

They were gone.

Ariyana didn't know if she would get used to that. It was as if something simultaneously opened and folded in upon itself at the same time. She shook her head, and, realizing that her mouth was open in a wide gape, she closed it and peered around.

Idrin had told her to head toward the star, or, as she called it, the sun. Ariyana looked behind her. The mountain range continued for miles with nothing but more meadow and trees beside it. The scree field in front of her appeared to be the only break in the mountain range, and according to Idrin, she would find the caves beyond that.

Not seeing any other alternatives that made more sense, Ariyana walked forward. She walked slowly, being careful where she put her feet. She couldn't hear anyone else but didn't want to take any chances of drawing attention to herself by being overly noisy. She also kept her tail off the ground and her wings folded against her back so that the bottoms of them wouldn't drag.

It was taking less of her focus to move her body around, and, though she couldn't claim that she was used to it yet, she felt comfortable.

Ariyana reached the edge of the scree field and looked up. She was surprised to find that the valley in the mountain range came down lower than she'd thought it would. The scree field led up to a group of boulders that surrounded a strange rock ledge that led forward through the valley. She could see the sky through the valley, but the rock ledge was too high for her to see anything else beyond that.

Ariyana took a few more steps forward, toward the sun, placing herself between the scree field and the trees to her left.

A huge blast of wind hit her, making the low flame along her feathers dance, and the leaves beside her hiss. Ariyana stopped and faced the wind. Her short, silver hair danced like thin ribbons across her neck. It wasn't just a simple wind that traveled through the valley to greet her. It was an unmistakable energy. It swirled and pulsed around her; it called to her.

The chill in her chest started to throb, and she pushed her fist between her breasts to calm the sensation, but it didn't help. Ariyana looked left, toward where the caves should be. She heard Vayle and Idrin's warnings in her mind: focus on her companions and not venture from the plan, but there was something here that she needed to see. She could feel it.

She looked left one last time. Ariyana shook her head, pushing the last of Vayle and Idrin's warning aside, and ran up the scree slope to the boulders.

Ariyana's talons caught nicely in the loose stones, allowing her to reach the boulders quickly, and her claws felt strong against the rough stone as she climbed them. She leapt from boulder to boulder with ease. Her arms and legs felt strong and powerful, and her tail adjusted constantly, balancing her each time she shifted. After one final leap and one last, graceful pull, she stood on the rock ledge without breaking a sweat. She smiled as she stretched and flexed her muscles.

Another swirl of energy flowed around her. Ariyana moved forward slowly as if caught in its current.

What she saw stopped her cold, and she tucked herself quickly into the side of the boulder on her left side. Ariyana had moved so quickly that she had slammed her left folded wing into a jagged point in the rock, and she had to stifle a groan of pain. She adjusted her wings and made sure that the burn of her feathers was low. It was the middle of the day on this planet, but she still didn't want to burn like a beacon on the ridge's edge. Now, stowed safely in a place she hoped would provide her obscurity, she stared, open-mouthed, at the bustle of life below her.

It was clear now that the mountain range wasn't just a mountain range. It was a caldera. It was one-tenth the size of the caldera on Draca and full of dozens and dozens of Aryllyns moving about in the routine of what appeared to be a regular day.

On the right-hand side of the caldera, there was a baby-blue lake tucked tightly against jagged peaks that curved inward over the silent water. It was an eerie scene—like the planet had a giant mouth and was consuming its own resources.

The left-hand side of the caldera was where all the activity was taking place. It was a large meadow of blue and grey vegetation that stretched out and nestled against a dark grey wall of shorter peaks pocketed along the bottom with half a dozen caves. In the middle of the meadow, the Aryllyns had built dozens of wooden structures in a large circle around a huge, light blue bonfire. The structures were not built for longevity. They had three walls that opened toward the bonfire and a rough roof. It was obvious to her that they were built to provide only the most basic protection from anything coming from the sky. It was also clear that these Aryllyns had been here for a while. It was a village built to provide unity, warmth, and protection to a group of people: a home. Ariyana could even see that their structures had distinct wear and tear and signs of reconstruction on them, and she could see a sizable amount of destroyed building material piled against the rock wall to the right of the last cave visible to her.

Ariyana's eyebrows pinched together.

The questions that she had asked before Rillac left to explore the energy signatures of the energy realm were spot on. All Rillac did was blow her off, making her feel like an idiot. Rillac had made her feel small-minded when, looking at them now, it was obvious that Kylor would bring them back here, where he had the greatest number of people surrounding him and knew his terrain perfectly. No one would be able to just slip in and take anything from him without him noticing.

What was the game then? What was she missing?

Even if all Rillac wanted to do was confirm that they were on Ora, it shouldn't have taken him a few hours to do it. Somewhere in this narrative, there was a lie that involved Rillac and Idrin, but she didn't know where. *Was it a lie of omission or something more than that?*

Ariyana stewed over her questions as she watched each Aryllyn move around the structures with purpose. Some tended to the flames of the huge bonfire, making the blue flame spark and dance around the dark wood that they threw along the edges; some worked metal objects into weapons over smaller blue fires spread throughout the village; some fixed structures; some trailed in and out of the caves; some sat in a circle along the outer edge of the structures, their eyes trained to the sky above; and others sat at the water's edge of the lake, diligently watching the calm water.

Everyone had a task, and everyone did their task without hesitation.

As she watched each Aryllyn's movement and purpose around the village, she noticed that same energy that had drawn her up here was shifting and morphing into something colder.

Ariyana concentrated. *No, not colder.* It was broken in places, hollow in others…unhealthy. She realized that the energy was familiar, though much stronger and more noticeable on this planet. She had felt it in the undercurrents of the energy that swirled around Draca, more specifically around the Aryllyns on Draca. It wasn't until this moment, connecting it to what she saw below her, that she was able to understand what it meant.

The truth hit Ariyana with such force that it took her breath away. She reeled and was immediately grateful for the strength of the boulder next to her.

But that strength quickly faded as the security that the boulder tried to offer Ariyana was no protection from the onslaught of rage that rushed up behind her.

Chapter 43

Kylor.

His rage had branded Ariyana on Earth, and now it circled around her like a swarm of angry bees.

It was nothing compared to the sorrow that she felt in her ryn, though. She did not try to escape, and she did not bother to look at him. She lay one hand on the cool, rough stone beside her and dug the fingertips of her other hand into the icy throb in her chest.

It didn't help.

"They're dying." The words left her without the effort of forming them. Ariyana stated them as matter-of-factly as the pain of the truth was blunt, and though she desperately searched the group of Aryllyns below for some sign that she was wrong, she knew that she wasn't.

As if a sharp blade had sliced between them, Kylor's movement and emotion stopped instantly below her.

Neither of them spoke.

Ariyana felt consumed by what she saw…*what she knew*, and the emptiness of Kylor's presence behind her gave nothing away. All she could feel was the heat of his gaze boring into her back. The urge to see his eyes overwhelmed her. It pushed aside the trauma of what he had done to her on Earth and the fear that she had had of facing him again. She needed to know.

Ariyana forced herself to break away from the sight of the Aryllyns in the caldera and faced him.

Their eyes locked fiercely.

Ariyana couldn't feel what he was feeling, but she could see it. Emotions that she couldn't name fought their way across his features and left dangerous, empty shadows in his eyes. She knew those eyes…knew that emptiness inside them. Familiarity rushed through her, and though he did not lay a hand upon her flesh, her head fell back, and a memory of the past consumed her.

***

Ariyana was winded and weak; her eyes were cast to the ground, and her chest was full of shattered ice and emptiness. Vayle cooed soothing words in her mind, but they were only sounds. The barrier to the darkness inside her had cracked, and the empty numbness that she'd tried to control was leaking out.

I cannot follow him! She cried into Vayle's mind, hot tears trailing down her cheeks. *He's lost to me. It is so dark without his energy to guide me.* Her knees buckled in anguish, and she fell back against the protection of Vayle's muzzle as Vayle tried to steady her companion.

Something else grabbed Ariyana's hand and pulled her back up onto her feet, overcoming the force of grief that had tried to pull her down. Her eyes swung up.

Not something…someone.

Kylor stood in front of her, conscious and aware, while his royal leader still lay unconscious at his feet from the bonding process. Dozens of emotions fought for dominance across his features, and shadows drifted across his eyes. His markings were dark blue and pulsed slowly. He pulled her up until her knees supported her. He kept her hand in his, the temperature of his body equalizing with the icy feeling of her own. His temperature felt like Vayle's, like it adjusted itself for her.

Ariyana searched his eyes. Had he heard her private thoughts? Had she lost control so badly that she had revealed the brokenness inside her? What would this show of weakness on her part mean for their alliance? She opened her mouth to speak, but he reached out with his other hand and laid it on her cheek. She saw her own anguish mirrored in his eyes as he wiped away a falling tear.

His royal leader started to rouse at his feet, and he released her to help him up. Ariyana adjusted her demeanor before Idrin was fully conscious, and Kylor had resumed his stance next to his leader without missing a beat.

***

Ariyana crashed back into the present with a jolt of surprise.

Kylor was standing in front of her, so close that his icy peppermint smell swirled around her. Being around him reminded her of drinking peppermint tea on the first day of freshly fallen snow in the mountains.

Kylor's expression was controlled now, and the only two emotions that he was showing were anger and annoyance.

Ariyana tried to step back but had forgotten about the rock wall and smashed clumsily into it.

Kylor stepped closer, not willing to give her the space that she'd attempted to put between them. "Where was your mind just now?" he demanded. His voice held the harshness that it had on Earth. Her muscles tensed instinctively. His brow ridges furrowed, and his annoyance swirled around her.

Ariyana leaned forward slightly, trying to relieve the discomfort of the rock digging into her wings, but Kylor stood firmly in front of her, limiting her movement. She furrowed her own brows to match his annoyed look. "I think that it was the day that I bonded with Idrin. It was just the two of you, and he was still unconscious. I only saw a small part of it, but I seemed to know that he was unconscious from the bonding process."

Understanding and familiarity crossed Kylor's features for a moment and then darkened back to anger. He leaned down close to her face. "A moment where we thought that we could trust you."

Ariyana's lip curled in a snarl, and she ground her teeth together. "I'm getting really tired of this trust crap from all of you. I don't remember much of anything from the past, and the little bits that do pop up are confusing. It's like being told a story from multiple points of view in, seemingly, no logical order. I think that all of you have made it abundantly clear that you're pissed at me, but you know what I've noticed?" She jabbed her finger in his face. "I've noticed that none of you are taking ownership for your parts in all of this."

Kylor's features iced over, and the nostril slits on his high cheekbones flared. "Ownership?" he hissed. He grabbed her wrist and pulled it up, forcing her palm into her face. Ariyana tried to pull free against his tightening grip, but he had her pressed tightly against the rock. Her wings were pressed awkwardly behind her, and there wasn't enough space between them to rip her arm free. "I have no patience for the words that you speak through a false innocence," he gritted out.

"I am neither false nor innocent," she shot back. "Would you let go—you're hurting me."

He squeezed tighter.

"What is the point of all this?" she asked. "After the memory that I saw of Idrin, I figured that you came to Earth to finish what he failed to complete all those years ago, but now, I'm wondering if you wanted me to see all of this. Is this why you came to Earth?" she asked. "Did you want me to understand? If so, why didn't you just approach me without violence? I already didn't feel like I belonged there, and your features were similar to what I saw in myself in my dream. Did not being violent even cross your mind?"

Confusion and irritation prickled against her skin. Kylor narrowed his eyes and squeezed the wrist of the hand that he held in front of her face. She turned her head to the side, but he grabbed her jaw in a vice-like grip and forced her to turn back. "I would prefer that you answer that," he sneered. "Did not being violent even cross your mind?"

He opened his thoughts to the memory and forced it into her mind. With both of his hands touching her exposed skin, she could not stop the memory from consuming her. Her eyes rolled back, her neck muscles tensed, and her talons curled into the loose stones. The memory of her hands covered in dry, lavender blood and the shame of what she had done consumed her. Her body trembled. Ariyana fought to escape it, but the shame threatened to pull her down. Three sets of vacant eyes looked up at her. Shock, disbelief, and pain distorted their faces, but it was their vacant eyes that blamed her for her betrayal. She recoiled and flexed against the memory. Unlike the other times that she had been pulled into a memory, Ariyana could feel the frayed, weak edges of this one. It was being forced upon her, not naturally recalled. So she tore at its weak edges until she felt it shred and break away, and the only thing that filled her vision was Kylor.

Ariyana pulled her head free of his grasp and snarled at him. "Don't ever do that again. You have no right to force memories into my mind. I will put a blade in your chest if you ever do that again." Tears burned in her eyes, though she would not let them fall.

"You'll put a blade in my chest like you did to my kin?" he snapped, his eyes were full of malice.

"Stop," she warned.

"Stop what?" Kylor asked. "Stop speaking the truth?"

"I said stop."

"A memory locked in the dark still exists. It does not matter if you refuse to shine a light on it." He squeezed her wrist tighter again, and she felt a tingling sensation at the base of her skull. He was trying to force the memory into her thoughts again.

Ariyana mentally pushed back on the connection that he had created, blocking his memory with her own thoughts. *I am not refusing! I remember...I remember their eyes.* She hurled the words into his thoughts and trailed off. *I remember as if someone showed me the memory, not like I lived it myself. But I'm not that person...I can't be.*

"It must be a luxury to pick and choose," Kylor said bitterly.

"I'm not asking you to understand," she said softly, closing her eyes. Ariyana took a deep breath and slowly opened them again. "I'm sorry that I took your brothers, your kinno, from you. I'm sorry that your people are dying. Please take the blood that I owe you from me and let my companions leave with Idrin."

Kylor released her wrist like she had burned him and stepped away from her. Dozens of emotions swirled around her as quickly as they clashed on his face.

Ariyana opened her mouth to speak, but a shrill, animal cry tore through the caldera below. Kylor's eyes widened, and a feeling of panic rushed along her skin like thousands of cactus thorns pressing against her. "Drivik," he hissed and rushed forward, maneuvering her between himself and the rock wall.

Chapter 44

Kylor's body was tense as he held her in place. At first, his eyes wildly searched the caldera and the sky, finally settling firmly on a single location around the lake.

His claws dug into the rock, and a low growl emanated from his throat.

Kylor was close before, but now, with his back pressing her against the rock wall, Ariyana felt overwhelmed and trapped. The memory of the trauma of what had happened on Earth started to flash in her mind: the hard rock wall at her back and the feeling of being impaled against it.

Ariyana struggled against his grasp, tearing at the arm that held her in place. She lifted her head, gasping for air. Her panicked mind zeroed in on the back of Kylor's neck, free of armor and protection. He had three horns on his head like the other Aryllyns that she had seen, but his middle horn, the one that would protect his neck from a straight-on, backward attack, had been broken: snapped off by Idrin when he'd banished Kylor. He was vulnerable in this position.

Ariyana growled and lurched her head forward, teeth bared, intent on sinking them into his flesh. His elbow flashed out and struck her hard in the forehead, whipping her head back against the rock. Before she could utter a sound of pain or protest, a clawed hand was clasped over her mouth, squeezing.

Ariyana's eyes watered from the impact and the ache in her jaw. Kylor pulled her forward and shoved her against the boulder on her left. He had his right hand over her mouth and his left over her upper wing bones, holding them against her back. His full weight pressed against her, pinning her tightly against the boulder.

She jerked against him but stopped when his voice shouted in her mind, *Quiet! Expend your energy on your surroundings instead of your useless struggles.*

He squeezed her face and pointed her head toward the lake. *There is danger here that you are incapable of fighting. And if you distract my people, and it gets into the caverns, your companions will die.*

It wasn't his threat that made Ariyana stop moving. It was the creature that pulled itself from the blue water that made her muscles freeze, and her blood run cold. It wasn't the creature's "alienness" that caught her off guard. After being around Draxins, Aryllyns, and whatever species Rillac was, she had accepted that her life would be full of the unfamiliar, but there was more to this creature than just being unknown to her. The moment that her eyes landed on it, she could feel its intent. *To kill.* She could also sense its intelligence. It was strategizing each step that it took. It did not step out of the lake onto the shore; it was climbing up the rock wall of the caldera to get an advantage over the Aryllyns below it.

Watching it climb was like watching a reptile climb a tree: gravity did not seem to affect it. It was covered in short, blue fur with yellow stripes on its shoulders and haunches. It lithely moved up the rock wall toward the jagged peaks. Its long, lean muscles kept it pulled in tight to the rock wall as it curved into an overhang over the lake. Its two, yellow-clawed hands drove into the stone like hot blades through ice, and its two, black talons on each foot easily found cracks and rock footholds to hook onto. It had seven thin, whip-like tails that trailed behind it, six of which were long with long, thin, yellow fins on the top of them. In the middle of the six tails was a seventh tail that was shorter than the others. It didn't have a fin, and whereas the six long tails ended in one sharp, curved, yellow, claw, the seventh ended in two.

It effortlessly pulled itself up and over the edge, turned, and stood on two long legs. Its upper legs were thick with muscles, and it had long ankles. Its two long, strong arms were pulled in close to its long torso.

It surveyed the Aryllyns below it with its large, inky eyes set into a long, rodent-like face. A low rumbling noise emanated from its throat, followed by another shrill cry.

This time, though, it was answered by a roaring battle cry from below.

"Rhyne," Kylor stated, a proud gleam in his eyes.

The word did not translate into anything understandable to Ariyana, but before she could ask Kylor what he meant, an Aryllyn pulled itself up onto the roof of one of the wooden structures.

She sensed the Aryllyn as soon as she laid eyes on it. It was female and was a vision of Amazon fierceness. Instead of wearing pieces of Tethryn exoskeleton like Kylor, she was wearing the skins of defeated Driviks.

The yellow stripes in the blue fur were cut in long patches that covered the front of her chest, ran over her shoulders, and down her upper back. Other patches of yellow stripes ran down her hips and covered her upper thighs. The rest of her body was protected strategically with patches of the Drivik's blue fur, the major areas being her abdominals and the backs of her legs, down her calves, and around her long ankles. Her white hair was cut short, uneven, and spiky with blue dye streaked through it around her three magnificent horns. The horns were in no way as large as Kylor's, but, for her size, they were sharp and strong.

It was then that Ariyana realized that "Rhyne" was not just a word, it was this female's name, and though it might not have had any other meaning assigned to it, she was the epitome of strength and fierceness.

The Drivik stood up on its two hind legs, dug its sharp talons into the rock, threw its arms back, and hissed.

It knew who she was.

Rhyne responded by crouching low, her muscles becoming tightly coiled springs, and drew out a small, dark blade that she waved at the Drivik in a "tsk tsk" manner.

The Drivik leaned back, its long ankles almost touching the rock, and sprang forward. Its strong quad muscles helped launch it off the edge and into a dive toward Rhyne.

Once it was in mid-air, strong, thin muscles moved out in long flaps from the base of its skull to the tops of its hip bones, reminding Ariyana of a flying squirrel. It glided toward Rhyne using the flaps on its six tails to control its direction.

Rhyne dashed forward in two long strides, the light blue markings on her face turning dark blue, reached the edge of the roof, and jumped.

The Drivik and Rhyne collided in a tangle of limbs and tails. Rhyne flipped their bodies and drove the Drivik into the ground with such force that it audibly wheezed.

The Drivik's tails slashed at Rhyne with lightning speed, but she evaded them just as quickly. It struck out with its left hand to slice its claws through her face, but she caught it and slammed it down, securing it to the ground with her right foot. Its right hand shot out to grab her, but she threw her blade from her right hand to her left and sliced the Drivik's hand off. It roared in pain, and its middle, two-clawed tail struck toward her exposed back like a scorpion set on paralyzing its prey. She swiveled, and, in a blur of slashes, she cut off the two-clawed stinger and the claw-tips of three of its other tails. It screeched and, in a show of desperation, wildly stabbed at her with its three remaining tails. Rhyne bent back with the grace and flexibility of a dancer, evading each strike. She swiveled again, throwing the blade back to her right hand, and shoved it under the Drivik's jaw, deep into the creature's skull. It made a sickening gurgling, gagging noise, and then finally fell completely limp.

Rhyne ripped the blade from the Drivik's head.

A dozen male Aryllyns rushed down to where the creature lay. She held the blade over her head in both of her hands and paused. The males formed a tight circle around her and dropped to their knees.

As she held her arms up, Ariyana noticed a sparkling, dark blue stone embedded in the pale, lavender flesh of her upper chest. Aryllyn females didn't appear to have breasts, but the stone glistened against her skin where a human female's cleavage would begin.

Rhyne's hands shot down, impaling the blade up to the hilt into the Drivik's chest just below the base of its throat. She ripped the blade through the chest cavity, and the sound of breaking bone and tearing meat rang out into the air. Now, no longer joined at the center, what appeared to be the Drivik's rib cage sprang apart, its chest exploding open and blue blood spraying across Rhyne's face and upper body and splattering across each male around her.

Rhyne dropped the blade to the ground and pulled her fingers down her face, creating a gruesome display of war paint.

Ariyana's gut wrenched. *Was that why her hair had blue dye in it? Was it Drivik blood?*

Without warning, she plunged her hands into the Drivik's chest and tore out a large blue organ. She brandished it toward the sky and roared. The males around her roared, and the rest of the Aryllyns in the village, now walking toward them, answered with roars of their own.

Ariyana's eyes were transfixed on the gory scene that played out below them. She couldn't take her eyes off the blue organ as it glistened in the sunlight. With closer focus, she realized that it wasn't just glistening from the sunlight, it also appeared to emanate a light of its own: a blue light that seemed to pulse.

She gasped and pulled away from Kylor. The light from the organ wasn't just pulsing on its own; it was pulsing in time with the chill in her chest. How the hell was that possible?

Kylor rounded on her, and she took a few steps away from him, staying close to the rock wall on her left.

What the hell was happening here? What had she just witnessed?

Her first encounter with Kylor on Earth had been violent. Her encounter with Idrin on Draca hadn't been much better, and the main memories that had come back about him involved him stabbing her in the chest. She was supposed to be bonded with this species, allied with them, but she knew so little about them. Or, if she was willing to fully accept that she had lived a whole other life with this species, then she would have to admit that there was so little that she remembered.

Ariyana had torn into the Tethryn on that dying planet without remorse, without question. She did it to protect her children, to protect Vayle…and to avenge the lives of the crystal species that had once thrived there.

Was this a similar situation? Was this Rhyne also protecting the Aryllyns on this planet from the Drivik? *Why did it matter?* she wondered. *Why did she feel panic rising in her chest?*

Devyn and Lexa.

Their faces flashed before her eyes in sudden realization. Her husband and best friend had been alone on this planet with Kylor's violent people and these terrifying Driviks. Were they still alive? Or had Rhyne performed the same ritual on her companions while she was on Draca, trying to figure out how to get to them?

Ariyana charged forward and pushed Kylor against the boulder, his right horn scraping a deep gouge through the stone. "Where are they?" she demanded. "Are they alive? Did Rhyne mercilessly tear open their chests and rip out their organs? Did you want me to come here to find them dead?" She pushed her forearm into his chest, shoving his back against the stone again. "Answer me!" Her body shook from the increase in adrenaline.

Kylor's gaze darkened quickly, and he shoved her away. His clenched fists shook. "Mercilessly?!" he snapped. "You dare to talk to me about lack of mercy? I do not kill the innocent. Where was your mercy when you killed my kin?"

Ariyana's anger mixed with the storm of emotions that were emanating from Kylor. Ariyana punched him in the face. Kylor's head whipped to the right. He narrowed his eyes as he turned to look at her. He spit blood at her feet and snarled. Ariyana clenched her fist and swung at him again. Kylor caught her wrist. He yanked her forward and glared into her eyes. "Do not ever strike me again," Kylor growled and pushed her arm into her chest, forcing her to take a couple of steps back.

"Where are Devyn and Lexa? Tell me. Now," Ariyana demanded sharply.

A cold smile curled the corner of Kylor's mouth, two fangs catching the light on his lower lip. "It only takes moments for you to waver between offering your blood in exchange for the lives of my lost kin and attacking me. Where in those false moments is your true self? What am I to believe is real? I only see weakness and lies. The thought that your once unique energy and fierceness could right the wrongs of the past was a pathetic notion."

"Fine. I shouldn't have hit you. I overreacted. I just watched Rhyne gut that Drivik. I freaked out when I thought about Devyn and Lexa being here in close proximity to that kind of danger. But I meant what I said," Ariyana urged. "If blood is owed, take mine." Ariyana whipped her tail forward. She grabbed one of her tail feathers, squeezed, and yanked her tail back behind her, slicing the sharp feather through the palm of her hand. She held her hand out, palm up, toward Kylor, silver blood dripping onto the ground between them. "I am not false. I didn't lie. Just take what I owe from me and let Devyn and Lexa leave."

Kylor's eyes widened. His pupils constricted into thin crescents before dilating into full moons, filling his eyes with black. The nose slits on his cheekbones opened, and he inhaled deeply. Kylor's eyes searched her eyes intensely. His arm muscles twitched like he was restraining himself, and his shoulders looked strained. His emotions had locked down when she had cut her hand, but his body language made it clear that he was holding back.

Ariyana stepped forward, and Kylor jerked back.

"You mean what you are offering," Kylor stated. "But you do not know what you mean." He glanced at her hand and shook his head. "No, not like this. The Driviks sense your uncontrolled energy. Get off my planet."

Ariyana clenched her injured fist, feeling the liquid silver slide down her palm to cover the wound, and brought her hand down to her side. "What? No, I'm not leaving without Devyn and Lexa."

"Get your companions and get off my planet," he growled, stepping forward.

"What was the point of all of this? Why did you want me to come here, Kylor? Why did you go to Earth and join me with my essence? This doesn't make sense. You clearly wanted me to come here, or you wouldn't have taken Devyn and Lexa."

Kylor grabbed her chin and squeezed. She tried to open her mouth to argue, but he cut her off. "They," he pointed vigorously at the caldera, "will decide that the only reason that Drivik showed up was because of your companions. I cannot protect your companions any longer now that the Driviks have ventured into the caldera. Take them now before the Driviks find them." He released her and leaned away.

Kylor wasn't telling her the real reason that he wanted her to leave. Whatever the reason was, it was important enough to sacrifice his only hold over her: her companions.

Ariyana shook her head and held Kylor's gaze. She wanted to argue, but his features were set and stubborn. She sighed, turned, and ran down the boulders and the scree field. There was something happening that she didn't understand, but she didn't have time to think it through.

Ariyana skidded the last few feet to the bottom and turned right toward the caves.

Chapter 45

The cave was an old lava tube, and its black stone seemed to swallow the light into its depths. Ariyana stepped into its endless expanse and, hesitantly, took a few more steps. She breathed a sigh of relief when her silver flame burned more brightly, lighting the way ahead and casting the shadows back to the confines of their cracks.

As a small child on Earth, her family had taken her to a couple of beach caves. This cave lacked the distinct smell of the ocean that those caves had possessed. As she traveled deeper, though, the air became familiarly damp and cold. The scent of rock moss and river stones was stronger in the cave.

She noticed that, at this depth, there were patches of what looked like some type of fine-haired, white fungus growing on the walls of the tunnel. She leaned in closer to take a look. It surprised her that the wall was covered in blue veins of vegetation, and that from that vegetation, the fine-haired, white fungus grew. She wondered if it was white to attract something, or if it was white because there was no sunlight down here.

A few feet down from the white patch was a section of the rock that didn't have any white fungus. It did, however, still have an intricate map of blue-veined vegetation. This part of the wall was characterized by large scrape marks and torn vegetation. Something was clearly eating it or using it in some way. She wondered whether it was the Aryllyns or some other creature. She hoped that it wasn't the Driviks. She turned back toward the descending tunnel and strained her ears, listening for any signs of danger.

At first, she could only hear her soft footsteps on the moist cave floor, but the deeper she got, the more she could hear the periodic drip, drip, drip of water, and the soft gurgling of streaming water. It made sense to her that there was running water somewhere in the cave because the air was fresh and cool. She wondered whether the streaming water led to the lake in the caldera or away from it.

Up ahead, the lava tube took a slight bend to the left, and she paused at the bend.

There was an opening to a chamber of some kind about 100 feet in front of her on the left, and a blue light glimmered from the opening. The blue light floated around the opening like a gentle fog, and in the fog danced tiny, honey-almond lights that shimmered and exploded like little fireworks. It was the same honey-almond color that encircled her friend, Lexa, after Ariyana had woken up from her transformation.

Ariyana listened intently. There was a murmuring voice behind the cave's background noises of dripping and streaming water. She didn't want to charge into a chamber full of Aryllyns unless she absolutely had to.

The intonation of the voice changed slightly, and Lexa's smoky voice rose clear and crisp in the cave's tunnel. Without thought, Ariyana bolted forward into the chamber, but stopped short at the sight in front of her. Lexa was on her knees in the middle of what appeared to be a moving circle of undulating white fungus. It traveled across her lap and over the soles of her exposed feet.

The moving mass of fungus was strange enough, but what alarmed Ariyana the most was the white fungus that wrapped around Lexa's neck— Lexa had her hands on it like she was trying to pry it away from her throat.

Ariyana moved forward. "Le—" she began. Her head whipped to the right and pain exploded through the left side of her face.

Ariyana stumbled a few steps to the side. Her wings unfurled to their fullest in the large chamber as she tried to catch her balance. The feathers through her hair and along her spinal ridge rose and ignited into a brilliant flame. She whirled toward the origin of the blow, her tail whipping around her side, the feathers at the tip flexed to a sharp point, and she came face to face with an all-to-familiar look of hatred and disgust.

Devyn.

"No one wants you here, demon!" Devyn spit the word at her, swinging his right fist at her head again.

Ariyana leapt back, dodging both his right fist and his left.

"I don't know what your lot is doing to her, but I don't want any part of your mind control or mating rituals," he said, his face pinched in revulsion.

"What—" she started to question his bizarre statement and glanced sideways at Lexa without thinking. A mistake. Devyn jumped at the opportunity and punched at her face again. She wasn't quick enough this time to jump out of the way, and his fist hit her in the temple.

"What the shit is wrong with you?!" Ariyana shouted. "Dammit, that hurts, you jackass!"

Devyn's eyes widened, and his arms fell to his sides. She clearly didn't look the same, but it was obvious that he recognized her voice. He eyed her from head to toe, which Ariyana found offensive, his expression changing from disbelief to utter rejection. He shook his head violently. "No. No," he denied. "I don't know what you are, but you," he waved his pointer finger at her body dismissively, "*that*…this thing…standing in front of me is not Ariyana. You may have her voice somehow, but you…it…isn't Ariyana." He stepped away from her, holding his other hand over his mouth like he was trying to stop himself from throwing up.

"Screw you, Devyn," Ariyana stated, annoyed. She took a step toward him. "There is a lot that has happened since we last saw each other. We need to talk."

Devyn's face turned red, and he grabbed her by the throat.

"Stop," Lexa said. The word was stated calmly, no threat lingered in the tone of the simply stated command.

Multiple things happened at once. Devyn's shoulders tensed, and vacant, unseeing eyes stared right through her; multiple swaths of white fungus broke from the cyclone of movement around Lexa, and moved toward Ariyana; and something shifted in the shadows on the opposite side of Ariyana.

Though Devyn's fingers circled around her throat, there was no tension in the grasp. Ariyana pulled back, crouched low in her stance, and held one hand out toward each threat, claws elongating and forearm feathers sharpening.

On her left an Aryllyn, shorter than Kylor, stepped out of the shadows. The Aryllyn's hands were raised in the familiar stance of showing no weapon or threat, but his eyes were not focused on her; they were solely aimed at Devyn.

The swaths of fungus on her right, though, continued their forward advance, moving like a group of insects. Once close enough, they reared up and revealed themselves to be three insect-like creatures that had broken off from the larger mass. They had multiple legs, each leg ending in a sharp, blue talon. They didn't have a face that she could discern, except each one had a thin mouth that had two large, white fangs protruding out. They each had two small mandibles, one on either side of their mouths, and those also ended in sharp, white fangs. The underbelly of the creatures was devoid of the white fungus, or maybe it was fur now that she had a closer look at it, and each had a long blue stripe that ran from the bottom of the mouth to its tail.

The creatures hissed at her in unison.

Viewing them as her bigger threat at the moment, she turned to fully face them, threw her arms out to her sides, flared her wings, and hissed back.

"Stop!" Lexa yelled. "It's okay, Ariyana. Please don't hurt them; they are just trying to protect me." She was still on her knees, but she had released the creature at her neck and was now moving her hands in a 'calm down' motion.

Ariyana relaxed her stance, folding her wings against her back and lowering her arms back down to her sides. Her feathers naturally relaxed, and her flame settled into a mild burn.

"What did these creatures do to Devyn?" Ariyana asked. She tried to sound calm, but her voice was laced with anxiety.

"That's not because of the Nierite," Lexa stated, a small mischievous grin curling her lips.

"The what?" Ariyana asked.

"The Nierite," a male voice said behind her.

Realizing that she had forgotten about the Aryllyn in the chamber and that he had managed to maneuver himself behind her, Ariyana whirled around to face him.

Realization dawned on her, now that she could fully see him. "I recognize you from Earth. You're Kylor's brother, or kin…or kinno…whatever. You're Kress. You cut my best friend, and then took her from me," she snarled. Her words came out harsher than she had intended, and he flinched slightly, but she wasn't about to apologize. Both Kylor and Kress had started all of this, and Kress had just stood by and watched while his brother beat her and nearly bled her to death on Earth. He would just have to deal with her attitude and get over it.

Kress cast his eyes to the ground and refused to look at her. "I am the youngest of our line. I am Kress, the weakest of Kylor's clan." His tone was even and respectful, except when he uttered his own name; it was the only word that was tinged with a small note of regret. "The creatures are called Nierites," he continued. "They are protective of your companion." He glanced over at Lexa when he said the word "companion" and quickly, glanced back down again.

"And Devyn?" Ariyana asked.

"He is well. I am holding his energy in stasis so that he does not harm anyone, anything, or himself. He is not a progressive creature and seems unwilling to accept change," Kress stated, his eyes focused on Devyn.

"What Kress is trying to say is that Devyn has been trying to fight or kill anything that gets close to him," Lexa chimed in. "He's been annoying." She rolled her eyes. "So Kress, in essence, shuts him off when he starts acting like a jackass. Problem solved." She smiled brightly, and the honey-almond energy around her shimmered warmly.

Ariyana narrowed her eyes at Kress. "Is this what you did to Lexa on Earth?"

He bowed his head slightly in confirmation and added, "But your companion was far stronger of mind and easily broke my hold."

He glanced sideways again, and Ariyana could hear the intrigue in his tone. Ariyana wondered if it was Lexa, herself, that fascinated him or her ability to break through his hold on her.

Lexa beamed, "That's cause I'm *fierce*." She waggled her eyebrows at Ariyana, clearly proud of herself.

Ariyana smiled, despite herself and the strangeness of their surroundings. She loved that, even with all this change, Lexa was still very much herself.

Ariyana eyed the mass of creatures swirling around Lexa and the one around her neck and tried to keep her tone calm and even. "We need to get going, Lexa. My boys are on another planet, and I came here to bring both you and Devyn to that planet." She wanted to say that she came here to bring them to safety, but given Lexa's good health, lack of injury, and overall good mood, she didn't feel that the word was appropriate. Ariyana gave her a small smile. "Can you walk over to me?"

Lexa smiled back and stood slowly. She adjusted each move that she made, making sure that she didn't hurt or jostle the Nierite around her.

"I'm going to miss these little guys," Lexa said.

She gently lifted the Nierite around her neck over her head and held it in front of her face. It unwound itself from both of her hands and crawled up the length of her right arm. It arched its back under her chin, affectionately caressing her. Then, it reared up on her left shoulder, facing her at eye level. Lexa cooed at it and placed her forehead against the top of the creature's head. Lexa's eyes were moist with tears. "I'll never forget you," she whispered and pulled away.

The creature swayed its upper body back and forth. As it moved, the white fur folded back on its head, revealing two glowing blue orbs. It cooed and hummed at Lexa, holding eye contact with her.

On Ariyana's left, Kress made a strange noise. Ariyana turned to look at him. His eyes were wide, and he took a couple of steps forward.

The creature whipped toward him and hissed. The other Nierites gathered between them, rearing up and blocking them from getting to Lexa.

The Nierite on Lexa's shoulder resumed eye contact with her, hummed soothingly and, without warning, drove its fangs into her chest.

Chapter 46

Lexa sucked in a deep breath, her head whipped backward, her eyes rolled back, and her body trembled as all her muscles tensed.

"Lexa!" Ariyana yelled. She flared her wings, and her silver flame crackled through her feathers. She had just leapt forward to start kicking her way through the Nierites to get to her friend when Lexa's head snapped forward, revealing glowing blue eyes.

"No…harm," Lexa stated, but it was not her voice that filled the chamber. It was neither male nor female and held the power of being spoken by many, not by an individual. It reminded her of Rillac, except that it was soothing and melodic.

The Nierite released her, moved across her chest, and settled its head on her right shoulder. It hummed and purred, and Lexa caressed it absent-mindedly as her body relaxed, and her eyes returned to their normal honey-almond color.

"They have no intention of harming me," Lexa said, reaching up under the creature's belly to touch her chest. The creature moved onto her shoulder and down her arm, revealing a blue stone embedded in her chest.

Ariyana whirled on Kress.

"What the hell does that mean? Rhyne has a stone just like that!" she demanded.

Kress held his stance, though he continued to avoid eye contact and looked momentarily taken aback by her words. "Unclear. Rhyne is the only other that was given a stone, but the circumstances were different." He glanced up at Lexa and back at the ground. "Driviks are formidable. Their strategy of attack and abilities are impressive. They seek out the strongest, focus on that opponent until it is defeated, and carry it off before it dies. Rhyne not only discovered that the Driviks were absorbing the essence of the Aryllyns that they took, but she was the first to survive an attack. Rhyne killed the Drivik before it could carry her off." Kress paused and closed his eyes for a moment.

When he opened them again, he continued. "Rhyne's injuries would not heal. She ranted that she needed to be taken down into the caverns to be protected. She said that if the Driviks took her, they would absorb her essence, her strength, and knowledge of our people. She was convinced that the Driviks learned from the species that they killed by absorbing the strength of their cores. Rhyne thrashed in pain for three planetary rotations. We had no charrid root or Lielycet to heal her. We protected her and waited for her end to come.

It was on that third day that the Nierite came to her. We had observed that they were drawn to the heat of the volcanic activity deeper within the tunnels. In this case, they were drawn to her pain. Kylor found Rhyne with that Nierite," Kress pointed at Lexa's arm, "with its fangs in her chest. The Nierite had given Rhyne a similar stone. Rhyne sat up, sucking in deep breaths of air, and as she did so, the stone shrank slightly, and her injuries healed before Kylor's watching gaze. Rhyne claims that the stone healed her and removed her pain. She calls the stone 'Battamii,' which translates to 'reliever of pain.'"

"But Lexa is not injured," Ariyana stated, and it was clear she was upset.

"I stated that the circumstances were different. Not all pain is visible on the surface of our flesh," Kress said, peering up and holding Ariyana's gaze for a moment. "Or maybe they are bonding with her in the only way that they know how."

Ariyana looked at the stone, then looked at Lexa, and finally, looked back at Kress. She hated the uncertainty of not knowing what the stone was for or what it meant. She wondered if Vayle might know.

"I need to get them to Draca," she said to herself out loud, "before anything else happens." She sighed heavily. "Can he be released?" she asked Kress, looking over at Devyn.

"When you are ready," he replied.

She stepped closer to Devyn. His face was relaxed, and his body was no longer tense. Both of his arms now hung limply at his sides. He looked peaceful.

Ariyana reached out and touched the scab on his forearm where she had bit him when he tried to wake her from her nightmare. The wound was red and angry. He clearly had not been able to take care of it while he was here. There was some dried blood around the edges of the injured skin.

Their fight felt like a lifetime ago. *Hell, this was the third planet that she had been to, and she had encountered so many new species that she was having trouble remembering what all of them were called. And all of that had happened since she last saw him.*

Her gaze drifted up to his face. She gently moved his brown hair out of his eyes and smiled.

She had done that the first time that he had kissed her. His gaze had been so intense that night. His pupils had been dilated, and she could only see herself in the dark pools of his eyes. No one had ever looked at her like that before.

She shifted a few more strands of hair out of his eyes and looked deep within their green depths. The image that looked back at her in his eyes was drastically altered: pale, porcelain skin, silver eyes, burning silver feathers through her hair, a mouth full of sharp teeth. *Of course he saw her as a monster.*

Could he ever be the man that he was before her nightmare became too overwhelming for him? The man that once adored her and stood by her side?

She ran her finger down the space between his eyes. There was no anger there. He might look like the man that he was before, but she couldn't hide from the truth that was staring back at her through his eyes—she was forever changed. "He looks like the Devyn I remember," Ariyana whispered. She glanced over at Lexa, who was watching her.

Lexa nestled the Nierite on her arm one more time and set it down with the others. She walked over to Ariyana, the Nierite moving to clear a path for her, and playfully bumped her shoulder against Ariyana's shoulder. "Ari, you've spent your life hiding from who you are. You can't be someone that you're not." Lexa laced her fingers through Ariyana's and lay her head on her shoulder. "Maybe it's time to admit to yourself that you aren't the person that *he* hoped you'd be."

Tears burned in Ariyana's eyes. She missed the version of Devyn who had made her believe that it was safe to love, that she was free to be herself.

She sighed and rested her cheek on Lexa's head, nestled on her shoulder. "You realize that he's going to fight us every step of the way?" Ariyana asked.

Lexa jumped in front of Ariyana, her eyes wild with mischief. "Let him fight," she said excitedly. "It's damn time that he had to take responsibility for his stupidity and terrible decision-making skills."

Ariyana looked over at Kress. "You can release him now."

Kress inclined his head toward her and took a few steps back into the shadows of the chamber.

Devyn burst into motion as if he had not been frozen in place. His arm stretched out, reaching for her throat, and he stumbled forward to grab her, surprise filling his eyes because she wasn't in the same spot as earlier. Lexa jumped out of the way and Ariyana, expecting the move, knocked his arm down, pivoted out of the way, and put her foot out, tripping him.

Unable to stop his forward momentum, he tripped and landed hard on the ground.

"Devyn, we don't have time for this," Ariyana stated. "I don't want to fight you, and I don't want to argue. We have to leave before things go from bad to worse here."

His head whipped up, his once gorgeous green eyes now daggers of rage. "Worse?" Devyn snapped and jumped to his feet. "How could this possibly get any worse than this? There is a part of me that wants to believe that I'm still on Earth, but those things," he glared over at the Nierite, "clearly are not creatures that live on Earth. Worse than that, though, is that you sound like my wife, but you look nothing like her. How is that possible? Am I imagining this? Is my mind grasping at anything familiar so that the stress of this scenario doesn't break me, or are you mimicking her voice to lull me into a false sense of security so that I do what you ask of me?"

"Neither," Ariyana stated incredulously. "It sounds like me because it is me, Devyn. I can't say that I fully comprehend what's happened or that I fully believe what I've been told so far, but I can say that it feels familiar, in here," she said, touching her chest. "I have had this sensation of ice shattering in my chest, or…sometimes it's like a pulse, in rhythm with my heartbeat, that spreads an icy chill through my body. I don't know, I'm not making sense, but whatever it is, it is responding to the individuals that I have met so far and the energy of the planets that I have visited." She stepped a little closer to him. He didn't step away, but he did narrow his eyes. "The individuals that I have met so far remember things that I saw in my nightly…dream." She paused and eyed him, waiting for him to correct her.

Devyn always referred to her dream as her nightmare, using the term with friends, family, and doctors, and correcting her irritably when she used the word "dream." When he didn't respond and only stared at her, Ariyana continued, "They say that it's a memory, that I lived with them a long time ago, and that I feel comfortable in this form because it's close to the way that I used to look." She reached out and laid her hand lightly on his forearm. She peered into his eyes, imploringly. "Isn't it wonderful, Devyn? I'm not crazy or sick. Everything that I saw was real and happened, just a long time ago…a distant memory that had to be remembered."

She tried to smile the smallest of reassuring smiles, trying desperately not to show any teeth.

His eyes became unreadable.

She remained quiet, hoping that he just needed a little time to process it all. If he could just accept this part of the story for now, she could explain the details of it while they were safe on Draca.

Devyn's eyes darkened, and his skin crackled with the storm brewing inside of him. He pushed her away, hard, forcing her wings to flare slightly to stop her from losing her balance. "Not crazy or sick. Fine. So, you're a liar, then?" He spit the words at her like he was throwing knives. He took a step toward her. "Is that it? You lied about being human; you lied about loving me; our marriage was a lie; everything was a lie!"

"No, of course not. I had no idea until Kylor…changed me, I guess. What happened is complicated, but my body changed into this, and some memories came back. I didn't lie to you. I was honest with you about my dream. I just didn't realize the full extent of what it meant."

He snorted.

"Is something funny?" she asked.

"You must be Ariyana, as always still full of delusions." He sneered at her. "Did your naïve little brain ever question that maybe these aliens…, these creatures are showing you what you want to see, telling you what you want to hear, so that you'll help them?"

"It's not a delusion. This is me. I have so much to learn about myself, and I can feel that there is even more than I can possibly imagine. Devyn, you supported me once, before we got married. Can't you support me again while we figure out the truth?"

He studied her face and scanned her body from head to toe. He laughed, only it wasn't a pleasant sound, it was harsh and full of animosity. "Truth? I don't want to be any part of your truth. You're a monster, Ariyana. If that's really who you are I thought that you were sweet and full of light, but all you've done is embarrass me, take from me, make me suffer, and refuse to take your medicine like I told you to. All because you couldn't sacrifice for your family. You selfishly made your dream more important than all of us… even putting it ahead of our needs, our lives. So, no, Ariyana, I will not support you. You're a monster, and maybe it's time that you live among them."

Ariyana's body shook with anger. It was the same argument, though the words had changed. He was still unwilling to accept her for who she was. She clenched her fists and opened her mouth, but it was Lexa who spoke.

"You're an idiot," Lexa said, loud and clear. Her energy was swirling around her like an angry windstorm. "You are not even worth the words that she spoke. I have stood by her side while you forced her to take that poison, while you abandoned her, threatened her, and left her to suffer. You were lucky to have her in your life, and all you did was throw her away."

Devyn turned to face her, his face red and his eyes wild. "You know what, Lexa, I'm so tired of your bullshit. If it's not one thing, it's something else with you. Always the faithful friend, in your own eyes, but what you never saw was that you just encouraged her delusions. You made it worse, not me."

Lexa stepped toward him, fist raised, and Devyn followed suit. Ariyana moved between them, feathers rising and wings unfurling. Devyn stopped cold in his tracks. His eyes went blank, and he fell to his knees.

Kylor.

Ariyana felt him again before she saw him. She turned just as he strode into the chamber. Kress moved up to stand behind him, slightly off to his side, his head down.

"Reason will not work with a mind that is simple and broken. A conflict with that broken creature will not solve itself here and will result in your discovery by either my people or the Driviks. Neither of which is desirable. I will guide your companion out under my hold." His eyes narrowed. "Call to your royal companion."

Her royal companion. The words were hurled at her with contempt.

Ariyana was exhausted. She was moving from one argument to the next and was getting tired of defending herself. She hadn't known what to expect when she decided to come here, but this "rescue" was an unexpected and confusing venture. She expected Devyn's ridiculous behavior, but Kylor was hard to get a read on. He seemed to want to kill her on Earth, then he led her here, and now he wanted to get rid of her with no explanation.

Ariyana studied Kylor's expression and wondered what had changed from their fight on Earth to now. *Was it something that she said earlier? Was it simply all about Idrin? Was he expecting her to arrive with Vayle?* She shook her head. She had too many questions, and based on his determined expression, he wasn't going to give her any answers. She broke his gaze and muttered, "He's not mine, you dumbass. Lexa," she said. "Time to say your goodbyes."

Ariyana closed her eyes and took two deep breaths. She listened to Lexa move around the chamber, sweetly talking to the Nierites, offering them her thanks and leaving them with her promises of return. She allowed Lexa's voice to fall away like distant background noise and thought of Arc's burning magnificence. A warm pull started at the back of her mind and quickly consumed her thoughts. *Now,* she thought, and severed the connection before it overwhelmed her completely.

Ariyana's eyes popped open. Her pupils were fully dilated and quickly constricted back to a 4-pointed star in each eye. She took two more deep breaths to steady herself.

"They are coming," Ariyana said to no one in particular.

Kylor bent down, raised Devyn's arms over his head, grabbed his upper torso, and threw him over his left shoulder.

Devyn was a six-foot, strong, athletic man who had always towered above her. It was disconcerting for Ariyana to watch him being tossed around like a ragdoll by a creature that easily stood at nine feet. Kylor and Kress walked out of the chamber.

Seeing the height difference between Devyn and Kylor made Ariyana think of her own height. Her transformation had made her taller as well, but here, in front of Devyn, she had been shorter than him, just like she was when she was human. She rolled her eyes. She felt sure that some therapist out there would love to analyze that crap, but she didn't have time for it today.

Lexa walked over to her. "I'm going to miss them," she said, looking sadly over her shoulder.

"They feel the same," Ariyana said. She couldn't hear the Nierites talking, but she could feel their emotions.

The chamber was full of sorrow.

Chapter 47

They stepped out of the tunnels and into the full light of midday. Ariyana's eyes adjusted instantly, but Lexa groaned and rubbed her eyes until they adjusted.

Kylor stood about twenty feet away in the open grassy area with Devyn lying on the ground at his feet. Kress stood on the other side of Devyn, watching him closely. Kylor had a strange expression on his face.

She and Lexa walked toward him and glanced down at Devyn. It occurred to Ariyana that it was strange that Devyn appeared so relaxed and peaceful, and her eyes widened when she realized why. "Why aren't Devyn's ears and nostrils bleeding like Lexa's were on Earth?" Ariyana asked, looking over at Kylor.

"Lexa possesses great strength and resistance to our hold. She fought us as fiercely as an Aryllyn siress," Kylor said, studying her face. "Her bond to you is complete, a true companion."

Ariyana arched a brow in confusion. "Devyn and I are also bonded. We are married and have two kids. Is that why he isn't bleeding? Because he and I have an intimate relationship?"

"You did not translate my words correctly. He is barely connected to you. He has been slowly shattering his energy bond to you. I can feel it through my hold on him. Some tendrils remain intact, but the rest is broken and sharp."

Ariyana glanced back down at Devyn and sighed. The information that Kylor shared didn't surprise her, *but it sure as hell hurt*. There was a part of her that was holding onto hope that maybe they could find a way back to each other, but knowing that Devyn was actively breaking his energy ties to her meant that he was clearly done with their relationship. He was pulling away.

Ariyana could feel Kylor's eyes on her but didn't want to face him or the truth. She opened her mouth to let him know to drop it when a light tingle rippled through the back of her mind. *Oh, thank goodness,* she thought. She had no interest in dealing with the information about Devyn at this time.

The air above the grassy area rippled and cracked, and in the next moment, Arc appeared with Idrin on his back. Icy air burst around them.

Arc looked down, saw Devyn, and landed close by.

Kylor and Kress moved away from the Draxin.

Lexa gasped. "Is that what Glacin looked like?"

"Different coloring, different feathers, different flame, but, yes, just as breathtaking as Arc is," Ariyana replied.

"Is that how we're getting back?" Lexa asked.

Ariyana smiled and nodded.

Lexa's eyes grew big with excitement. She jogged halfway over to Arc and stopped once she was closer to Kress. "You and I will meet again," she stated coldly, glaring deep into Kress's eyes. "You owe me blood, and I always ensure that no debt goes unpaid."

Kress's brow ridge raised in response.

Lexa turned and jogged the rest of the way over to Arc.

"The companion, on the ground, is broken and has no reason. You will need to maintain the hold on his mind," Kylor stated, peering up at Idrin.

Arc hissed.

"Do not speak to me," Idrin snapped. "Tehkaric do not have words that matter to the Aryllyn. I will discover how you left this planet. We will know soon who aided you, and the fate of the individual will be far worse than your own." He raised his head, purposefully showing Kylor that he would neither look at him nor lower himself to his level.

Kylor's body tensed, but he kept his mouth closed. He moved further back, standing in front of the tree line next to the caldera.

Idrin leaned down and scooped Lexa up, placing her in front of him. He looked over at Ariyana.

"We leave now," Idrin demanded.

Ariyana's face twisted into a frown. "You need to learn how to talk to people," she stated, shaking her head.

Ariyana glanced over at Kylor, searching his eyes and emotions for answers. She didn't understand why he wanted her here, but, no matter how hard she concentrated, he kept himself guarded.

She turned and walked over to Arc. She hated leaving, knowing that Kylor and his people needed something.

Idrin lowered his hand to her. Ariyana glanced back one more time, then took his hand. The temperature difference between the two of them was uncomfortable as he hoisted her up and helped her mount Arc behind him. She folded her wing joints down so that her wings were flush against her lower back and would not catch the wind as they phased.

Arc scooped Devyn up in his claws and flapped his wings, lifting them off the ground.

"This doesn't feel right," Ariyana said out loud to no one in particular.

"Your companions are safe. What more do you require?" Idrin asked, not bothering to turn around.

They flew higher.

"To understand," Ariyana stated.

"To understand what?" he shot back, irritation lacing his tone.

"All of this has happened for a reason, but I do not know what that reason is. He would not—"

"He is Tehkaric!" Idrin turned and snapped at her. "You cannot reason with Tehkaric. They are nothing. They have no loyalty. You cannot hope to understand or reason with something that has no loyalty."

"Nor can you reason with ignorance, I suppose," she snapped back.

His markings pulsed to a dark purple. He glared at her, sucked in a deep breath through the slits on his cheekbones, then turned away from her. "Focus on Draca. I will focus on the hold with your companions, or I'll force you into unconsciousness to make the journey easier," he snarled.

Ariyana had raised her arm and clenched her fist with the intention of hitting him when the energy around her changed. "No," she breathed.

A shrill cry filled the air, followed by multiple other answering cries wailing from the side of the caldera.

"Ari? What the hell is that?" Lexa questioned, her voice quavering.

"Driviks," Ariyana whispered as she frantically searched the area for the source of the sounds. "Shit!" she exclaimed once she saw them.

There were at least five that she could see. They were running on all fours and traveling fast. Chunks of soil, grass, and rocks were flinging into the air with each push of their back legs. There was a large Drivik in front, running ahead, and it was flanked, two to each side, by the remaining Driviks.

Ariyana looked down at Kylor.

He had a blade in each hand, and they glinted in the sunlight. His gaze shot up to meet hers, and he aggressively waved his hand at her in a shooing motion. "Leave!" he shouted.

"Kress!" Lexa screamed out.

Kress looked up at Lexa, his eyes heavy with concern. He gave her a slight shake of his head, palmed two blades of his own, and readied his stance for battle.

Ariyana looked at her friend in surprise, but Lexa was already looking at her, her eyes pleading.

"We have to help them," Ariyana said to Idrin.

"Help?" Idrin asked, his voice full of disdain.

"Kylor and Kress!" Ariyana exclaimed urgently. "There are too many. They will be torn to pieces."

"They are Tehkaric. I will not risk my ryn, my companion's ryn, or your ryn to save something that does not deserve the air it breathes. They are already dead. Let their bodies realize the truth."

"Is your pride really more important than your people?" Ariyana asked.

"None of my people exist on this planet," he snapped. His eyes narrowed at her, daring her to challenge him.

Her eyes widened in disbelief. "Take Lexa and Devyn to Draca. Then return for me," Ariyana demanded.

"You dare to order me around?" Idrin asked through gritted teeth.

Ariyana stood and flared her wings. "You're an idiot," she said and jumped.

Idrin turned to face Lexa, who was now staring at him. "What is an idiot?" he asked.

Lexa considered him for a moment, a small smile playing at the corner of her mouth, and lifted one shoulder in a slight, non-committal shrug. "Well, in short…you," she quipped and flashed a mocking smile.

"Gah!" he snarled. His hand whipped out and wrapped around her throat. Her eyes widened in surprise and maybe a touch of fear before her eyes closed, and her body slumped forward, completely unconscious.

The corner of Idrin's mouth curled in amusement. He didn't have to touch her to put her under the hold, but since she was disrespectful, he'd decided to teach her a lesson. He adjusted Lexa on Arc's neck. Her breathing was steady, and her mind was blank. She would be easy to transport.

As Ariyana dove toward the Driviks, Idrin peered down at her one last time and shook his head. She was proving to be even more of a pain in his existence than she had been before. "Draca," he commanded Arc.

Arc's feathers rippled on his wings in agitation. He rumbled his protest, but knew Idrin's mind was set. Arc prepared his body to phase.

Neither of them knew what they would be returning to, and Arc was not ready for Vayle's anger when they arrived without her companion in tow, but he also knew that they couldn't join the battle with two humans to protect.

The air shimmered and cracked around Arc, and cold consumed him as he phased them into the energy realm.

Chapter 48

Ariyana pulled her wings in tight against her body as she hurtled toward the surface. She didn't glance up to watch Arc phase. She didn't need to. The air above her flexed and chilled for a moment and returned to normal. She felt a sigh of relief. *At least Lexa and Devyn would be safe…well, safer than they would be if they had stayed here.*

The five Driviks were gaining ground on Kylor and Kress but had not noticed her yet. They were panting and drooling as they charged forward, their blue fur slick with what looked like sweat. They were intensely focused on the Aryllyns in front of them, their black eyes wild.

The lead Drivik broke off from the pack, picked up speed, and charged straight for Kylor. Kylor leaned into his stance, clanged his blades together, and roared.

The energy around Ariyana pulsated against her body as if she were caught in a current of the planet's life force. *No, not the planet*, she realized. *It was the Drivik's energy.* She had noticed a subtle throb of energy when the Drivik had risen out of the lake earlier, before it attacked Rhyne, but she had dismissed its importance. It was undeniable now, and the more it pressed against her body, the more she realized how much she wanted that energy: how hungry she was for it.

The icy throb in Ariyana's chest responded to the pulsating energy around her. Her body tensed in response. Her skin felt too tight around her as if it could split from the energy building inside.

Ariyana aimed for the lead Drivik, not attempting to slow down. Energy burst inside her, and without thought, she allowed it to consume her.

Ariyana flipped her body, diving feet first now. She flared her talons and crashed into the Drivik, driving its head and upper body into the ground. Rocks and soil exploded around them. Her talons pierced through its eyes, deep into its skull, and through its flesh at the base of its neck. She used the force of the impact to drive her talons in as deep as they would go. She flared and flapped her wings violently, jerking herself upward. She tore and twisted the Drivik's head, snapping its neck. She flapped again, dropped its lifeless body, and landed face-to-face with a furious Kylor.

"Have you lost all reasonable thought?" Kylor snarled. "You were told to leave! I do not accept your aid, and I will not risk my ryn to save yours. Leave Ora! Now!"

Ariyana ignored Kylor, whirled, and stood between him and Kress and the four slowly approaching Drivik. She leapt over the small crater that contained the dead Drivik and shook her wings, flaring them out to their fullest. She raised every feather through her hair, along her spinal ridge, and down her tail, causing them to burst into a brighter flame. She whipped her tail out to the side, lashing it and contracting the long feathers at the end into a deadly point. Her second skin moved across her body with purpose, extending off the body piece that hugged her close like a strapless one-piece bathing suit, and solidified into protective armor around her upper thighs, down into intricate plates that covered her calves, and along her upper arms. She threw her arms out to the sides, elongating her claws, and roared.

The four Driviks stopped twenty feet away from her, raised up on their hind legs, bared their sharp fangs, whipped their tails, and hissed and clicked at her.

Kylor spoke behind her, but his words held no meaning to Ariyana. All her body understood and recognized were the four creatures in front of her. Only one truth existed at that moment: if she let even one of these creatures live, it would kill any Aryllyn that it could get its claws into, and she wasn't going to let that happen.

The Driviks chittered at each other and fanned out into a half circle in front of her.

Before she had killed the lead Drivik, they had been solely focused on Kylor and Kress. Now their black, unblinking eyes shimmered only with the brilliance of her silver flame.

Ariyana's body hummed with energy, just like it had on that dying planet when she'd fought the Tethryn.

The Driviks clicked, barked, chittered, and hissed at each other, clearly communicating.

Well, Ariyana thought, *better not give them any more time to plan their attack.* She dug her talons into the ground and flexed her muscles.

"You cannot defeat four," Kylor barked behind her.

"Oh, shut up," Ariyana hissed and charged.

The Driviks sprinted forward in response. The two directly in front of her charged her head-on, and the two on the outside fanned out farther, appearing to try to surround her. The two in front of her remained high on their hind legs, while the other two ran on four legs to pick up their speed.

After three long strides, Ariyana flared her right wing and hugged her left wing around her side. Her wing caught the air, yanking her back. She folded it into her body and allowed her body to fall on her left side. The momentum from her forward motion, combined with the smoothness of the grass and her wing wrapped around her body, caused her to slide.

The two Driviks in front of her had initiated their jump when she had flared her right wing, so they were currently aimed at the area where her upper body would have been. Ariyana arched and sharpened the feathers along her right wing as the Driviks leapt over her. The feathers sliced through the Drivik on the right, gutting him from neck to navel.

Ariyana's hand shot out, grabbing the ankle of the Drivik on the left. She dug her left talons into the ground and arched her body up and right between the two leaping Driviks. She slammed her right foot down and dug her claws deep into the Drivik's ankle. She flared her wings, arresting her forward momentum, flapped her wings once as hard as she could, and pivoted. The Drivik's body arched in a circle, and she slammed it into the other Drivik with a loud "squelching" sound as the other Drivik's entrails fell out of the deep gash that she had made.

The sliced Drivik fell motionless in its own mess of entrails and blood. The other one rolled, shrieking, off to the side. It was covered in blood and gore and was pulling at its shredded ankle.

The other two Driviks were charging in fast. One leapt at Ariyana's front, and the other leapt at her back. She launched into the air, flapped her wings once, and then tucked them into her back again. The Driviks collided and landed in a small heap of limbs and tails. She shot back down, intending to land on both of them, but one popped up quickly. She landed hard on the other, dug her talons into its right shoulder, and slammed her sharpened tail through its upper left chest. Its gurgling shriek tore through the air.

The other Drivik slashed at her—first left and then right. Ariyana reared back, dodging both blows, but was unable to finish the Drivik on the ground.

The two Driviks hissed and growled at each other, jaws snapping but not connecting with flesh. It reminded Ariyana of a display of dominance that she had seen between animals on Earth.

The injured Drivik remained low, eyes cast down, while the healthier one stood tall, glaring at Ariyana. The healthier one roared at the injured one. It stood, blue blood streaming down its chest, its left arm hanging limply at its side, and hissed at Ariyana. With a burst of energy, it charged her. She kicked out and struck it square in the chest. Blue blood burst from its mouth, and it staggered backward. She jumped forward and grabbed it by the throat. It flailed in her grasp and attempted to whip its tails at her. She drove her claws into its jaw, shoved her foot into its chest, and ripped its jaw and throat out. It sputtered and blood sprayed from the wound. She released it, leapt back, and it slammed to the ground in a grisly "splat."

The healthier Drivik roared at her, its entire body shaking with rage. The earlier Drivik with the injured ankle stood, unsteadily, on three limbs and limped toward the healthier one, its injured ankle dragging behind it.

A roar sounded from the right. The Driviks whipped their heads to the side to see Kylor and Kress charging straight toward them.

Ariyana took advantage of the distraction and lunged forward.

Kylor and Kress collided with the injured Drivik. It tried to defend itself. It slashed at Kylor and whipped its tails at Kress, but in its weakened state, it was no match for the two Aryllyns.

Kress sliced at each tail that struck at him, slicing off the clawed tips. Then, grabbing the middle tail with the stinger on it, he pushed his full weight forward into the Drivik, driving both a blade and the creature's own stinger into its back.

The Drivik lurched forward and Kylor shoved his blade into its throat. He twisted the blade and roughly shoved it through the rest of its throat. Kylor and Kress pulled their blades out at the same time, and the Drivik hit the ground with a loud, wet thud.

The sound of its body hitting the ground was echoed by Ariyana colliding with the other Drivik. It made a loud 'umph' noise as she knocked the air out of its lungs and cracked a few of its ribs. They hit the ground hard and rolled. The Drivik thrashed at her, claws raking over her armor, and its stinger striking at her chest, but her armor held strong, deflecting the assault.

Her body moved without any thought in her mind of what was possible. It just reacted as if it knew what to do.

Ariyana leapt to her feet. She pulled the webbing in tight against her wing bones, leaving the arms of her wing bones covered by raised, sharpened feathers. They looked like insect legs covered in blades.

The Drivik jumped up and hissed at her, drool and blood dripping from its fangs.

They circled each other, neither of them daring to allow their backs to be exposed to the other.

A branch in a tree snapped nearby, and her senses instinctively expanded outward beyond the Drivik in front of her, trying to determine the nature of the threat, if any.

Ariyana broke eye contact to glance left and right, and the Drivik rushed toward her. She snarled and ran toward it. It lurched and snapped. She swerved right, its jaws clamping shut on the empty air to the left of her head, and she punched it in the temple. Bone crunched. It shrieked. Three claw-tipped tails stabbed at her torso. She whipped her right arm up, blocking them, and punched it in the face with her left hand.

The flaps on the sides of its neck and body extended out like a cobra's hood, and it hissed. Ariyana grabbed its right flap and pulled its head down, kneeing it in the face. Its head whipped back, she released it, and kicked it in the chest. More ribs broke. The Drivik fell backward and slid across the ground.

Ariyana walked toward it slowly. It was done. These creatures were no match for her new form, and it was time to show them that they couldn't mess with her or the other Aryllyns on this planet.

Ariyana snarled and started to reach out to grab the Drivik when another snapping branch had her whirling around. She hadn't noticed it before, but their fighting had pushed them closer to the trees, and, though she had not been certain before, she could feel the new Drivik's energy now. Unfortunately, she only realized what was happening as it was leaping toward her from a branch. She only had enough time to raise her arms before it slammed her body to the ground.

Chapter 49

Ariyana heard fighting going on around her, out of eyesight, and assumed that it must have meant that Kylor and Kress were taking care of another Drivik.

The Drivik on top of her snapped wildly at Ariyana's face, and being pinned against the ground seriously limited her body's movement. She pushed at its torso, trying to get it off her, but its short, blue fur was slimy, and her hands kept sliding off it.

It stabbed two of its claw-tipped tails at her face. Ariyana raised the feathers on her forearm and slashed at them, cutting off their tips. It grabbed the side of her face, pushing her left cheek into the ground and shrieked at her. It whipped two other tails at her face, stabbing down toward her right eye, but she caught one in each hand and snapped them backward, exposing the bone. It shrieked again. It raised its head up, mouth opening wide, six fangs popping out like a snake, three on each side, and it snapped at her. It caught her where her neck and right shoulder met. Her armor protected her from all but two fangs, and they sank in deep.

Ariyana screamed.

Instantly, her lungs began to burn, and her mind began to fog. She grabbed the side of its face with her left hand, but her fingers were already numb, and they slid uselessly through its fur. Ariyana's mind struggled to come up with other options when all of a sudden the Drivik was ripped off her.

Ariyana pulled herself up into a crouching position and wobbled, silver blood trickling from her shoulder and down her side.

The Drivik twisted and writhed in front of her, held by some unseen hand. Then, blood sprayed across her face from a large gash across it throat. The creature's body hit the ground with a wet slap, and an exquisite warrior, standing over its still form, threw its head in front of Ariyana's feet. She jumped up and back, staggered, and wheezed.

The trees and meadow morphed into the egg chamber, a Tethryn head lying on the rock floor beside her. Ariyana gasped, squeezed her eyes shut, and shook her head. No, it wasn't real. She knew that it wasn't real, it couldn't be.

Ariyana opened her eyes.

The warrior stood firm, adorned with the hides of dead Driviks, a blade in her right hand, and blood dripping from her long, clawed fingers.

The warrior morphed into Glacin's face, fangs dripping with yellow blood, but only for a moment, before morphing back into the Aryllyn she had seen earlier.

Rhyne.

Ariyana's eyes blazed, and a warning filled her mind.

None of the Aryllyns on this planet were her allies.

Ariyana raised the feathers on her forearms defensively and stumbled back.

Rhyne advanced on her.

"No," Ariyana whispered as she struggled to take in breaths of air. She continued to stumble and trip as she moved out into the large, meadow-like area. Her flame flickered, she sucked in desperate breaths of air, and black dots flickered in her vision. Her fingers tingled. Her wings were heavy. Her skin felt like it was burning.

"Rhyne!" Kylor yelled.

"It is Aris!" Rhyne yelled back. "It is her. We kill her. This ends."

"My name…is…not…Aris," Ariyana wheezed.

Rhyne glared at her like she had committed the greatest offense.

Ariyana's mind struggled to comprehend Rhyne's behavior and formulate a response that would make sense. Her throat felt like it was constricting. She couldn't breathe. She clutched at her throat and fell backward.

"Your pain has only just begun, Tehkara," Rhyne hissed. "Drivik venom liquefies. It burns your nerves and boils your blood. Your muscles will contract until your bones break and your flesh tears from strain. I will stand above you and witness your slow death."

"Rhyne," Kylor said sharply.

Rhyne whirled on him. "Why do you hesitate? You—"

The air above Ariyana rippled and tore open, Arc exploding through it. He landed roughly behind Ariyana and slammed his tail between her and Rhyne, protecting her.

Arc roared at Rhyne.

Rhyne palmed two blades and clanged them together at Idrin, roaring back.

Idrin, on Arc's back, ignored her. He jumped off, scooped Ariyana into his arms, and mounted Arc again. He secured her in front of him. He stabilized her neck so that her head wouldn't loll forward, and he wrapped his arm around her waist.

Kylor stepped forward, pushing Rhyne to the side.

"Drivik venom," Kylor stated, loud enough for Idrin to hear.

Idrin looked down at him and growled deep in his throat.

"Ariyana understands the truth without words being spoken," Kylor said, trying to get Idrin to understand part of what had happened.

"Tehkaric words are not truth!" Idrin spit the words out, then roared at Arc, who immediately charged forward.

The last thing that Ariyana saw before she lost consciousness was Rhyne, blades drawn and eyes burning fiercely with anger, and Kylor, weaponless, standing next to her with nothing but concern etched into his features.

Chapter 50

Ariyana's eyes popped open, and she sucked in a breath that hitched in her throat. Everything hurt: most notably the area between her neck and right shoulder. She clenched her jaw until the bone ached and moved her left hand up to her shoulder.

It was wet.

Wait, no, that wasn't the full truth.

The pain had been so distracting that Ariyana hadn't immediately taken in her full surroundings. Her body was submerged in water. The back of her head rested on a hard surface above the water while the rest of her body sprawled out in the shallow liquid.

Ariyana shifted her left wing and raised the long feathers along her wing's forearm. The feathers vibrated above the surface of the water causing the water to churn around her neck.

Aggravation swirled around Ariyana as if the feeling had substance and form. It pushed on her, stung her, and held her breath hostage in her throat.

Ariyana gasped and attempted to sit up as Vayle appeared next to her and stopped her by putting a clawed paw over her body.

Calm. Vayle scolded her.

"Then get your emotions under control," Ariyana countered.

Vayle rumbled deep in her throat, but lifted her forelimb, releasing Ariyana's body, and shielded her emotions.

Vayle walked in a wide circle around where Ariyana reclined. Her multi-faceted eyes stayed fixed on Ariyana.

Drivik venom is difficult to remove from the body. Again, your body was not healing. I suggest that you do not move. Your body would not do well with the added stress of Lielycet toxin.

Ariyana lowered her gaze to the green water surrounding her body. The pool of Lielycet was large enough to fit her entire body and flashed with tiny sparks of green lightning. At the edge, where the Lielycet touched the stone, there was a layer of what looked like black ash or black dirt…something small and granular.

"Where are we?" Ariyana asked.

In the egg chamber. You could not be alone. Vayle's voice held a hint of pain with her last sentence causing Ariyana to glance back up at her.

"Why is the Lielycet sparking, and what is that stuff along the edges?"

It is healing you. It is dying to heal you! Vayle barked. She slammed her tail down on the rock floor sending a tremor through the Lielycet that rippled around her body. Ariyana held her breath, expecting the Lielycet to react, but relaxed when nothing happened.

"Why are they dying?"

Vayle's aggravation filled the chamber again. *Drivik venom is unknown to their species. They have deemed your life more worthy than their own lives, and those that lie with you now have agreed to cut themselves off from the species to heal you and protect the rest from contamination. They give you their lives to save yours.* She whipped her head toward Ariyana and hissed, baring her long fangs.

Vayle's emotions combined with Ariyana's pain and guilt. Why was she feeling guilty? And why did that guilt feel tinged with loneliness and regret? She felt out of control. Her emotions refused to settle down.

Familiarity in what she felt made her pause. Vayle's reaction to her, and her reaction to the Lielycet: something wasn't adding up.

Ariyana sat up, pushed off the side of the pool, and spun around into a crouch. Her tail and wings whipped through the Lielycets, triggering their defenses and turning the pool red. Pain tore through the half-healed wounds on her body as the Lielycets covering her body released their toxin and she collapsed on the rock floor next to the small pool. She yelled out and clutched her right shoulder. Vayle made a pained noise and stepped toward her.

"No!" Ariyana hissed, dragging her body away from both the pool and Vayle. She snapped her head up at Vayle. "If you have something that you would like to say, Vayle, just damn well spit it out!"

Vayle growled. *You risked your life to save theirs! How could you be so reckless? What thought entered your mind to make you think that was permissible?*

"Permissible?" Ariyana spit out. "I don't need your permission. Life is life, and their lives matter as much as mine does! I did not think twice about it; I just acted. Those creatures were there because of us…because of me. Kylor and Kress did not deserve to die because of that."

Kylor went to Earth, an impossible venture, to find you, for reasons unknown. When his intentions for you did not succeed, he abducted your mate and companion and held them on his planet. The Driviks were drawn to your energy, but you were there because of the path that he chose to take. Vayle flared her wings and scraped her tail across the rock floor. *Does your ryn believe that Kylor cared whether he might kill you on Earth, Aris?* Vayle hissed as the name left her thoughts. Ariyana flinched and glared at her. *Ari.* Vayle corrected, her tone harsh.

"I refused to stand by and watch as Driviks tore them apart. There is no excuse for that. I realize that I do not remember everything, but they do not deserve to die, no matter what Kylor did to me on Earth," Ariyana said. She pulled herself up on her forearm, pushing with her left wing, and groaned as the skin on her right shoulder pulled from the movement. She was uncertain about how she felt about the little that she remembered of Kylor, the events that took place on Earth, and the events that took place on Ora. She also felt guilty about his kin, and she didn't know how to process what she was learning about herself. With uncertainty being as plentiful as the air she was breathing, she didn't want to make a rash decision to let them die, not to mention that the decision had made itself on Ora. She acted on instinct, and it was her instincts alone that drove her to dive between them and danger.

Vayle roared and slammed her wing claws into the rock floor between them. *Did my people that followed him into a blind battle deserve to die? Did Idrin's? Do you dare to place more worth on Kylor's life than those that I lost due to his recklessness?*

Rage slammed into Ariyana. Her forearm gave out and her body slapped against the rock floor. The Lielycet on her body reacted again to the violent motion and a fresh burst of toxin flowed into her wounds.

The pain and frustration burst inside her. Vayle's rage added to it, and Ariyana struck her fist on the ground. "Did Kylor's kin deserve to die?" She roared at her, "Did they? They were innocent in what happened, and I murdered them! I did! If you want to compare who deserves what, then why don't we start there?" She dug her claws into the ground and pulled herself up into a crouch. She wavered slightly, but held her ground and raised her eyes up to meet Vayle's piercing glare. "Why would your people follow him if not of their own accord? You're angry and hurt that they died, but have you considered that they followed him because they believed in his cause?"

Vayle's head pulled back like a snake about to strike, her fangs elongating. Her crest rose, and her feathers burst into an inferno.

Ariyana groaned and stood. Her wings hung limply at her back, throwing her off her balance, but her tail found purchase on the ground, offering support to her instability.

Ariyana held Vayle's stare, unwilling to back down. "I keep running through the memory, trying to piece together what happened from the limited information. I know that I killed his kin, his brothers, though I can't recall the full memory. I remember the guilt, the blood, the knowledge that what was done could not be undone, but what really stood out, when I remember sitting in that chamber, trying to rub the blood off my hands, was the loneliness." She held her hands out, palms up, as if she could see the dried blood caked on her hands again. "I was alone; it was empty… I was spiraling. But I was on Draca. How is that possible, Vayle? How could I be alone on your planet? Where were you?" Ariyana hissed. "The Lielycet choosing to sacrifice themselves to save me feels all too familiar, doesn't it? You're not angry at Kylor. You're angry at me. Your people followed Kylor willingly to protect me, to hopefully eliminate the threat to my life, and, in turn, eliminate the threat to yours. But they died, and you abandoned me to both mourn and deal with your hatred of what I had caused among your people. Now you hate me again for the decision that I forced among the Lielycets, don't you? Admit your true anger, guilt, and regret, Vayle! Say it!"

Ariyana's breath exploded from her lungs, and she flew across the chamber, hitting the ground and rolling away. She never registered Vayle's movement, only felt the blow of her tail across her chest.

Surprisingly, Ariyana's ribs were not broken, but her right wing was pinned under her in an unnatural position. She wheezed painfully.

"Ari!" Lexa's voice echoed down the tunnel and throughout the chamber, but Ariyana didn't call out to her. She kept her focus on Vayle.

Shame filled the chamber, and Vayle collapsed on the floor as if the energy in her body had abandoned her.

Ariyana rolled her body to the side, easing the pressure on her broken wing, and met Vayle's gaze. Her face no longer showed any signs of anger. Instead, Vayle's eyes glistened with sorrow, and her body looked broken and defeated.

"This goes back as far as Glacin, doesn't it?" Ariyana asked. "You sacrificed for me; you cared for me; you fought for me and with me, but when it comes down to it, it turns out that both of us have scars from Glacin's death that have not healed." She rolled the rest of the way off her wing and groaned and cursed through the pain. Her body ached, and her vision was blurred. The Drivik venom, Lielycet toxin, and injuries were taking their toll. A wave of unconsciousness tried to crash over her, but she jerked her head roughly to the side, shaking it off.

Ariyana's lungs burned from what felt like a lack of oxygen. She sucked in a few uneasy breaths and looked back at Vayle. "You targeted your anger at Kylor when it really should have been targeted at me. You pulled away from me, and because of that, I lost control. Then, I was gone, and you didn't know what that meant. Now I'm back, and you still don't know what that means. Well, neither do I, but what I can tell you is that if we want to try to heal, we're going to have to work through it together. You'll have to get to know me for who I am now, and I'll have to do the same for you. And the only way that we can do that is by being honest."

Ariyana paused, giving Vayle a chance to chime in or rail on her, but she did neither, she just stared at her.

"I spent my life on Earth desperate to fit in," Ariyana continued. "I don't want that anymore. I want to be myself. I want to belong with people that accept me for who I am."

"Look, you pulsing-face-tattooed ass, you can either move on your own, or I'll move you myself, and let me tell you, if you make me move you, you will not enjoy it." Ariyana heard Lexa say.

Ariyana peered over to the tunnel opening.

Idrin was standing in front of Lexa, keeping her from entering the egg chamber, and Lexa had a finger pointed directly at his face.

"Lex," Ariyana whispered.

"Move!" Lexa yelled and shoved him.

Idrin stumbled left, caught off guard by Lexa's strength, and she dashed around him, running over to Ariyana. Lexa practically slid across the floor the last few feet and stopped at Ariyana's side. "Oh, Ari, what is happening? Why aren't you healing? Why aren't you in the Lielycet pool? Come on." She fussed over her, lifting up her arms and checking on her wings. Then she lifted her up, supporting her weight, and helped her walk back to the pool. "You look worse than you did when they brought you back. Why?"

She will not heal while her body is under stress, Vayle said, finally speaking.

"Is that right?" Lexa barked. "Then, why don't you stop fighting with her? Maybe your 'pain-in-the-ass' attitude is what's stressing her out!"

Ariyana looked at Lexa in shock. One, she was surprised that Lexa had heard Vayle, and two, she was not expecting her bluntness.

Lexa noticed Ariyana's expression and "Tsked" at her.

She adjusted her arm under Ariyana's armpits, shouldering more of her weight, and half-walked, half-dragged her back to the Lielycet pool.

They reached the side of the pool, and Lexa stepped in first. She was gentle with her footsteps, sliding them into the Lielycet pool as if she was slowly testing the water's temperature. Ariyana was less gentle, but because Lexa guided her, she didn't cause the Lielycet to react.

Lexa moved in front of her and pulled Ariyana's body weight onto her chest.

"Can you move your wings slightly so that I can guide you back down onto your back?" Lexa asked.

Ariyana winced and nodded. She marveled at her friend's strength. Ariyana had grown taller when she changed, and she knew that her wings and armored body made her heavier, too, but Lexa didn't appear to be under any strain at all as she moved Ariyana around. She wondered if it had to do with their connection. She'd seen changes in her children before she left for Ora, so maybe Lexa'd changed, too. Her eyes lowered to the stone in Lexa's chest. *Or maybe the stone was changing her.* She thought to herself. It was hard to say.

Ariyana glanced back up at Lexa's face and noticed that her brows were furrowed, and her eyes were wide. She followed her gaze to her shoulder and sucked in a breath. The bite mark consisted of two punctures on top of her shoulder, the one closest to her neck being the deeper of the two. They were covered in bright green Lielycet and were still slowly oozing silver blood.

"I'm worried," Lexa stated. "That doesn't look good, and everyone here seems to think that you should have healed by now. Do you think that it's the venom? If that other female Aryllyn could heal from it, don't you think that you should be able to also?"

Ariyana let Lexa lay her back. She adjusted her broken wing as best as she could, and sighed as the Lielycet filled her wounds. It stung at first and then slowly numbed.

Lexa sat down next to her, tucking her legs under her, sitting on her feet. "Seriously, what's going on?" Lexa asked. "I don't understand what the two of you were arguing about, and I don't understand how the events that you were both talking about would be stopping you from healing now."

Ariyana didn't know where to begin, and she didn't know how to explain things that she didn't fully understand herself. She and Kylor had a painful history between them that she had only just scratched the surface of, but she didn't feel that it warranted leaving him to die. *Would she have felt different if she remembered everything?* She didn't think so. Even with what she remembered and the anger that she felt over what he had done to her on Earth, it never dawned on her to just leave him. She had seen what was about to happen, and she had acted.

Vayle didn't understand that. She expected Ariyana to be who she was before, but Ariyana didn't think that that would ever be possible again. "My body has changed so much that I don't even recognize my own reflection, and yet, it feels familiar. But my mind, my thoughts are still me…, the person that I was on Earth, except for these flashes that I have of a past that I don't remember." Ariyana's hearts began to race, and the ice in her chest throbbed. It felt like shards of ice raced through her veins. Her tail lashed back and forth under her in the shallow water.

Lexa caught it, wrapping her fingers firmly but gently under the muscled appendage, stopping it. She placed her other hand on top of the hand that Ariyana pressed into her chest, bringing Ariyana's attention up to her gaze.

"Try to calm yourself," Lexa soothed. "It is a difficult task to reconcile yourself as you are today with a person who once was. As you were growing up on Earth, you only remembered the events surrounding Glacin's death, but you did not know for certain that it meant you were anything other than the person that you appeared to be. You did not remember that." Lexa peered over at Vayle for a moment, considering her, and looked back at Ariyana. "You mostly lived your life as a human, affected by what you thought was a dream of Glacin, but not affected by an entire life lived and lost as another version of yourself. You became 'Ariyana' as much as any other human becomes who they are." She reached up from Ariyana's chest and ran her hand over the feathers in her hair. "Just because you look like you do now does not mean that 'Ariyana' has to disappear completely as you resume a life that you once lived here among these people. What you said to Vayle earlier is true. If each of you wants to heal, you'll have to work through it together, and the main way to do that is by getting to know each other again."

Ariyana wrapped her tail around Lexa's back and gave her a small smile.

Vayle lifted herself up, moved over to the pool, and lay down, wrapping her body and tail around the pool.

"I'm afraid that I won't like the person that I was," Ariyana whispered, tears beading in the corners of her eyes.

Lexa leaned down and put her forehead on Ariyana's.

"I'm not afraid," Lexa said, her own eyes shiny from tears. "It didn't matter what you remembered or didn't remember on Earth. You were you, and I loved you the first moment that I saw you. I knew that our lives would forever be on the same path, and that I would stand by your side no matter what. I knew who you were the moment that you walked into that chamber on Ora, just like I knew you the moment that my eyes opened on Earth. Aris…Ariyana…or my Ari…your soul will never change, and neither will our bond."

Vayle's tail feathers fanned out, the tips lightly caressing the other side of Ariyana's body. *Your human companion is wise beyond her youth. Your ryn will never change. Time brings change, and, as many solar rotations as I have lived through, I know that to be true.* Vayle rumbled low in her throat, and her feathers vibrated slowly along her spinal ridge. *Glacin chose you and chose to die protecting you. That was not a reckless choice. He knew you, the infinite you, and decided that this universe could not survive without you.* A tear fell from the corner of her multi-faceted eye, down her jawline, and onto the rock floor. *Your past holds great pain, but I agree with Lexa—we are better suited if we face it together.*

Lexa smiled, big and bright, and her honey-almond-colored energy burned around her.

Vayle lifted her head and shook it as if she was shaking off the emotion.

*But first, Ari…*Vayle paused, a wave of warmth washing over Ariyana.

Lexa's face beamed at the use of her nickname for Ariyana.

We need you to heal so that we can discuss what happened on Ora. I understand why you helped Kylor. Glacin would never have turned his back on someone in need. In that you are the same. She groaned. *But there is an unanswered issue that must be resolved.*

Lexa and Ariyana held Vayle's gaze, her discomfort spreading through the chamber like a low fog.

How did Kylor and Kress phase to Earth? Lexa has no memory of her journey to Ora. We must discover who among my people has betrayed us.

Chapter 51

It took Ariyana another planetary rotation, or day as she would say on Earth, to heal enough to be able to stand without anyone's help. It might take her another day or two to have her full strength back, but she was certainly strong enough to check in on Devyn and her children.

Vayle had been right about needing to figure out how Kylor was able to make his way off Ora, but her family needed to come first.

Lexa told Ariyana that her boys had checked on her a few times while she was unconscious and that they had been tentative when they reached out to touch her hands. That told Ariyana that she needed to assure them that she was well and whole. Lexa also assured her that her children had not been alone with Devyn while she was healing. Idrin had Rays stay with them or close by. He had been concerned that Devyn might either lash out at Alec and Kai for the changes that were taking place with their bodies or that he might try to leave the chamber and potentially hurt someone because they weren't human. Ariyana was grateful for this. She knew that Lexa had spent most of her time with them, but while Lexa was with her, it felt better knowing that there was someone else there that the boys trusted.

As she approached the chamber that they were staying in, she heard Devyn's voice carry down the tunnel, "…believe that nothing has changed, but you both saw what I saw and know that this isn't true. She isn't the wife or mother that we knew."

"That isn't true. She is more herself than she's ever been allowed to be."

It took Ariyana a moment to realize that it was Alec's voice saying that. The playful tone of a six-year-old was gone. He spoke with the confidence of a young man, his tone matter-of-fact. She felt a pang of guilt over taking so long to heal. She had seen changes in her children before she left, and now she wondered what else she had missed.

She heard a noise ahead of her and saw Rays walking toward her. She must have been waiting outside of the chamber to give Devyn and the boys the illusion of privacy. When they were close enough to each other, Rays nodded at her and walked past.

"Why?" Devyn demanded. "Because now her physical appearance matches her appearance from her nightmare? Couldn't one of these creatures be manipulating all of you to get what they want? Maybe one of them has infected her, causing her body to change, so that they can use her, convince her that she belongs here for some corrupt purpose. And maybe both of you are changing because you've been infected too." He paused, and she heard the shuffling of feet. "We need to leave…all of us, before this goes too far. We aren't safe on this planet. We need to get your mother back to Earth before she changes beyond our control. And it may already be too late. Lexa told me that she killed some creatures on that planet where she found us… She killed them. Could you ever have imagined that your mother would be capable of such a thing?"

"She isn't infected and neither are we." Kai's voice was firm, no longer cheery. "She is no longer safe on Earth because of you, and now, you are showing her that she isn't safe *with* you either because you refuse to accept her for who she is."

"We know the truth. We saw it," Alec said. "You do not have to let your fear of the unknown blind you. Mom is meant to be here…; we are meant to be here."

"This is bigger than the three of us," Kai said. "Bigger than your negativity."

Devyn's anger blasted out of the chamber and down the tunnel like a wave of heat. Ariyana didn't realize that she had stopped walking until she clutched the uneven surface of the rock wall harder, bracing for the impact of his angry voice. "How dare you both take that tone with me!" Devyn shouted. "I know what is best for us. I know what is safe. And it is too dangerous to stay anywhere near your mother when she is acting like this…when…when she looks the way she does."

Ariyana's own anger flared. *When she was acting like this? Like she was having some childish temper tantrum? This wasn't going to change. He wasn't going to see her as anything other than an inconvenience in their life…a stain on the canvas of their picturesque family.*

She felt a gentle tug across her thoughts and recognized the warmth of her children's emotions. They had sensed her and were offering her comfort. Ariyana took a deep breath, relaxed her muscles, and let her children's comforting emotions wrap around her like a protective cloak. She raised her chin, shook her wings out to settle her feathers, and walked the rest of the way down the tunnel and into the chamber. Alec and Kai were facing the entrance and greeted her with a warm smile.

Devyn whipped around like a mouse that just realized that the hawk had cornered it, and though he reeked of fear and anger, his face was etched with scorn. "Why do you still look like that?" he snapped. "You shouldn't be here looking like that. You'll frighten the boys."

Ariyana didn't need to lean to the side to peer around Devyn to see them, but she made a show of it anyway. She swallowed the sharp inhale of breath that hitched in her throat. Though she saw no fear on their faces, she saw the changes that were obvious when she heard their voices.

Neither of her sons looked like little kids anymore. They looked closer to eleven or thirteen, both taller and more muscular than before she'd left. Alec's brown hair was streaked with silver and Kai's blond curls were tipped in silver. They both also had light silver swirls showing under the skin on their faces, chest, and arms. She controlled her expression so that Devyn would not see her surprise. "There isn't any fear in their eyes," she stated.

Devyn's head whipped around to look at them and then back at her. His eyes narrowed. "Why can't you just go back to the way you were?" he snarled.

"Trapped…inside my own mind, behind a haze of poison? Alone? In a crowd of people that didn't want me to be who I really was?" Ariyana snapped. "How could you expect me to go back to that?"

"So then you'll tear everything that I know and love away from me?" Devyn's eyes glistened and his hands shook. "You'll abandon me like I'm nothing?"

"The way that I am does not mean that I am abandoning you, Devyn." Ariyana softened her tone. "My dream meant that there was more inside of me than I could have possibly imagined, but it never meant that you didn't also have a place inside my soul." She took a tentative step toward him.

Devyn didn't step back. He held her gaze, his eyes pleading with her. She slowly closed the distance between them. She stopped a couple of feet in front of him. He studied her face, emotions warring across his features. Ariyana held still, careful not to lose the momentary calm between them. "If this is your life now, you do not need me," he said, finally speaking, some type of clarity showing through.

She hated that this was what he felt, but she had longed to hear him say the words. His anger came from fear, and he was finally voicing that fear. Ariyana reached out to touch his forearm but accidentally laid her hand on the injury that she had given him, the bite mark from days ago—at least she thought it was days ago. He flinched, and the emotion that he showed a moment ago was nothing more than a shadow that vanished in the glare of his anger. He shoved her away with such force that she tripped over her tail and landed ungracefully on the ground.

"Mom!" Alec and Kai called out, running over to her.

Devyn glared down at her. "Why couldn't you have been the sweet girl that you appeared to be? Why did you lie to me about what was really wrong with you?" He swept his hands wildly out to his sides. "Why couldn't you just take the pills so that we could be happy?" He spit each question at her like a snake spitting venom. The boys helped her to her feet, and she caressed each of their cheeks at the same time. "And you've poisoned them on top of it!" he exclaimed.

Ariyana glanced up at him and sighed. "I don't think that you really want to talk about poisoning people right now." She felt a warm ripple across her thoughts. *Her boys.* She looked down into their pleading eyes and understood that they were urging her to give him some space. *They were right. This wasn't going to get any better, and he clearly needed more time to process what was going on without her confusing matters for him.*

She gave them a weak smile and looked back at him. "I couldn't share what I didn't know, and a life built on lies isn't fulfilling to anyone. I never meant to cause you pain." She placed her hand over her hearts. "I love you, Devyn. I always have, and I always will. I hope that someday you'll see that too… no matter what I look like or what I dream about." She squeezed her children's shoulders. "I think that it would be best if I give you guys some more time to talk on your own. I can come back after sundown. Devyn, this isn't the best time, but before I go, have you remembered anything about how you arrived on Ora with Lexa?"

"I told you already; I don't remember," he said, glaring at her. "There was an explosion on Earth, and then I woke up on that planet with all those creatures. That's it."

She gave him a small smile and nodded. Then, she turned and walked out of the chamber. Each step tore at Ariyana's hearts. Each step tore at her resolve. *For so long, she had wanted to be what he wanted, but at what cost…her health? Her sanity? She couldn't lie anymore to make him happy. He had to find that himself.*

She wiped at her eyes as she came around a bend in the tunnel and almost collided into Rillac. Ariyana's wings flared out for balance as she abruptly stopped in front of Rillac's domineering form. "Shit!" she shouted. "What are you doing? You scared the crap out of me."

Rillac stared down at her, scales rippling, inky eyes swallowing her up. *So brave to save him, but gratitude will never come. He bonded with you believing you were worth fighting for. Now he wishes you dead.*

Ariyana's mind quickly became overwhelmed with echo over echo over echo of different voices all saying the same thing at the same time. "Go to hell," she hissed, trying to get around him.

Rillac's torso moved in a serpentine motion, swaying in front of her. *Hell? This is unknown.* Rillac's body hummed with interest. *Why are you desperate for his understanding?*

Frustration spiked in her chest, and she narrowed her eyes. "*There is no desperation.*"

Rillac leaned down until his Doberman-like snout was next to her ear. *You shimmer with desperation.* He nuzzled through the long feathers around her ear and then pulled back slightly. All she could see was her own reflection staring back at her in the mask of gold scales around Rillac's eyes. The air felt thick with the scent of salt and clay.

Ariyana pulled her head away and stepped back, sneering. "Tell me, Rillac, do you feed on pain and anger and heartbreak? Is that why you've come? To satiate your need?"

Only came to offer praise. Rillac's tone was matter-of-fact. *You saved your companions. You defeated Driviks. You survived their venom. Only praise.* Rillac's head inclined slightly. *Brave, though most companions have not forgiven you.* Another head nod, this one toward Devyn's chamber. *Others do not accept you.*

"Good talk," she said curtly. "Thanks for the praise." Ariyana moved to get around again. "If you'll excuse me, I need a break from all this praising." Rillac's arm shot out, and she stopped abruptly.

How was Kylor defeated? Rillac's tone was neutral, but the space between them became colder.

She watched Rillac's body language carefully. "I didn't defeat him. He let me take them."

Kylor beat you. He nearly killed you on that planet he found you on.

She didn't appreciate Rillac's bluntness or the disregard for her emotions that were tied to the experience. "Yeah, I remember," Ariyana snapped. "I don't get it either."

He let you leave?

"I told you, yes," she snapped again. The line of questioning was wearing on her nerves, especially considering that she still felt raw from her short conversation with Devyn.

Rillac glanced in the direction of Devyn's chamber. *Devyn is important. Why?*

Ariyana wasn't sure what Rillac was looking for. "Why is anyone important to someone else? They create something together…; they struggle together. It is no different for Devyn and me."

It is different. The scales rippled around Rillac's eyes, the golden scales reflecting the black vastness of his eyes for a moment before glimmering pure gold again. It gave the illusion of a darkening mood washing over Rillac's features. The effect chilled Ariyana. *Your bonding to him created younglings. This is his importance?*

"We created a family, yes, if that is what you are asking," she said. She had a nagging feeling that she needed to be careful about what she said to Rillac, so she kept her response short and vague. Rillac considered her for a moment, glancing from her to Devyn's chamber. She felt a strange warmth caress her body. It took her a moment to realize that it was coming from Rillac. She arched a brow, considering the sensation.

Rillac reached out to the side of Ariyana's face, and she flinched. He paused, showing that even though her flinch was subtle, it was noticed. *Why do you recoil?* Rillac asked, confusion filling the space between them.

The warmth that caressed her now had ribbons of emotion flowing through it that Ariyana could only describe as…hurt. *Oddly enough, it truly felt like she had hurt Rillac's feelings.* She felt a pang of guilt. She couldn't stop the feeling from building inside of her. The desire to please others was second nature to her and failing that made her feel guilty.

She had spent her whole childhood trying to please her family, to show them that she could be a normal child, and every time that she failed and her dream consumed her, she felt guilty over failing. Ariyana had tried to please Devyn, too, by being the wife that he wanted her to be, by taking the medicine that he wanted her to take, and by pretending that her nightmare, as he made her believe that her dream was, didn't control her night after night. But she had come to the end of her rope the morning that they fought, and her whole life had upended. She finally decided that she couldn't spend her life pleasing others without thought for herself. She needed to come first too, sometimes, and it wasn't her job to make everyone else happy. Unfortunately, though, it would take her a while to unlearn feeling guilty even if she knew why she was feeling the emotion.

She rolled her shoulders and shook her wings slightly to ease the tension in her muscles. Her reaction was justified and clearly Rillac needed to be reminded of that. "The last time that you touched me, you threw me out of the flight chamber to fall to my death," she scoffed.

A necessary challenge to test your true strength. There were no emotions in the words as they drifted through her thoughts. *You achieved self-realization without all the drama of your emotions.*

She lifted her tail, swayed it back and forth and leaned back, putting more distance between them without taking a physical step backward. "You mean you cut through the bullshit? Is that it?" she stated, her tail flicking as her agitation grew.

That does not translate.

"You can't solve every problem by cutting the emotion out of it, Rillac. I have a lot to learn, a lot to understand, and a lot to remember, and we're not going to get me there by throwing me out of the flight chamber each time. Feeling the emotions that come with everything is a part of that process…an important part."

That is not the Torin way. Rillac stated, staring at her.

She stared back and shook her head. "Is that your form of an apology?"

What is apology?

"You agree that you were wrong and say that you are sorry."

Weak. Like the Aryllyn language, there are no words for "apology" or "sorry" in the Torin language. Rillac's tone was condescending as the English words were imitated in her mind. *The results of our people cannot be argued with.*

Ariyana studied the expressionless eyes that stared back at her. It was wrong of her to expect Rillac to behave like a human, just as it was wrong for him to expect her to behave like a Torin. They were different species that would behave as their cultures had taught them to. Maybe that's where her discomfort was coming from as well, from the fact that she didn't understand.

She ran her tongue across her sharp teeth and sighed. Ariyana laid her tail down on the ground and leaned forward on the balls of her feet, closing the distance that she had put between them. "I think that we both have a lot to learn from each other. I can't expect you to behave like a human like me, just as you can't expect me to behave like a Torin. We will have to work on finding a common ground." Rillac reached out again. She schooled her features as Rillac ran a black claw through the feathers around her ear.

Agreed, though you are not human.

The words hit her like a slap across the face. *Rillac was right.* At her core, she still identified as human, though her body told a different story. She wondered what she truly believed about herself. *She had a lot to unpack, and if she'd been on Earth now, she would have been in desperate need of talking to a therapist. But considering where she was, it appeared that she would have to take that journey on her own.* She wondered if her personality or beliefs would change as she remembered more about the past.

Rillac made a strange noise, bringing her thoughts back to the moment. She hoped that she had kept those musings to herself and had not opened up a one-sided dialogue in Rillac's mind.

Rillac ran his claws musingly through her silver hair, letting the strands fall away slowly as his hand moved.

You are whole now, and that is cause for celebration. Rillac lowered his hand and moved to the side so that she could pass if she wanted to. *It is time to return to Tor.*

Chapter 52

"Tor?" Ariyana exclaimed. "Why would we go to Tor? I just got back from Ora with Lexa and Devyn. I haven't fully healed yet, and Devyn is in no state to travel to a different planet. He's barely dealing with his journey from Earth to Ora, let alone his most recent trip from Ora to here. He's on the verge of a breakdown." She shook her head violently back and forth. "No, not now. We need to let everyone settle in before we suggest another trip. And anyway, I was just checking on my family. Vayle has already stated that our next focus needs to be on how Kylor has managed to get on and off of Ora. Neither Devyn nor Lexa seems to remember. I agree with her on that. I think that celebrating now would be premature."

Rillac stepped forward and moved in front of her again, his fathomless eyes locking on hers.

She didn't have the strength to argue with Rillac, just as she didn't have the strength to argue with Devyn anymore today. Her limbs felt heavy, making it feel impossible to hold her wings up any longer. She hated the idea of not settling her argument with Devyn, but she was no good to him or her children if she didn't get some rest and allow her body to heal. She tried to convince herself that she only needed an hour or two, and she'd feel like a different person, but the look that Rillac leveled on her told her that she wouldn't get the chance to find out.

The scales on Rillac's body rippled in small waves from face to feet, their iridescence catching the light from her silver flame. *Agree.* His tone was cool. *Vayle is desperate to catch the traitor among her people. The urgency is clear.* Rillac lowered his head down so that his eyes were level with her eyes. *The Draxins are here…the Aryllyns are here…to see truth. But Torins are on Tor. Torins cannot see truth in your completeness. Only on Tor will Torins see. Vayle's urgency is clear, but Vayle's urgency needs allies if a traitor hides among her people.*

"So what are you saying?" Ariyana asked. "Torins won't help the Draxins unless I prove the truth of my completeness? Isn't discovering the traitor more important? What if it's one of her most trusted people? We could be wasting precious time by going back and forth."

Energy burst out of Rillac's body for the briefest of moments, making it seem like it was exuding nothing but fire. As quickly as Ariyana sensed it, though, it was gone. There was no longer any movement in the scales, they had stopped in mid-ripple, leaving the scales along his flank standing on end and giving Rillac the appearance of being covered in spikes.

Then, Rillac's energy changed again. It rolled off in warm waves, caressing her exposed skin. It felt purposeful, triggering Ariyana's instincts. She stood completely still and kept her mouth shut as if she was standing in front of a dangerous predator.

The energy that I felt a moment ago, the wave of fire, felt more natural than the energy that Rillac's releasing now, she thought to herself.

So far, Rillac had been strategic in the energy that was released. She didn't trust it. She had already learned her lesson with Rillac. She had not learned how to master her control over how each individual's energy affected her. She knew that he would use anything that she did or said against her. So, she just watched.

After a few moments, Rillac rose back up on both hind legs and walled off all emotions. *You are correct. There is an urgency to talk to Vayle and give you time to heal. The time to do both has come.* Rillac glanced in the direction of the chamber that Devyn was in as if he could look through the tunnel wall. *What does your companion remember of his arrival on Ora?*

She found it strange that Rillac kept looking toward Devyn's chamber. When she combined that with the abrupt wall that she now felt and the repetitive inquiries for information that had already been given, it made her feel even more uneasy.

Out of all of the companions that Ariyana had discovered that she'd had, her connection to Rillac felt unnatural and cold. She and Idrin clearly had a "difficult" relationship, considering how it ended, but she felt the connection between them like it was truly a part of herself—losing it would do harm to the rhythm of her ryn.

Rillac was different, though. She only felt the energy or emotions that were allowed to flow between them, and so far, they only made her feel uncomfortable and exposed. It felt like Rillac was using certain waves of energy and bursts of emotions to manipulate her.

Ariyana wondered if her instincts were leading her in the correct direction or if she was being too paranoid. She didn't fully understand the Torin way, and that lack of knowledge could lead to a misunderstanding between them. Both Vayle and Idrin trusted Rillac with their lives and the lives of their people, and that trust came from the countless years that they had spent together.

Ariyana gave her head a small shake, struggling with her inner turmoil. She owed Vayle for everything that Vayle had done so far, and she owed Idrin, though he made it hard for her to feel that way with all the attitude that he was always giving her.

But, even with all that attitude and the memory of him stabbing her, she was still giving Idrin a chance. In truth, she was giving herself a chance…a chance to remember and an opportunity to figure out where she fit into all this. Hell, she'd fought multiple Drivik to save Kylor, just days, at least she thought it was only days, after he'd beaten and nearly killed her on Earth.

If she was honest with herself, she felt strange with them too, but she was still trying. *Maybe I need to spend some time getting to know Rillac and the Torin people. Maybe that would chase away the strange feeling that I have when I'm around Rillac,* she thought to herself. It would be hard to push her uncertainties to the side, but it was worth it so that they could give their companionship a chance. A small smile spread across her lips. *What harm was there in trying?*

"He didn't remember anything on Ora, and he seems more focused on my appearance and disloyalty than trying to remember anything," she said.

Rillac inclined his head. *It is time to consult with Vayle.* He held two arms out in the direction of the egg chamber. *Come.* Rillac stepped aside yet again and waved her toward the egg chamber.

She shook her wings, easing the built-up tension in her back muscles, and walked forward. Rillac stepped forward as well, keeping pace next to her.

She glanced up and wondered about Rillac's peripheral vision. Rillac's eyes were too black for Ariyana to tell what they were pointed toward.

She glanced down at Rillac's side. The silence between them was becoming awkward.

She watched the scales move with each step. The tiny ripples of each scale looked like rhythmic waves. It was mesmerizing. Without thought, she reached out and touched one of the scales. Rillac's muscles tensed, and the scales around the scale that she'd touched spiked straight out. She jerked her hand away, and his head whipped in her direction.

Ariyana stepped away and rubbed her fingers together—they felt cold and tingly where she'd touched the scale. She didn't understand what just happened. It didn't seem likely that she had hurt Rillac, though the instant recoil away from her made it seem like she had.

She had attacked Rillac after she was thrown out of the flight chamber. Could Rillac be reacting to her based on their previous altercation? It didn't fit the persona that Rillac had presented to her so far. "Did I hurt you?" she asked, looking up apologetically.

Rillac's upper shoulders rolled. He shook his torso slightly, settling the scales smoothly back in place. *Unexpected.* The word was clipped in her mind as if Rillac was still trying to piece together what to say. *It has been many solar cycles. It is unfamiliar.*

"I will ask next time," Ariyana said.

Unnecessary. Time will bring familiarity.

Rillac's tone was neutral; there was no warmth behind what was said. Rillac stepped closer to her and stood as if each scale was now ready for her appraisal. When she didn't move, Rillac nodded once at her, indicating that she could touch the scales again. She didn't want to cause any offense, so she reached out and ran a hand along them.

They were cool and smooth, reminding her of snake skin. As her hand moved, each scale reacted to her touch, rippling under her hand and moving it along the body. As her hand moved, the scales seemed to warm, and a calming sensation flitted over her thoughts. She took her hand away and looked up. Rillac was watching her with a strange intensity.

She cleared her throat. "I remembered something earlier about arriving on your planet. I think that it was the first time that we...," she paused, feeling a stab of pain over the memory. She had met Rillac with Vayle, not Glacin, and the pain of losing him was stronger in that memory. She cleared her throat again and continued, "I think that it was the first time that we met you." She flashed a quick smile. "In that memory, you stood out among your people. I don't remember anyone looking like you do—all black scales except for the golden band across your eyes. I've noticed small changes in your coloration as your scales move. Can you control it, or are Torins born with specific colorations?"

Each Torin is unique, the leader standing out among the rest. Rillac's head raised and nodded toward the tunnel. A clear indication that they needed to keep moving.

Rillac turned and headed down the tunnel, not waiting for her. It wasn't lost on her that Rillac didn't answer her question. She peered down at the hand that she had touched Rillac with and rubbed the tips of her fingers together again. They still felt strange and cold, like she had tapped into something that she wasn't supposed to feel. She didn't understand.

She shook her wings again and followed.

Chapter 53

"Ari!" Lexa yelled and jumped up to hug Ariyana.

Ariyana caught her friend and hugged her, burying her face in Lexa's hair. She drew in a deep breath, letting Lexa's citrus and cloves scent fill her nose. It felt calming, and she wished that she could stay like this with her friend forever.

Lexa laughed, pulling her out of her thoughts. "It's so weird hugging you with these huge wings, not to mention that you're much taller than me now." Ariyana set her down. Lexa reached out for one of Ariyana's wings, and Ariyana extended it toward her. Lexa ran her hand along the long, silver feathers and curled her fingers in the silver flame. "It's wild that the flame doesn't burn me, but it's even wilder that when I touch it, I can feel you…the real you, Ari. It's incredible."

Ariyana smiled and leaned down to hug her again. She wrapped both her arms and both wings around Lexa. "I'm happy that you're here."

They drew away from each other, and Lexa looked back at Vayle. Ariyana looked back as well and was happy to see that her companion was standing up strong and sturdy, her body no longer showing any signs of injury or pain.

Lexa glanced back at Ariyana. Her eyes glistened with the threat of tears. "I didn't want to overwhelm you before, but it's scary how close we got to losing you. Idrin said that you killed a bunch of Drivik but that one of them bit you. Vayle thinks that your strength combined with the help of the Lielycet is what helped you. Do you know if anyone else was bitten? Was it just you?" she asked. She picked at her cuticles, clearly avoiding eye contact with Ariyana.

Ariyana remembered Lexa screaming out for Kress when the Drivik charged toward them, and the way that Lexa's eyes begged her to save them before she jumped. She wondered what had happened on Ora before Ariyana had arrived because even though Lexa had threatened Kress before they left, she seemed awfully concerned about his well-being.

Ariyana gave her a soft, comforting smile. "I was the only one. The others were fine when Idrin brought me back here."

Lexa's shoulders relaxed, and, finally looking up at Ariyana, she smiled.

Ariyana studied her friend and thought about all of the Lielycet that had died to save her. Then, she remembered the argument that she and Vayle had had while she was trying to heal. It dawned on her that she wasn't sure of the specifics. "I feel very lucky that the Lielycet knew what to do even though Drivik venom is foreign to them," she said. "Do you know what happened?" Lexa looked deep into Ariyana's eyes, and for the first time, Ariyana saw that Lexa was hesitant to answer her. "What's wrong?" Ariyana asked her.

"I guess I'm not sure how to describe how it's possible, but I can hear them…all of them. The Lielycet. I heard them as soon as Idrin removed his hold over me, and I can hear all of them now." She peered over Ariyana's shoulder to the area where the pool of Lielycet had been. Ariyana turned and looked at it too. It was empty now except for a thin layer of what appeared to be moist, dark ash.

"When Idrin brought you back, I felt a rush of panic. My mind raced trying to come up with a plan to help you," Lexa continued, looking back at her. "It was when Idrin and Vayle were arguing that I heard the Lielycets in my thoughts. They said that they would help. I don't know if I asked or if I demanded, but, looking back, I feel like I just expected them to help you, and they did, without any hesitation. I'm struggling, Ari, because I feel like I forced them to do it even when I felt the truth that those that helped were going to die. I'm not saying that I think that I have control over them, but what if I somehow made them think that they had to? And what kind of person am I, if I did?" she asked, her eyes shiny with unshed tears.

Ariyana grabbed her hand and squeezed it. "There are a lot of changes that are taking place, but I don't believe for one moment that that means the core of who you are is changing. If it were, you wouldn't look back on their loss as a sacrifice that needed to be honored; you'd look back on it as cold and necessary. I'm grateful for what the Lielycet did, and I am grateful for your new ability to communicate with them." Ariyana hugged her again and looked her square in the eyes. "What do we always say to each other? 'We'll figure this out together.'"

This time, Lexa smiled back.

Vayle shifted behind her, and Lexa's expression quickly changed; she glanced self-consciously to the side.

Ariyana stepped around her, giving her shoulder a gentle squeeze as she went by.

Vayle's wings were relaxed and tucked in against her sides. Her flame burned gently through her feathers. Warmth and connection washed over Ariyana as she approached Vayle.

"I spoke to Devyn," Ariyana said. "He hasn't remembered anything new about how he arrived on Ora."

Vayle lay her head down, and Ariyana ran her hand along the burning feathers of her eye ridge. Vayle closed her eye and leaned into the touch. Ariyana's silver flame swirled around Vayle's red flame, creating little tornados as her hand moved.

Your features are strained. The conversation has drained the strength of your energy. Vayle's voice was a soothing balm through her mind.

"Devyn needs time and a little space. We can give him that while we figure this out," Ariyana said. Vayle nudged her with her head, a gesture of affection, and Ariyana ran her hand along her eye ridge again.

Rillac stepped toward them, and the sound of talons scraping along the rock floor filled the chamber. Vayle opened her eyes and Ariyana turned around. It was clear that Rillac wanted their attention.

What is the next step? The human companions are of no help to discover the truth. Is there a plan? Rillac asked.

Lexa sneered, though Rillac missed the expression because his back was toward her. Ariyana hid a small smile.

I understand your desire to bring Ari back to Tor so that she can connect with your people again. Vayle's tone was even. *I long for the same thing.* She continued, *It must be safe for all of us, though, and right now we are exposed and vulnerable. Someone is helping Kylor move through the energy realm. Among our combined people, only the Draxins have displayed that ability. I have been searching through Lexa's and Devyn's memories for familiar energies but have felt none. Arc sent his senses out while on Ora and also felt nothing familiar. That tells me that we are either dealing with an unfamiliar species or that someone within our people has found a way to mask their energy, tamp it down, or hide it completely. We must strengthen the bond between Ari's core companions, her Nexus.* She lifted her head up high. *We must strengthen the bond between each of us so that we might find the one helping him. Only then can we find our way back to the paths laid out before us.*

"Is it possible to change or hide your energy?" Lexa asked.

Idrin walked up next to her. "We are not sure what is possible now. There was a time that I would have said no, but Arc and I barely felt Ora's inner energy while we were there, whereas Ari felt it strongly and clearly."

"How is that possible?" Lexa's eyebrows were pinched together.

"She is stronger and more intensely connected to all energy, but the fact that she could feel it and we barely could means that someone has found a way to mute it. And if they are muting the energy of an entire planet to cover up their presence, we are dealing with a very dangerous individual."

"Why do you think that that makes them dangerous?" Ariyana asked.

An energy presence is a precious thing. It burns as brightly as the stars, though you cannot see it with your eyes, you feel it with your ryn. Could you imagine trying to mute the light of a star? Or changing its color to hide within it? Or altering the wavelength of the energy it emits to mask its very presence? Neither can I, Vayle said. Ariyana didn't realize that she was shaking her head until Vayle said that. *We are dealing with someone I do not believe we have encountered. I believe that if we strengthen our bond, we can figure out who it is and how to defeat them.*

Ariyana peered up at Vayle and put her hand on her neck. "How do we strengthen our bond? Will that also include Devyn?" Ariyana asked.

Yes. The three of you were on Earth together at the same time when this individual would have arrived. I believe that if I can connect with the three of you while you remember your last moments on Earth, I might be able to sense something that can help us.

"Lexa!" Alec and Kai called out, running into the egg chamber.

The abrupt, unexpected intrusion made Ariyana think that something had happened. She whirled around. "Where's your father?" she demanded. "Did something happen?"

They looked at her, their eyes wide with surprise. "No, nothing happened," Alec said.

"Dad wanted to rest," Kai added.

"So, since you were feeling better, we wanted to find Lexa and show her our favorite eggs," Alec said.

"Are we in trouble for coming in here?" Kai asked.

"No, of course not," Ariyana tried to backtrack her panic. "You guys just scared me."

The boys looked at each other, back at Ariyana, and at each other again. Her response seemed to mollify them because they each grabbed one of Lexa's hands and dragged her over to the clutch, excitedly pointing at their favorite eggs.

Idrin walked up closer to Ariyana. "It would be good to add the young to your plan. Their memories could help as well," he said.

Vayle's head shifted up slightly, her version of a nod. Vayle's presence drifted over Ariyana's mind, like she was about to add something to their conversation, but then Ariyana's throat began to burn.

Ariyana heard Vayle roar and Idrin yell "No!" The egg chamber faded away, and Rillac's face consumed her mind.

Confusion filled her thoughts.

Rillac had ahold of her throat.

No, not hers. The edges of her vision were blurry, and it felt like she was peering through a window. She clearly saw Rillac's face and felt a burning sensation in her throat, but her body's sensations didn't match the movement that she saw happening.

There was struggling, and then an arm with a healing bite mark flew toward Rillac's face. It was stopped well before it made contact and was held in front of wide eyes. Devyn's eyes…Devyn's eyes that showed her everything.

Tor. Rillac stated the word clearly, without emotion. Was Rillac projecting the word into Devyn's mind or her own?

"What is a 'Tor?'" Devyn's voice was a harsh whisper. He clearly had one of Rillac's clawed hands wrapped around his throat.

Rillac's head tilted to the side, and a black claw ran down Devyn's forehead, lightly over his quickly closed eye, and down his cheek. Ariyana could feel everything through her connection with Devyn. As Rillac moved the black claw, the smaller, curved, white claw scraped over Devyn's other cheek. Rillac stopped when the claws reached Devyn's jawline. Rillac scraped the white claw back and forth along the soft flesh under his chin.

Tor is the next step. Must come. Only Vayle may join you. Other companions and younglings must stay on Draca. Expect your swift arrival.

Rillac pressed the white claw into Devyn's throat. Both Devyn and Ariyana screamed.

Rillac's face vanished, and Vayle's head appeared over her.

"-uck is Rillac?" Lexa's voice demanded.

"Rillac took… Devyn…" Ariyana forced the words out between gasps of breath, "…to Tor." She felt exhausted and winded.

She was lying on her back, her head in Idrin's lap. Lexa was kneeling by her side, one of her hands secured tightly in her grasp. Alec and Kai were peeking over Lexa's shoulders, their foreheads furrowed in concern. Vayle's head was hovering over Ariyana's body, looking down at her.

Ariyana attempted to sit up, but her core muscles refused to work correctly. She groaned.

"You mean that Rillac and Devyn were *taken* to Tor by the traitor that is helping Kylor?" Idrin demanded. "Rillac cannot take Devyn any-where without help, and there is nowhere on Draca that one can hide. Tell us, what did you see when the images flashed through your mind? You must have seen some hint of the individual that has betrayed us? Better yet, what did you feel?"

"I only saw Rillac's face. I saw no other. I felt no other." Ariyana urged them. "We need to leave. We need to get to Tor."

Idrin pushed Ariyana's upper body into a sitting position. The forced movement seemed to remind her muscles how to work again, or, better yet, seemed to remind her mind how her body worked.

"Impossible!" he exclaimed, rising to his feet. "I will not dismiss innumerable cycles of our alliance because you are too weak to correctly interpret a vision that you just saw. Rillac was protecting Devyn for you, prioritizing your companion over safety, while you are too blinded by your time away to see the truth."

Ariyana shot to her feet. The chamber spun, but Lexa was next to her instantly, holding her up by grasping her hand, creating the pillar of strength that she needed to right her world again. Clearly, her body wasn't all the way better yet.

She squeezed Lexa's hand and glared at Idrin. "Rillac pierced Devyn's skin with that damn white claw, delivering a dose of toxin into his system that made him pass out. I sa..." she paused, realizing that, *no, she didn't see it*, "I felt it! I felt Rillac do it."

"Proves nothing," Idrin hissed. "That is the easiest way to phase with an unwilling passenger. Every Draxin and Aryllyn knows that. Again, Rillac did it to ensure that your companion was not harmed."

Exasperated, Ariyana turned to look at Lexa and Vayle. They were both studying her. Lexa's eyes bounced back and forth between her eyes. *What was she looking for?* "I hope that you're right," she said finally. "I hope that I am misinterpreting what I saw. I'm pretty sure that none of us wants to lose anyone else." She added the last statement with a bite in her tone. She wanted to get some distance between herself and the group, a chance to think, but Arc burst into the chamber.

Vayle snarled, and Idrin yelled, "Impossible!"

Ariyana knew that Arc had confirmed what she had already accepted: neither Rillac nor Devyn was on Draca. Ariyana thought about what she saw through Devyn's eyes. She heard Rillac's voice again: *Tor is the next step. Must come. Only Vayle may join you. Other companions and younglings must stay on Draca. Expect your swift arrival.*

"It's confirmed then," Ariyana stated, and everyone turned to her again. "I heard Rillac speak when I saw through Devyn's eyes. That's why I initially told all of you that Rillac took him to Tor. Rillac said that the next step was to go to Tor, but it was clearly stated that only Vayle and I could go."

This new detail did not go over well, as the entire group erupted into protest.

"A lie!" Idrin growled. "You are angry because we do not agree. We never agree, Ari," he dragged out the sound of her name as though it disgusted him, "Why should now be any different. You have no say over whether or not I may go to Tor."

"Please do not do this without us," Lexa pleaded, placing her hand on Ariyana's forearm. She was noticeably trying to take a calmer approach. "We'd be stronger together, more capable of fighting whatever lies in wait on that planet."

"My argument to go has nothing to do with you, Human," snapped Idrin. "I do not need more weakness at my side during a battle."

"Excuse me?! Don't species shame me!" Lexa was in Idrin's face, on her tiptoes, pulling on his armor around his neck to drag his head down close to hers. "You haven't seen me fight to judge me, you worthless piece of crap!"

He bared his sharp teeth and hissed at her.

Alec and Kai, not wanting to be anywhere near the fight that was about to break out, ran over to the clutch and sat down by their favorite eggs.

"We don't have a choice," Ariyana cut in. "Vayle and I must go alone."

Idrin's head whipped toward her, and he shoved Lexa away. Lexa's body tensed, ready to hit him, but Ariyana shot her a look that made her clench her fists at her sides and step back…for now.

"Unacceptable!" he growled, his right hand slashed angrily through the air in front of him. "You don't know what you'll be flying into."

"We'll have each other!" Ariyana motioned between herself and Vayle.

"It is not worth the risk."

"So, we leave Devyn there?" Ariyana demanded, disbelief making her voice crack. "What if this traitor, so to speak, decides that Devyn should not live? Do we just leave him to his fate? Maybe it is time for you to accept that this could be the fastest way to find out what really happened with this whole situation: Kylor showing up on Earth, torturing me, joining me with my essence, reigniting my companionships, Devyn and Lexa being taken to Ora, rescuing them, and now Vayle and I ending up on Tor. This has to be part of a bigger picture—one that we've been questioning since we found each other again. It's time to end this…time to figure out who's been working with Kylor, and now…," she paused, knowing that she had to be careful with her words, "… figuring out who took Rillac and Devyn."

"By charging in without support? Worse yet, you would be the only support that Vayle has to keep her safe. I am not willing to take that risk. You cannot control your body. You are overcome with others' emotions or memories. You are weak…*reckless*. You have already put Vayle in harm's way and almost gotten yourself killed."

Ariyana's blood felt like it was boiling. If she'd still had red blood, she was sure that her cheeks would have been flushed with crimson. "You refused to help me on Ora!" she snapped. "You refused to put yourself in harm's way for companions of mine that you did not know."

"And here you are again, asking her to do the same," he snarled, glaring at Ariyana.

Her wings flared out behind her. "What's the real problem here, Idrin? What is it about Devyn that you don't like? Cause it's clearly him who bothers you. Is it because I gave him children but not you in our past life together?" The words came out before she could stop them, and she immediately regretted them. She'd remembered a statement about her not wanting to have young, and she threw it in his face without thinking.

His half-moon pupils dilated to full moons, blackness consuming his eyes. He stomped toward her, hatred etched in his features and swirling around her in what felt like a torrent of wind.

Enough! Vayle exclaimed. *This gets us nowhere. This choice is mine. It is neither of yours. Ari, you cannot travel to Tor without my help. Idrin, Arc cannot leave Draca if I order him to stay. I agree that this is a trap of sorts, but I also agree that this unknown problem must be resolved. Ari and I will go to Tor alone. Arc, you will stay here with Idrin and guard both my clutch and Ari's human companions.*

"Vayle, you are making a mistake. I forbid you to force me to stay," Idrin stated through clenched teeth. His hands were balled into tight fists at his side.

She calmly angled her head toward him. *You have been adamant about our people following each other's rules and laws. I am the Queen of my people, and though Arc is your companion, he falls under my reign, not yours. If you can find a way to Tor without a Draxin, so be it. Until that moment, you will keep your 'forbids' to yourself and your people.*

Pale lavender blood dripped from his clenched fists, and his body shook from his tense muscles. Alec and Kai whispered something to each other, and Lexa glanced at her from the corner of her eye. The moment was a little too intense for everyone. Ariyana knew that Idrin's goal really was to keep Vayle safe, and she felt more regret over what she said to him. She also knew what it felt like to be pushed to the side when you wanted to help. She found it difficult to make eye contact with him.

Arc. Vayle called, and Arc took a few steps toward her. *You must guard the clutch and Ari's humans. I do not know what game is being played here, so we cannot take any chances. If we run into trouble, I expect you to gather our forces and come to my aid on Tor.* She looked back at Idrin. *I truly hope that you will also answer that call, though I will not demand it out of respect.*

Idrin gave her a tight nod and walked over to his companion.

Be on alert, all of you. Vayle continued. *We must expect the worst and be prepared for anything.*

Alec and Kai clasped their hands between them. An electric blue light radiated from their clasped hands, and they nodded respectfully.

Lexa watched them, glanced back at Ariyana, and gave her a small smile. "Go. We will take care of everything here. Clearly, we will be ready for anything," Lexa said.

Vayle nodded, ruffled her wings, and walked toward the tunnel opening without another word. Ariyana knew that it meant that she needed to follow. She squeezed Lexa's hand, kissed her children's cheeks, and walked over to Idrin. They stared at each other. After a few moments, he nodded and gestured at Vayle with his chin. She felt the need to touch him, to offer some apology for what she had said, but her body didn't move. She peered down at his hand and back up into his eyes. She returned his nod, ruffled her own wings, and turned to follow Vayle.

As she walked into the tunnel, she peered back into the egg chamber and tried to memorize the features of the faces of the people that she loved.

Ariyana made a silent vow to them that she would be back, that Devyn and Vayle would be safe, and that they would all be together again soon.

Chapter 54

Vayle watched her as she walked into the flight chamber.

We are both strong, Ari. We have healed. We will not fail at whatever is presented to us. If Kylor is responsible, we will listen to what he has to say. It is long overdue.

"His people are dying. Though he did not ask me for help on Ora that must be what he wants. If this is all his doing, how can we help him? Idrin is strict about the laws of his people. We can no more change his laws than he can change yours," Ariyana said.

I do not know. But we must first open the communication. We will figure it out from there.

Ariyana walked up to Vayle's side, nodding. Vayle leaned down and Ariyana pulled herself up on top of her shoulders. Vayle's red flame swirled through Ariyana's silver flame, like they were dancing together. Vayle's body temperature lowered slightly to match Ariyana's, and Ariyana released a breath that she didn't know that she was holding. Vayle's scent reminded her of roasted hazelnuts, sweet and fresh. She would describe it as "earthy" but knew that that didn't truly fit since Vayle was not from Earth. However it was described, it just made her feel at peace, like she was sitting where she belonged.

She ran her hands under the feathers of Vayle's neck. She couldn't help the uncertainty that was creeping into her thoughts. Her body felt healed, as did Vayle's, *but what did that mean about their minds?* She had felt broken on Earth, always pulled between the pain and loss that the night would bring and the order and calm that she needed to project around her family during the day. She had failed miserably there, and it felt worse being on Draca. She had discovered that her nightly dream was a recurring memory of losing her first companion, and now she was surrounded by a life with other companions that she hadn't known existed. If she could fully accept all that, it should be her true path forward. Unfortunately, knowledge only submerged her deeper into her pain and constantly reminded her of the companion she had lost. *How could she face the consequences of the life that she didn't remember? What if Idrin was right, and she fell short yet again?*

Vayle rumbled under her and shook her neck as if to ease the tension that was building there. She did not speak to Ariyana, but she projected the feeling back to her that she had felt just a moment ago, feeling at peace with her companion, feeling like she was where and with whom she belonged. Ariyana let the feeling flow through her and said, "You're right, whatever we face, we face together."

Agreed. Trust what I say and be ready to leave if we have to. No matter what. She waited for Ariyana to nod before she continued. *I will show you Tor. Lie down against my neck and hold the image in your mind. We will see it together.*

Ariyana nodded again and lay down along her neck.

A planet with a bright turquoise light filled her mind. She held onto the image but didn't force her way into it, remembering what happened last time. She squeezed her eyes shut. The air over her back and wings turned to ice. She heard a cracking, shattering noise, felt a pulsing energy across her skin, heard more cracking and shattering, and was finally surrounded by warm, moist air.

You may open your eyes.

Ariyana sat up and sucked in a breath. Warm ocean air and the sweet smell of vegetation filled her nostrils.

Tor.

The sun was low in the sky. The air was warm but held a cool promise of the night to come. There were two full moons already visible in the early evening sky; they were close to each other, positioned diagonally.

The sight was breathtaking in the aqua-colored sky. They had one moon on Earth, and though it was beautiful, it didn't have the same power and intrigue as the two moons on this planet. They had a few big impact craters on their surfaces, but not as many as Earth's moon, so they appeared to shine more brightly.

The moons rose in the sky like two lovers caught in the force of each other's bond to one another, an eternal dance of rising, falling, and rotating. *Beautiful.* She wished for a moment that she and Vayle could join that dance, that they could be two burning stars, dipping and turning in the force of their connection.

A splashing noise jerked Ariyana's attention away from the sky toward the vast ocean expanding out around them.

Vayle dove lower and ran the tips of her wing's longest feathers along the surface. She was agile in her flight and curved expertly around and over the waves, not getting splashed or allowing Ariyana to get wet.

Ariyana watched the undulating turquoise water and marveled at how the crests of the waves sparkled with iridescence.

The memory that she'd seen of her first time on Tor flashed through her mind. The ocean's rhythmic dance and sparkling turquoise water had reminded her then of Glacin's flame, just as it did in this moment. Ariyana didn't hold the memory back; she let it flow through her bond to Vayle.

Vayle's wing joints shifted slightly under Ariyana's legs; a small sigh, just like in Ariyana's memory.

Tor is not an easy place for you. It reminds you of loss and suffering, and that was before this strange incident with Rillac. As I said in that moment, I say now: though you walk a path that feels alone, you are not. We travel as one, one ryn, bonded companions that are stronger together than apart. I will let no harm come to you.

Ariyana lay along Vayle's neck and ran her hands under the feathers of her crest, placing them on top of the sensitive scales that were protected there.

"Things felt uncertain the first time we came here, but still hopeful. The energy feels different here somehow, and I fear that we must not let our guard down. Maybe Rillac just wanted us here as soon as possible, but my instincts tell me that I can't push aside the alarm bells that I have felt since I came back into your lives. I know that we will protect each other, no matter what happens on that island, but are we truly ready to face the possibility that Rillac…" she trailed off, unsure how to finish her thought. She pushed her face against the softness of Vayle's feathers and found her resolve. "We will figure it out together." Her words were strong, and there was no waver in her voice.

Vayle's throat rumbled in response.

Ariyana lifted herself back up into a sitting position just in time to see the white stone and sand of the island coming into view. Whether they were ready or not, it was time to find Rillac and face the unknown in the hope of discovering the truth.

Vayle landed in their usual spot as Ariyana remembered it: a wide, flat area of white rock at the cliff's edge that led to the center of what was a busy village.

But it wasn't busy. In fact, the water vegetation farms were not being tended to, and both full and empty baskets were strewn everywhere. Every Torin, except for one, seemed to be either gone completely or missing.

Vayle flapped her wings in agitation, as if she was trying to decide if she should take off again. Finally, she fell forward onto her arms, indicating that she had chosen to stay. But not without first slamming her tail down on the same fractured scar that she had left in the white stone on their first visit to Tor—her show of dominance on a planet that was not under her rule.

Ariyana leapt off Vayle's back, landing gracefully in front of Vayle's tail. She stood up slowly and flapped her wings a few times, letting the flames on her feathers grow until her wings seemed consumed by nothing but silver fire. *Neither of them would let anyone cow them.*

Rillac stood about fifty feet in front of her, at the mouth of the main path into the village. Devyn stood at the side, and Rillac's hand was gripping Devyn's shoulder. Ariyana couldn't see Rillac's claws digging into Devyn's shoulder, and from where she stood there were no obvious creases, no drops of blood, but Devyn's face was lined with strain from the effort to keep himself standing.

Vayle roared and threw her wings back in a wide flare, sending tendrils of flame into the air around her. *Explain! Now!*

Rillac didn't move, didn't speak.

Rillac's cold, unblinking eyes stared forward, devoid of emotion. Not even a single scale rippled across Rillac's body. Nothing happened. Until Devyn's left eye began to squint and the left side of his jaw began to clench tightly.

"This is wrong," Ariyana whispered, maybe to herself, maybe to Vayle, she wasn't sure.

Rillac! We are allies. Explain what is happening. Why do you hold one of your fellow companions against his will?

This elicited a deep growl from Rillac.

The feathers along Ariyana's spinal ridge rose, and her tail twitched, her long tail feathers flexing to sharp points. Her second skin, her thin silver armor, moved instinctively on its own, providing more protection over her vital organs. It also moved over her claws and talons, sharpening them further into lethal weapons.

It was the sound that hit her before the energy, but even then, it was too late. *The humming, the vibration, it was everywhere…*all around her.

She had whipped around to run to Vayle when the impact caught her in the chest and sent her skidding across the white rock toward the village. Her left wing caught between her and the ground and took the majority of the damage from the rough stone, but the pain barely registered as she jumped to her feet to charge back toward Vayle. Only there was no clear path back to her companion, because Vayle was now caught in an onslaught of dozens of Tethryn, all focused solely on bringing her down.

"Vayle!" Ariyana screamed. The sound erupted from her ryn as if her soul had been given the voice it needed to finally release its pain.

Vayle roared and reared up in response. The Tethryn slashed and bit at her, screeching and chittering loudly at each other. Vayle pivoted, crushing two by stepping on them; she kicked back, knocking over a few, and whirled, cutting those closest to her with her tail. The ones that she injured didn't move, but the others continued to advance.

"Fly!" Ariyana screamed, trying to encourage her companion to take her escape by diving off the cliff behind her. But in response, the sky shattered and exploded above her, and dozens of Tethryn dove toward Vayle's exposed back. As they fell, they sliced deep gashes into her scales and tore deep chunks of feathers from her body. They screeched and wailed as they touched her flame and burned alive, but their sacrifice left imperfections in her protections that allowed those that fell after them to cut her deeper and wound her further.

The air was thick with moisture and the scent of blood. The sounds of the Tethryn screeching and wailing and Vayle roaring and howling made it suffocating.

Vayle limped and slipped in her own blood as more Tethryn phased around her body. They sliced at her hind legs, her tail, her neck, and no matter how she defended herself, more came to fill in for the dead that piled around her.

Ariyana roared and jumped toward the closest Tethryn, claws extended, talons poised, but she was kicked in the stomach and sent skidding back across the white rock.

The wind was knocked out of her, but she rolled over, tearing at the ground to get back up, the need to save Vayle more important than air. She managed a half breath and sprinted forward on all fours this time, planning to pounce at the last minute, when something large drove down on her back between her shoulder blades, not only shoving her chest into the stone ground but her face as well. She choked on blood, bits of rock, and her own cries of pain as she tried to drag in a breath.

Something grabbed her by the throat, hauled her up, and slammed her down, not just once on her front, but twice, the second time on her back, her left wing breaking along what felt like her radius bone. She shrilled. Vayle's cries mixed with Ariyana's until it was impossible to distinguish which ones belonged to who.

Ariyana rolled slightly toward Vayle and blinked through the blood blurring her vision.

Vayle's flame was low. The Tethryn were on her still—tearing, biting, slicing, and pulling at the scales of her wings.

"No!" Ariyana begged, though the word was barely a whisper of sound on her lips between her gasps of breath.

Hold! Rillac's voice was abrasive against her thoughts but still brought relief as she saw that the Tethryn did as they were commanded and stopped tearing at Vayle's body. They still held her but they no longer moved. Vayle collapsed in her own blood and her eyes half closed from the pain and exhaustion. *She was still breathing, though. She was still alive*, and Ariyana would cling to that with all she had.

Ariyana gingerly rolled the rest of the way onto her side, and, clutching her injured wing to her left side, she pushed herself into a wobbly standing position, facing Rillac, who still held Devyn by the shoulder.

"Well, I guess that clears up the 'We're allies' crap, doesn't it?" Ariyana asked dryly.

Not an ally. Not a companion. Keep your offensive words to yourself, or the Tethryn will continue. Rillac answered coldly and in one tone. Ariyana hadn't noticed it before when Rillac commanded the Tethryn to stop, but the words were only spoken in Rillac's unique tone—harsh, unyielding, and abrasive.

"You did all that because Vayle said you were our ally and companion?" she scoffed.

Rillac tensed, Devyn hollered, and Vayle whimpered.

"Okay," Ariyana backtracked, hands up. "Trust me, I have no problem not calling you any of that."

Finally. Words of spoken truth from your mouth. Now we begin.

Chapter 55

Ariyana's hearts sank as she took stock of her surroundings, her broken body, Vayle's broken body, and Devyn's pain. They had probably only arrived about ten minutes earlier, and so much had happened to show them how vastly unprepared they were for any possibility, and even with all that damage inflicted and knowledge gained, Rillac only now thought that they were beginning. *Beginning what exactly?* The thought sent chills through her body.

She kept her eyes focused on Rillac, but sent her thoughts directly to Vayle.

How bad are your wounds?

*They have bitten to the bone on my right wing. If they sever it….*Vayle trailed off.

But Ariyana didn't need her to finish. She already knew what it meant for a Draxin to lose one or both of their wings. She would die. Draxins could withstand a lot, but losing a wing that was covered in burning feathers, a large portion of her ryn, was the equivalent of a human losing too much blood.

Ariyana flexed her back muscles and painfully adjusted her left wing. Her wing joints were still intact, and the humerus bone of both wings felt solid. She willed her silver armor along her left wing bones to solidify over the break, acting like a cast of sorts.

"Raesor is here?" Ariyana asked, glancing around the quiet paths of the village. She expected him to step out like some 'big super villain reveal' in a movie. But it didn't happen. Nothing moved.

No. Rillac's tone was neutral, though the voice in her thoughts was still abrasive.

"But you're working with him?" she asked.

Working with him? You speak strangely. Rillac's tone sounded annoyed. *No work is done for anyone unless it meets my needs.*

"I don't understand. I thought that the point was to stop them from destroying planets, not to join with them," she stated impatiently.

Not companions with Raesor. The scales around Rillac's eyes rippled, and Devyn groaned, the tension lines in his forehead deepening. *Your goals were never mine.*

"I speak strangely?" she yelled the question. "You always speak so cryptically. I don't freaking understand! Why ally with us if our goals didn't align? You could have just gone your own way."

Raesor is exceptionally powerful. He was searching for something. When a powerful creature searches for something, it is either necessary to possess the object or the power itself. Patience is a great tool when it comes to survival and the acquisition of power. Patience is my strength. Finding power is my talent. Rillac's scales rippled aggressively. *It took hundreds of cycles to figure out what he was looking for. Do you even know?*

Ariyana remembered her strange conversation with Raesor on the dying planet. He had clearly wanted to hurt her, told her that she would be judged, but more importantly than all that, he had made it clear that he was looking for *her. Her.* Not her allies, not the other creatures on the planets that he destroyed. *Just her.*

She chanced a sideways glance over at Vayle and quickly looked back at Rillac. "Me," she replied, her lip curled in a snarl.

Correct. No sense. You are weak, worthless, unable to adapt, and yet a creature as powerful as he sought you out. Understanding was necessary. Tests were arranged. Rillac visibly squeezed Devyn's shoulder, and Devyn cried out.

"Stop! Why are you doing that? Just let him go," she demanded.

Phasing is one of my talents, but my energy has limits. Rillac continued as if she hadn't spoken. *Everyone can be manipulated, even the powerful. Raesor lost many Tethryn each time he tried to face you. Many losses, many setbacks. Just look at the interaction you shared on the dying planet. Better plans lead to better outcomes. Test you. Injure those close to you. Break you down. When emotional and physical self are at their lowest—strike! You forced plan changes many times, but patience is my strength. It has been easy to weave my energy through each of yours for all these cycles. Easy to hide. Easy to watch. Easy to manipulate.*

Her chest felt tight, and the icy throb inside her threatened to shatter as her mind raced to understand everything that he was telling her. She couldn't keep up with the answers that were unraveling before her. "It was you," she stated. "You brought Kylor and Kress to Earth."

So simple. The energy burst you released made it easy to convince them to go. But a test was still required.

"That dead planet. You made me see it," she realized. "You forced me to focus on it. You wanted me to face him."

Wanted to see what would happen. Disappointing. You have so much strength behind you. Too much work left to be done. The hope was that the separation from your companions for so long would have weakened you, but they did not hesitate to protect you yet again. Needed to regress you back to where you were at your weakest. Again. Success would have been had if you hadn't slipped away before the time was right.

"Weakest?" The word came out as barely a whisper as the realization hit her. "You?" she hissed.

Vayle howled.

"You brought the Tethryn to Draca all those cycles ago. Glacin and Evix died because of you!" she yelled the words, wishing that they were knives that she could throw at Rillac instead.

Patience. Rillac said the word like it made sense of everything. *Death is a natural part of life and discovery.*

Vayle started to struggle.

There is no desire to kill the queen of the Draxins, as the Draxins will be essential in moving Tethryn throughout the universe over time, but other means will be discovered if necessary.

The threat was clear.

Ariyana closed her eyes and pleaded with Vayle to settle. She didn't have the words she needed to convey her fear and panic in this moment, so Ariyana sent the feelings themselves to her. Vayle was in no position to fight or protect herself. Ariyana was caught between a rock and a hard place, with Vayle being held by the Tethryn and Devyn being held by Rillac. She would lose one, if not both, of them if she made a move.

There was the solitude of the planet to consider as well.

They were alone on this island—alone in the sense that she couldn't feel beyond their collective energies. She felt Rillac and Devyn, Vayle and the Tethryn, and, of course, herself, but nothing beyond that. The ocean no longer undulated with its own current, and the vegetation no longer flourished. She was being cut off from all of it, and there was only one way that was possible.

Rillac.

They had suspected that someone was masking their energy signature or maybe hiding in plain sight. Turned out, it was both. Rillac was the traitor, strategically moving everyone around to fit his plan. How far did this go?

The ground no longer felt solid under her feet, the air no longer breathable. She was missing most of her memories from her past with the Draxins, Aryllyns, and Torins. Each moment was a struggle to maintain her grip on reality. *Only a couple of weeks ago—was it a couple of weeks? She wasn't even sure—she had been struggling with her dreams of Glacin on Earth and her relationship with her husband because of that dream. Then Kylor showed up and beat and nearly killed her, forcing her physical appearance to change as he "joined" her with her essence. This change brought flashes of memories and a past that she wasn't sure she wanted to accept. So much pain. So much loss. So much still unknown. And now she stood before Rillac, her supposed companion, who'd just decided to share that it was all a lie…a means to an end.*

How would she be able to figure out what was true and what was maneuvered by Rillac? Her hearts hammered in her chest, and she could hear Vayle's heart doing the same. She wanted to drop to her knees and hold her head in her hands, *but why? What would she gain from dropping down and letting Rillac see that she was defeated? Nothing!*

Even if she had remembered her entire past with Rillac, even if she had accepted it, this would still have thrown her. *She didn't remember trusting Rillac, but Vayle and Idrin did, not only with their lives, but their people's lives, and, in the end, it meant nothing to the Torin.*

All that death meant nothing to Rillac. She repeated the phrase to herself again—it was just a means to an end.

She listened to Vayle's ragged breathing and opened her eyes to stare straight into Rillac's.

"So, who's going to die, Rillac?" she asked, enjoying how annoyed she sounded. "That is the point, right? Someone has to die."

Rillac cocked his head to the side and considered her for a moment. The energy flowing around her felt amused.

A trade.

"What?" she blurted. It didn't make sense. After all the intricate things that Rillac had put into play—whispers in ears, testing her, killing those closest to her. How could it all come down to just a trade? What could Rillac possibly want?

You are weak without your companions. Rillac responded. *They are the pillars of your foundation. Without them, you are a wandering blight upon the universe. There is no use for power that cannot be obtained, controlled, or easily directed. There is no use for any of your companions on their own, except for the Draxins, who can phase. There is also no use for Raesor. He has no pillars and wanders in his own way. What Raesor does have, though, is knowledge. At first, it was believed that he had knowledge of unique power destinations, energy realm destinations. He obtained what he has from where he has been and what he has done. Just as it has been possible for me. The true, unique asset was seen after digging deeper into his mind: an energy unlike any other, located somewhere in the energy realm. It is necessary to obtain that location, but it cannot be taken; it has to be shown. An energy base like that will rival even his own…an energy base that I, and I alone, will build up on my own.* Rillac roughly pushed Devyn a few steps forward but still kept him tightly secured. *It is simple. Raesor says that he needs you. Devyn for you. No more fighting, no more talking, no more death. Devyn goes to Vayle. We go to Raesor. Done.*

"I don't understand what game you're playing at here?" She shook her head, glancing between Rillac and Devyn. "Why even do all of this? Why throw me out of the flight chamber? Why constantly insult me? Challenge me? Allow me to rescue Devyn and Lexa on my own? Why convince me we are companions? Why?!"

Rillac made a gesture that reminded her of a shrug. *Your energy might have been the greater power. Maybe Earth was the final destination or held the truth about what he saw. The true power destination was unknown. Inferior power is not desired. Hundreds of cycles have been necessary to gain what you see before you.* Rillac straightened, held out two top arms, and flexed the scales in rippling waves. Though the scales looked black from where she stood, when they rippled, their iridescence caught the light from the setting sun, and Rillac radiated the beauty of a god. Rillac continued. *Inferior power would destroy what you see and regress the power that has been obtained. That is why patience is important. Coming from nothing, transforming into true energy. You say, 'Testing you. Convincing you. Challenging you.' These are easy pieces to move around to see what you're worth. Nothing.*

It appeared that Rillac had spent cycles judging her worth and found her lacking. Rillac's words spun circles in her mind, abrasive and cold. She didn't feel any shame or remorse coming from Rillac; everything he said was just a statement of fact. She either made the trade and went with Rillac, or both Devyn and Vayle would die. Then, once they were dead, she would be forced to go anyway. This was her opportunity to save those she cared about.

Her skin tingled with the anxiety that she felt. She needed time to piece through the information that Rillac had admitted to her, to come up with a plan that would ensure that the rest of her companions and family were safe, but it was a luxury that wasn't available to her. *She wouldn't trust Rillac; she couldn't, but she could try to manipulate him the same way that she had been manipulated. Maybe if she led Rillac astray a little, it would give them the extra amount of time they needed either to escape or call for help.*

Ariyana schooled her features as much as she could so that when she turned around to look at Vayle she wouldn't look like she was about to break down. When their gazes locked, she almost lost control, but she swallowed her pain and continued.

They are going to let you leave, and I'm going to need you to take Devyn with you. She told Vayle calmly.

No. Vayle objected, the word cut short in her mind. Vayle's body strained under the Tethryn's hold, and fresh red blood covered the polished, white stone.

The colors conflicted dangerously with each other like fire attacking ice, and multiple images flooded Ariyana's mind.

She saw Glacin lying on his stomach in the egg chamber, covered in turquoise blood, his flame desperate to burn…for his own life source to spark again, only no flame would burn.

She saw Tethryn lying at her feet, their slick, yellow blood covering her hands, arms, and chest as she'd torn through body after body to try to save Glacin on Draca, and then Vayle and her own children on the dying planet.

She saw her hands covered in lavender blood as she heard alliances that she'd helped create break down because she'd lost control.

She saw her own red blood splashed across the granite rocks on Earth as Kylor tortured her and forced her back into a creature that she had once been.

So much blood…too much blood on her hands. She could stop it from happening again, so she would.

Lexa will help Devyn figure out how to guide the boys, and I hope that you will too.

Enough! Vayle yelled. *This is not a discussion. I will not leave you here with Rillac. I will not allow you to trade yourself.*

You are correct, Vayle. There is no discussion. Take him to Draca, heal. I will go to Raesor and find out what is going on; find out why he has been looking for me. I am sure that when everything is said and done, I will be able to find my way back to you.

Lies! You do not even believe the words that you speak. I can feel it. Vayle countered.

I won't let you die. I cannot watch another one of my Draxin companions be torn apart. I don't think that I could survive it. Ariyana's words were barely a whisper over Vayle's thoughts.

How dare you imply that I could? Vayle snapped.

This is a waste of time. Rillac interrupted. *It is clear that both of you wish the other to know that a connection exists between the two of you. One does. But it is not the connection you assume.*

The statement completely caught Ariyana off guard, and she found herself whipping around, her mouth open, with a soundless "What?" on her lips.

Vayle's scales seemed to pale, and panic wafted off of her like a sour smell. *Rillac. Don't.* she warned.

Ariyana's eyes darted between the two of them, taking in their body postures, their expressions, and the tension, most of which was coming from Vayle.

Rillac only felt amused.

Rillac squeezed Devyn's shoulder again, causing him to wince. A swirl of satisfaction drifted around Ariyana, and it disgusted her when she realized that the emotion came from Rillac.

Rillac enjoyed watching Devyn's pain response.

Pain is an interesting motivator, is it not? Rillac asked.

Ariyana raised an eyebrow in response.

"Would you stop being a dick and get on with it?" Ariyana demanded out loud so that Devyn could hear her.

Your Glacin was one creature that could not be predicted. He brought you to Draca and taught you how to take physical form before it was determined that you were what Raesor was looking for. Rillac curled two black claws on another hand. *Things would have been easier if we had secured you before you established companions. So, taking Glacin out of your life was the next step. But he was unpredictable yet again. He forced a connection between you and Vayle by forcing you inside the clutch. He knew that he was going to die, knew that Evix was going to die. He forced both of you to bond so that you would protect each other. Not a natural connection, a forced connection. Vayle didn't trust you, Aris.* The name came across like a hiss in her mind, and she glared at Rillac. *She was forced to look after you, forced to care for you, forced to feel anything for you.*

It does not matter how our bond was forged! Vayle roared. *We needed each other; Glacin knew that. Our bond grew from that need. It is stronger than any bond that I have known before.*

"Is this true?" Ariyana asked, her voice felt quiet and weak. She felt sick to her stomach thinking that something as precious as a bond between the two of them had been forced. It was a connection that she felt when she dreamed of Glacin, a bond that was mutually desired. She never would have imagined that such a thing could be forced.

Did you not tell her? Rillac asked Vayle.

I will not play into your hands on this one, Rillac. You are clever, but she is my companion, and there are no words that can destroy that. Her words then softened as she spoke to Ariyana. *Ari, it does not matter how we began, it only matters how we continue. Do not let Rillac divide us.*

Ariyana glanced at her and gave her a weak, small smile. Then, she looked at Devyn and met his gaze. For the first time since…actually, she couldn't remember when, he looked at her with sympathy and empathy in his eyes. He felt the pain of what had just been shared. He felt her pain, and it was hurting him too. It was what she needed to seal her resolve.

"The best way to keep the majority of us together is to make the trade," Ariyana said clearly and confidently. "I agree to your terms, Rillac."

Vayle's keening cry tore through the air around them as the sun sparked its last flash of light before disappearing below the horizon.

Chapter 56

Vayle's cries cut off suddenly, and Ariyana whipped around in alarm. Vayle was still distressed. Ariyana saw her thrashing, saw her mouth open in a silent roar, saw her claws and talons raking the white stone, but she heard nothing, felt nothing. Ariyana turned back to Rillac, her brows pinched in confusion.

Energy can be manipulated too. Rillac stated.

Ariyana didn't know this creature at all. How could Rillac sever her connection to Vayle so easily? Hell, how could Rillac sever both her and Vayle's connection to the planet's energy and keep it severed without, what appeared to her, any effort?

She thought back to her encounter with Raesor. It didn't appear that Raesor used an ability like this while they fought. Granted, in the scheme of things, the fight hadn't lasted that long, and it wasn't possible that she had been exposed to everything that he was capable of. Inwardly, she hoped that between the two, Rillac or Raesor, Raesor would not be as strong as Rillac was. Otherwise, it might be harder than she thought for her to get back to her companions and her family.

Rillac's head cocked to the side again. Devyn's body began to tremble, and his mouth twisted in a grimace of pain. His left knee buckled, but his body didn't crumple to the ground. Rillac held him up like a rag doll.

"Damn it! Stop!" Ariyana demanded, hands out, palms facing Rillac. "You don't need to hurt him. I'm ready. Let's make the trade. I'll come to you, and Devyn can go to Vayle. You drop the energy boundary around Vayle so that she can reach out to Arc and let him know to come and get them. Then, you and I—"

No. Rillac's harsh answer cut her off. The word echoed through her mind painfully, and she flinched.

"Excuse me? What the hell do you mean '*No*?'" She snapped back.

That was not the arrangement.

"Screw you! That *was* the arrangement. I go with you so that we can go to Raesor, and Devyn goes with Vayle. Done, negotiations are over."

Correct, negotiations are over. The trade is you for Devyn. That is it. The trade has nothing to do with Vayle. Vayle must now negotiate for herself, her people, her planet, and the safety of the Aryllyns.

"You lied," Ariyana snarled. "Deal's off. I won't let you hurt her or strong-arm her into a situation where only you benefit."

You have less awareness of your surroundings than it was believed you had. You are in no position to make demands upon anyone. Devyn's whole body started convulsing, and a small trickle of blood came out of his left nostril. *Vayle must negotiate for herself, and her decisions have nothing to do with you, companion or not. It would not have mattered what you decided. It is up to Vayle and Vayle alone what happens to her, her people, and her planet.* Rillac held Devyn's shaking body out in her direction. *Decide now, or he dies.*

Ariyana was still stuck between the same rock and a hard place that she had been before. She couldn't think straight. She was cut off from Vayle's thoughts and emotions. She was overwhelmed by Devyn's pain washing over her in wave after wave of what felt like lava crashing over her already sensitive skin. The icy throb in her chest was threatening to shatter inside her, shredding the last of what was keeping her whole inside.

Without thinking, her body stumbled forward a couple of steps. "Let him go," she said. Her words were quiet but thick with emotion.

Devyn slumped in Rillac's grasp, the unknown torture stopping immediately. His eyes closed halfway, and he sucked in huge gasps of breath. That was when she felt it, both inside her body and against her skin. The air froze around them. Devyn's exhalations misted around his face. The chill in Ariyana's chest responded, changing from a steady throb to one that grew in intensity with each pulse, mirroring the expanding cold around her. Fractures spread out in the air next to Rillac like ice splitting after hot liquid is poured on top of it. The fractures exploded into puffs of fresh powder, and there, in their stead, stood Kylor, healthy, unmarred, and clearly annoyed.

The chill in Ariyana's chest had burst in a pulse of cold waves through her body, but it all ceased the moment Kylor was visible. Now, as she stood there, the chill below her hearts became subdued and tolerable, no longer threatening to freeze her from the inside out.

While her insides might have calmed down at his presence, her mind was a torrent of negative emotions. "What the hell is he doing here?" she spat. Her logical thoughts told her that she should focus on the abilities that Rillac was showing her: phasing Kylor here without moving a muscle, phasing the Tethryn here in sizeable numbers, and keeping the Tethryn under a physical hold. Rillac was able to do all that with what appeared to be little thought or effort. Rillac's abilities were staggering and not something to underestimate.

Even with all those logical thoughts scraping at the back of her mind, Ariyana couldn't stop her emotions from taking charge. She and Kylor had unfinished business. Seeing him made her react in ways that, yet again, she had not had the time to work through. Her hearts raced from a stab of fear that she hated that she felt, but he had beaten her, tortured her, and taken her control away, all while keeping Lexa in a dormant state in front of her. Now he was just a few feet away from Devyn. She felt angry because he forced her to join with her essence, again taking away her control and ability to decide for herself. And now she felt oddly betrayed, as it was clear that he had partnered with Rillac, a creature that just moments ago had admitted to killing her Glacin, Vayle's Evix, and countless others to attain his precious knowledge. Their last encounter on Ora had left her with more questions than answers, but did those answers matter anymore if Kylor was allied in some way with Rillac, or, worse yet, had played some part in Glacin's death?

Ariyana looked over at Vayle's torn and broken body and tried to fit the Kylor that she had spoken to on Ora into this current situation. Something wasn't adding up, but then again, her mind was reeling—too many thoughts, too many questions, too many emotions, and not enough memories for her to rely on. How could she make an informed decision if she still didn't understand what was going on?

As if her thoughts had been shouted instead of spoken internally, Rillac responded by adding, *"Your decision has been made—the only one that you had any authority to make. The rest is up to Vayle."*

"Why is *he* here?" Ariyana pressed, leveling her gaze at Kylor this time. Kylor surprised her as he met her gaze and held it. He peered deep into her eyes as if he had been waiting for her to look at him. She couldn't read his expression, though. She had no idea if he was staring at her in defiance or challenge. She also couldn't feel him. He was keeping his emotions tightly hidden behind a stone wall.

Plans change, Rillac stated, pulling Ariyana's attention back to their conversation, but as her eyes shifted from Kylor to Rillac, she noticed that Kylor's gaze flickered with an emotion that she recognized, though she couldn't name it, and he quickly averted his gaze. *Vayle must negotiate for her people and her planet if she wants to be protected from the Tethryn.* Rillac continued. *Part of that negotiation will involve bringing Kylor's people to Draca permanently.*

"Idrin needs to be a part of that decision, not just Vayle," Ariyana snapped.

Annoyance and disgust emanated from Rillac in heavy waves. *Idrin? Idrin is Tehkara on Draca. He has no planet to call home, no one to keep him and his people safe. Vayle allows Idrin to play leader while standing on her soil because she knows that the true power of that planet lies in her connection to it, not his. He is connected to nothing without his bond to Arc. And nothing he shall become again if he refuses the deal that Vayle strikes today.*

Ariyana couldn't help but agree with some of what Rillac had said. She hadn't thought about Idrin's situation from that perspective. He and his people were just as homeless as Kylor was. She hated the word that he used, Tehkara, because it had been thrown in her face many times, but she felt an odd satisfaction at realizing that Idrin was in a similar situation to both her and Kylor. With all his ridiculous attitude and posturing, he was just as lost in this universe as she was.

Ariyana glanced back at Kylor, but his eyes remained focused away from her. She wondered why. *Rillac had just backed him up, if she wasn't mistaken? Rillac had just all but stated that Idrin's high and mighty behavior was unjustified. She would have thought that Kylor would be pleased to hear that stated out loud.* But his expression said otherwise.

Before Ariyana could question it further, Rillac released the hold on Devyn, both freeing him and shoving him forward at the same time. Devyn, not expecting to be let go and pushed, stumbled forward and fell onto his hands and knees. Devyn's eyes were wide with shock. He whipped his head toward Rillac as if to confirm that he had truly been released. Rillac gave him a slight nod in Ariyana's direction.

Devyn pulled himself to his feet clumsily and rolled the shoulder that Rillac had been grasping earlier. He kept his eyes locked on Rillac but stumbled forward a few steps. Then, he stopped and grasped his head, digging his fingers into his temples. Ariyana didn't hear anything and didn't notice Rillac moving, but she wondered if Rillac's hold had yet to leave Devyn completely. It made her feel helpless. *Devyn had been through so much in such a short period of time and hadn't been treated very nicely through most of it.* She felt a pang of guilt at knowing that she, unfortunately, had added to a good chunk of that.

Then, she immediately chastised herself. *Yes, Devyn had been through a lot recently, but so had she. There wasn't an innocent party here, and, as far as she was concerned, they both had a lot of apologizing to do.* She tentatively stepped forward a couple of steps. "Devyn," she said softly.

Devyn's head whipped around at the sound of her voice, and Ariyana braced herself for an accusatory glare or a stream of insults, but instead, his usually steady, confident green eyes appeared frantic and scared—almost crazed. The Devyn she had known, who'd exuded both mental and physical health, now looked frail and broken. Where was the man who, just moments ago, had looked at her with empathy in his gaze?

"It's okay," she soothed. "Come over here. Let's get you somewhere safe."

Devyn perked up at the use of the word *safe* and half-stumbled, half-ran toward her. She allowed herself to smile slightly, careful not to show her teeth, and hoped that the look that she was giving him was an encouraging one.

Devyn tripped over one of his own feet when he was a couple of feet in front of Ariyana and plowed right into her. His hands landed roughly on her shoulders, and he would have knocked her backward if she hadn't caught both of them by bracing herself upright, pushing her tail against the ground like a tripod, and adjusting her center of gravity by moving her wings slightly. He let his momentum completely close the distance between them and wrapped her in a tight embrace. Ariyana tensed, not expecting the affectionate response. The last few times that they had seen each other, he had been disgusted by her appearance and had been quite vocal about it.

Devyn had always smelled good. His skin seemed like it was covered in the barest hint of citrus and coconut oil. Ariyana let his scent fill her nose. It amazed her that she could still smell him. She figured that being on different planets for a few days and bathing in a Lielycet pool would have removed all traces of the smell that she was so familiar with, but it was clearly just a part of him. It was nice to feel his body against hers, but after a few moments, it started to grow uncomfortable and somewhat painful. His body temperature was too hot for her colder one. How could she tell him without hurting his feelings that his body was burning her? Before she had to think about it further, he grasped her shoulders and jerked her body away from him.

"I don't know how I didn't see it before, but I can see you in there now." His eyes darted back and forth between hers. "The eyes are different, but their expression…their energy…their light are the same. Same…" he said, letting the word trail off. Then, his eyebrows pinched together like he was both surprised and concerned. Devyn hardened his gaze, focusing on her right eye alone, and sputtered, "I'm so sorry. This is all my fault."

"What?" she asked, too shocked to say anything else. This was such a change from when they'd last talked that Ariyana wasn't sure what to say.

He squeezed her shoulders and gave her a little shake. "It is my fault," he stressed, his eyes huge and pleading. "I'm—" He stopped talking, glanced to the left, and then back at her. Her own lips had parted to ask him what was wrong when she felt it.

But it was already too late.

Chapter 57

The air froze and fractured around Devyn, his breath crystallizing along his lips and in tiny clouds in front of his mouth. His eyes widened. His fingers dug into Ariyana's shoulders, and he jerked her body to her left. His back arched. His face contorted into a mixture of pain and fear, his mouth opened in a silent scream. There was a sickening sound of bone breaking and flesh tearing. Something warm and wet covered her chest, neck, and face. And pain lanced through the right side of her chest—hot and agonizing, like a fire-heated, metal rod being shoved through her body.

Ariyana heard someone yell "No!" but wasn't sure who it was.

She stared in disbelief at the grisly scene in front of her. Devyn's back was oddly bent, his chest arched toward her, and a long, sharp, black object protruded from his chest and impaled into hers. The wound around the unknown object was surrounded by torn flesh, bits of bone, and blood. There was so much blood—the front of his shirt was covered in it, and, as Ariyana watched, the red stain continued to expand outward on the cloth. She was vaguely aware that she had an injury in her own chest. It was hard to distinguish between his pain and hers. His fingers continued to dig into her shoulders. It was as if he was afraid that she would disappear, that if he didn't keep touching her, she would vanish and he'd never see her again.

Movement above Devyn's left ear caught Ariyana's attention. The air next to and slightly above Devyn's head shimmered, cracked, and puffed into a cloud of white powder, creating a hazy, winter mist. The creature was unmistakable, though it managed to half-conceal itself by keeping the phase portal open.

Rillac.

Rillac's iridescent scales glinted like gems in the mist as they caught bits of light from her flame.

Rillac pulled the object from their chests, slamming Ariyana's body into Devyn's. The force of the impact caused Devyn to cough and sputter, covering Ariyana in more blood. Rillac held the bloody object up next to Devyn's head. Rillac curled and uncurled the two black claws that had been straightened into a weapon just moments ago. He'd used his arm to impale them.

Pain tore through Ariyana as Devyn's knees buckled against her. His head lolled back and flopped forward, hitting hard against her shoulder. He gurgled and choked on his own blood as it filled his mouth. He was becoming limp in her arms as his strength drained out of him. His body seemed caught in fight-or-flight mode, though, as his feet uselessly flopped against the ground, trying to find purchase to get him upright. Ariyana struggled to keep him from falling to the ground. She was short of breath, and the stabbing pain in her chest was getting worse. Her right lung wasn't working, and the obvious lack of oxygen was taking its toll.

Devyn jerked left and back. Ariyana's foot flew out to adjust their balance. She tripped over one of his feet and tried to compensate with her other foot. She stepped in something warm and wet. The slick surface combined with Devyn's weight made her slip, and they both crashed to the ground.

Devyn's back hit hard, the back of his head smashing against the white stone, and Ariyana collapsed on top of him. She pulled as much of her body weight off him as she could, so afraid that she was hurting him more, but his unfocused eyes and pale skin told her that he wasn't feeling much of anything.

The only true light that she had was her flame. Its silver light danced across the large pool of red that they had slipped in—Devyn's blood. It was all around them and all over them.

Ariyana's hands darted out to his chest, and she pressed down on the wound as hard as she could with her own wavering strength. "No…no…no," she repeated over and over again in a weak plea. But the blood wouldn't stop. The wound went straight through his body, and she watched in horror as the dark crimson pool spread out on the white stone around his shoulders and head like an ominous aura. Panic welled inside of her, and tears burned in her eyes.

Ariyana tried to shift more of her body weight onto her arms to try to apply more pressure, but her elbows collapsed. She caught herself on her forearms on his chest and struggled to catch her breath. She looked down at Devyn's chest and saw that his crimson blood was swirled with silver—*her blood.*

She glanced at her own chest and saw the wound on the right side of her body. It wasn't nearly as bad as Devyn's because it didn't go all the way through, but it was clear that she had a collapsed lung and was bleeding profusely. She kept one hand on Devyn's chest and placed her other hand on her own chest. "Devyn," she whispered, searching his face. "Devyn, please, can you hear me?" *Nothing.* He just lay there, making a gurgling noise here and there.

Ariyana heard a scraping sound on the stone, and her head jerked up. She expected to see Rillac standing over them, but instead, Rillac was back by Kylor's side, calmly watching her, flicking blood and gore from his black claws.

Rillac's body posture denoted boredom.

Kylor's appearance was the exact opposite of Rillac's. His mouth was open in what looked like shock and horror, and one of his feet was pulled forward as if he was in mid-step toward them. Ariyana wasn't sure what it meant, and she didn't care. She growled at both of them. "I agreed to go with you. Why hurt him?" she asked, her voice weak and strained as she gasped for breath. "Take him to Draca. Heal him. There is no need for him to die."

Humans must be an incredibly gullible species. Rillac stated with no emotion in the words. *A plan was discussed, and you believed it without question. Very trusting…though you always were. And predictable. Especially once the pattern is discovered. The argument with Idrin revealed the secret. Though you cover yourself in armor, you let your guard down around those you care about. You don't even realize that you do it. You leave the most important part of your body exposed and vulnerable—your hearts. Is it because you long for them, crave them, need them? Your body and armor react to that need and leave your hearts unprotected. Doesn't seem instinctual…must be emotional. You certainly have enough of that. Which is the reason that you are not needed. You are nothing. Both you and Devyn will die choking on your own blood, and once you take your last breath, Vayle will follow.*

Kylor's head whipped toward Rillac. His entire body tensed, and his hands clenched into fists at his side. He opened his mouth to argue but Rillac's arm shot out, a hand latching around Kylor's throat.

Keep your threats in your throat, Tehkaric. You were no better than that. Rillac hissed in their minds, gesturing a hand toward Ariyana. *The plan was…*

Ariyana could still hear Rillac's voice in her mind, but she could no longer hear the words. They faded to the background, no longer mattering to her. Her eyes slowly lowered back down to Devyn's face. *Everything was a lie. A lie that Devyn was paying for with his life. A lie that she would soon pay for with hers.*

She took her hand away from her chest and placed it on Devyn's cheek. She didn't care about her wound anymore. "Please," she whispered. "You can't go."

Vayle roared behind her. Ariyana turned and saw that the Tethryn had renewed their attack on her body—stabbing and biting where her flame had extinguished.

The Tethryn that had been standing on the outskirts of the group of Tethryn that were attacking Vayle turned and slowly advanced on Ariyana.

It felt impossible. *How in the hell could she save Vayle, Devyn, and herself from all of these Tethryn, not to mention that all three of them were critically injured?* Her mind raced for a solution, but that ended quickly when her body filled with fresh bursts of pain as Vayle's agony spread to her through their bond.

Ariyana couldn't concentrate. Her body was being bombarded from every direction: her skin burned where Vayle was being attacked, her stab wound wasn't healing and still bled, and her insides felt shredded from the emotional chaos. She couldn't hold it back any longer—she screamed.

Her body hunched forward from the effort, and Devyn's eyes popped open just as Ariyana's eyes met his. They were frantic and pleading as they searched hers for a solution. Fresh tears burned in her eyes as she shook her head in shame. She couldn't heal him. His mouth moved as if he was saying something, but she couldn't hear anything. She leaned down close to his mouth and pressed her ear against his lips.

"Mus…t…s…ee…" Devyn rasped.

Ariyana was confused and started to lift her head away so that she could look at him again when his hand shot up and grasped the back of her neck. She flinched and attempted to jerk away, but Devyn's hand had landed perfectly—he had found her akra points.

Chapter 58

"Ariyana?"

The name, *her name*, floated around her calmly, but she couldn't see anything. *Why couldn't she see anything?* She felt her heart rates rising and panic starting to kick in. *Where was Devyn? Who had taken him away from her?*

Something strong and unyielding grabbed her shoulders. "Ariyana, it's okay, just open your eyes," the familiar voice told her.

Were her eyes closed? She didn't remember closing them. She obeyed and opened them. She was shocked to see that she was home. *Home! On Earth, of all places,* and standing in her favorite spot in the meadow close to her parents' cabin, with a very healthy Devyn standing in front of her with an unsure smile on his face.

"Devyn! You're—" she exclaimed, and then stopped abruptly when she moved forward to throw her arms around his neck. She stared in disbelief at her arms and hands, turning them one way and then the other, expecting the illusion to wear off, but it didn't. She was human again.

With wide eyes, she examined the meadow more closely.

The meadow itself looked the same—beautiful, lush, full of spring flowers, up to the line of pine trees that circled around it. That was where things changed. As the pine trees spread out toward the mountains in the distance, things became progressively more blurry and darker, like her mind couldn't remember the details, and the sun refused to shine anywhere else except for the area around them.

Confused, Ariyana looked back at Devyn and flinched. Devyn's white shirt had a red stain in the center of his chest, and it was growing outward. Blood was streaming out of both corners of his mouth, dripping on his white shirt and adding to the grisly stain that was growing in the center.

The sight of him made everything come rushing back.

Devyn had been stabbed through the chest by Rillac because Rillac had betrayed all of them. Devyn was dying and had grabbed Ariyana by the back of the neck, landing on her akra points, and had clearly pulled her mind into his thoughts.

"Please," he begged, collapsing to his knees in front of her.

Ariyana rushed forward and put her left hand on his cheek. She closed her eyes and slid her right hand behind his neck and down between his shoulder blades. She felt the solidness of Devyn's body and knew that she was doing it to Devyn's real body, not his projected mental image of himself. She easily found his akra points, the center of energy in his body, and closed the connection between them.

Devyn's wound slowly disappeared, and Ariyana's human form slowly transformed back into her porcelain-colored skin, silver feathers and hair, and her bright silver flame.

"There you are," Devyn said affectionately, surprising her. He stood up slowly and touched her cheek. She flinched, not knowing what to expect, and then relaxed when all he did was stroke her cheek and outline the small, burning feathers around her eyes. "How is this possible?" he asked.

"I stopped us in this moment," she said, looking down. "But I won't be able to hold it forever. I can't heal you." She felt ashamed that she couldn't help him.

Devyn grabbed her right hand and squeezed. "This is exactly what I need—a moment with you where no one can interrupt us." She gave him a weak smile. "I need you to know and see the truth, Ariyana," he said softly.

With his words, the meadow around them faded away, and their old college campus took shape around them. Devyn stood on the grassy hill in the quad that looked down at the campus coffee shop on the edge. It was a normal, beautiful early morning on campus. The coffee shop was packed with students picking up their morning caffeine before classes began.

As Devyn watched, Ariyana and Lexa walked out of the coffee shop, laughing at something and walking toward the main lecture hall. At exactly the moment that Ariyana stepped around the corner of the building, the sun broke through the morning clouds and seemed to shine right on her. It was as if her body absorbed the light like someone would suck in a breath of fresh air. Only for her, the more the sun shone down on her, the more her skin glowed with a faint silver light.

Ariyana glanced over at Devyn in surprise. "Have I always done that?" she asked.

He met her gaze and shook his head. "No," Devyn said casually. "I only saw it happen a handful of times, and Lexa's never mentioned it. She can't keep anything to herself when it comes to you, so I'm sure that she would have said something if she had seen it."

"What could it have meant?"

"I don't know for sure. Maybe that you were happy? Maybe that a subconscious part of you was trying to reach out to your companions? We may never know, but it meant that my whole world stopped in that moment. I fell in love with you. I didn't even know your name, and it didn't matter. I loved you and knew that I would protect you."

Ariyana leaned away from him, confused. His words didn't match up with how he had treated her the last few years. "That doesn't make sense, Devyn. Things have been tense between us for years and that's putting it mildly."

The campus scene faded away, and the meadow took shape around them again. He reached for her hands, grasping them, rubbing his thumbs across her wrists. "Please keep watching. I promise it will make sense. I need you to see," he pleaded with her. She nodded.

He gestured across the meadow to the path where she and Lexa usually broke out of the tree line to run the outer rim of the meadow. There stood Devyn in a handsome tux; he had looked so incredible that day. Standing with him was an officiant. On either side of them stood their families, Lexa, and Devyn's best friend. On the ground between them lay a long turquoise cloth that ran all the way to the tree line.

It was their wedding day, and any minute, Ariyana would break through the tree line, arm-in-arm with her father, to become Devyn's wife.

She saw movement through the trees and then, there she was, Ariyana, in a gorgeously simple white satin wedding dress, stepping into the meadow. In that moment, the sun burned through the light clouds and covered her in its radiance. Again, she saw herself absorb its light and emit a silver glow of her own.

Ariyana watched Devyn's face, the one that was waiting for his bride to stand by his side, and couldn't believe the look of pure joy that lit up his features. It had been so long since she had seen it that she had forgotten how he used to look at her.

The Devyn standing next to her sighed. "In that moment, I didn't think that I would ever be that happy again, but then came the day that you told me you were pregnant, and we found out that we were having twin boys. My heart felt so full of love."

The meadow morphed around them into a hospital room. Ariyana was in labor. Devyn was standing next to her, and there was a doctor and a few nurses helping with the delivery.

The Devyn standing next to her looked down at the ground. Confused, Ariyana turned to watch as her sons were born.

The Ariyana that was in labor was doing her breathing exercises and pushing when she was instructed to push. Everything was progressing normally until the nurse told her that a big one was coming and that she was going to need to bear down and push as hard as she could. When that contraction finally hit, Ariyana bore down. All of a sudden, though, her entire body seized up, her eyes rolled back into her head, her jaw clenched, her heart raced, and she started panting. The doctor jumped up, ordering the nurses to roll her over onto her side. They pushed past Devyn and started to shift her when her body went completely limp, and the only sound echoing off every surface in the room was the high-pitched noise of three flat-lined hearts.

Both the Devyn in the hospital room and the Devyn next to her yelled, *"No!"* The Devyn in the hospital room ran to his pregnant wife, and the Devyn next to her collapsed to his knees. He buried his face in his hands and rocked his upper body.

Ariyana heard the doctor say something about a defibrillator, but he was caught off guard by the Ariyana on the bed, sitting straight up, eyes popping open, and sucking in a huge breath. A wave of silver energy burst from Ariyana's upright body, and she collapsed back onto the delivery table, whispering Glacin's name. The room settled back into the chaos of babies being born when three vibrant heartbeats resumed their normal rates.

Ariyana remembered getting stuck in her dream during labor, but she really had no idea how that had been for Devyn. She also had no idea that she had released a wave of energy during that time. She kneeled down next to Devyn and put her hand over his clasped fist. "I had no idea that's how bad it was. I'm sorry that you had to go through that alone," she said.

Devyn glanced up at her, his eyes red with tears. "All three of you were dead for twenty-five seconds. I lost my whole world for twenty-five seconds," he said hoarsely.

"I'm so sorry," she said, placing her hand on his forearm. "So, that's what happened? That's what changed things for you? Why you became so distant and angry about my dream? Forcing me to go on medication?"

Devyn's gaze hardened. "No, you don't understand. I never changed how I felt. I still supported and loved you, and I never would have asked you to take something that made you sick. It wasn't me who changed, Ariyana. It was who was in charge of my body that changed."

Chapter 59

Ariyana shot to her feet.

"What did you just say?" she asked, her voice sounding squeakier than she intended.

Devyn stood up next to her, though he moved more slowly than she did.

"You saw the burst of energy that I saw, right? The blast of silver light? I think it was like a beacon of some kind because Rillac showed up the next night...*on Earth.*" He paused and looked down at the ground again. "We were still in the hospital, and you were nursing the twins. I decided to run down to the cafeteria to see if I could get a little food before they closed for the night. I had taken the stairs. One moment, no one was there; the next, that creature that calls itself Rillac was standing right in front of me. As you can imagine, I freaked out. It was clearly not a creature of Earth. But it had a hold of my neck before I could even think to scream. It told me that it had been watching us. Its voice sounded like thousands of voices screaming in my mind, and it also sounded like one harsh, male voice that seemed to dominate every part of me. I didn't know what Rillac was, but when I could think independently, and he used his one dominant voice, I thought of him as a 'him' because all I knew was the sound. It was painful. He told me that I would be a vessel for him to keep an eye on you without actually being here every moment. Then, he took this white claw and punctured my neck. I felt something hot spread through my whole body. It became hard to think. I saw him cut a line across his palm, and he clasped his hand to my mouth. I wanted to struggle and pull away, but my body wouldn't respond. I just let the blood drain down my throat." Finally, he raised his eyes to meet hers. "Ever since that day, I felt like I was watching my life take place on an old, low-resolution TV. I heard myself talking, I felt myself moving, but I had no control over those functions. It was a nightmare. All I could do was sit inside my body and watch as your heart broke day after day; watch as you withered away from the medicine that was making you sick; watch as you were dragged from test to test and a little bit more of you died each time you went in."

"So all those terrible things? All those fights? All those threats?" she asked.

"They weren't me. They were him." He shook his head. "He would come back every few weeks to make sure that he hadn't lost control, to renew his hold over my mind, and to make sure that you were deteriorating."

Ariyana felt relieved that she hadn't been wrong about the man that she'd married. He hadn't changed, he'd just been "taken over." But it was quickly followed by a rush of grief. Devyn's life with his family had been stolen from him, and now his own life would be stolen too.

A loud but very slow *lub dub* sound echoed around them. The sound pulled the shadows from beyond the meadow toward them, and then pushed them back.

Ariyana was losing her hold on this moment. Devyn only had a couple of heartbeats left before he died.

He stared at her and smiled, though it did not touch his eyes.

"I don't have much time," he said bluntly. "And honestly, neither do you. Rillac is looking for something. Having Rillac in my head for so long worked both ways—I learned a bit about him too. First of all, he's a sociopath. He feels nothing for anyone else and only cares about himself. He will manipulate the universe if he can find a way. One thing that I wasn't so sure about was whether he was trying to break you or kill you. Even now, stabbing you in the chest, I'm not sure what his intention was. He would have kept you a secret for as long as he could, manipulating you, if you hadn't sent out the larger silver energy blast on your thirtieth birthday. That one was so big that Vayle found you and came to get you. He had to put a whole new plan in place to ensure that they didn't know that he already knew about you." He grabbed one of her hands and held it tightly. "He convinced Kylor that he had to go to Earth to get you, *join* you to your essence, and make you remember. He told him that was the only way to save his people."

Another *lub dub* echoed around them. This time the shadows didn't push back. They pulled closer and loomed.

Devyn looked up at the sky. His body swayed a little, and Ariyana caught him before he fell. She eased him down to the ground. He winced and looked at his chest. A bright red dot was forming on his shirt and getting bigger by the moment.

"We take our heartbeats for granted, don't we?" he asked, his voice quiet. "It's not until you get down to the last couple that you realize that you're not ready to lose them."

Tears burned in her eyes, and she put his hands to her lips for a light kiss. "Devyn, I want to stop this from happening," she said.

"No, it's too late for me. I knew years ago that Rillac would never let me live. There is just so little time and still too much to share." He put his hand on her chest. "I moved you to the side for a reason. He missed your hearts. You will heal, and you will be there to care for our children. There is one thing that he hasn't figured out, and that's how you've truly been able to stop the Tethryn. He doesn't know about the other energy that is growing inside of you. Hell, you probably aren't fully aware of it either." He coughed and pointed to the side. "Watch."

The meadow melted away, and Ariyana was lying on her back at her parents' cabin, and Devyn was on top of her, trying to get her to wake up from her most intense dream yet. But she was still fighting the dream as she came to. She latched onto his forearm and wouldn't let go, no matter how hard he tried to pry her teeth from his flesh. Then, something seemed to snap in place, a realization maybe, because her eyes widened and she stared straight at him.

"There," Devyn said next to her. "Do you see it?"

She sucked in a breath. She did see it. Her eyes were surrounded by silver flames, but not just her silver flame, because surrounding that was a flame that was as black as the darkest, starless sky.

"It's incredible, isn't it?" Devyn asked her, knowing that she saw what he saw. "I don't think that Rillac has been able to see what you're capable of. Maybe it's because he's seeing things through my eyes instead of his own? Has he ever been around you when your flame is surrounded in black fire?"

She thought about it, thought about the memories that others had shared with her, thought about the events that had taken place, and thought about her dream.

"Not that I can remember."

"Good," Devyn said. "I can tell from your expression that you know that energy. You've actually used it before, haven't you? Is that why Vayle and Idrin are somewhat uncertain of you?"

"Uncertain? I guess you could say that. And you've probably seen and heard a lot more than I have."

"That's nothing to worry about. They are your companions, and they won't abandon you. I need you to worry about the real threat. You have to figure out how to use that energy again. You have to kill Rillac, Ariyana, and after that, you have to kill Raesor. Raesor wants something inside of you. I don't know what, but I do know that. And Rillac will want it too, once he figures out what it is. He won't stop until he has it. This leaves you dangerously open to attack." Devyn stopped talking and pulled himself next to her. "I can see the doubt in your eyes, my Yana."

That got her attention. Devyn only called her *Yana* in their most intimate of moments. No one knew about the nickname except for the two of them. She met his eyes, intense and full of passion. Her thoughts swam, caught up in the intensity of their private memories. She glanced down at his lips and back up to his eyes. He held her gaze and smiled.

"It blows my mind how different you are in this form. It's hard to control myself when your emotions emanate from you in powerful waves." He put his hands on either side of her face and kissed her. He kissed her like the world was ending, which, for him, it felt like it was. He kissed her until he had to pull away to breathe. "Rillac's been in my head since the day after our twins were born. He was controlling my body and my words on Earth, on Ora, and on Draca. And I couldn't stop him. He said what he wanted and took what he wanted, all the while forcing me to watch. Once he figures out that I saved you and that you are what he is looking for, he won't stop hunting you or our children." He held her hands tightly. "I am finally myself again, free of his rotten poison in my body and in my thoughts. I am so grateful that I will die as myself."

As if on cue, another *lub dub* echoed around them slowly, and the shadows pushed their way toward them like grasping claws—only a small amount of light remained fixed on their bodies.

"This will hurt when I die, but I beg you not to give up," he said, his voice tired and empty now. He was fading. "You have to keep our children safe, and you have to keep yourself safe." He placed his hand over her hearts. "You are the key to saving this universe. I can feel it. It doesn't matter what name you go by. Aris, Ariyana, Ari…my sweet Yana—your energy is more powerful than he will ever imagine." He tried to suck in deep breaths, but they gurgled in his throat. He collapsed back, and she caught him in her arms. "Do whatever it takes to them all." He grasped at his throat, trying to dislodge some imaginary hand that he felt there.

Ariyana was losing her control over his body. Their connection was no longer enough. She pulled him into her lap, pressing her tail along his side and arching her wings around them. She wanted him to feel like there was nothing else in this moment except for them. Tears streamed down her face, and her flame flickered. The image of her in their combined minds didn't have any visible injuries, but she could feel where her body was broken and bruised because the pain still transferred through. The bloodstain grew and grew, and his eyes started to glaze over as his body went into shock.

"No, please don't go. I can't lose you too. It will break me," she whispered, holding his face close to hers.

His fingers twitched toward her, and she grabbed his hand and held it to her cheek.

His lips parted but no sound came out. Instead, his warm voice traveled lightly through her thoughts like a fading breeze. *No tears. You didn't break on Earth, and you won't break here. You are stronger than all of us. You will see. And you could never lose me. I have been, and always will be, part of your energy. I knew it the first time I laid eyes on your silver glow. I have only ever wanted to protect you, to love you, and to take my last breath in your arms. I…I love…you…Yana.*

And then, his whole body relaxed. She heard his last breath as it passed his parted lips, and she saw his energy, his ryn, leave his eyes. His hand became heavy in hers and tried to fall out of her grasp, but she squeezed it and pressed it harder to her cheek.

"Devyn," she sobbed. She wanted his eyes to look at her again. She wanted his hand to feel her again. She wanted him back. She wanted more time.

But there was no more time, and the connection between them was shattering. The meadow and pine trees fractured like they were made of glass, and, as they shattered and fell around her, they exploded into bursts of dust and sand. Each time something shattered and burst, she felt something shatter inside her chest, slicing through her. She groaned, clutching her chest, and leaned over his body.

As she watched, large cracks spread through the image of Devyn's body, growing and spreading and revealing the true image beneath it—white stone and pools of blood so large they looked black. When the image was fully consumed in cracks, it burst, and Devyn's dead body lying on the white stone of Tor came into clear view.

Consumed with agony and anguish from their shattered connection, Ariyana screamed.

Chapter 60

Ariyana's body felt like it was collapsing in on itself: bones breaking, muscles tearing, blood boiling, skin burning. But it was deeper than that; deeper than even her soul. Her energy was fracturing. She could feel that her bond to Devyn was completely shattered. *What was left?* Pain. It fractured and expanded. It fractured and expanded again. The pressure was too much to bear. She wanted to die too, to just curl up next to his body and let her soul follow his into the next life.

Ariyana felt the right side of her body hit something hard. She didn't have the strength to care. Pain was her only companion, and it demanded everything from her. Her skin felt too tight. She longed for it to split open and release the building pressure inside her body. Instead, it grew. It grew until another sensation burst from the center of her chest: the icy throb that usually dominated her body's focus. Instead of bringing its constant chill, it brought relief and focus. And *an ache.* Not an ache from pain, but an ache born from the desire to consume.

Rillac had cut Devyn's life short and not just from death. He had taken Devyn's freedom and his individuality. Rillac took and took and took without any concerns for those that were hurt. She could take too. Ariyana could feel the need growing inside of her—the need to take, the need to consume, the need to hurt Rillac.

Ariyana channeled her emotions to the center of her chest. She didn't try to control them or tamp them down. She let them build. She let herself feel all of it—the pain of injury, the anguish of loss, the rage of being controlled, the hurt of betrayal. *All of it.*

Ariyana's emotions spread throughout her core like a darkness. She felt a small moment of hesitation when she recognized the darkness, realizing that if she let it go, it would consume her, and she might not be able to control it. *But what had being in control done for her lately? Nothing. She was trusting the wrong individuals; she was losing more people that she cared about; she was being used.*

Screw it. And, as if she were the only one holding back a horde of people with just her raised arms, she let them fall. She released all her control and let the soothing balm of darkness course through her.

Ariyana's eyes opened, and her pupils dilated. Her four-pointed-star pupils grew until her eyes appeared to be as black as Rillac's.

Ariyana was lying on her side, with Devyn lying in front of her, his left hand still grasped in her right. His hand looked so small in hers. Losing Devyn had not only changed the energy inside of her, but it had also transformed her body. Her limbs were longer and stronger. Her armor covered more of her body. Her claws and talons had lengthened. Her flame was brighter.

Ariyana pulled herself up, equalizing the support of her body weight across her four limbs. Liquid dripped from the feathers of her right wing: Devyn's blood. She had fallen over into the crimson pool when their bond shattered. It felt fitting. *She should wear Devyn's blood on her body like war paint while she tore Rillac's body apart.*

Though it was still dark, her dilated eyes showed her every detail that she needed to see. Rillac stood about forty feet from her, with a hand still wrapped around Kylor's throat. It felt like she had held the connection with Devyn for hours, but based on Rillac's position, barely any time had passed. Rillac was also fully focused on Kylor. This meant that Ariyana's cries of loss and transformation had remained internal, confined within her deteriorating connection to her husband, to Devyn.

Ariyana turned to look at Vayle, who was still surrounded by Tethryn, pulling, tearing, and biting at her, and a small number of Tethryn were also advancing on her and Devyn's body.

Ariyana weighed the threats. The darkness consuming her changed the lens with which she viewed the scenario around her. Of course, she still felt the need to save Vayle, to ensure that she wasn't taken from her, but her mind approached a resolution more methodically than before.

The Tethryn needed to be stopped, both those advancing on her and those attacking Vayle, but a direct attack was not the logical choice. She saw the connection that each Tethryn had to the others; hell, she even felt it. It was a misty, black ribbon of energy that flowed from one to the other, and, as she tracked the energy, she knew the destination before her eyes settled on Rillac.

Destroying Rillac would sever the connection, and without a connection, a siren guiding their actions, they would be easy to subdue.

Ariyana's body tightened, reacting to Rillac without thought. Her wings tensed, the long feathers along her wing bones lifting, lengthening, and sharpening. She raised her tail off the ground as she leaned forward, countering the weight that she put on her arms. Her tail swayed from side to side. The long feathers along her spinal ridge and down her tail rose and sharpened like the hackles of a wolf. Her armor thickened across her chest, both filling and covering the seeping wound that no longer consumed her thoughts. Then, thin, silver tendrils crawled down her arms and forearms, creating intricate patterns along her skin and culminating in a bone-like pattern on her hands, which coated her claws until they elongated and sharpened into deadly weapons.

Two more armored plates formed flexibly over her hips and down her thighs, tendrils branching out across her legs, around her calves and ankles, and branching out along her feet, creating the same bone-like pattern and coating her talons until they pierced the stone.

Ariyana's jaw ached, and she felt her teeth elongate. She wanted to tear Rillac's throat out.

Rillac and Kylor were deep in some kind of conversation, one that Ariyana could not hear, until Kylor's eye ridges pinched together, his lips tightened, and his eyes darkened.

Then, one word and one word alone boomed inside her mind. "Tehkaric!" It was Rillac's voice, harsh and grating, throwing that word at Kylor like a blade.

Tehkaric, traitor, it tore through her. Rillac was spitting it at Kylor, not her, but it ravaged her all the same. "Betrayer!" she roared at Rillac. She slammed her tail down once on the right and once on the left, her sharp feathers leaving gashes in the stone. "I will rip your heart from your chest and feed it to you!"

Rillac slowly turned and looked at her, pulling Kylor closer to him as he held her gaze. Rillac's energy held an air of both intrigue *and boredom*.

Ariyana felt it and growled: a deep, guttural sound. His callous reaction taunted the darkness inside of her, and it begged to be released. The pressure increased throughout her body, its intensity most noticeable around her eyes.

Ariyana slammed her fists down hard on the ground and roared again. Black flame erupted around her silver flame, starting at the feathers around her eyes, moving through the feathers in her hair, along her wings, down her spinal ridge, and across her tail. And the white stone fractured around her, deep gashes that radiated away from her. Her wings flared out, the black flame billowing around her feathers, around her body, like an ominous cloak. The flame was so intense that it appeared to move like a liquid around her.

She remained on all fours: predator stalking prey. She reached her hand forward and dug her claws into the stone. Ariyana lifted her leg to step over Devyn's arm, and her eyes swept over to gaze at his face once more. Leaving his body unprotected hurt her hearts, though she knew that he was in a place now where she would no longer need to protect him, and she was grateful, in that moment, for all they had been to each other.

Ariyana stepped beyond Devyn and swung her gaze back toward Rillac. She narrowed her eyes and curled her upper lip in a growl. "I will kill you, Rillac," she hissed.

Her talons dug into the stone; her muscles coiled, and she sprang forward into a charge. Her arms flew forward, her body elongating, and her legs stretched out behind her. Her clawed hands hit the ground, tearing easily, violently into stone, and she pulled her body forward, her back legs digging into the rock to give her more momentum.

Two more strides and she would reach Rillac.

Claws hit the ground again, tearing deep gouges into the stone, her legs flung forward, talons finding purchase next.

One more stride and she would tear through Rillac's neck.

It was then that she felt it. It was unmistakable. The darkness that coursed through her and all around her muted the sensation, but she felt it all the same. The icy throb in her chest reacted to it. It called to her. If that wasn't enough, in that moment, Kylor's eyes met hers and widened in shock.

Time slowed down.

Ariyana dug her talons in deeper and pushed off the ground with all her strength, claws outstretched, sharp teeth bared. She dove, determined to grab ahold of Rillac before the phase was complete.

She braced for the cold she knew was coming, but it still hit her like a slap to the face, even as she kept her eyes locked on her prize—the determination in her piercing gaze, her secret promise to end Rillac.

The gold scales around Rillac's eyes rippled. Rillac's head leaned slightly toward Kylor as he side-stepped right, with Kylor in tow, out of her projected path.

In mid-leap, Ariyana was not able to adjust her forward momentum. She stretched her left arm toward Rillac and flared her left wing, extending her wing's sharp feathers toward Rillac's face, but it was too late. Rillac's body was already faded, like a ghost standing under a streetlamp on a cool, misty night. Rillac was in energy form. Ariyana was in physical form. Her wing's feathers sliced through the haze that was the left side of his face. With eyes narrowed and a hand wrapped tightly around Kylor's throat, Rillac and Kylor faded.

We shall see. Rillac said in her mind before the air around them burst into a flurry of icy crystals.

Ariyana slammed into the ground, gouging her claws and talons into the stone, sliding to the side, trying to stop her forward momentum. "Coward!" she roared.

The energy bubble that Rillac had secured around them burst. Vayle's cries and emotions hit Ariyana like a tidal wave. The Tethryn all turned and advanced on Vayle like a horde of angry insects.

A sickening wet crunch filled the air, and Vayle howled in agony, a howl that Ariyana was all too familiar with. She knew that howl; she remembered that howl. It was the howl that tore from Glacin's throat as the Tethryn descended on him in her dream, in her memory.

"No!" she screamed. She scrambled on the ground, finding the purchase that she needed, and charged toward Vayle. *ARC! NOW!* She screamed in her mind, hoping that she had enough energy to get the message to Arc on Draca.

If he heard her, he would come.

Chapter 61

Too much damage was being done too quickly. Ariyana just wasn't close enough yet to save Vayle.

Then, she saw it—the black, misty energy that connected the Tethryn had not disappeared when Rillac left. Like ominous steam, it appeared to be coming out of the ground from the trenches of some deep, dark place. It flowed into the Tethryn that were closest to her first, and then through the others around it, connecting them.

The realization of what she needed to do hit her, and she skidded to a stop.

"With the connection that all of you share with each other, I would have thought that you would have remembered me," she said loudly and drove her claws deep into the ground.

The energy inside of her instantly felt the energy of the Tethryn. She knew that some minerals were excellent conductors on Earth, and she wondered what the white stone was made of. She must not have felt it before because she was so focused on Rillac, but now that she did, she hungered for it, craved it as she had in her dream of Glacin's death.

The fresh reminder of losing Glacin added fuel to the raging hunger inside of her, and she pulled on the energy of the closest Tethryn. Surprisingly, her body reacted as if the action that she took was as natural as pulling air into her lungs.

The Tethryn froze, its limbs trembled, and it shrieked. Its cries filled the air around them and echoed through her mind.

The sounds of the creature's distress spread through the energy of Ariyana's darkness and woke something primal inside of her; something that had been sleeping *was now wide awake.* She pulled harder, filling every cell inside her body with the creature's energy.

Its cries cut off in a dry wheeze, and it crumbled in on itself like a log burned down to nothing but ash, erased by a gentle breeze.

Ariyana sucked in a quick breath and yanked her claws from the ground. Her hands buzzed with energy that wanted to be expended, though her core hungered for more. She sensed the Tethryn around her. They were hesitant and uneasy.

Ariyana's eyes were open, but she felt like she had never seen things as clearly as she saw them now. The "physicalness" of the environment around her faded, showing everything's true energy form within it.

The white stone beneath her hands and feet swirled with turquoise ribbons that began and ended with the ocean around them; the Tethryn in front of her glowed with yellow energy woven with black energy that misted through it and out of it, connecting each Tethryn to the others; Vayle burned with golden-red energy.

It was Vayle's energy, or lack thereof, that pulled Ariyana's thoughts back into focus. Vayle burned, but not as vibrantly as she should, and parts of her body were growing darker, her wings the darkest compared to the rest of her body.

This shot a fresh burst of panic and anger through Ariyana. Vayle could not survive without her wings, and Ariyana had moments before the Tethryn ripped them off. She lurched toward the next closest Tethryn and leapt. In mid-air, she felt the physical realm above her flex and expand, and the chill in her chest reacted. She expected the bursts of light above her before they occurred, energy ribbons of every color exploded in her periphery.

Idrin and Arc had arrived, and they were not alone.

Ariyana felt Idrin's presence in her mind. He was trying to connect, but she pushed back, keeping her full concentration on the Tethryn she'd gone for.

The creature had been in mid-pivot when Ariyana leapt toward it. It had raised its top limb to knock her away, but it hadn't moved fast enough. Her long claws and talons, clad in their new armor, easily punched through the exoskeleton plates of its neck. The instant connection rushed through her. She felt every part of the creature—the pain that contributed to its ear-piercing screech, its recognition of her, and, more importantly, its connection to the Tethryn on this planet.

Ariyana's black flame whipped out in dark tendrils, lashing at and attaching to the Tethryn's now flailing body. It uselessly swiped at her, only to jerk away as more flame lashed out at its defenseless limbs. Its screeches grew louder, and she reveled in them, letting them fill her and drive her forward. She would make sure these creatures felt the pain that they had inflicted on her, on Vayle, on the Aryllyns.

The Tethryn's back legs gave out as it crumpled toward the ground. Ariyana flung her right hand up, piercing her claws through the creature's right eye before it could pull the soft orb back into the folds of its face.

She needed its mind.

Its screech turned into a wail, and its large bat-like ears popped up like it was going to attempt to take flight. She grabbed its right ear with her left hand and tore it down, disorienting it more.

It pulled itself forward, trying to regain its footing, trying to knock her off, but her body had already started pulling its energy into her, and it was growing too weak.

Ariyana dug in deeper, relishing in the connection that she felt to all the Tethryn around her.

A slight sensation in the back of her mind made her pause. It was familiar, and it was weak, and it was Vayle, and time was running out. Ariyana had become so lost in savoring the feeling of the Tethryn's energy in her body that she had momentarily lost track of her objective. The Tethryn were now connected to her, but it wasn't stopping them from trying to tear apart those that she cared about. She felt every injury that every Tethryn was inflicting on Vayle and every injury that every Tethryn was inflicting on the Draxins and Aryllyns that had come to her aid.

Ariyana roared; her black flame exploded around her, seeking out and locating every Tethryn on the planet. It only took seconds before it had found all of them, and when it did, she pulled.

Screeches and wails filled the air around her as their energy filled her, fueling not only a hunger that she didn't know that she had, but pushing her reach among the Tethryn out beyond those that stood on this world. She felt the energy of her black flame pushing beyond the energy realm and into the physical realm of the closest Tethryn and latching onto them.

It was intoxicating. She could eradicate every last Tethryn through her connection with the withering Tethryn under her. It was as easy as breathing. *She could avenge Glacin. She could avenge Devyn. She could find Rillac. She could*—

The abrupt stop of the pull of energy hit her so hard that she felt like she had hit a wall. She cried out in frustration.

A presence that was both familiar and unknown was in her mind. *We've been here before. ENOUGH!*

The last word cut like a sharp knife, instantly severing her connection and forcing her black energy to snap back into herself. It was so abrupt that it blasted her backward, her claws and talons ripping out of the dead Tethryn that she had used as a conduit. It slammed her back hard into the physical realm.

Ariyana grunted and slammed her fist on the ground. She leapt up to her feet and searched around with wild eyes, trying to find a live Tethryn to connect to again. All she saw were lifeless husks: Tethryn that were already crumbling in on themselves, their ashes catching the wind out to the turquoise sea.

Her body trembled with anger, frustration, *need. She wasn't done yet. She was still hungry.*

She jumped forward, landing on all fours, and growled. The long silver feathers along her spinal ridge raised, and the silver flame burst into black again. She needed to leave. She needed to get to the location of that voice in her mind. Something deep inside her told her that she needed its energy most of all.

Her wings flared out, and she turned to run and take flight off the cliff's edge when a soft, barely audible, silvery voice said a name. *Ariyana. Her name.* She stopped abruptly and shook her head. *She knew that voice.* It was an anchor, a lifeline, a pleading call for her help.

Her eyes snapped back into focus—the star-filled sky, the vast, dark, turquoise sea, the white stone. She felt the dark energy pull inside herself, unravel, and reveal itself as the many emotions that she allowed to consume her.

Ariyana.

Vayle.

Ariyana stood and spun to see her companion collapsed on the white stone, her broken wings sprawled out on either side of her, her head too heavy to keep up, and her red blood pooled around her. Her flame only burned lightly around her eyes, through her crest, and along her spinal ridge. The rest of her body was torn, broken, and soaked in blood. Next to Vayle's neck lay the lifeless body of her Devyn. Once freed from the Tethryn, she must have pulled her broken body to him to try to protect what was left of Ariyana's husband.

"Idrin! Arc!" Ariyana cried out as she ran toward her, but they were already about to land.

Ariyana fell to her knees by Vayle's head, tucking her cheek against the soft skin under Vayle's right eye. Idrin didn't speak to Ariyana. He stood there and barked out orders to all of the Draxins and Aryllyns that had come to fight. Vayle wasn't strong enough to get back to Draca, but she didn't have a lot of time left. They needed to get her to the Lielycet pools immediately. It was the only way that she would survive.

"We're going to get you back. You're going to be fine. I promise," she whispered to Vayle. "I can't lose you too."

No one can hurt his energy where it is. Vayle whispered in Ariyana's thought. *His body was a vessel for the connection that you shared, and no one can take that from you. Just as no one can take mine from you. I feel the energy of the ancestors calling to me from the stars. Do you see them, Ariyana?*

Vayle's eyes were glazing over as she stared up into the night sky.

Ariyana felt the truth that Vayle had already accepted. They would be able to get her back to Draca in time, but she wouldn't survive the healing process of the Lielycet.

Ariyana stood and whirled on Idrin as he ran over. Most of the Draxins had landed around Vayle, getting ready to phase her back to Draca.

Idrin's eyes were wild, his half-moon pupils fully dilated, consuming his eyes. His markings were dark purple, almost black in the light from her silver flame. His body was covered in gashes and blood, both his and the Tethryn's, marring his beautiful skin where it showed.

"Grab Devyn's body. We can't leave him here. Let's go," she ordered.

Idrin gave her an abrupt nod, not arguing for once, turned on his heel, and delicately picked up Devyn's body. He swiftly mounted Arc, and Arc walked closer to Vayle.

With all of the Draxins in place, the air around all of them started to freeze and crack. Ariyana leapt up onto Vayle's back; her own body tingled with anticipation. She felt rather than knew what she had to do, and she felt certain that the only way it would work was while they were briefly in the energy realm.

She raised her hands up and glanced back at Idrin as the air around them fractured and her chest filled with the icy throb of the energy realm. So far, she had learned that the energy realm needed a destination and an anchor, or your energy could be cast adrift, lost in the realm without purpose. That took focus. Unfortunately, what she had to do meant that she had to focus on Vayle and Vayle alone. She hoped that her connection to Vayle would anchor her enough to travel with her to Draca, and, looking back at Idrin, she hoped that her eyes conveyed the things that she wasn't sure how to say.

Worry clouded his eyes just as the fractures exploded, and Ariyana slammed her hands down onto Vayle's neck, driving her claws into her golden scales, and pushing all of the energy that she had stolen from the Tethryn into her companion.

Chapter 62

It was bitterly cold, and she hurt everywhere. Only after a moment did she understand why—she was solid again, fully in the physical realm, and lying atop a hard, stone surface.

Something touched her, and her eyes quickly opened. Something stood next to her—it was blurry and unrecognizable. She shoved it and jumped to her feet. She groaned and clutched the arm that she had been lying on. It didn't feel broken, but it was badly bruised. She must have landed on it.

"You are clearly not dead," the thing she'd pushed said. She knew that voice—it was Idrin. She blinked rapidly, clearing her vision, and smiled when he came into view.

"Did it work?" Ariyana demanded, ignoring both her happiness that she hadn't been left behind and her previous dislike of him.

"I will not retaliate for you pushing me," he said in an angry tone and got to his feet.

Ariyana's vision cleared the rest of the way, and she saw Vayle being settled into a huge pool of Lielycet. She hadn't seen this chamber before, or at least, she didn't remember having seen it. It was nearly double the size of the egg chamber, and the Lielycet pool took up half of it. It was also deep enough that Vayle's entire body was easily submerged.

Vayle groaned loudly as her head was settled on the side of the pool, and Ariyana's hearts beat with happiness. *It worked. She was okay!*

Ariyana pushed past Idrin, who had managed to stand, shoved roughly to the side by Ariyana again. He barked out a protest, but she ignored him and ran to the edge of the pool where Vayle's head now lay. "Are you okay?" Ariyana asked, her voice tired and full of emotion. She ran her hand along Vayle's eye ridge.

Vayle's eye focused on Ariyana. *You could have been lost in the energy realm. That was a dangerous decision. How did you know it would work?*

Ariyana didn't want to admit that she hadn't been sure it would and that she'd been following her instincts alone, so she smiled briefly and said, "I couldn't let you die."

That is not an answer.

Vayle was frustrated, and Ariyana opened her mouth to try to soothe her when she felt it. Something was wrong here. Something was off. Something drastic had changed.

She stood. Vayle said something in her mind, but Ariyana didn't hear the words past the panic that was rising in her chest. "No," she whispered, the word falling from her lips on an exhale. Then, she turned and ran from the chamber.

She didn't remember the chamber she had just been in, but her body still seemed to know where she needed to go. The tunnel walls flew by in a blur as she made her way to the egg chamber. Ariyana burst into the chamber, her breath heaving in her chest. She felt an instant rush of relief as she saw the clutch sitting safely in the center, burning brightly, but it quickly died inside of her when the creature standing in front of the clutch turned around to face her.

"*You!*" she yelled, charging him, all of her anger spilling from her like waves of burning air. She punched him across the face, and he fell back against the rocky floor. Ariyana leapt on top of him and hit him again. "Where the hell is he?! Where the hell is your brother, Kress? If you are here, he can't be far behind," she yelled. She pulled her arm back to hit him again, but someone grabbed her and threw her off. She quickly regained her balance, whipped around, flared her wings, and came face-to face with…Lexa.

Startled, Ariyana stepped back.

"What are you doing?" she demanded, after she regained her composure.

"Stop, Ari," Lexa said, her hands raised, palms toward her. "You don't understand."

It was then that Ariyana took Lexa's demeanor and appearance in fully. Lexa was badly bruised and bleeding. Her shirt and pants were torn, gashes in her skin showing through the ripped clothing. More than that, though, was the panic and pain in her eyes. Ariyana's hearts sank, and her chest heaved in large breaths. "Where are my children?" she asked, tears burning in her eyes and fear threatening to choke the air from her lungs.

Lexa's eyes filled with fresh tears, and her face twisted into sorrow, shame, and fear. "I fought them, Ari. I'm so sorry. I fought them. But there were too many, and they kept coming, appearing out of thin air."

"Where are my children?" Ariyana yelled; her world felt like it was crashing in on her.

Lexa sobbed and looked at the ground, shaking her head violently back and forth. Ariyana grabbed her and squeezed her shoulders. Lexa whimpered but finally looked back in her eyes. "He took them. I don't know how he did it, but he phased here, and he took them."

"Who?" Ariyana demanded, her tone rough with panic.

Lexa held her gaze. "Rillac," she said softly.

Chapter 63

Ariyana roared and pushed Lexa aside. Lexa stumbled and fell. Ariyana stepped toward her and flared her wings, her body towering over Lexa. Her rage pulsed out of her in powerful hot waves.

Lexa gasped and made a pained noise. "What are you doing, Ari?" She clutched at her chest and tried to scramble backward. "I can't breathe. It hurts."

Ariyana flapped her wings out roughly, the silver flame along her sharp feathers turning black.

Before she knew it, Kress was in front of her, shoving her back. "You must stop," he demanded. "It's Lexa, your companion. She is not your enemy. She fought back with everything that she had."

Ariyana's focus shifted immediately to Kress, her waves of hot energy shifting to target him.

Kress groaned, and his knees almost gave out. Instead, he caught himself and stepped backward. Ariyana stalked forward, nothing but rage filling her mind, blinding her to any logical thought.

"Ari, stop!" Lexa yelled.

Ariyana heard words and knew that they came from Lexa, but acting on them didn't cross her mind. It was as if she understood the meaning of the words but didn't possess the means to execute them. All she was aware of was the need to hurt. *Kress didn't belong. He and his brother had kidnapped both Lexa and Devyn. They'd started this. If they had not taken Devyn to Ora, he never would have been brought into all of this. He never would have died!* She channeled all of her fury and all of her pain into her energy and pushed it toward Kress.

Kress groaned louder, and, no longer able to stay upright, he collapsed to his knees.

Ariyana slammed her tail down hard onto the rock floor and clenched her fists at her sides, silver blood trickling between her fingers as her claws dug into the meat of her own hands. "Where are my children?" she demanded. "Where did Rillac take them? Take me there now!"

Kress groaned. He clutched at his temples, his eyes were squeezed tightly shut, and his teeth were clenched.

"Now!" she yelled, pushing more of her energy toward him.

A blinding pain smashed into Ariyana's left temple, and she stumbled to the right, lost her balance, tripped, and fell to her knees, catching herself with her hands. She shook the haze from her vision and whipped her head up to see Lexa standing between her and Kress. Lexa was favoring her right leg, which appeared to have even more gashes across it, and was rubbing the knuckles of her right hand. Her face was scrunched up in pain, either from hitting Ariyana or from all the injuries to her own body, or both.

Ariyana pushed to her feet and got into Lexa's face. Her quick movement startled Lexa, but she held her ground in front of Kress.

Someone made a hissing noise behind her, and Ariyana felt Idrin and Arc burst into the chamber.

"How—" Idrin began, but Ariyana growled and cut her right hand through the air in a motion that demanded silence.

She snarled at Lexa.

Lexa lifted her shoulders and shook her head slightly. "I told you to stop, but you wouldn't listen. I didn't want to do that, but you're not yourself. The Ari I know would never hurt me like that."

Lexa's words stung and broke through the haze of Ariyana's rage. She was right. She would never purposefully hurt Lexa, but the Lexa that she knew also wouldn't support someone who had hurt her.

"You're protecting him," Ariyana gritted out. She had intended the sentence to come out as a question, but it came out as a statement, a statement laced with all the hurt and betrayal that Ariyana felt.

"He protected me. I would have died if he weren't here. Rillac appeared out of nowhere with these huge, bug-like creatures. Kress called them Tethryn. And they started attacking. I held them back at the tunnel entrance over there."

Ariyana peered over and saw multiple dead Tethryn lying on the floor in the tunnel. Then, she looked back at Lexa.

"I kept the boys behind me and stabbed and cut at anything that came near the tunnel entrance, but Rillac phased behind me, and I wasn't ready for that. Rillac sliced at my legs and tried to stab me in the chest. I fought back, but Rillac kicked me toward the tunnel, grabbed the boys, and phased away. I would have died if Kress hadn't stabbed through the Tethryn in the tunnel and fended them off."

"He is a traitor just like his traitor brother!" Ariyana barked. "He probably came along to distract you while Rillac got away with my children."

"Kylor and I are not traitors," Kress said, his tone even but laced with anger.

"Both of you have been a part of this the whole time—this whole game of betrayal." She waved her arms in an arching circle around her. "I should have ended this on that stupid planet. I never should have saved your worthless asses from those Driviks. If I had known that you would just turn around and betray—"

Kress stood quickly and cut her off. "We are not traitors! I told you that already. That is not a word that you have any right to throw at us."

"Ari, he's telling the truth." Lexa gently touched Ariyana's arm. "They've been trying to help us this whole time."

"Help us?" Ariyana screeched, ripping her arm away. "Devyn is dead, Lexa! Dead! How in the hell does that help us?"

Lexa flinched and sucked in a shaky breath, her hand flying up to cover her mouth. "What? No? How is that possible?"

"Rillac shoved an arm through Devyn's chest in front of me, that's how. Rillac wanted to kill me too, but Devyn saved me. He pushed me to the side to ensure that Rillac didn't pierce my hearts. He protected me, even after everything that we've been through. He broke through Rillac's control and saved me. But you want to know who didn't help me? Kylor, that's who. He just stood there right next to Rillac, while Rillac took yet another one of my companions from me." She pointed an angry finger at Kress's face. "Your brother, your kin, your whatever, he just stood there doing what exactly, not being a traitor?"

Kress's gaze darkened. It surprised Ariyana to see him like that. She had only ever seen him acting in a submissive way. There was clearly more to him than he let on while he was around Kylor.

"That was never part of any plan that was discussed. That has to be Rillac. Rillac wants something from the energy realm. This is either a test to see if you can get it, or your children will be forced to try."

The mention of Rillac using her children to get anything made her spiral out of control. *They were out of her reach. She couldn't protect them. She hadn't even been able to protect Devyn, and he had been right next to her. How in the hell could she help them if she didn't even know where they were?*

"I…I…" She stumbled back away from Lexa and Kress. Vayle roared in her chamber and the sound carried through the tunnels like a haunting call of warning. Arc made a low humming noise in his throat, and Idrin took a couple steps toward her.

Ariyana's eyes drifted behind her, peering at Idrin over her wings. His eyes were full of confusion and concern. He couldn't help her either.

Her head lolled back toward Lexa, who was reaching for her. "There is more to all of this. We have to listen to Kress. I think that he can help us. We need to heal. I need you to heal. *Ari*, are you listening to me? Please, we need to slow down and figure this out together."

"Together," Ariyana repeated the word as it echoed through her mind. *Could there really be a "together" anymore? Glacin was gone. Devyn was gone. Rillac had stolen her children and was using them for some unknown reason.* Lexa trusted Kress, one of the two Aryllyns that had kidnapped her and brother to the one that stood by and let her husband die. Idrin had already tried to kill her in a past life together. Vayle was another companion that she wanted to trust, but even she was still so unpredictable. She didn't have all of her memories back, but she did remember that Vayle had abandoned her when she needed her most. *What did "together" really mean?* It felt to her like their "together" no longer existed, and now she had nothing left…nothing left except for pain, loss, and fear.

The air around Ariyana started to feel icy, though she wasn't sure why. She felt weak and no longer wanted to hold onto any form of control. She heard Lexa gasp somewhere in her mind. She felt Vayle and Idrin trying to reach her, but she pushed them away. She heard someone, maybe Idrin, say, "That is impossible. Grab her!" Then the world around her felt like it crumbled away. She was no longer strong enough to remain standing, so she let go and fell backward, her eyes rolling back into darkness.

The last thing that Ariyana felt was the ghost of warmth flow through the fingertips of her left hand as she fell through a thin layer of ice…into darkness.

Chapter 64

Floating…weightless…Ariyana regained consciousness slowly. Her body felt whole, though it also felt limitless. She sensed where she began and ended, and she sensed beyond that. She felt countless other sensations that were not a part of her and yet were bound to her in some way. If she only concentrated on one, she could pull herself toward it, but she did not want that…*not yet.*

She wanted the quiet of where she drifted right now. It was a strange quiet: not the quiet that comes from no one talking, but from the absolute absence of sound itself. She felt the space around her move and flex against her, but the movement did not create any noise.

She also no longer felt the cold against her skin. Her body felt the same temperature throughout, her core in balance with the space surrounding her.

She thought her eyes were open, though she could not see anything, and she wondered what it meant.

Her mind pieced together the things that she was certain about. She had lost Glacin, she had lost Devyn, and her children had been taken from her. Her world felt like it had crumbled in on her, and she felt like she had nothing left but pain, loss, and fear. She remembered falling and then falling through something that felt like a barrier of ice.

Cold. Ice. Quiet.

The words floated across her thoughts. And then she realized what had happened. She didn't know how she did it, but she had phased. *By herself no less.* She was in the energy realm, and she had arrived there without help from Vayle or any other Draxin.

Of course that was where she was. She already knew that; it was her mind that needed to catch up. As if she had turned on a light switch, the realm around her burst into color. She could see every color, both imaginable and unimaginable, take shape around her. It was both beautiful and frightening at the same time.

Like the majority of humans, Ariyana had only seen pictures of space. Vayle had told her that she had traveled a lot through space and the energy realm with both her and Glacin, but those memories had not come back to her yet. This seemed like the first time she had gazed upon the realm of space.

It looked like she was in the middle of a nebula, looking out at pinpricks of light of every color. Parts of the realm were swirling, some were collapsing in on themselves, and others were exploding outward. Nothing in the realm appeared to be stationary, except for her.

This sparked a small fear inside of her. She remembered being told that it was vital to have a destination point when entering the realm because without a destination, one could be cast adrift, forever lost in the infinite realm.

Ariyana thought about her children. She had no idea where to start looking for them. Rillac had the ability to phase without a Draxin, and this meant that her children could be anywhere in the universe. She wondered whether she would potentially find some clues as to where Rillac might have traveled to if she started looking for them back on Tor, would she potentially find some clues as to where Rillac might have traveled to. Maybe she could find out where Rillac had been and follow a trail from there.

She shook the idea away by shaking her head. *There had to be a more strategic way to find them—a faster way.*

Then, she thought about Vayle, Idrin, and Lexa on Draca. She had left them without an explanation, and they were probably worried sick about her. She was entertaining the barest thought about returning to them when she felt her body tug backward. She quickly cut the thought off and whipped her head back to look behind her.

There was an unmistakable light that stood out in the nebula-like clouds of color. It reminded her of standing on Earth's surface at night, looking up at the sky and knowing that the brightest star you were looking at wasn't a star at all, but was a planet.

Ariyana knew, without a doubt, that the bright, green light that twinkled at her from far away was Draca. It was the same color as the Lielycet pools on Draca. Vayle had told her that the Lielycet were the "lifeblood" of the planet. *So, it must be Draca.*

Something shimmery caught her eye to the right. She glanced over to find what had caught her attention, but there wasn't anything there necessarily. There were plenty of pinpricks of light and nebula-like gases moving and shifting around, but nothing that shimmered.

She peered back over at the bright, green light.

There it was again—a shimmer to her right, but when she looked at it straight on, it vanished again. She shifted her head back and forth while keeping her eyes locked on one spot. That's when she noticed it. There was an area that shimmered slightly when the light caught it just right. She wasn't sure how big it was because it was hard to get a good look at it, but it was there nonetheless.

She started to reach her hand out toward it when she felt a gentle tug against her chest. She looked down and saw a thin, very faint ribbon of green light that came out of her chest where her hearts were and flowed all the way to the bright, green light of Draca. Drawn in by the energy touching her, she twisted her fingers through the ribbon. She was surprised that it did not break but instead eagerly wrapped around her fingers and held steady on its trajectory toward Draca.

The ribbon welcomed her interaction with it. It followed her movement as she wiggled her fingers. Then, she felt another tug. This time it originated from Draca, and she swore that she felt Vayle on the other side.

Vayle was looking for her.

But she wasn't ready. She released the energy and threw her arms down to her sides. She looked away from the bright, green light of Draca and let her eyes wander among the trillions of lights in the realm around her. Maybe if she concentrated hard enough, she could find the energy of her children and lead herself to them.

She closed her eyes and thought of them—she thought of the day that they were born; she thought of their warm eyes and bright smiles; she thought of their connection and the bright, blue light that they could create; she thought of them lying on the ground in the egg chamber, running their hands along the two eggs, making colorful designs with their fingers; she thought of them holding hands in the chamber with Devyn, trying to soothe their father, not knowing that he was being controlled by Rillac.

Ariyana concentrated and concentrated, sending her thoughts out all around her, hoping for a tug or a pull from somewhere, but it never came. She felt her hearts sink. She felt lightheaded, and she knew that if she'd still had red blood coursing through her veins, it would all have drained from her face right that moment. Fear was taking up space in her hearts.

Was it possible that Rillac had killed her children? Was it possible that Rillac had already brought her children to Raesor and he had killed them? Is that why she couldn't feel them? Were they gone?

She grabbed her temples and shook her head violently, trying to physically shake the thoughts from her head. *NO!* She yelled the word in her mind. *No, it wasn't possible that her children were gone. She would feel it. She knew that she would.* Losing Glacin and Devyn had shattered her inside, but losing her children would destroy her. She had to think about this logically.

Rillac was clearly prepared to keep them hidden from her. Rillac had created that energy barrier around them on Tor without any outward signs of effort. That had to be what Rillac was doing now. The problem was that she had no idea how long Rillac could keep an energy barrier around her children.

She stopped pushing her thoughts out and closed her eyes.

She thought about Glacin. She couldn't remember how long it had been since she'd had a dream about him. The memory of him seemed to come to her when she slept, but she couldn't remember the last time that she had slept naturally. *Would the memory of his death come back to her if she closed her eyes to sleep?*

She felt a pang of sadness and longed for all of her memories to come back to her. She didn't only want to remember him as he died. She wanted to remember him as they'd created a life together. She wanted to remember him the way that Vayle did—to remember him before the Tethryn.

Ariyana felt empty inside without him, and that emptiness was growing now that she had lost Devyn too. She expected her thoughts to tell her that maybe she should return to Vayle, Idrin, and Lexa. She expected herself to long to go back to them, to re-enforce their bonds, and mourn together, but she couldn't bring herself to do it.

She was still struggling with the memory that Idrin had stabbed her. She was struggling with the new knowledge that Glacin had forced a bond between her and Vayle and that she had been a part of that. She struggled with Lexa's decision about Kress—she had protected him over her.

She had too many questions within herself, and she couldn't face Vayle, Idrin, or Lexa without answers.

She needed to go somewhere where a stray thought didn't have the power to pull her there before she was ready. She needed to go somewhere where there were no companions and no Tethryn. She needed a place where she could find the answers within.

Before Ariyana knew it, her body was moving through the energy realm. She felt a burst of cold and slammed against something so hard that she lost consciousness.

Chapter 65

Cold.

It filtered in through the boundaries of unconsciousness like roots looking for vulnerabilities in unyielding soil. It was as intense as the first crack between the physical realm and the energy realm just before phasing, but instead of fading, it remained.

It surrounded her; it filled her; it forced her to awaken. It felt as though the icy throb in her chest was connected to the cold around her and allowed it to spread through her like growing crystals of ice.

She was lying on something hard and uneven, but her body did not feel uncomfortable from her position.

She forced her eyes open and strained as her eyes tried to adjust themselves through what looked like tunnel vision.

All the color of the energy realm was gone. There was only black surrounding her now.

She continued to search the dark depths above her, blinking her eyes to try to clear them, when thousands of lights burst into focus, some brighter and larger than others.

Stars, she realized.

Ariyana was looking up at the blackest sky that she could remember. It looked like a sea of ink was churning restlessly around pinpoints of light. There was no depth to what she was looking at. She reached out to see if she could touch it.

Her hand and forearm caught her attention as they moved through her field of vision. They were covered in little white fluffs. As she watched, they fell off of her skin and fluttered around her face.

Snow.

She pushed herself up into a sitting position and took in the scene around her. From what she could see and what she could sense, she was on a lifeless planet. She couldn't feel any other species, and she couldn't see any vegetation.

Her body went through the motions of sighing, but, by the true definition of a sigh, she did not push out a long, audible breath. She couldn't believe that she hadn't noticed it yet, but she wasn't even breathing. There was no oxygen, no atmosphere on this planet, but, oddly enough, it did not matter. She felt strong and healthy, not weak or panicked because she wasn't breathing. In fact, she wasn't consciously holding her breath. Her body just seemed to know what to do. It existed.

She pulled her wings down to inspect her feathers. They burned steadily and brightly. She had so much to learn about her body and realized that these were the moments when she wished that she could remember her past. *Was the energy of her flame connecting her to an energy source that she couldn't see? Was that energy source what was keeping her alive?* She shook her head. She had no way of knowing for sure and hoped that someday the truth would make itself known.

She pulled her attention back toward the scenery around her. Everything was covered in ice, and, with the help of three moons in the night sky, it all shimmered and glistened. She clearly had some control over what she did when she phased because she hadn't accidentally phased to the sunny side of the planet. She had no idea how hot things would get, but if the extreme cold that she felt now was any indication of what would happen on the opposite side, she didn't want to find out.

She also noticed that she was close to the edge of a cliff. She leaned over and looked down. It was at least a hundred-foot drop to the ground.

Something moved around her left thigh and around her waist and startled her. She hastily searched her body and the ground and was surprised to discover that she was actually sitting in a silver plant. She had thought that there wasn't any life, but she was wrong. What life that was left was settled and thriving around her.

She ran her hands along the succulent-like stems and leaves, and it shimmered and reacted to her touch, the plant's vine-like stems wrapping delicately around her fingers and wrist. She marveled at its silver color as her flame glistened on the surface of it, and she wondered if it was the plant's natural color or if it was feeding off her energy. She wasn't in any pain, so she didn't think that the plant was trying to harm her.

When she'd first awoken, she was solely focused on figuring out her surroundings. She was caught in the moment, and that meant that her thoughts had not yet wandered to the pain of what had happened. All that changed when the little silver vines wrapped delicately around her fingers.

An image of her sons wrapping their little fingers around her own fingers after they were born filled her thoughts at the plant's touch, and with that image came all the memories that hadn't haunted her yet... *Glacin, Devyn, Rillac, the Tethryn, and her children.* Everything crashed into Ariyana all at once.

She had not lost the memories, they just had not broken through the thin layer of ice that attempted to keep them secure in her mind.

The fresh pain of all she'd lost was crushing. Devyn was gone, he had died and saved her life in the process, and her children had been taken from her. She could not sense where they were and had no idea what Rillac planned to do with them.

She carefully crawled out of the plant and perched on the edge of the cliff. She tucked her knees against her chest, dug her talons into the cliff-edge, and folded her wings out behind her, covering and protecting the freshly growing plant that continued to reach for her and entwine its vines around her.

She felt the tears freezing in the feathers around her eyes as she stared blankly and without purpose at the icy expanse of the planet in front of her.

A strange and yet familiar sensation flitted across her mind.

Idrin, she thought, her upper lip lifting in a silent snarl.

She leapt to her feet and whirled, ready to demand that he give her the space that she required, and then, she froze.

It wasn't Idrin. It was Kylor.

He stood on an icy ledge about fifty feet away from her. His eyes bored into hers, though his expression was blank.

White-hot rage tore through her, dripped off of her, and undulated out.

The last time she had laid eyes on Kylor, he had been with Rillac.

His brow ridges twitched and pinched slightly together: the only indication that he could feel her rage as it blasted across his body.

He leapt down from the ledge and stood still, not attempting to approach her but making sure to maintain eye contact.

Her wings flared, her crest raised around her ears, through her hair, and down her spinal ridge, and, as she crouched, her tail whipped behind her. She dug her talons into the soil for purchase as her body coiled to react.

There was no oxygen to talk, but his words floated through her thoughts with ease.

I came here to talk, not fight. His words were direct but gently spoken, like a parent trying to soothe an angry child.

They only added fuel to the inferno inside of her.

Where is Rillac? Did Rillac bring you here? Where are my children?

The words roared through her mind, and, not caring if she had projected them to him or kept them to herself, she charged.

Chapter 66

Gravity was lower on this planet, and she felt less pressure on her body. It felt like there was nothing restricting her path forward.

She slammed into Kylor with her arms crisscrossed across her chest, and on impact, she pushed her arms outward, driving as much force into his body as she could. It was easy to knock him off balance, and he slammed back into the rock wall. Cracks splintered out around his point of contact.

He pushed off the rock wall, seemingly unfazed. He held her glare but, again, did not advance on her.

Where is he? This is all your fault. Devyn is dead because of you! My children are missing because of you!

She bared her teeth at him and punched him in the gut. His upper body collapsed toward her, and she drove her elbow upward into his chin, whipping his head back and forcing him to stumble back into the wall. Blood sprayed from a cut in his lip and instantly froze in droplets as it fell to the ground from a thin trickle down his chin.

She slammed into his body as his body hit the wall and pinned him in place by pressing her forearm into his neck at an angle that both cut off his circulation and dug the side of his face into the rock.

Dammit! Say something. How did you get here?

Still no reaction. Still no response.

She dug her talons into the ground to give her more purchase and drove her forearm deeper into his throat. He grimaced but didn't attempt to fight back.

She pushed into his throat and then leapt back a few feet.

He faced her and took a step away from the wall.

She kicked him square in the chest. He flung back, hit the wall, and stumbled forward. She caught his chin with her knee and punched him in the temple. She side-stepped as he fell, pivoted toward him, and kicked him in the side of his rib cage.

He skidded a few feet, clenched his jaw, and squeezed his eyes shut. Then, slowly, he opened his eyes and peered up at her.

Fight back! She screamed the words in his mind.

Why? he asked, finally speaking again, his tone tinged with a bit of frustration. *Do you want me to hurt you? Do you need to feel the pain?*

He rolled onto his hands and knees and slowly stood. Once he was standing, he dropped his hands down to his sides and locked gazes with her again.

I do feel pain! she screamed. *I feel nothing but pain.*

She lurched forward and punched him in the left temple, and his head whipped to the right. She grabbed his left horn, its sharp edge and point slicing into her hand, and pulled his head down to her rising knee. It connected with his jaw and sent him stumbling back again.

He caught his balance and locked gazes with her again.

Stop just staring at me, she demanded.

Silver blood trickled and froze on her hand, but she didn't care.

Tell me where Rillac is, or I will kill you.

Kylor just stood there, never letting his eyes waver from hers. His cheek was swollen and covered in abrasions, and both his lip and eye were covered in frozen blood.

I did not come here to fight you. His voice filled her thoughts. Each word was perfectly pronounced.

She snarled. *Fine. Then, you came here to die!* She hissed the words to him and followed them with waves of white-hot energy. They blasted out of her with the force of a ryn burst.

He staggered, but she was in front of him before he could respond. She punched him in the face, and kicked him in the chest—once, twice— until he slammed back and hit the wall again.

She stepped forward and punched him below his ribs.

His upper body came forward. She grabbed him by the throat and slammed his head back against the wall, once, twice, three times, until his middle horn made a large dent in the stone. She held him in place, and her right wing claw shot forward and impaled the rock wall at eye level, right next to his head.

He didn't blink…didn't flinch…just stared deep into her eyes.

Her body shook from the rage building up inside of her.

He's dead! She roared into his mind. She grabbed his jaw like he had done to her on Earth and pressed his head back into the wall. She waited until a flicker of pain flashed through his eyes and whipped her tail forward, impaling him through the left shoulder. His mouth opened in a silent scream that filled her mind instead of the air.

His eyes cast down to the ground for the briefest of moments before looking back into hers, and she felt it. It was brief but unmistakable, and due to their proximity and contact with each other, it passed right through her.

Regret.

The emotion was so unexpected that it acted like a splash of cold water to the face.

She saw shame in his eyes, and it brought her back to her own shame. The memory of her hands covered in dried lavender-colored blood; the memory of the bite mark on Devyn's forearm… They filled her mind and brought a clarity to the moment that she wasn't prepared for.

She was ashamed. She had allowed herself to lose control again. She pulled her tail out of his shoulder, and he winced. She pulled her wing claw out of the rock and backed away from him.

She glanced between him and the dead landscape around her as she slowly inched backward to the cliff's edge.

Everything on this planet was caught in its last moment, frozen in time, and it finally made sense why her mind would bring her here. She was stuck in multiple last moments, unable to move forward: Glacin's death, killing Kylor's brothers, Idrin running a blade through her chest, Devyn's death, her children's abduction.

She was trapped in the cold emptiness inside. Her chest felt heavy from the weight of the expanding freeze.

She was losing her hold again. The ground was falling away. She tore at the skin on her chest, desperately trying to dig out the icy spike. She needed the darkness. She needed the quiet. She wanted the cliff's edge so that she could fall until she phased.

A hand grabbed her upper arm and yanked her back until she hit something hard.

Stay in this moment. Concentrate on my voice, Kylor soothed.

He had pulled her back roughly, and now they were so close that the only thing that kept them from touching was his hold on her arm, keeping her in place.

He looked down at her and, though he eased his grip, he did not let go, and she did not push him away.

His body was not warm. It was cool but soothing. She felt her body temperature adjust to his proximity. The icy throb inside her chest slowed. Her second skin, her armor, stopped moving and snugged against her skin where it was. Her shoulders and wings slumped, no longer feeling the tension of her anxiety.

She glanced up and found his eyes boring into hers. His features were schooled, though his eyes were intense. Their weight upon her made her take a step back.

He didn't try to stop her. His hand trailed down her arm, his claws lightly running over the feathers on her forearm and across her palm before dropping to his side.

You have lost much. We all have. There are too many that are depending on us—your young, your companions, my people. You do not have the luxury of blissful emptiness.

There is no luxury in the emptiness that I feel, she hurled the words through her thoughts. *Have I not lost enough, felt enough, bled enough to step away to mourn and gather my thoughts?*

Have not I? he countered. *Have I not given you my pain three times over? Have my kin not sacrificed enough of their blood at your feet?*

She took another step away from him, a fresh wave of shame washing over her.

His brows pinched together, and he held a hand up to her. *I did not come here to tear this wound open again for either of us.*

Then, why did you come here? she asked, glancing up at him. *How did you get here? And why should I listen to anything that you have to say?*

You must return to your companions. You have been gone too long, and there is much to do to try to find your young.

It wasn't lost on her that he hadn't answered her questions, but one of his comments caught her off guard.

What do you mean I have been gone too long? I've only been gone a few hours. Vayle still needs to heal…and Lexa. She added her friend in hesitantly as the memory of what took place between them flashed through her thoughts. Lexa had defended Kress and taken his side just as he had defended her and protected Lexa from her, of all people. *I'm sure they are fine.* She whispered the words through his mind.

He took a heavy step forward, aggression radiating around him.

Hours? he demanded. *I do not understand the measure of time, but based on your dismissal of my statement, it is not an accurate measure of how long you have been gone. It has been several planetary rotations since you disappeared. Vayle is healed, Lexa is healed, and your companions have spent countless rotations searching the cold expanse of the energy realm for you. An urgency has now been reached, and you have no choice but to drop your mental boundaries, let Vayle back in, and get back to Draca.*

I disagree. I am not subject to her rules or Idrin's laws. I will return when I am damn well ready, and that probably won't be until I have figured out a way to find and save my children.

His lip curled into what looked like a snarl. *How has that progressed? From what I have witnessed, you are wasting time trapped in your own misery. You refuse to move forward because you only exist in the events of the past. It is a great weakness that I see inside of you.* He looked her up and down. *Such a waste of such incredible energy, held down by the binds of broken shadows.*

The words hit her harder than she could have imagined. It was as if Rillac was standing in front of her again, telling her that she was nothing, that she would never meet her full potential.

Her wings flared back, her flame burning brighter, and she closed the distance between them.

Like I give a shit that a liar and a traitor thinks that they see weakness inside of me, she shot back, her shoulders squaring in defiance.

How dare you spit those words at me! What memory do you have that shows truth? His lip lifted in a snarl that she could not hear, and his markings darkened.

Her mind went blank as she struggled for a response. This argument felt all too familiar. Her face pinched in anger. *I don't need memories. I know what I saw.* Her fist clenched, and she raised it to punch him.

You saw a moment in time. There was no truth in that moment.

Her eyes narrowed in a glare, and the muscles in her upper body coiled to punch him in the face. His hands shot out before she knew what was happening and circled around her throat. His fingertips found her akra points, her energy center. Her eyes widened as realization hit her.

No— Her words cut off. He broke through the initial boundaries of her mind with ease. She had been too distracted by her anger to protect herself. She pushed back on him, desperate to expel him from her mind. Her hands flew up to his wrists, and she pulled and tore at his hands. She dug her claws into his flesh. She roared into his mind. She strained to break his hold on her mentally and physically.

He winced but showed no other sign of reaction to her efforts.

She bared her teeth at him and brought her leg up to kick him in the chest.

He cocked his head to the side, dug his fingertips into her neck, and pushed his thumbs into her chin, lifting her eyes up to meet his.

Enough. He said the word firmly in her mind, and it shattered through more of her control.

Her head slumped into his thumbs, and her leg dropped back down to the ground.

Don't…do…this…. Her eyes pleaded with him. She wasn't ready to go back. She wasn't ready to assume the responsibility that everyone wanted her to. She wanted time to figure out her place in all of this. She needed time to find her children.

His eyes searched hers empathetically. *This was not my desire. I hoped that you would see reason on your own, but you are too consumed by your pain, by your past. I want you to understand the truth, no matter the victor. I want you to realize the need to overwhelm you now to get through your mental blocks, but you will not until you return to your companions, return to Vayle. If there was more time to allow you to mourn, I would not hesitate to give it to you. But there is none. You must learn, as I have, that the many are more important than the one. You must solidify the alliance. Only you can bring everyone back together, and then, I promise that you will find your children. I hope that you can believe that.*

Please…too shattered… The gentle plea not to force her drifted across his thoughts. She did not want to be forced to do anything ever again. She wanted to do this on her own when she was ready.

A tear crystallized in the feathers around her eyes.

His expression remained intense but there was no indication of disgust as there had been before when she had used "Please." The Aryllyns had no respect for pleading. They didn't even have an Aryllyn word that translated to please. They had only understood the meaning behind the word.

He pulled his face down to hers until their eyes were level with each other. He dug his fingertips into the back of her neck. Her body continued to shake from the tension in her muscles as she fought to keep him from breaking through the last of her barriers.

Vayle! He pushed her companion's name into her thoughts, and it shattered the last of her hold as it created an instant connection with her. Vayle's emotions, needs, and instincts filled her mind and exploded out of her.

Kylor's fingers spasmed, forcing him to release his contact with her akra points. He kept his hands hovering around her neck, though, as if he expected that he might have to force her back into her connection with Vayle if she broke it.

Ariyana didn't care. She no longer felt concern over Kylor's proximity to her. In fact, she no longer felt concerned about anything that had bothered her moments before. She was consumed by Vayle, by her urgency… her instincts. Something was wrong, and the only thing that mattered was getting back to Vayle.

She stared at Kylor but didn't see him as she had before. It was as if she could see right through him.

She took a step back. Kylor's fingers trailed across the skin of her neck, but he didn't try to stop her.

Vayle. The name delicately drifted through her thoughts. Kylor wasn't sure if Ariyana was calling to Vayle, or if she was talking to him, or if she was just projecting where she needed to be.

Something twined around her fingers, and she looked down to find the silver, vine-like plant trying to hold onto her. She had a distant memory of lying in it, mourning those that she had lost, but it seemed so long ago. How did she find herself back in the middle of it?

Again, it didn't matter. She didn't care. She couldn't worry about why she was here and what she was doing. Vayle needed her, and she needed to get to her.

She took another step back and stepped out of the silver plant. The air around her grew colder and shimmered. She felt lighter knowing that she only needed to concentrate on one thing, her companion, to phase.

More urgency slammed into her, and her eyes rolled back as she absorbed it.

Ari! Vayle screamed into her mind, solidifying the connection. Ariyana felt her need to hide from Vayle drain away from her. She felt her desire to pretend to be something else shatter. She felt her fear of not knowing disappear. Vayle's anxiety and need for her filled her. *How could she have forgotten what that felt like? She had felt the same way about Glacin. She was wrong to pull away, and it was time to fix that.*

She closed her eyes, spread her wings, and fell back over the cliff. The air fractured around her as the energy realm opened up and enveloped her. Vayle was her destination. She fully released her control and allowed Vayle's energy to embrace her. Ariyana knew then that she shouldn't have doubted it before. There was only one way forward, only one way to solve the conflicts before them… only one way to save her children, *and that was together.*

Epilogue

Instinctively, Kylor lurched forward, reaching out to grab Ariyana, even though he knew that she was phasing. He felt the air grow colder and saw the air shimmer and fracture around her, but watching her fall, even if for only a moment, felt unnatural to him.

He was now standing in the middle of the silver plant, the charrid root, and ice crystals filled the air around him. Once the energy realm closed, the tiny crystals burst toward him, and, without either an atmosphere or a sufficient amount of gravity, they floated around him.

There was no sound, but he imagined that he could hear the cracking and fracturing of the charrid root around his feet. With Ariyana here, the plant had thrived, even while she had fought him and hadn't been close to it. The plant had not succumbed to the frozen air around it. It had grown, stretched, and strained to reach Ariyana, just as it had tried to do as she fell. But once Ariyana was fully consumed within the energy realm, the charrid root flash froze, capturing it in its last moment, still stretching toward the last place that she had stood. Now the plant stood around him like a fragile, lifeless crystalline structure.

Kylor reached out and snapped off the end of one of the reaching vines. He held it in his hand for a moment and pressed it against his forehead. Its silver color reminded him of Ariyana, and its frozen, lifeless form reminded him of the glazed look in her eyes before she phased.

Ariyana's eyes had pleaded with Kylor, and he hadn't felt disgusted or lost any respect for her. Kylor had no desire to force the connection. He'd watched while Devyn accidentally forced a connection with her in the mere moments before Devyn had died, and Kylor had seen what that had done to her. Kylor hated the glazed-over look that she'd had when the connection was obtained. He hated how she'd stared right through him. He turned and made his way over to the ledge that he'd jumped down from before he and Ariyana had fought. Kylor pulled himself up and turned to stare out at the desolate landscape around him. Aryll had once been so vibrant and colorful. Now it was bleak and cold and filled with the skeletons of the past.

Kylor felt his new companion land behind him, but he didn't turn around. Kylor kept his feelings blocked off from the Draxin. He wasn't ready to show him how the whole interaction with Ariyana had affected him.

Do you believe that she sensed my presence here? The question floated through Kylor's thoughts.

Kylor shook his head. *There was no indication of that.*

Good. It is time to prepare for the next step.

Kylor held up the piece of the charrid root in his hand. *It should not be possible. She brought it back without even trying. One tiny spark of life on this whole dead planet without willing it to happen. And it wanted to survive for her even when she was not next to it. Imagine what she could be capable of if she tried.* The charrid root started to crumble in Kylor's hand as the life drained from it more with each passing moment. *We were right about her. We need her to fix this.* Kylor looked down at the ground, and his shoulders slumped slightly. *She is only half herself without her young, though. She is unbalanced and chaotic without them. Finding them will have to be one of our first goals.*

Agreed, but not until later. We must secure our positions first. We will offer guidance afterward.

You understand that Vayle and Ari may not accept us, even if we follow Draxin law. Kylor added.

Draxin law is what matters, but, yes, you are correct, they may still not accept it. Does that mean that you wish to step away from the plan?

Kylor shook his head in response. He held up the charrid root as it turned into ice dust in his hand. *This is proof enough that we are on the correct path. Vayle will help her now. We will secure our positions; we will find her young, and we will help her to heal all of this. Aryll will thrive yet again. The universe will thrive yet again, and it will all be due to the power that lies within her.*

Agreed. We move forward whether she is ready or not.

Kylor turned his head to look at the Draxin. He was still caught off guard by its unusual coloring. Rillac had left Kylor behind on Tor after killing Devyn and phasing a horde of Tethryn onto the surface. Rillac had believed that the Tethryn would kill Ariyana, Vayle, Kylor, and anyone else who arrived to intervene. Kylor had found a weapon and started killing as many Tethryn as he could. The nature of the battle had changed dramatically when Ariyana burst into black flames and started pulling the Tethryn's energy into herself. Draxins had already phased to Tor with their Aryllyn companions and joined the fight, but Ariyana had seemed unaware of this and was hungrily absorbing as much energy as she could. Unfortunately, the Draxin standing next to him now was caught in the crossfire.

Three Tethryn had been phased onto the planet from the sky and had landed on his back. The Tethryn had killed his Aryllyn companion and had latched onto his scaled flesh to rip him apart as much as they could before they burned in his flames. When Ariyana had begun pulling the Tethryn's energy into her body, she could not tell the difference between the Tethryn's energy and the Draxin's energy. She had just pulled. The Draxin would have died if Ariyana had not stopped as suddenly as she did.

When Kylor had found the Draxin, he actually assumed that the creature was dead. The Draxin had been vibrantly colored with blue scales, purple membranous wings, and long, green feathers. But when Kylor found him, his scales were white with blue outlines, his wing membranes were white with purple spots, and his feathers were white with green tips. His flame had been green before the battle, but his still, pale body held no sign of a spark when Kylor approached him. It had appeared that when his energy was pulled from his body, his color had drained away as well.

Kylor had knelt down by the Draxin's head, feeling overwhelmed with loss. He'd just experienced Ariyana losing her human mate, and looking at this Draxin's needless death had reminded Kylor of losing his own Draxin companion. Kylor had trailed his right hand under the Draxin's eye. A spark of energy had zapped from his hand to the Draxin's scales on contact, and the Draxin's eyes popped open. Kylor had fallen back, startled. The Draxin then leapt to its feet and burst into white flames tipped with green. The Draxin had pressed its muzzle against Kylor's chest, its opalescent eyes staring deep into Kylor's eyes, and Kylor had felt the familiar pull of bonding. There had been no doubt in Kylor's mind that he would accept, even though he did not know this Draxin. He had known that connection, had missed it, longed for it, and accepted it freely.

The memory faded, and Kylor reached out and ran his hand over the Draxin's eye ridge. *Have you chosen a name?*

The Draxin nodded. *Stolik died on Tor. Scian will die with him.* The Draxin took a step forward, lowered its head, and stared into Kylor's eyes. *I have been digging through your memories.*

Oh? Kylor replied, schooling his features to look unfazed, though his chest grew tight with apprehension.

What did your Sire and your clan people call your Siress?

Kreya, the Rune Seeker, Kylor stated, his brow ridges pinched together in confusion.

Kreya had the ability to find ancient energy sources in the realm. She combined them with her energy and your Sire's energy to create some of the strongest energy sparks that the clans had ever seen.

Correct, Kylor confirmed, though the Draxin had not posed the information as a question.

I found those same sources. That ancient energy flows through me just as it flows through you. We bonded instantly because of the energy bond that we already share. The Draxin lifted his head up to his full height and flared his wings out to their fullest. *I have decided. I am Rune.*

Kylor nodded once in respect. He kneeled down, grabbed a handful of frozen soil, and rubbed it between his hands until both palms were coated with a thin layer of rock dust. He took his right hand and rubbed a thin layer of dust diagonally across his own neck. He took his left hand and rubbed a thin layer of dust down Rune's neck scales. *In respect of our old ways, I am honored to call you my companion.*

The ritual of sharing the soil of each species' planet had not been performed since the Aryllyn people were one people, not fractured into two groups, but Rune straightened even more to show his pride. Rune glanced down at Kylor, gave him a slight nod, and ended the ritual by repeating the same phrase. *In respect of our old ways, I am honored to call you my companion.*

Rune's expression changed quickly. His eyes squeezed shut, and his body went rigid. The discomfort passed as quickly as it started, though, and Rune's expression relaxed. He looked down at Kylor. *It is time, Kylor. I can feel the call.*

Kylor pulled himself up onto Rune's neck, settling himself in front of Rune's wings. He felt Rune's gentle attempt to connect to his thoughts to phase, but he pushed it away to stare out at the frozen expanse around him.

I feel your conflict. You are off-balance, and your resolve is wavering. We must be aligned now for this to succeed. What lies ahead will hurt, and one stray thought could ruin us.

Kylor stared at the spot where Ari had phased. *Does he know the truth?* Kylor thought to himself. Kylor felt off-balance when it came to her. His resolve wavered whenever he was around Ari. The conflict between them wasn't settled; the wound still bled. But he couldn't stop the feelings that arose when she was hurting. He had felt it when she collapsed on Aryll after she bonded with Idrin; he had felt it on Ora when she said that she was sorry for taking his kinno from him; and he had felt it on Tor when Rillac killed her human companion.

This will not be the last time that you will stand on Aryll. Rune stated, interrupting Kylor's thoughts.

Kylor focused on the landscape again, but this time, he imagined Aryll as it once was: light grey sand and rocks with flecks of clear crystals and pink stones; healthy clusters of charrid roots interspersed among vibrant vegetation; hundreds of Aryllyns, living in clans among each other, connected and thriving. *His planet and his people were his main objective, and he couldn't lose sight of that. Ari was the key.* Kylor made her a silent promise. *What is shattered can heal, Ari. We will show you.*

Kylor leaned down, pressing his chest into Rune's neck, and released his thoughts to his companion. Rune's scales vibrated under Kylor. *A low growl. Rune was pleased.*

The air around them shimmered, froze, and started to fracture. Kylor tensed his muscles, readying them for quick adjustments. Rune charged forward, both leaping off the ledge and phasing into the energy realm at the same time.

Their destination was set: Draca.

Acknowledgments

To my family: Michael, Talus, Kyrin, Ethel, Gene, Jesse, Kevin, and Sandra. This book would not have been possible without your support, encouragement, and commitment to cheering me on. I am grateful for all of you.

To my editors/publishers: Dianne Pearce and her husband, David Yurkovich. Thank you so much for all of your support, hard work, insights on where I could strengthen my storytelling skills, and, above all, making sure that my unique voice shone through. I appreciate both of you.

To my friend/tattoo artist: Guf at Tattoo Royale. Thank you for the incredible cover art! I am so grateful for all of the time that you have spent with me, making my characters not only come to life on my skin but on paper too. All of the character concept art that you have drawn for me has truly made my characters come to life. You inspire me, Guf!

To my friend, Marc Blackwood. You are such an incredible photographer. I had a blast working with you during the photo shoots that we did together. You are so talented and fun to work with.

About the Author

 Athena Plencner grew up on the East Coast. She moved out to San Diego, California during her sophomore year of high school and vows that she may never leave. When she isn't exploring new worlds on the page, she's busy creating them—writing fantasy drawn to imaginative realms and stories that explore what lies beyond the familiar. Away from the keyboard, she finds inspiration on the trail, fueled by long runs and adventures that keep her moving as fast as her ideas.

Website: athena-plencner.com
Instagram: @athenaplencner
Facebook: facebook.com/athena.plencner